UNCLEAN SPIRITS

AND BONUS NOVELLA *DRAG HUNT*

GODS & MONSTERS

An Abaddon Books™ Publication
www.abaddonbooks.com
abaddon@rebellion.co.uk

Collected edition published in 2018 by Abaddon Books™
Rebellion Intellectual Property Limited, Riverside House
Osney Mead, Oxford, OX2 0ES, UK.

10 9 8 7 6 5 4 3 2 1

Editor: David Thomas Moore
Cover art: Sam Gretton
Design: Sam Gretton, Oz Osborne and Maz Smith
Marketing and PR: Remy Njambi
Editor-in-Chief: Jonathan Oliver
Head of Books and Comics Publishing: Ben Smith
Creative Director and CEO: Jason Kingsley
Chief Technical Officer: Chris Kingsley

ISBN: 978-1-78108-615-5

CHUCK WENDIG
UNCLEAN
SPIRITS

PART ONE
LOVE DIES

CHAPTER ONE
The Bloom Is Off The Rose

LIFE, SLICED INTO tiny moments. Cason Cole beneath a shattered door. Smells: eggy gunpowder smoke, rose petals, sweat, sex. Sounds: someone screaming. Another someone gurgling. A high-pitched *eeeeeeeeee* in the deep of Cason's ear.

Pain along his shoulders. Arcing like a lightning whip.

Pain in his nose, too. Mouth full of blood.

Older wounds—the ghosts of injuries from fights long over—stir restless beneath his skin, above his bones, within his joints.

His own breath. Loud against the door above him.

Blink. Blink.

What the *fuck* just happened?

THIS IS WHAT the fuck just happened:

Cason sits there in the hallway. Flipping through a magazine—*Us Weekly*, not a magazine he'd ever want to read, but it was there and besides, he's not reading it anyway.

His eyes hover over a story about some teen pop star sticking it to some other not-so-teen pop star, but he's not taking in any of the

9

information, not really. He's thinking that he feels like a rat caught in a chain-link fence, tail lashing and teeth gnashing. He's thinking how the teenage pop star—a boy with bright eyes and classic dimples—might look like his own son were Barney that age. He's thinking that he's a piece of shit, that all his choices aren't choices at all but really just a pair of mean shackles and they're holding him here, to this magazine, to this hallway, to E. and the Croskey twins and this Philadelphia brownstone—to this tits-up asshole of a job that he'll never be able to leave.

An RC car whizzes suddenly past.

It looks like a little remote control dune buggy. Its toy engine goes *vvvvzzzz* as it bolts down the length of the hallway, over the literally spit-polished heart pine floor.

It's dragging something.

A small cloth satchel. Cream white. Flap snapped closed.

It heads toward the end of the hall.

Cason stands. Knows that it's probably just one of the Croskey twins playing around again, those narcissistic nitwits. They're twenty-five, but they act half that. This is probably Aiden, if he had to guess—Aiden's the giddier, bubblier of the two. Ivan, on the other hand, can be sharp and mean like the stinger of a stepped-on scorpion, and he's less inclined for physical games—his are all in the head.

The car is headed around the hallway toward E.'s door, though, and that's a no-no. For a half-second Cason entertains the idea of just letting it play out—letting the car thump against the closed door of E.'s chamber, interrupting whatever (or more like *whoever*) E.'s doing, and that'll be that. E. will emerge and his wrath will be swift and unparalleled as it always is. And maybe, just maybe, Aiden will learn the nature of cause-and-effect. Things we do in this life have consequence, a fact that seems to have escaped him and his brother so far.

But Cason knows that's not how it will go. Aiden's a favorite. A flavor-of-the-month that's gone on three months too long. E. is, for whatever reason, fascinated with the Croskeys—the Croskeys think it's wonderful tanning in the warm spotlight, but they don't realize that E. is 'fascinated' in the way a praying mantis is 'fascinated' with a buzzing bee. When E. is done with them, the twins will find out what it's like to be cast out of the firelight, left to wander the darkness feeling a kind of profound, *surgical* loneliness, as if a sharp knife cut something precious from your insides. Something that doesn't kill you. But that leaves you dead anyway.

Cason's seen it before.

E. is cruel, callow, callous. Cason doesn't want to be on the receiving end of that... malicious whimsy. Or whimsical malice. Whatever. He's been there before.

Better then to catch the RC car before it gets too far.

Cason jogs after it. Rounds the corner.

His heart catches in his chest like a thread on a splinter—

That little thing is fast. It's already there. At E.'s closed door.

Cason sprints.

The RC car pauses. Then backs up a few feet.

Vvvvzzzzzzz.

The toy surges forward again into the door.

Thump.

Two more times in quick succession—*thump, thump,* like it's knocking to be let in—and then Cason catches it, scooping it up in his arms. Wheels spinning against his forearm, antenna almost jabbing him in the eye. Bag dangling.

Cason shakes his head, starts to walk away.

But then the hallway shimmers. Like it's not real. Like everything is suddenly a sheet of foil or a sequined dress rippling in a wind. The humidity in the room jacks up by a hundred per cent.

Cason feels dizzy. Sweat in the lines of his palms. Mouth dry.

He's here.

The door unlocks and opens and Cason feels perfumed breath hit his neck, crawl up his nose—the smell of roses. Apropos, given his boss' name: E. Rose.

"What's that?" E. asks.

Cason turns. E.'s naked. Erection standing tall like a toddler's arm fervently clutching a toy. Everywhere else, he's not a big man; in fact, he's fairly small—five-five, thin arms, thin legs, cheekbones like shards of glass, lips sculpted onto his face as if by little scalpel blades. Boyish. E.'s olive skin shines from sweat.

"I..." Cason's not sure what to say. "I don't know."

"You interrupted us."

A damp chill grips the air.

Behind E., Cason catches sight of another naked someone—no, more than one. Then, the smell: sweat and sex and latex and lubricant. Commingling in their own orgy of odors. From inside the room, one of the somebodies—a man with a high-pitched titter of a voice—says, "Come back inside. We were just about to see if it would fit!"

Then, a woman's voice, heady, druggy, ecstatic: "I can take anything."

E. ignores them and holds out a hand to Cason. "I want to see that."

Cason offers a feeble nod, hands over the car—and there, as E. reaches for it, is that sudden spike of undesired desire: his body tightens as hope surges, hope that E.'s finger will touch his own, just a momentary brush, an electric flash of skin-on-skin. He doesn't understand it, doesn't ask for it, doesn't swing that way but it's there just the same—and it's been there since the day he started working for E. as a bodyguard five years ago.

But no. E. just takes the remote control dune buggy. Holds it up and stares at it, lip in a sneer, brow in a quizzical knit—as if turning it one way makes it junk, and turning it the other way makes it art. He shakes the bag, and what emanates sounds like metal chips or stone pieces rattling together. "I suppose we could use it."

"What is it?" calls the man from inside the room.

The woman: "Bring it. I want to play."

E. flicks the antenna. *Twonnnng*. "Fine. We'll take it. Go away."

Then the man-who-is-most-certainly-not-a-man turns and goes back inside, carrying both the RC car and the bag that was attached to it.

The door closes with a pitiless *click*, and suddenly it's like—*whoosh*, the air is gone from the room, the ride is over, the magic is ended and real life will now resume. E. shows his face and everything seems brighter, shinier, stranger. And when he leaves it feels like a bag has been put back over your head, like cataracts have been thumb-pressed upon your eyes.

Inside, Cason hears the rev of the RC engine. *Vzz, vzz, vzz.*

The woman laughs. Then cries out in some measure of pleasure that turns to pain—and then back to pleasure again.

Cason shakes his head.

And that's when the bomb goes off.

CASON DRAWS A deep breath. Shoves the half-shattered door off himself.

When he stands, he stands into a miasma of smoke.

He pushes through it. Staggering, dizzy, into E.'s chamber. It's dark. He takes out his cell, hits a button—the window of light from the phone isn't much, but it's something. He shines it back and forth, a lighthouse beacon in the mist.

There—the light causes the man's naked flesh to glitter, and at first Cason's not sure why but then he sees: little metal shards, bright and polished, are sticking out of his skin. Arms. Thighs. Face. His body is alive and his eyes turn and wander in the sockets, like he's looking for something but seeing nothing. His hands are steepled over his cock and a low gurgle comes from the back of his throat. Blood runs to the floor in little black rivulets, pooling under his asscheeks.

The woman sits nearby. Also naked. Pert little wine glass breasts defying gravity, pointing up. The nipples gleam. Not from shards of metal but from alligator clamps chomping down on the nubbins. She's not as badly hurt—she's bleeding, too, mostly up her arms. Her head is wobbly; it tilts uncertain upon her neck, gazing up at Cason. Her mouth is a muddy lipstick streak from lips to ears: a clownish grin.

"I don't understand," she says, each word a breathless squeak.

"Where is he?" Cason asks.

She mumbles something incomprehensible.

Cason raises his voice. "Where. Is. He?"

She points with trembling finger, and Cason moves through the room. Past an overturned chaise. Over a dead lamp. Hip-bumping a leather horse.

And there he is.

E.

Laying against a lush mahogany desk, body a glittery disco ball of tiny metal shards that sparkle in the light of Cason's cell phone.

E.'s nose and mouth are bubbles of spit and blood. Inflating and popping.

"Not s-s-supposed to happen," E. says.

E. tries to blink, but a shrapnel piece juts from his left eye.

"I hate you," Cason says. Forcing those words out is like making yourself puke. But just like puking, it feels better having let loose.

"You sh... should thank me."

"Fuck you."

E. extends a trembling, spasming hand. "Help."

Cason stands there. He knows he should help. Should reach out and scoop up his boss—and just the thought of that makes his heart flutter in his chest, that uninvited thrill of the promise of skin on skin. "I..."

But then whatever Cason was going to say or do no longer matters. E.'s body suddenly stiffens—one good eye going wide, mouth stretching open far, too far, lips curling back to show the teeth. A gassy hiss from the back of his throat—a hiss that brings words, words that are not English but some foreign, even alien tongue.

Then: an abrupt punch of air, a thunderclap of wind. Cason falls like a marionette whose strings were cut all at once, and it's like something's been stolen from him. He feels lighter—empty, somehow, a pitted fruit gnawed from the inside. He starts to lose his grip on consciousness, like it's an oil-slick cord slipping through his palms. Feelings of shame and guilt war with a woozy, drunken bliss: the feelings of waking up after a one night stand magnified by a hundred, *by a thousand*.

He wrenches his head from the floor, and then he sees—

E. is like a doll, being pulled apart at the seams by invisible hands. Rents in flesh. Skin pulled from skin. Bloating then falling—from the open, bloodless wounds, a puff of feathers, both white and gold. Rising on the expulsions of air, then drifting back to the ground.

Raining over Cason.

The skin—really, the skin-suit—deflates.

Two wails rise nearby: the man and the woman, these most recent sexual conquests of E. Rose, sobbing into their hands, pulling at their hair with bloody fingers.

Cason stands. Almost falls.

As he runs to the door, an impossible thought flies into his head and won't leave, a moth trapped in a lantern glass.

That thought:

I'm free.

He laughs. He can't help himself.

CHAPTER TWO
Liberation

CASON NEEDS TO leave.

His skin itches. His brow is hot. He feels drunk—a drunk that see-saws between giddy, insensate bliss and a dispirited wave of vomit and disappointment.

Down the steps. Boots on plush carpet. Everything in dark wood and antique bronze. It used to feel rich and elegant: he a bulldog sitting in the lap of luxury. Now it all feels hollow and empty. Like a building on a studio backlot. The wallpaper seems to bubble up. The floors have lost their shine. Light bulbs flicker in rusted fixtures.

In the second floor parlor, he finds the Croskey twins.

Ivan is curled up in a fetal position on a glass-top coffee table. Biting into his own forearm—blood running down his jawline to his ear, to the table. As he bites, he sobs.

Aiden stands across the room, bashing his head against the slate-top mantled corner of the fireplace. He's breaking his own skull. As Cason stands there, the corner finally cracks through the top of his head—a broken egg, the yolk scrambled. Aiden babbles something, then falls backward with a *thud*.

"Holy shit," Cason says.

You have to leave.

Ivan continues to blubber and bite. Aiden's heels twitch against the floor.

You're free.

Cason unroots his feet from this horrible room and heads to the second set of steps. He almost falls down them, he's so eager to escape, but he steadies himself. At the bottom, he sees the front door in the foyer—and the guard who was supposed to be manning the door is there. Joe-Joe Kerns. Big sonofabitch. Head like a waxed cue ball. And now he's dead. Laying in a crumpled heap on the floor like a sack of spilled potatoes. Head bashed in with something.

Then: a boot scuff.

Cason wheels.

The man standing by the laundry chute—a wrought iron hatch now open—is in a dirty t-shirt and a pair of slashed-up grease-stained corduroys, but it's his face that draws all the attention. Guy's got a mug that looks like it's been through a wood chipper. Eyes bulging wide, utterly lidless. Lips gone. Ears just puckered holes. Cheeks, forehead, chin, all puffy with the lacework of scars, curls and spirals, and hard, perpendicular slashes. At first Cason thinks—*Was this guy in the blast?* But the scars and wounds are old. Shiny and swollen with time.

"Who are you?" Cason asks.

Then he sees: the man holds a small black box with a pair of shiny antennae and two control sticks. A remote.

"You did this," Cason says.

But the man just smiles—a smile made all the bigger by the lack of lips—and in this wretched rictus grin he offers teeth that are white, *too* white, and then he presses a finger to that grinning slit as if to say *shhhhh*.

The man drops the remote on the floor.

Then he dives headfirst through the laundry chute.

The iron door bangs shut.

Cason's not even sure he saw what he saw.

It doesn't matter.

It doesn't involve you.

You're free.

He goes to the front door, steps over Joe-Joe's cooling body, and makes his escape.

HE'S HAD BUDDIES who did stints upstate, and buddies who ended up at Curran-Fromhold here in town—maybe assault, maybe battery, often robbery, never more than a dozen years in—and this, Cason thinks, is what it must be like to get out.

He steps onto the Olde City sidewalk. It's night. Nobody's around. The air is warm. It's not like he hasn't been outside for the last ten years, but this—*this* is different. He smells the air and it stinks of the chemical shit-stain that pervades Philly, but just now it doesn't smell so bad. That bitter burn odor smells like freedom.

The air, crisper than usual. Everything, hyper-real.

Then: sirens rise in the distance.

The bomb.

Cason sees glass glittery on the sidewalk. He looks up: the upper floor windows are all blown out. Snakes of smoke rise from the holes, drift toward the starless sky.

The sirens get closer.

At first, he thinks—*I don't know where to go*—but that's not true at all. He knows exactly where he wants to go, and before he even realizes it, his feet are carrying him toward the corner of Chestnut (not far from Independence Hall, a fact that until now had been nowhere near appropriate but that suddenly felt utterly prescient).

Cars. Bleary lights. He looks at his watch: 8pm.

A couple ducks past him, arms linked at the crook. Giggling, suddenly stopping to mash their mouths together and play a speed round of tonsil hockey.

A homeless dude in Hawaiian shorts and a grungy polo sits nearby. Head leaning back against a brick wall, snoring. A skinny dog slumbers in his lap.

Across the street, two kids with skateboards scream obscenities and threats at one another: *fuck you, no fuck you, you piece of shit, suck my dick if you think I'mma—*

Whatever. Cason hates this town. Always has. Always will.

He flags a cab and gets in.

"WHERE TO, CHIEF?"

Big black dude driving the taxi; looks too big for the car. His accent is—well, Cason doesn't know. African, if he had to guess.

"Uh, hold on," Cason says. He pulls his wallet. Fishes through money—not much else in the wallet besides that—and feels a cold spike of panic lance his heart. He can't find it. It's not here. *It's not here.*

But then, it *is* there. Tucked in the fold of a fiver.

He goes to hand the little piece of paper across the seat, but the cabbie's behind a Plexiglas divider. Instead, he reads it off.

The cabbie laughs. "That's... that's not in the city, my man."

"I know. It's up in Bucks County."

"Yeah. Yeah. I don't drive there."

"Please. You have to."

"No. No. This isn't—this isn't what I do, chief. You find another cab. Okay?"

"Not okay. Here, look—" Cason starts pulling out money. "Hundred bucks. Fifty now. Fifty when I get there."

The cabbie turns and stares at him through the scratched up Plexiglas. Guy's got a stare that could make a tiger show its belly. "Seventy-five now. Seventy-five when we get there. That's it. That's the deal, man."

"Fine. Yeah. That's the deal, then." Cason fishes out money. Counts it. Pops it in the little drawer and pushes it through.

The cab pulls away from the curb.

THE CRACKLE OF *fire.*

Windshield glass on asphalt.

Blood on the road.

Cason tries to get his hands under him, but it's they're like rubber bands without any tension and everything feels slippery and melty and scorched like burned butter—

He rolls onto his back. His head feels ten times bigger. A medicine ball on a broomstick. Feeling like a dozen kids are kicking it all at once. Whoomp whoomp whoomp whoomp.

Smells smoke.

Oh, god. God, no.

Alison. And Barney.

No, no, no, no, NO.

He sits up—whole body feels like he's been in the ring with all the fighters he's ever fought, Muay Thai and Jeet Kune Do and Greco-Roman motherfuckers all at once—but somehow he hinges his body and pushes through the pain to sit, then stand.

His car, the Honda, is off to the side of the road. The white SUV that t-boned them—a Yukon full-size—has a crumpled front-end but otherwise looks fine. No driver there.

But the Honda is on fire.

Cason runs toward the vehicle that's bright and hot like the tip of a flare.

Alison starts to scream.

It's not a horror movie scream, it's not a just-saw-a-mouse-in-the-kitchen scream. It's a jagged, jerking thing, as alive a thing as it can be—it's the scream of someone burning to death.

Alison is burning.

And Barney—

"HEY, MAN, YOU from Philly?"

Cason shudders awake like a man rising out of cold water. He sucks in a hard gasp of air and looks around. The cab. Plexiglas. Torn-and-taped seat. Big dude driving.

"What?" Cason asks.

"You asleep?"

"What? No; well. Was." He shakes his head, pushes the sleepiness back to the margins. Still hears the distant echo of that scream in the back of his mind. "What'd you wanna know again?"

"I didn't mean to wake you, chief. I just ask: you from the city?"

"Kenzo. Kensington."

"Yeah, man. I know Kensington."

"I don't live there anymore. Area turned to shit. It's all drugs and jailhouse tats and—it's trouble. Everything there is trouble."

Outside, the sodium lights of the turnpike whizz past as they head north.

"You got family back there?"

Cason blinks. *Family.* "A brother." *A useless insane fuck of a brother.* "You?"

"Got a big damn family, man. Big damn family. Brothers and sisters and cousins and my mother and more cousins and—you know. Big damn family. Right? Still live with them over in Gray's Ferry."

"Sorry to hear that," Cason says, regretting the words as soon as they tumble out of his mouth, like so much ash. "Wait, hold up, I don't mean anything by it—"

"No, chief, you're right. It's shit there. It's all shit. Everybody mad at everybody else. Last week a woman got stabbed there, you know? Right on the corner. Drug corner or something. They don't know if one of the dealers did it or one of the white-boy Catholics who are mad at the dealers, but it doesn't even matter. Because a woman is dead."

"That's Philadelphia." *That's why I hate this town.*

"My brothers all want to pray, you see? They want to pray it all away."

"They church folk?"

"No, no, Islam. Nation of Islam."

"You're Muslim?"

"Not me, man. Not me. I don't believe in made-up fairy tales, right? That's all bullshit, man. It's all bullshit. You believe in that?"

I just saw a man turn to a skin-suit filled with feathers. A man who made me his indentured servant for the last five years because of a 'bargain' we made. A man who had a power over other people like I've never seen before and will hopefully never see again.

He says none of that. Instead he just says, "I don't know what I believe anymore."

"That's the truth, man. That's the truth of it all."

"Truth." Cason rubs his eyes. "Yup."

"Where we going, anyway?"

"I told you. Bucks County. Doylestown. You need the address again?"

"No, man, I got that, I mean, what you got there? Who you got?"

"Family."

"Not the brother."

"Different family."

"Parents?"

Cason shakes his head. "Both dead."

"Wife? Kids?"

"I, ah, don't know." It's an honest answer, but not a good one.

"Okay, okay, that's cool, chief. That's all cool."

CHAPTER THREE
Homecoming

DOYLESTOWN. SUBURB OF Philly. Tree-lined streets. Little boutique shops. Old movie theater still up and running, the marquee bulbs pushing back the night. A town for nice people. A town for people with money.

The cab sits at a light. A gaggle of white kids comes out of a corner Starbucks, lingering and loitering in the middle of the street. Laughing. Playing grab-ass with one another. The cabbie blows the horn, rolls down the window, yells at the kids: "Hey! Fuck this, man! Move, move! Move your shit-cans!" Way he says *shit-cans* it almost sounds to Cason like *chickens*. The mob of kids break apart, mopey and indignant.

The car eases through the intersection. Turns down a residential street.

The closer they get, the more anxious Cason feels. He gnaws at a thumbnail. Chews the inside of his cheek. Feet tapping. Knuckles popping. He wants to punch something. Kick it. Slam his head into it. Every nervous habit built up over his thirty-five years of life come back to haunt him; ghosts of the body lured by the séance of a reunion he never thought would—or *could*—happen.

"This is it up here, man," the cabbie says. No way to pull into the curb—too many cars parked on the street—but there's no traffic, so he just pulls the car up and stops.

Cason stares. The house isn't a big one—just a little white square plopped between a pair of old and mighty Victorians, each of those probably a mansion containing mansions. But the little white house is nice in its own way—flowers out front, a big tree giving the patch of lawn some shade, shutters slapped with a fresh coat of barn-red paint. Even a little house like this in a *town* like this probably cost bank. Money that came from where, he doesn't know. And is afraid to ask.

"Hey," the cabbie says, snapping his fingers. "I see what this is now."

"I don't follow."

"You're seeing a lady. *Your* lady. But you have not seen her in a long while. And you worry she does not want to see *you*. Maybe you two, separated. Maybe a divorce. Do I have this right, man?"

"Separated," Cason says. True enough.

"I tell you what. I drive around a few times. I give it ten minutes. If you don't come back out inside ten minutes I know your lady still likes you and you don't need a ride."

"All right. I appreciate that."

"My name's Tundu, but people, they just call me 'T.'"

"Cason. Cason Cole."

Tundu—'T.'—continues to stare at Cason. Unblinking.

"What?"

"Still gonna need that money, my man."

Right. Cason thumbs another seventy-five bucks out of his wallet, and into the drawer it goes.

"Good luck, chief."

"I'm gonna need it."

And with that, Cason steps out of the cab.

HE HASN'T FELT this way in a long, long time. Hell—he hasn't felt much *at all* in a long, long time. Being with E. was like what he heard happens to meth-heads: the first high is the best high and everything after that is just diminishing returns as the dragon you're chasing flies further and further away. Worse, it blows out your brain's ability to make dopamine, and so the only way you feel anything resembling joy or happiness or excitement is by—drum roll please—smoking more crystal.

Being around E. was the high—everything brighter and shinier, all the sharp edges rounder, all the hard surfaces softer. All is glitter, all is gold. But then he'd go back into his room or into the basement or out to some club and it'd be that magic trick where someone pulls the tablecloth out from under the place settings, except here the trick fucked up and all the shit fell to the floor—silverware clattering, plates breaking, wine spilling on once-nice carpets.

But this, *this*...

Cason feels alive again.

Giddy and sick and nervous.

Like a kid on Prom night about to see his date in her dress for the first time. No! Like a kid *asking* a girl to Prom—and not knowing how she'll answer. That sour pit of battery acid in the gut. The shallow breathing. The heart doing laps.

He walks up to the front door. It's just past nine and the lights are still on inside—squares of golden glow like portals in the blue-dark.

Cason holds his breath.

Says a small prayer to whatever saint is listening.

Then knocks.

Footsteps on the other side. *Thump thump thump thump.*

Little feet. Quick succession.

The door opens and there stands his son.

Barney. Now seven years old. Cason feels like he's looking in a mirror—a circus mirror, maybe, a mirror that takes off his age and vacuums up all the excess paunch he's built up over the last few years, but they share many features. The mop-tangle of black hair. The dark little eyes. Strong nose above thin lips.

"Hey, buddy," Cason says. Eyes burning with tears that he blinks back.

Barney just stares. Takes one step backward.

He doesn't know me. He doesn't remember. Jesus, how could he?
A flutter of curtains at the window.
Then—
Alison.
Red hair pulled back in a ponytail. Pale as a swan with a long neck to match. Long and graceful and thin as a reed, and even the floppy yellow latex dishwashing gloves that go to her elbows and drip soap suds can't cheapen her beauty.

"Al," he says. He can't say her full name because his voice is about to crack and he knows he'll sob, and this moment can't be all blubbering bullshit tears.

She sees him.

She recognizes him.

Her eyes narrow—

She takes a half-step back into the kitchen. He hears something—metal on metal.

Then she's back. And she's got a stainless steel skillet in her hand.

Alison moves fast. Says something to the boy, who retreats into the hall as she pushes past, coming at Cason with the speed and determination of a starving cheetah—he backpedals off the stoop and back down to the walkway, almost tripping over a couple of solar lights stuck into the grass.

His reflexes are like boots stuck in mud. He hasn't been in a fight—hasn't been a *fighter*—in years. He throws up his arm but between almost tripping and straight-up not-believing this is even happening, he's too slow.

The skillet cracks him across the head.

Fireworks flash behind the dark of his eye—he staggers backward, falls onto his side, onto his hip. "Alison! Alison, it's Cason—"

Wham. The skillet comes down between his shoulder blades. Once. Twice. A third time. Hard, too—she's stronger than she looks. She always was, maybe, but this is different. This is power a human does not normally possess. He turns, stops the next attack by catching her wrist—

"Alison," he pleads.

But her eyes are wild. Frenzied. Barely even human.

This isn't anger. Or bitterness. Or lost love.

She wants him dead. Genuine bonafide grade-A *dead*.

The spell. The curse. Whatever the fuck it is, it's still 'on.' Still *active*.

And then the frozen wall slams down inside his head and a terrible thought is captured there in the ice: *You're not free at all, Cason.*

Alison bares her teeth and hisses. He gives her hand a twist and the fingers open—the skillet thuds into the grass. She screeches like an owl. Mouth open. Hungry teeth ready to bite. Cason's muscle memory kicks in; he's older, slower, sloppier, but written into his body are reflexes that cannot easily be deprogrammed—

Her anger, hot and present, still falls against the old ghosts of his training. Cason twists his body beneath her, reaches up, flips her onto her back—the air blasting out of her lungs, her eyes losing focus.

"Al, please, don't do this." Maybe if he can just—get through to her somehow? Clear the fog, move the clouds, pull her back down to earth. "It's me. It's Case. Baby, c'mon, think, *think*—"

Suddenly—there's Barney. Standing next to him. Face the very model of placid, child-like innocence. The undisturbed waters of a mountain lake.

Moon eyes and pursed lips.

And a glint of gold. A ribbon of window-light caught in a small blade.

A paring knife, by the look of it.

"Hey, buddy," Cason says, and he's about to ask, *Whatcha doin' with that—*

Barney stabs the knife into Cason's back.

Pain blooms like a bloody rose.

Cason cries out. Tumbles off Alison with the knife still stuck. Gets his feet under him—starts to run, but then the dewy grass is slick under the soles of his boots and he goes down again. She's on him. Fists beating into the sides of his head. One hand grabs the knife, starts yanking it like a lever.

The boy hurries over to the skillet, picks it up with a mad, empty gleam in his eye.

Cason's mind is a pinball machine on full tilt. But through it all, a single thought screaming louder and louder: *Don't hurt her don't hurt her don't hurt either of them—*

Run.

He grabs her arm, shifts his weight and twists—

Alison flips over his shoulder onto her back.

Barney's mouth opens. A keening wails from the back of his throat—not a human sound, but the sound of storms and wind and rain tearing through an open window.

Everything's a blur—Cason's back up, feet planted on the lawn, then on the sidewalk, careful not to trip on concrete buckled by tree roots swelling underneath. Barney's after him, skillet spinning in the child's grip. Before Cason knows what's happening, he's slamming hard against a yellow car door in the street—

Big black hands grab his shoulders, pull him into the passenger seat through an open window. His feet still dangling—a skillet cracks hard against his ankle. It'll bruise, but the thickness of his boot saves it from anything worse than that.

"Holy shit, man!" Tundu cries, then steps on the gas like a man trying to break another man's neck just by standing on it—

Tires squeal.

The car moves and Cason tumbles inside.

THEY SIT IN the car for a while. Nobody saying shit. Tundu occasionally gives Cason a look—an incredulous and expectant *whoa-what-the-fuck* look—but Cason just tries to keep his eyes forward. He leans forward, plants the heels of his hands on the cab's dash. As if doing that will steady the world and force it all to make sense.

Tundu pulls the cab south out of town. Back on the highway, heading toward the turnpike. Finally, Tundu speaks: "Yo. Man. You got a knife sticking out of your back."

"Uh-huh," Cason says.

"You're bleeding."

"Yeah."

"On my seats."

A hard swallow. A sniff, a blink. "Sorry."

"You need a hospital."

"I'm good."

That does it. Tundu topples off the ledge, and with him falls any sense of calmness or propriety: "You got a fucking knife! In your fucking back! Hey! Man! Some little kid was hitting you with a frying pan! Some crazy bitch beating you up on the lawn! What the hell, man? What the *hell* was all that about?"

"She's... not a crazy bitch." Cason's jaw sets tight. "Something is wrong with her."

"Yeah. She's *crazy* like a *crazy bitch*."

"I said she's not a bitch. And she's not crazy, either. She's got a, a..." He wants to say, *she's got a spell put on her*, but he bites those words in half before they get out of his mouth. "She's my wife, okay? That was my wife and son."

Tundu's gaze darkens. Eyes narrow to suspicious slits. "What'd you do?"

"Huh?"

"To them. What'd you do to them to make them want to kill you like that?"

"Nothing."

"That wasn't nothing. That was something."

How to say this without sounding like a lunatic? "Somebody lied to them. About me. Told them things that make me seem like a different person." That itself is a lie, but it sounds far more believable than the truth. "I thought... I thought it had been enough time and they'd learned the truth by now or that they were, I dunno, *over* it. I guess they're not."

The spell should've been broken.

The very thought that this is still happening, that they don't just want to be away from him but want him actually *dead* robs his body of strength, his mind of will. He wants to open the door and just roll out onto the highway. Face scraped off. Body dragged under the too-many tires of a tractor-trailer. Cason slumps against the window.

"That's... that's tough, man." Tundu's gaze falls back onto the road.

"It is. And I don't know what to do about it. Nothing, I guess. Not a damn thing."

"Maybe she'll come around. A few more weeks. Months."

"It's been five years."

"Oh."

Another span of silence.

"Where am I taking you?" Tundu says, following signs toward the turnpike.

"I don't... I don't even know." With E. dead and Alison still treating him like an enemy of the state, where *is* there to go? "Back to the city. Motel or something. I still got some cash left."

"Shit. You can stay with me."

"Huh?"

"No, man, it's nothing weird—but my one younger brother just moved out, so the couch is open. It's not too comfortable—I tell you, it's like sleeping on a bag of rocks, you know? But you can stay for the night."

"I don't want to put you out."

Tundu waves it off. "You already put me out. Too late for that." He offers a smile to show he's not mad. A big smile. Toothy. A deep basso laugh follows. Cason didn't think people even laughed like that: *HA HA HA HA.* "Besides, I make you pay me. I need the money."

"Just tonight. Then I'll be out of your hair."

"I don't got no hair, man."

"It's a saying. An expression."

"Right, right." Tundu nods. "Hey, you still got a knife in your back."

"It's not puncturing anything important. Not too deep. Long as I lean forward in the seat I'm okay. I'll take it out at your place—you got a shower? Gonna bleed more when I pull it out."

"You paying, then it's cool by me, chief. Cool by me."

CHAPTER FOUR
Mother May I?

CASON PULLS AT the doors, hands scalded, the palms blistering as he tries to open one, then the other, then back to the first door again. The window is cracking, warping. Inside it's all dancing orange light and greasy black smoke and the shadow of a body—his wife's body, thrashing around like a moth burning against a lamp bulb.

Then the body stops moving.

He can't even see the car seat in the back.

Alison. Barney.

Taken from him.

He falls backward. Onto the road's shoulder. Cason rolls, presses his forehead against the ground hard enough to draw blood. The skin on his hands is soft and shiny and red and he drags them against the gravel. Flesh sloughs off. He doesn't even feel the pain, which sucks because he wants to feel it, needs to feel it.

That's when it all stops.

The flames lay still behind the glass. A burger wrapper blowing nearby stops in mid-tumble and stands impossibly on its paper corner, poised but never falling. The air is warm and unmoving. Cason feels light-headed.

That's when he sees a car pulling up.

THE ROAD IS rough and the memory is broken as the cab skips across a pothole. Cason blinks, tries to figure out where they are. All he sees are trees. Dark trees lining an empty back road. The fuck?

"This isn't the turnpike," he says.

Tundu says nothing. Hands at 10 and 2 on the wheel.

"Hey," Cason says again. "Where are we?"

Tundu's head shifts, lolling limp against his shoulder. Mouth wide in a gaping, drunken smile. Tongue out. Eyes rolled way back into his skull.

A moan drifts from the cabbie's lips.

Cason goes to shake him, but then—

Pop!

The cab shudders. Another three noises in swift succession. *Pop! Pop! Pop!* The car sinks on one corner, then the others. The tires are blown.

The engine gutters; dashboard lights flicker before going dark.

The cab drifts another ten, twelve feet, then stops.

From the hood, a *tink-tink-tink* of the cooling engine.

Tundu slumps against the steering wheel. His head honks the horn: a droning beep. Cason pushes him back into the seat. Worry bleeds into his gut, forming a septic pool. He reaches out, tries the key. Nothing. Not a spark. Dead battery. Or something else, something far stranger and far worse.

Turns out, though, that Cason doesn't know what *strange* even is— but he learns fast. Ahead, headlights cut holes through the night as a car heads toward the cab. When Cason shifts in his seat, he hears a *squish squish squish* by his feet and a sudden smell rises in the cab: the smell of the beach, of the ocean, of brine and salt and dead fish.

Water is seeping into the cab. Rising one inch, then two, then three around his boots. Milky foam pools around the leather.

Cason cries out, pops the door, tumbles out onto the empty road. Trees sway and hiss above in a sudden wind, shushing him as that car grows closer.

This all seems suddenly too familiar.

No, not again, not possible, he's dead...

The approaching car is a pearlescent white. A Lexus, by the look of it. It stops about ten yards away. Dust and pollen caught in the beams. Cason feels blinded.

The driver—

He sees a shape, a shape that doesn't make sense, with margins that shift and seem impossibly inhuman...

The back door on the driver side pops open.

One figure steps out, leading a second someone by a length of... chain? Both women, by their shapes. The leading figure is tall, hair long around her shoulders, and even witnessing her shadow Cason feels the world shift like a listing boat—the curves are perfect, the lines elegant and inalienable, and again he smells the sea, but now the smell is heady, lush, intoxicating. A call by the waves to wade in and drown in the deep.

He swoons, almost falls.

The other woman stands bound in a straitjacket, which is in turn swaddled in lengths of golden chain. Hair a mad black porcupine tangle. She shakes her head like a dog with an ear infection, sobbing and muttering. But Cason can't look at her for long; his eyes are drawn back to the first woman, dragged there like a fish reeled toward the fisher.

"Kneel," the tall woman says. Her voice is sonorous, and syrupy sweet. And without flaw. Cason can't help it—it's like someone else owns his legs. He does as she commands, knees hitting the road hard.

He sees then she's not wearing any shoes.

Bare feet pad against the road as she approaches, weightless as light across water.

The forest seems to ease toward her, then away from her.

"You killed my son," she says.

He feels like he's drowning in her presence.

"I... don't know what that means..." he says, gasping for air.

"Eros. My son. You did what is not to be done. You killed him."

Eros. E. E. Rose E-Rose Eros. "I didn't—it wasn't me—"

"The truth, now." Sand and shore and sea, the smell crawling into his nostrils. "How did you do it? How did you manage to kill what cannot be killed? We kill one another, but you are not allowed such fortune. To you that door is locked. Where did you find the key? And what key did you find?"

He shakes his head. "I swear, I don't know what you mean."

She backhands him.

His head rocks. He tastes blood. He loves it. He *hates* that he loves it.

"You found a way to kill him. To *undo* him from the tapestry, to chip his face from the frieze. Even the Great Usurper did not kill—but you do?" She pulls him close, and it's now he can see her face. Her beauty washes over him like a tide. Golden hair like liquid light. Lips like bleeding pomegranate. Eyes cut from alabaster and emerald and onyx. Her exquisite face twists with pity and disgust. "One of the weak-kneed striplings—a squealing pink piglet—ends my son's time, a time that should have been an *eternity*?"

She lets go of the chain—it drops to the ground, rattling against the asphalt.

Both of her hands close around Cason's throat.

Her touch is like a kiss. Even as she tightens her grip. Even as she lifts him high, legs dangling, tongue growing fat in his mouth with the blood pulsing at his temples. He finds himself wanting to taste those lips, to crawl inside her and forever be lost among the labyrinth of her guts, her lungs, her heart—he knows this is wrong, that this is as artificial as a drug-high, as manufactured as the magic E. cast on others, but he can't help it. Even as darkness bleeds in at the edges of his vision he welcomes it.

"I'm going to keep squeezing," she says, her breath fragrant, her words honeyed. "I'm going to let my fingers join in the middle, your neck melting beneath my palms, your head rolling off your shoulders. Then I shall take your head and I will have it bronzed. I'll use it as a trashcan. Or an ashtray. Or a place where guests may scrape *filth* from their *boots*. Would you like that?"

He barely manages to nod.

She smiles.

A glorious last reward, that smile.

But then inside his mind, he sees their faces: Alison. Barney. First he hears his wife burning, then he sees them both alive again—the boy's kind eyes, his wife's sweet smile, and a small voice reminds him: *they were stolen from you by this woman's son, by the man she calls Eros, and now she's going to steal you from them.*

No. That can't happen.

He has to fix this.

He has to fight.

It takes all his effort to speak—

"I... didn't... kill... him."

Moving his hands is like moving mountains. His muscles ache with desire; his flesh resists. And still he manages, inch by inch, to bring his right hand up to the woman's jaw and grip it while the other hand reaches back behind him and—

It's like pissing on the Mona Lisa or installing a cheap Wal-Mart ceiling fan in the Sistine Chapel, but it has to happen just the same: Cason wrenches the paring knife from his back and sticks it in the side of the woman's neck.

The woman screams—

And flings him into the trees.

His body hits an old oak—branches shake and green leaves flutter into the dark as he thumps against a tangle of roots pushing up out of soft earth.

Things happen—things that Cason in a million years could've never foreseen.

The woman in straitjacket-and-chains laugh-sobs—a sound so sharp and unnatural that Cason can feel it vibrating in his teeth. Her silhouette flexes and swells—the straitjacket tears and the chain falls away, piling on the ground at her feet.

Her shape now includes a pair of long, dark wings.

And with them, the woman takes flight. Her ascent is imperfect—clumsy, herky-jerky, like she hasn't used the things in years—but still she catches air and carries herself fast above the trees. The rush of air. Her cackling weepy cry growing swiftly distant.

The beautiful woman cries out. Screaming at the night sky the strangest exclamation—so strange that Cason is sure he could not be hearing her correctly.

Cason scoots back against the tree, catching his breath, taking all of this in. He thinks suddenly to turn tail and run into the woods, darting between trees and hurtling into darkness—but then he fears that whatever just took flight will come for him there. A fear that would once seem irrational but now seems like good practical thinking.

The driver of the Lexus pops the door and steps onto the road.

The driver is a woman. But not human.

In fact, Cason's starting to think that none of these people are human.

The driver wears an outfit like a chauffeur—a too-thin body tucked away in a black suit that's all hard angles. But her eyes are black pools, and as she steps alongside the front of the car, the wash from the headlights shows that they're not black but red, red and wet like blood, like no eyes even exist but for pockets of dripping crimson.

The driver's fingers are long, too long, tipped with talons that belong on a golden eagle or a big fucking owl.

Fabric rips.

The chauffeur's outfit—like the straitjacket before—tears, though this time it does not fall away in a pile of ribbons, but rather accommodates the pair of black bat-like wings that unfurl like fiddleheads from the driver's back.

"Go!" the beautiful woman screams, pointing to the sky. "Find her!"

The driver takes flight with none of the clumsiness of the other woman. Her wings flutter like those of a bat or a small bird, shooting the monster straight up and above the trees until she, too, is gone.

The beautiful woman turns back toward Cason.

Oh, shit.

"You," she says, pointing. He still feels the gravity of desire, but he's able to steel himself against it. He stands—his body is wracked with pain. From the pain radiating in his throat to the hole in his back, to the fact he was just thrown against a tree.

The woman glides toward him. She plucks the knife from her neck and tosses it behind her—the blade bounces into a pothole. Cason sees no blood. Just a hole.

"You have no idea what you've done."

"Who the fuck *are* you?" Cason says. He tries to yell the words, but they come out as tattered gasps. "*What* the fuck are you?"

The woman stops. Regains her composure.

"You really don't know, do you? You killed one of us and you don't even know what we are."

"I swear," he pleads. "I didn't kill any of you. I... worked for your son. I didn't kill him. Someone else—this guy, I think this guy did it, this guy with a face full of—" Cason mimes all the cuts and scars with his fingers. "His face was a, a, a mess. Eyelids gone. Lips, too. It was him. I'm sure of it."

She says nothing. Is that a flicker of recognition across her face?

The woman approaches. Cason can't help it—he flinches.

Her hand is empty until, with a twist and a flourish, her palm is full with a lush red apple. Skin the color of spilt blood. Stem dark and black like a dried worm.

Gently, she places the apple in his lap.

"You will find this man for me. And when you do, I want you to look into a mirror and hold up this apple. You will take a bite of the apple and then I will come to you. Do you understand?"

Jaw tight, he gives her a curt nod—as if doing anything more would give her license to finish the job she started, tearing his head off and making him love every anguished second of it. The thought sends shivers through his body. Makes him hard.

"Good. You do that, I will pay you in endless riches." She draws a deep breath. "But fail me, and you and all you love will see hurt like your pitiful human mind could never imagine. The ants once slighted me and now they stay underground to escape my wrath. Do you see?"

"Okay." It's the stupidest thing to say, but he doesn't know what else there is, so he says nothing else.

"Now, if you'll excuse me, I've a mess to clean up."

With that, she walks back through the lights of the Lexus, her body once more reduced to dark curves as lush as the apple in his lap. She enters the car through the driver's door, and the Lexus slides down the road like a retreating shadow.

CHAPTER FIVE
Click Your Heels Together

THE MAN THAT gets out of the car can barely be called that—he's so clean, so boyish, not a hair out of place, smelling of plain and simple soap. He's got a deep-deep-vee t-shirt and a pair of skinny jeans and he walks over to Cason on the side of the road and what he says is as forthright as words can come: "Your wife and child are burning alive right now. I can stop that from happening."

And that's all he has to say. Cason cares nothing for conditions, wants to hear none of the details of the deal. Because no proviso or clause could possibly be worse than the death of his wife and his baby boy. Cason says yes. Not once, not twice, but a dozen times. Yes, yes, yes, the word falling out of him between hitching sobs, around snot-bubble nose and saliva-string lips.

The boyish lad touches his brow and smiles. "Good. Now it's time to come home, Cason."

HE SMELLS SAUSAGE cooking. Cason lurches up on the couch, almost throws up. Feels his cheek sting from where the rough-hewn cushions bit into the skin, leaving hashtags.

Pain rides him like a horse. His back itches. Something tugs at the skin there: a bandage. He feels its margins under his shirt with probing fingers.

Two black kids—one boy, one girl—run past him. The girl chasing the boy with a fat cockroach squirming betwixt thumb and forefinger.

The living room isn't much to look at—peeling water-stained wallpaper of a paisley variety, striations of mold on the ceiling, ragged berber carpet bubbling up in spots. A small flat-screen television sits in the corner on an overturned plastic storage container. The screen is spider-webbed in the corner, the plastic around it cracked—but it still shows a picture. Some PBS kids' show. *Sid the Science Kid.* The show is warped by shadow.

From another room, the girl yelps. Then screams. "Abasi hit me with a shoe!"

The boy yells: "Afrika chased me with a bug!"

"Shoe!"

"Bug!"

"Hey you kids!" Tundu yells, coming into the room, shaking a spatula. Both of the children re-enter the room. Afrika is rubbing her head. Abasi looks quietly pleased with himself. Cason sees neither shoe nor cockroach. "Afrika, what do I tell you about picking up bugs? And Abasi: *no hitting your cousin with a shoe.*"

"I can hit her with something else?" Abasi asks.

Tundu flicks the boy in the ear and sends them both running.

He sees Cason. Waves the spatula. "Hey, chief. You're up."

"Yeah. Uh." He rubs his eyes. "This your place?"

"You betcha, man. You betcha. Hey. I got breakfast. Eggs. Sausage. And, aah, doughnuts. You like doughnuts?"

Cason looks down at his paunch, shrugs. "Guess I do."

THE TABLE ISN'T much of a table—it's a boxy fold-up card table shoved into the corner of a (barely) walk-in kitchen. Torn-up linoleum lines the floor. The only two appliances in the room are an avocado-green oven and a harvest-gold fridge.

But it smells good in here. Tundu puts a paper plate down, and on it sits a big floppy egg atop a couple sausage patties. On a smaller plate, Cason gets a doughnut that isn't like any doughnut he's ever seen—it's triangular, like an empanada, and crusted with sugar and busted-up peanut pieces and drizzled with a zig-zag of honey.

Cason goes there first. When he breaks the 'doughnut' open, a cloud of cardamom perfume hits him square in the nose. Unexpected, but only serves to make him hungrier. He tears into it like a starving dog.

"What the hell is this?" Cason asks, cheeks bulging.

"I told you. Doughnut."

"Ish no doughnut."

"It's a... a Kenyan doughnut, let's say. Mandazi."

"Ish good."

"Yeah, yeah. Not bad, not bad." Tundu sits, starts digging into eggs.

Cason says, "About last night."

"Mm. What about it?"

"How much did you see?"

"I saw everything, man."

"Everything."

"Your wife beating the shit out of you. The... the little boy with the skillet? I see it all, chief. I see it all." Tundu laughs.

"And the thing with the Lexus? And the woman and the..." He lets his words drift.

"Whaddya you mean, man? That lady scramble your brain with that pan."

A thought strikes Cason: *did any of that really happen?*

"Maybe so." He rubs his neck. It still feels sore.

"So whatchoo gonna do now, Mister Cole?"

"Cason. Or Case." He cuts into the sausage. "I don't really know. Yesterday I had a job, and it was a shitty job, but it was a job. And that job gave me a place to stay, and now..." He chews. "Both of those things are gone."

"What'd you do for work?"

"Bodyguard bullshit. For someone who didn't need his body guarded." *Because with a touch of his finger he could have you flailing like a fucking Muppet.* "Used to be a fighter, though. Once upon a time."

"A fighter. Like, boxer." Tundu mimics the sweet science, both fists up in a comical boxer stance. He fake-punches the air in front of Cason's head.

"MMA. Mixed martial arts. Little bit of hapkido, bit of Brazilian jiu jitsu."

"You any good?"

"Was. Called me 'The Beast.' They said I was a rising star."

"Why'd you give it up?"

"I...." He thrusts his tongue into the pocket of his cheek. "I just did."

"Well, Cason the Fighter-Man, you can stay here for the rest of the week if you like. Cheap! I can even put in a word for you at the cab company. Boss is a real shit, you know—he's both the turd and the fly eating the turd—but the job is the job and driving a cab is a bit of all right, man. Gives you time to *think*."

"Thanks, T., I appreciate it. And I'll think about it. Hey, can I grab a shower?"

THE HOT WATER'S a scorcher and the cold water's like a winter puddle, and the shower offers nothing in between. Cason goes with the hot. Leaves him lobster red, but the pain is good. Makes him feel alive. Keyed up.

The bathroom itself isn't much to look at. All Pepto pink tile. Small, too. One bathroom for a big family and the counter is evidence of that—everybody's things crowd the counter, leaving little space. Soaps and off-brand toothpaste and a box of tampons and a spilled paper cup of Q-tips and cottonballs.

The mirror's clean, but cracked. Smudged with fog from a too-hot shower.

Cason stands, fresh out of the shower. With the flat of his hand he opens up a patch of clean mirror and takes a good long look at himself.

Jesus.

He looks like microwaved hell.

He's let himself go. Once his body was a series of knife-edges; now it's dull and rounded. Muscle that forgot it was muscle and settled on being fat, instead.

Settled.

That word. That's what he's done.

He gave everything up that night on the highway. Had to. Wanted to. It was the only way. Not that it made sense. But you hit a certain point where you see that things don't add up and you just stop caring. You tune out. Look away. Stare at the wall. Pretend that the car accident never happened. That your family was never in danger, that it was all just a dream. That the man who saved them—and by proxy, *you*—is nobody special, even though you've seen him wield power over others, a seductive *sway* that can't be chalked up to a smooth chest and a dab of Drakkar Noir under the ears. Most of all, pretend that not seeing your family is *your* decision, not some proclamation from on-high, some supernatural law whose contravention brings down some serious and inexplicable shit.

Cason leans forward, fists finding rare real estate on the counter.

Face once handsome, now tired. Old scars and contusions rising to the surface like sunken wrecks beneath a shrinking sea.

He used to stand like this before a fight. Bobbing. Ducking. Throwing fake punches like Tundu did at the table. Give himself a little pep talk.

And that's what he does now.

"You're going to get them back," he says. "You love them. They love you. Something is in your way and you're going to find that obstacle and you're going to remove it. If it's got a pulse, you'll wring the life out of it until it's gone. And if it's something worse..." His mind flashes back to last night. A woman *exuding* beauty the way a broken reactor bleeds radiation. A lunatic with wings. A monstrous driver—oh, *also* with wings.

Was any of that real?

Maybe it wasn't.

Of course, if that wasn't real—well, soon as he starts picking those paint chips off the wall, the whole image starts to flake away.

And behind it lies a troubling tableau—if she wasn't real, if E. Rose (Eros?) wasn't real, then that means his family hates him just to hate him, wants him dead because of something he did; and that can't be right.

Because all he did was want them to still be alive.

And now he wants to be with them again.

Cason towels off one last time, resolving to once more plow the fallow field that is his body—tighten and toughen and strengthen. If there's a fight ahead, then he'd better be ready to throw a few punches and take twice as many in return.

OUTSIDE IN THE living room, Abasi's got one long arm extended to the ceiling. Afrika is jumping for it, but in this game she's destined to be the loser.

That's when Cason sees what he's holding.

A big red apple. The stem as black as the Devil's umbilical stump.

Suddenly there's a woman there wearing a nightgown and shaking an old clam-shell cell phone at the two children, her hair wild and frizzy.

"Hey, you kids are too damn loud." She's got Tundu's accent. Sister. Wife. Cason doesn't even know. "Gimme that."

She reaches for the apple, but Abasi plays keepaway with her, too, ducking her hand and his cousin's hand like he's got no bones at all—just bending and twisting out of their reach and darting suddenly to the other side of the small living room.

"Mom!" Afrika yells. "I want the apple!"

"That's actually mine—" Cason tries, but his voice is lost underneath the little girl's sudden shriek. Abasi just laughs and goes to take a big bite of the fat fruit.

Cason has no idea what that'll do. All he knows is, the apple is more than an apple. It's proof that last night happened. It's—

Well, it's goddamn magic, is what it is.

Cason races to grab the apple out of the boy's hand, but Tundu is there first, appearing like Batman to save the day.

"That's not yours, little man," Tundu says, swiping the fruit and flipping it quick to Cason. "That's *his*. What I tell you? You don't take people's things. You do that again I'll slap your butt so hard it'll be white. You hear me?"

Abasi pouts and runs into the kitchen. Afrika hurries after him and her mother follows, pressing the phone to her ear.

As she passes, Cason tries to introduce himself but it's to no avail—she just flips up her hand and keeps talking: "Yeah, yeah, yeah, Irene, no, no, you need to—listen to me—you need to just go to the salon and get it done—listen now, listen, your feet look like dead birds! Everybody says so..."

Tundu shrugs after she's gone. "Family, you know?"

"I know. Least yours isn't trying to kill you."

"Sometimes I wish they would, man. You wanna go? I take you to meet Mister Urbanski—he's the taxi boss. Like I said: real shithead, that guy, but the job is the job."

Cason shakes his head. "Not today. I got somebody I gotta go meet."

"Employer?"

"My brother. You mind giving me a ride?"

CHAPTER SIX
Whiskey's Thicker Than Blood

TUNDU PULLS THE cab up to the corner at H Street and Ontario—not far from the elementary school Cason went to, once. He thinks suddenly about what it'd be like if Barney went to that school. What he'd go through every day. The fights. The drugs. The teachers paid a pittance to teach an overstuffed classroom of kids that'd rather hit you with a book than read one.

"That the place?" Tundu asks. He lifts his chin, gestures toward the corner bar. Dirty red overhang. Sign that reads GIL'S BAR in white. Also smudged with the filthy fingerprints of this perpetually grimy city.

Cason nods. "Yeah."

"You got my number?"

"Mm. What do I owe you?"

Another big laugh from Tundu. "Don't worry, chief. I'm calculating. Mister Tallyman. Up here." He taps his forehead in the center with a thick tree-root finger.

Cason claps him on the shoulder and exits the cab.

The city breathes heat. It's not even summer yet and the whole town's got a muggy, gummy feel to it. And it smells like a sewer system backing up.

Into the bar, then.

Bell jingles. It's cool in here. Ceiling fan blows air scented with spilled beer and old wood. It's dark and dim, like an old forgotten bar should be. A few old salts lined up at the watering hole. A woman in her 40s—heavy-lidded eyes look over pock-marked cheeks into a tall glass of something boozy. Like a witch at her cauldron.

And it's only 10:00 in the morning.

But these people don't matter.

Only the man behind the bar matters.

Connor—'Conny'—looks up. He's younger than Cason but somehow looks older. Bonier, for sure—all bedknobs and broomsticks, this guy. Whiskery wire-brush chin. Dark, deep-set eyes. His nose is a mountain with many smaller peaks. Soon as he makes eyes on Cason, he clucks his tongue, shakes his head.

"Cason, you fuck," Conny says. Big bright smile. Contains no happiness. First thing he does as Cason walks up is start pouring a beer. "Yuengling lager, unless you want one of those fuckin' hoity-froofy craft beers. Which I don't have, by the fuckin' way."

Cason takes the beer. Doesn't drink it. "Conny. Been a while."

"A while? Been a fuckin' ice age." Conny leans in, squinting. Lowers his voice a little. "Hey, by the way, heard about your guy's house getting' blown to fuckin' hell's asshole and back. Supposing you're out a job." He leans back, resumes his normal too-loud volume. "Don't think you're gettin' work here, you lazy shit. Unless you feel like swabbing Flynn's syphilitic spit from his pint glass, ain't that right, Flynn?" Conny throws a glance toward the nearest old salt, a bald, liver-spotted eagle of a man whose white beard is mopping the bar. Flynn says nothing, just shoots up a crusty old middle finger. "Flynn, you old fuckin' prick, you're the best. I mean that."

Cason's turn to lower his voice. "How'd you know? About the thing."

"The explosion? I know all, big brother."

"Can we—can we talk about this somewhere else?"

"Don't think we need to. These fine fuckin' patrons are my friends and compatriots." He offers a sloppy hand gesture to indicate the whole of the bar. "Each and every one of them, you see."

Another eat-shit-and-die look from Flynn, the Bar-Top Mop.

"Fine. I need—"

"A job, and I told you no."

"I don't need a job."

"Good. Because Father was fairly clear about that point."

"I'm sure he was. I need *information*."

Conny flips up a rag, starts scrubbing the dark wood of the bar-top. He ignores the statement, as he's wont to do. "What're you up to now, then? Going back to the ring? More of that? That your plan?"

"No. I'm looking for—"

"You look like shit, by the way. Like a pile of deflated truck tires decided to put the deep dicking to a big jar of marshmallow fluff and you're the baby they had. What happened to you? You know, even in your prime I coulda fuckin' taken you."

"We both know that's not true."

"Hey! *Hey*." Conny thrusts out both his wire-brush chin and a waggling index finger. "Don't you disparage me, elder brother. I coulda taken you then, and I sure as sheep shit could take you now."

This, Cason thinks, is what it comes down to in the end with them. It always does.

Except this time, doubt pulls at his gut like a grabbing hand. He really has gone to pot. Hasn't had to throw many punches during his time with E.—it's not that E. didn't make people mad, it's just that he had this *way* of defusing any bomb that came his way.

Well. Except for that one *actual* bomb.

Still, this is happening whether Cason likes it or not. Because here comes Conny around the far side of the bar, craning his bony neck left and right, the spine crackling like a sheet of bubble wrap in the hands of a rage-fueled toddler. He starts shoving aside tables— pushing a chair with his foot, hip-checking a two-top to the edges.

"Here?" Cason asks. "*Now*?"

"That's right. Ohhh, now I see why you wanted to take this conversation elsewhere. You were afraid these fine patrons were going to see me kick your fuckin' nuts so hard they rattle around your empty skull like a pair of lottery balls. Well, *too bad*, brother."

"Let's do this, then." Cason gets into a basic stance—one foot ahead, one behind, hips turned. Body coiled like a whip. At least, that's the theory. He feels sluggy. Like his frame is carrying extra meat—and it is. Worst part of it is that his body doesn't even feel like his own. It's like taking somebody's shitty beater car for a drive when you once tooled around in a Ferrari.

"Hey-hey, watch that fuckin' table there—" Conny says, pointing a finger.

Cason turns to check. Finds no table there—

When he looks back to Conny, a hard fist pops him in the mouth. Cason staggers. Tastes pennies. Sees stars.

Conny spreads his arms out wide, braying like a donkey. "Oh ho ho! Conny Cole gets *first blood* and the crowd goes—"

Conny goes down. Doesn't even see the kick snapping for the side of his head. Cason's boot clips him across the temple and Conny literally spins like a drunken ice skater before falling forward, face-first, into his own bar. Bottles and pint glasses rattle.

And that's where Conny stays. Propped up by his own chin on the bar-top. Like a beached whale baking in the sun. He moans.

Flynn doesn't even look away from his pint glass. The haggard lady in the corner gives a sloppy three-clap round of applause and then falls silent once more.

Cason walks up behind his brother.

Which, as it turns out, is a little like walking up behind a rattlesnake.

Suddenly Conny moves fast—his face is like a twisted rag milked of all its moisture, and in his hand he's got a beer bottle. He pivots, slams the bottle against the bar to break it—

And it doesn't break. It just *thunks* dully against the wood.

He tries again. And again. *Thunk. Thunk.*

"Godfuckindamnit!" He turns, wings the bottle at Cason's head. It's an easy projectile to dodge. It sails against the far wall of the bar and shatters. Suds everywhere. Rising cloud of beer-stink. It was a full bottle, the dumb-ass.

That finally gets a response from Flynn. The old man's shoulders jiggle like a couple bowls of Jello and he emits a rough, raspy sound that might be a chuckle.

Red-faced and with all his meager bird muscles corded tight, Conny wheels on Flynn and screams. Spit gathers at the stretched margins of his mouth. "You old fuckin' kid-toucher motherfucker, get the fuck out of my bar!" When Flynn doesn't move, Conny mutters, "... you laugh at *me*..." then grabs the old man's pint glass and dumps it in his lap. Flynn backpedals off his stool, nearly falling down in the process. *"Now get the fuck out of my bar!"*

Flynn hobbles out of the bar, muttering and cursing, wiping beer from his lap.

Cason gives it some time.

Conny stands, sallow chest rising and falling behind his white t-shirt. He's got a Neanderthal hunch to him—something weighing him down. Shame, rage, something else, Cason doesn't know. But that's Conny. Now and forever. Classic.

Also classic Conny? He suddenly straightens up, offers a big mouthful of smiling yellow teeth, then says all bright and chipper: "So, it was information you wanted, big brother?"

THE BACK ROOM of the bar is even dimmer and danker than the bar itself. A small desk sits in the corner, heaped and mounded with papers and kept books. The walls aren't wood, but rather cheap wood paneling. On which hang beer posters and unlit neon from twenty years ago—St. Pauli's Girl, and Dab Beer, and Spuds Mackenzie in a Hawaiian shirt surrounded by a couple of tease-haired bikini babes.

Conny pulls a pair of shot glasses with one hand and they clink together as he deposits them upon the top of the small round table. Appearing in his hands, as if by magic, is a bottle of Bushmill's with the green label: ten-year.

He fills both shotglasses till they're overflowing, then slides one to Cason.

"*Slainte*," Conny says, then tilts his head back and fills his throat with the whiskey.

Cason knows that if he wants the prize, he's got to reach for the ring—and here that means drinking with his shit-heel younger brother.

The whiskey turns his throat into a barrel fire. Ragged and hot at first, but then suddenly communal and comforting.

"Whatcha need, Case? Spill it."

"I want the person who bombed my boss's brownstone."

"*Bombed my boss's brownstone.* Sounds like some kinky fuckin' sex move, don't it? You know, like, *I took her back to my bed and I bombed her boss's brownstone if you know what I fuckin' mean.* Brownstone tells me it's something to do with the ol' stink-eye, the dirty rosebud, the—well." Conny takes the bottle, pours himself another. "So who did the deed?"

"I was hoping you could tell me."

"Got a description? Or you just pissing in the fuckin' wind here?"

Cason tells him. Describes the freak best as he can. Says he was cut up like a snowflake made out of paper. And as he talks, he can see that Conny knows who he's talking about. So it's doubly surprising when Conny says, "Don't know him."

"Don't lie to me."

"Not lying. Don't know him. Know *of* him. But we're not girlfriends or anything."

"Who is he?"

"He's a madman. Bats in his belfry; shit, he's got bats and spiders and starving owls and a little one-eyed monkey playing the same tune over and over again on a dirty mouth-harp. He's a bomber. Showed up on the scene about five years ago. Got a real fuckin' bug up his ass about blowing things up. He's got a, whaddya call it, a signature: he likes to pack his bombs with... things. Things that make shrapnel. Forks and knives and toys and whatever else he thinks will best sign the crime." Conny breathes deep through his nose. "They call him Cicatrix. I don't know what the fuck that means. I think it's a bug or something."

"It's scar tissue," Cason says, then shifts uncomfortably in his seat. This isn't somebody he wants to tangle with. But he feels compelled. Whoever that woman was last night—the one who gave him the apple and threatened to pull his head off his shoulders—she has power. Power potentially beyond what her 'son' was capable of generating.

If he found the killer, maybe, just maybe, she could help him understand why his wife and son still won't talk to him. Why they still want him *dead*. Like they're programmed to do it. Perfect world scenario, she can even help him undo whatever grim magic is keeping the 'program' in place.

"Where is he? How do I find him?"

"I don't think you want to do that, Case."

"Conny. I need this."

"Do you. Do you." Conny draws a deep breath. Doesn't slam back the shot this time and instead just sips at it noisily, like someone slurping soup. "I'll look into it. Give me your number. I'll call you in a day or three. But you'll owe me for this."

"We're brothers."

"This goes beyond that. This goes *miles* beyond. Like I need this whackaloon coming in here with a bomb made of baby dolls and blowing the one thing I got going for me sky fuckin' high. This is favor territory. You owe me. Say it."

The words taste like mud and ash. "I owe you."

"Good."

Cason stands. Heads for the door. Conny lifts his head.

"Hey. Whatever happened with you and the woman? The wife. She leave you?"

"Something like that."

"I never met her."

"No."

"Did Dad?"

"He didn't want to."

"Sounds like him. You had a son, too."

Cason doesn't even answer. Just a grunt of acknowledgment.

"I'd sure like to meet them someday. If you work things out."

"I'm gonna work things out. One way or another."

Because it's all I have.

CHAPTER SEVEN
Lawn Skillet

MORNING SUN GLEAMS off the stainless steel skillet. Alison squints as the light hits her eye. She stares out the window, wondering just how her skillet walked its way outside.

Had to be Barney.

He's a kid. He has phases. Last week it was hiding his toys in the bathroom cabinets. Two months ago he thought he could run really fast like the Flash, so he'd run around the house going "*zhhhhoooooooom*" until he nearly passed out, dizzy. His fourth birthday marked a month-long stint of digging holes in the backyard as he became convinced from some book or cartoon that someone had buried treasure back there.

"Barney," she calls.

The fast-approaching *thumpthumpthump* of feet and, voila, there he stands. Shirt off. Pajama pants hiked up to his belly button like some old man. He smiles big, showcasing the gap in his lower teeth—he's already losing them. (Her heart hurts for a moment—they grow up so fast. Time slips by and all you have are memories—and even some of them fall through your fingers if you're not careful.)

"Hi, Mom."

"Barn, can I ask you something?"

"Um. Um. Okay."

"Did you put the—" But her question halts as her breath catches. Blood.

He's got blood on his hands.

Mommy alarm goes off in her head. Klaxons of worry. She hurries over, starts scanning him over and patting him down like an officer of the TSA looking for a bomb on a passenger—looking for cuts, contusions, anything to explain the blood that's dried on the back of his hand.

"Are you okay?" she asks, still checking. Nothing so far.

"Um. Um. I dunno?" That's his default answer when he's not sure if he's in trouble or not. *I dunno.* She tries to explain.

"Sweetie, I just want to see if you're hurt."

"I'm not hurt, Mommy."

She holds up his hand to show him. "Is this blood?"

"I dunno." Is he being cagey? Or honest?

"Is it something other than blood?" She smells it. Ponders licking it. Could be jelly or ketchup or... no. Too dark. Too brown. It's blood. She's sure of it.

"I dunno."

She goes through the scenarios. Blood that came from where? A hangnail? Maybe he was picking his nose, got a gusher. It happens. It's not like he'd hurt a neighborhood animal. The Burtons next door have a cat and Barn's only crime there is that he wants to hug and squeeze the cat a little too aggressively (a child's love cares little for restraint, after all)—but that doesn't explain blood.

Fine, then. Back to the original mystery—maybe one answer will offer another. Kids are like that, sometimes. You're missing an earring and later you ask the tiny human why he keeps messing with that tree stump and you find out he's been hoarding things from inside the house and hiding them inside the stump (along with lots of bugs alive and dead, like some kind of insect graveyard where the living visit the deceased and leave things like Mommy's earrings as tribute). That actually happened. So:

"Why'd you put Mommy's frying pan on the lawn?"

"I dunno." Eyes shifting left and right. Then followed by his feet. "I didn't?"

"Did you?"

"I didn't." Hedging his bets again: "I dunno."

Parental exasperation takes hold. Sometimes she pursues these mysteries to their meaningless conclusions, other times—like now, blessedly—she realizes that the answer will have very little utility and the illumination won't buy her back the time it took to get to the truth. Better instead to just go get the damn pan off the lawn.

She sighs, turns, opens the front door to go reclaim her wayward skillet.

And that's when she sees the woman on her lawn.

She's got a wild mane of unkempt hair, dark as a storm cloud and with the same lack of symmetry. T-shirt a size or two too big. Pair of baggy cargo shorts. If Alison had to describe it, she'd say the woman has an Edward Scissorhands vibe going on.

The woman is staring down into the grass. Nudging something with her foot.

"Uh, hello?" Alison says. Barney appears at her side and looks out.

"Whozat?" Barney asks.

"I have no idea." Alison snaps her fingers at the woman. "Hey. Hello."

The woman bends down, picks up the skillet from the lawn.

She proceeds to smell it. Then lick it. Then make a frowny face with eyebrows cocked and lips twisted.

"Is this yours?" the woman asks, holding up the skillet by the handle the same way one might hold a pair of mysterious dirty underwear found in a swimming pool. The pan dangles between thumb and forefinger.

Alison offers a lame, bewildered nod.

The woman lets the skillet fall back to the lawn. Thudding into the grass. With that, she begins walking toward the house. Toward Alison and her son.

Again, the Mommy Alarm. Def-Con going up a notch. Or down—whichever is the one where the worry escalates and the klaxons get louder. Something about this woman isn't right. She walks with her shoulders tight, her elbows pinched to her sides like they're not used to hanging loose. The woman's chin is pressed to her chest, and she offers only a piercing, guarded stare as she fast approaches.

"No, no," Alison starts to say, "no, we don't want any," a default response to anyone coming to the door, though she can't imagine what this lady could possibly be selling (perhaps the Satanic Bible).

But then calmness sweeps over her. It's like—she feels something sliding along the margins of her mind, and at first it calls to mind a snake, but that changes and then it's like a pair of warm hands cupping her mind from beneath, the way one might gently hold and stroke a cat or a puppy, and that sensation washes over her like a warm, sudsy tide.

The woman stands on the walkway.

"I'd like to come in," the woman says.

"Okay," Alison says. To her own surprise.

"My name is Psyche." *Sy-kee.* "I am the daughter of a king and queen."

Alison sits on the living room couch, the woman sitting not across from her but next to her, the way that a pair of teens might sit when going out on a first date. Neither of them look at one another. Psyche seems to shy away—like she's forced to sit next to an uncle who smells like body odor, or next to a grabby jam-handed toddler.

It's very off-putting.

"My name is Alison." She clears her throat. "Daughter of a... an accountant and a housewife."

"Yes," Psyche says. "I see your bloodline. The connections our heritage affords. A tangle of vines. All the way back and forward to the boy. Barney."

"Please don't... hurt my son."

Alison somehow had the presence of mind to send Barney upstairs to his room for now to read a book. Though her initial response was such a wave of comfort and familiarity she almost picked him up and plopped him down on this stranger's lap.

Not a normal response. Not at all. Alison feels like the bottom is falling out and she's slipping down toward the dark. She wants to get up from the couch, but she feels rooted here. Again she finds something running along the edges of her mind. Teasing. Testing. Probing. Fingers. Invisible, impossible fingers. Soon pulling things apart the way one pulls apart a warm dinner roll.

"You smell like that man," Psyche says. "But your mind doesn't."

"I don't understand."

"I don't either. I don't know him. But I could smell things on him—loyalty for family, a wellspring of love, an even deeper river of anger. A bloodline that runs deep and strange, farther afield than I can yet suss out. And, of course, I could smell my husband's life essence on him. Because he killed him. I think. The man murdered my husband." Psyche stares. An unswerving gaze like you'd see in cats. "But he's not inside your mind."

Alison's skin crawls. And yet she seems unable to get off the couch—she can barely even twitch a finger. Sweat rises warm on her brow, then cools in the breeze of the ceiling fan spinning above.

"I don't know who you mean," Alison says. Voice quavering.

"I smell him on your lawn. His grief. His blood."

"Please—"

"But you have holes in your mind, Alison. Human-shaped holes."

"*Please*. Please, please. Leave." Hot tears press at the corners of her eyes.

"Someone removed something from you." Suddenly, Psyche nods—and a little lunatic laugh rises up and out of her like a flurry of bubbles. "Of course. Of course. I see, now. Not all of it, but I see. I see my love's fingerprints." Another laugh. "My true love has been there. Inside you." Alison blanches and the stranger shakes her head. "Oh. Not like that. He would never—not *you*. You're too plain."

A spike of fear and anger rises inside Alison—

And instantly it's tamped back down again by a mental hand.

"I'm going to show you something now. Are you ready?"

"No, no. I'm not ready."

Psyche shrugs. "That's too bad. Because you need to see."

Though Alison's eyes are already open it's like her eyelids are being ripped off, her eyes—her inner eye, her third eye—exposed to the bright noon-day sun.

It's a face she recognizes, a face of—

Cason.

And then all turns to red curtains drawn dark over the light and yellowjacket wings and the shooshing thundering river of blood in her ears and—

CHAPTER EIGHT
Bomberman

COUPLE DAYS LATER, Cason stands in front of a falafel place on South Street. Smells of hot grease and steamed pita reach up his nose and hit that primal part of his brain—his stomach tightens, and hunger growls like a bear in a cave.

Behind him, Tundu honks the horn—"Hey, you good?"

Cason nods, gives a thumbs-up. Tundu pulls the cab away. Back to work.

Now, no time for food. Instead he looks down at the address on a curling piece of paper, an address given to him last night when Conny called right around midnight. His brother didn't say much. Just this address followed by, "You fuckin' owe me, remember."

The address took him here. To a falafel joint. Yehuda's. He's never felt compelled to have one before, but right now, his stomach is making a strong case to try one.

He quick steps out of the way as a black kid pedals by on a BMX bike. Cason almost falls into a gum tree—literally, a tree spackled with hundreds if not *thousands* of smooshed pieces of gum. Couple tourists—white girls with too big sunglasses, sunglasses that make them look like old women or praying mantises or something—hurry past. Again, he's reminded: *You need to get your reflexes back, old man. That kid almost cut you off at the knees and those skinny girls' elbows are sharp enough to make you bleed.*

It's then Cason sees that to the left of the food counter is a plain door. No address or number listed. Maybe the guy lives upstairs. Two more stories above the restaurants. Probably full of apartments. Hell, Cason's first apartment of his own town was above a bar. A bar that played loud shitty pop music till two o'clock in the morning.

Fine. To the door, then.

He tries opening it, but isn't surprised to find it locked.

Sure enough, a list of apartments—the labels all faded.

He runs his finger down all the buzzer buttons, mumbles something into the speaker. The door *clicks*. Bingo.

THESE ARE NOT nice apartments.

In the stairwell, Cason finds a grungy Schnauzer eating fast food out of a Burger King bag, chasing flies away with his tail. At a door on the second floor, he hears someone wailing and someone weeping—they call to mind the sounds you might hear at an old asylum, with madmen and women screaming at invisible intruders.

By the numbers, the apartment Cason's looking for is on the third floor.

Up to it, then.

First door on the right has an Asian girl in a leopard-print top and a zebra-print skirt pounding on it. She's not using her hand to pound on it, though—she's using the bottom of a bottle of Asti Spumante. She's yelling, "Hey! You Jew! Open up! I want to celebrate with you! I got the job!" *Thump thump thump.* "Jew!"

As Cason ekes past, she shoots him a look, her eyes daggers. "What are you looking at, asshole?"

He just shakes his head and keeps walking.

Door he's looking for is right around a bend. Last door in the hallway.

Apartment 313.

Down the hall, the echoing thumps of the bottle on the door. ("Jew! Open up!")

Cason's not really sure what his next move should be. What the hell was he thinking? Guy's got a maimed face and a penchant for blowing things up with his own special brand of shrapnel panache, and Cason's going to just—what? Knock on the door?

Fuck it. He knocks on the door.

Nothing.

(*Thump thump thump, "Jew! Job! I want sex!"*)

And that ends Cason's one and only plan.

Well—he's got one more item on the menu, a back-up plan that has no chance of working, because in this town, who leaves their doors unlocked?

He tries the doorknob. The door squeaks open.

No shit.

LIGHT FILTERS THROUGH gauzy, tobacco-stained curtains. In the beams whirl an endless dance of dust motes and cat hairs. Cason doesn't actually *see* a cat, but he smells it—the ammonia stink of spent kitty litter.

The apartment isn't much to look at, size-wise. One room with a kitchen and a bathroom glommed onto it. The guy's bed is a rumpled pull-out couch, covered with the remnants of various snack foods: broken tortilla chips, Cheeto dust, M&Ms laying strewn about like the cracked, chipped teeth of a colorful clown.

Makes Tundu's place look like the Taj Mahal.

What matters, though, are the walls. Or rather, what's on them.

Cason thinks: *So he's a tinfoil-hat type.*

All across the walls are photos, newspaper clippings, print-outs, documents, and more, all stuck to the wall with little thin carpenter nails. He begins scanning the walls—there, a blurry photo of a woman in blue walking in a wheat field. Here, an article about a man struck by lightning in his own house. Articles about bank failures and 9/11 and the Spanish Flu of 1918. Wikipedia articles covering a weird array of topics: triremes, Viking axes, volcanoes,

Homeric epics, Nazi occultism, hallucinogenic drug use, jaguars.

Many of them strung together with red thread wound around one nail, then to the next, then to the next. Forming connections that make no sense to Cason. Nor anybody else but maybe this man, this bomber—the 'Cicatrix.'

It's like the guy's walls are a one-man-band crazy-ass version of the Internet.

As Cason winds his way through the apartment, his index finger tracing his own invisible (and ill-conceived) connections between things, he sees something on the floor that gives his heart a reason to gallop with swift and heavy hoof.

It's a shoebox. With his name on it in thick permanent marker. CASON COLE.

Beneath it, a question mark: ?

It's not dusty like everything else. It's been opened recently.

Cason opens it. And immediately wishes he didn't.

The underside of the lid is affixed to another piece of red thread, like that which connects the images and articles on the walls—and when Cason opens the box, the thread tugs on something, and then that something *gives*.

He hears a *snick*.

He catches sight of a small canister inside the box.

A bomb, he thinks.

And there's a slow-motion moment where anger strikes him— anger that he was so stupid, anger that he hasn't found a way to bring his family back together, anger that he hasn't punished those who put him in this situation.

There's a hiss—and a cone of white fog blasts up and hits him square in the face. His hand slams the cardboard lid back down, crushing the box and killing the spray, but it's already too late. His face burns like he just pressed it into a plate of hot peppers. His nose runs. His throat starts to close. The corners of his eyes tear up and those tears burn like blown-out match-tips.

He can't see. Can barely breathe. Cason shoots to his feet, almost falls—

Behind him, he hears the door.

The room shakes. Footsteps. Closing in. Fast.

This is a trap.

He pivots on his heel, throws a clumsy kick wide—it goes nowhere, *swish*. But there's a scuff to his left and then something hard jabs under his armpit and his whole world turns from *swarm of fire ants* to *thrown into the witch's oven* as his darkness brightens with pain and light and his body goes rigid—

—he thinks about the man struck by lightning inside his own home—

—about Barney and how he looks so much like a *little boy* now—

—about that time he fought Choo-Choo Ortega in Vegas, and how that crazy sonofabitch almost choked him out but how after one good reversal he was able to get Ortega in a hold and rain a hail of ground-and-pound blows on him till Choo-Choo tapped out—

—about how he doesn't want to go out like this—

He lets himself go. Releases himself from the misery like in the old days, in the octagon days. Doesn't ignore the pain so much as disappear beneath it. He opens his eyes: a new misery, but fuck it. Past the watery curtain his vision looks like a melting masterpiece of running paint, but he can see movement, and there's an exaggerated rictus swimming across his vision like some mad cackling Jack-o-Lantern.

Cason stabs out with a straight punch. Connects. His enemy gurgles, yelps—

Opportunity. He throws another punch low and up—connects with his enemy's gut, hits hard enough he imagines it sinking deep, grabbing his opponent's heart, and squeezing it like it's an overripe grapefruit.

A new thought strikes him:

To win is to escape.

He shoves his foe out of the way and makes a bolt for the door. Or at least the door-shaped smear of brown at the far side of the room.

But his opponent has other ideas.

He hears the sound of a gun's hammer drawn back.

Only two options. Flee or stay. His life now in that regrettable role of being left only to hope—a trembling kitten beneath the dangling Sword of Damocles, the blade held up by only a little red thread.

Cason doesn't know which option affords him the best chance. But he's blind. And his face feels like napalm still burning.

He stops. Panting. Out of breath and out of shape.

"Don't move." The voice, rough and rusty like a can full of nails and screws. The words imperfect, too—hissed over lips that aren't lips but caterpillars of scar tissue, irregular and inflexible. "You want answers, yeah?"

"Go to hell."

"Been there and back again. You want to know the score? You want to know what they did to you and your family? You want to know *who they are?* I can pull back the curtain. I can set the stage. You want to see? Then let me show you."

CHAPTER NINE
Ex Nihilo

"Do you think I'm pretty?"

Psyche asks the question idly, as she tugs back the curtains on the bedroom window and stares out and up into the sky. Looking for anything with wings. The Driver is coming one way or another, soon as it catches her scent. She's done a great deal to distort and disturb the psychic imprint she leaves in her wake—but eventually the Driver will figure that out.

So, in the meantime then, idle conversation.

It's a lie, this idleness. The question neither empty nor casual. But the way she asks it: flip, one-off, like it's a half-formed thought.

"I think you're the most beautiful woman I've ever seen," Alison says. Her words take on a dreamy, listless quality.

"Thank you," Psyche says. But the woman's words do little to soothe the kinks out of her tangled nerves—after all, Alison is only saying that because Psyche is *making* her. Which makes it all the more surprising when the woman adds:

"You're the most beautiful and... the most... horrible."

That last part, a struggle to get out. Those final three words lose the dreamy vibe as a coldness creeps in, a stinging saline slush. Psyche didn't make her say those words. And couldn't stop her, either.

Psyche's just... rusty, is all. That's what she tells herself. Honestly, she's been rusty ever since Zeus abandoned them and Aphrodite made her a captive.

"Yes," she says in response, still watching pale clouds crawl across the washed-out watercolor sky. "I am horrible. But you don't know what I've been through, do you? My poor husband. His horrid mother. I tried, you know. I tried to make it all *work*. I did things in pursuit of her approval that I never thought I could do. Finally I'd done enough to earn her esteem and stave off her jealousy... and for a time it was fine. But then the Usurper came and three decades ago threw us all out of our houses." *Even Zeus, beautiful Zeus.* She sighs. "And now here we are. My husband is dead. Yours is a killer. I'm trying to make things right."

"Yes, of course," Alison says. Once more her voice soft and slow. "You don't deserve what they did to you. You've proven yourself again and again. And you're so pretty. I'd do anything to be allowed to kiss any part of you. Anything at all for any part."

Psyche turns, shrugs. "You're just saying that because I'm making you. Besides, I am still stung over the demise of my husband. I couldn't dare share myself with another." Though, of course, he was by no means chaste, was he? Gave himself up to whatever warm mouth or open hole he found appealing on a given evening. Used them up and left them as dry, gormless husks yearning only for his touch for the rest of their short, inadequate lives.

But he never gave his soul to anyone. That she's sure of. Because it's hers. Or was, at least. Now it's gone. She can't feel it anymore. Can't touch it. His mind and heart, closed forever—no, not merely closed, but walled off, sealed away with endless bricks piled atop one another. It deadens her. Psyche feels no grief—only an empty raggedy hole where grief once should've lived. When she found out that he was gone, the sorrow welled up within her and spouted like a geyser—screams of rage and visions of madness—and then she found her wings and fled to the skies. But soon after, it was like the sorrow was milk in a glass and she'd spilled it all—and now the glass would no longer fill.

Alison continues to clean the weapons strewn across her bed. Barney sleeping in the middle—Psyche couldn't abide the child's questions. Incessant. Like the whining buzz of a gnat venturing into your ear canal—*ugh*. Children. So she reached into the child's mind and turned his conscious mind *off* for a time—easy enough to do, as the mind is her domain, and his is like a simple toy. Now he sleeps, and Alison brings and cleans the weapons.

Weapons is a bit of a misnomer. Kitchen implements, mostly. Knives and forks and other stabby things. Two screwdrivers. A sharpened toothbrush. A whittled broomstick. But the piece de resistance, a real weapon: a small rosewood-handled .38 special revolver. Now gleaming thanks to Alison obsessively polishing it, staring into the blue-black barrel with dead eyes.

It won't stop the Driver, but it'll slow it down. Alison will make a wonderful sacrifice should it come to that. The child, too, if need be. And, if the Driver does not come, then she will be armed when it comes time to kill the woman's husband.

Psyche will enjoy that. Or so she tells herself. She hopes that empty hole inside her heart can at least be filled with happiness over an enemy's pain, if not grief over her husband being ripped from the grand and cosmic tapestry.

"I'm... hungry." Alison's voice is again small, steely, cold.

"Oh. Yes." Psyche *hrms*. Alison looks pale and peckish. Humans need to eat, don't they? Such frail little beasties. With such curious origins, too. Did man come out of nothing? Or was he born from chaos? Or the sea? Or from clay? Or from two divine parents who fucked and squirted him out on the dusty desert ground? The truth is, she doesn't know. Nobody seems to (though they'll be sure to tell you otherwise)—not Zeus, not Shiva, not Marduk or Inanna. Lucifer once told a story that said men were not made in the Usurper's image but rather were the manifestation of sin—sprung out of the Devil's head fully-formed. A lie perhaps stolen in a way from Athena. Matters little now. Nobody's seen the Devil in years. And he was always a liar, anyway.

Everybody has their own tale to tell and no proof that there's truth in the telling.

But one thing that seems certain: humans, however they came about, are weak.

And they need to eat. *Ugh.*

"Go," Psyche waves her off. "Go make yourself a... whatever it is you eat." She feels for the woman's mind and a cascade of images spring forth: a bowl of cereal, a hot sandwich, a plate of noodles, a crisp wet salad. And interspersed within, an image of Alison putting the snub-barrel gun to Psyche's temple and pulling the trigger. A crass fantasy and one that will yield no fruit, but Psyche decides that the human may keep it for now.

Alison sets the gun down. "I... Barney. Food."

"The boy doesn't need to eat. He's asleep. All of him is asleep. Even his hungers."

"But—"

"I said go."

She gives a small, hard psychic shove.

Alison's eyes lose focus and she stumbles out of the room. Psyche calls after in a sing-songy voice:

"Don't be long, precious. For soon we hunt."

CHAPTER TEN
Show, Don't Tell

THE SEPTA BUS stinks like the worst smells of humanity. Body odor and stale urine. Foot odor. Spilled beer. The vinegar tang of goulash. The sour stench of kim chi—Cason knows it's kim chi because, sure enough, there's some barefoot Korean guy with a Tupperware container in his lap digging into it with a spoon and shoving fermented cabbage in his mouth with great gooey slurps.

Sitting next to Cason is the man known as Cicatrix—sitting so close that you might almost suggest he was *cuddling up*, though the gun under the tented newspaper pressed into Cason's ribs defies that definition.

Cason watches him. The man's foam-slick tongue wets lips made only of scar tissue. His finger—a crooked twig, puffy with cracked calluses—probes the crater in his head that was once an ear but is now just a *hole*. He's trying to figure out how old the man is. Older than him, surely. Late 40s? Early 50s? Older still? The maimed face offers too few clues—all buried beneath criss-crossing furrows of scar tissue. Scar tissue that Cason can now see continues well beyond his face—down his neck, around his arms, each finger laced with a mesh of old slices and gashes.

The man jabs Cason in the ribs with the gun.

"You like staring at me?"

"Not really."

"I dunno about that. Way you and everybody else on this bus is watching me I half expect some of you to hike down your shorts and start diddling yourselves. Maybe I should put up a website. Charge people for the peep." All the man's consonants are hissed and whispered as they come out of his ruined mouth—some are lost entirely, dropped into a dark hole and forever forgotten.

Cason blinks raw, red eyes. Sniffs. His nose is still crusted with mucus—the so-called Cicatrix didn't give him time to clean up. He just grabbed a newspaper and a crumpled paper bag and used the gun to politely *urge* Cason onto the bus.

"What the hell was in that canister, anyway?"

"Tiger piss and pickle juice," the man growls. "Whaddya think it was? Pepper spray. Capsaicin. My own special brew. I used a couple of those ghost chilis—the, ahhh, naga booty whatevers. Stuff's so potent it'll eat the chrome off a bumper." His bloodshot eyes roll around in their lidless sockets and point toward Cason. "Speakawhich, seems like it worked as designed. You look like you shoved your face in a bee-hive. Your face is almost as ugly as mine, and I look like a human garbage fire."

"Fuck you."

"Yeah, yeah, fuck me. Such a nice Kenzo boy."

So he knows more about me than I do about him. "Where we going, anyway? Heading south, but why? Where? Thought you were going to tell me what's going on."

"I said *show* you. Showing's always so much better than telling. You rather *hear* about an elephant butt-fucking a pony, or you rather *see* it?"

Cason's twisted face gives him the answer.

"Bad choice, maybe. Point is, I tell you what I tell you, even after all you've seen, you probably won't believe me. But if I *show* you, you'll get it lickety-split." The freak fishes in his pocket, pulls out a plastic bottle of unlabeled eyedrops, pops a few in each eye. "Gotta moisten the old jeepers-creepers, you know."

"Fine. Whatever. Where we headed? Might as well tell me, because I'll see when we get there."

"North of the airport. Eastwick."

Eastwick's a shithole. So much of the city is. Run-down houses. Some flooded and damp—that whole area's on a marshy plain. Then there's the dump sites: the area's the closest thing you can get to 'rural' living inside the city margins, with tracts of open land here and there. Companies have been using that land to dump trash and chemicals and medical waste. Burying it sometimes; other times, maybe not so much with the burying and more with the 'leaving it out in the open.'

"And what's in the bag?"

"You'll see. Why spoil the fun?"

THE BUS LEAVES them in a cloud of fumes.

"Walk," Cicatrix says.

They move to cross an empty parking lot, leaving road traffic behind. They head toward a sidestreet lined with grungy townhomes.

The freak stays behind. Gun still hidden under the newspaper, bag tucked under his armpit. Cason starts to think that he can take him. He has to move fast—no move is faster than a bullet, but that's not the point. The point is to disarm. Or point the gun elsewhere. He just needs opportunity. But when?

"So. Cicatrix. Quite a name."

"Not a name. More like a... *nom de plume*. A CB handle."

"Got a real name?"

"Steve. Bob. Delbert. John Jacob Jingle-titties."

Cason shrugs. "I'll just call you Trixie, then."

"No, I don't think you will."

"Sure thing, Trixie."

"Watch your mouth."

"No problem, Trix. Hey, I dated a girl named Trixie once. Had a dog named Trixie, too—cutest little poopsy-doodle poodle."

"I swear to—you know I have a gun, right?"

"Trixie's a good gun moll name. I bet you tuck it in your garter belt—"

"Frank!" the freak yells. Spit flecking the back of Cason's neck. "My name's Frank, mmkay? Frank Polcyn. Now, I know what you're thinking, *Cason Cole.* You're thinking now'd be a real good time to do some of your fancy ninja fu-fu shit and kick the gun out of my hand or twist my wrist or whatever wily bullshit you got up your sleeves. You do, you'll never know. You'll never know why your boss was some kind of freaky seduction magnet. You'll never know how I unzipped him like a fucking Members Only jacket. You'll never know why your wife and son turned on you."

Cason stops. Fingers tightening into fists.

He's frazzled. He's waving his hands around like a drowning man. And he's right. Now's a good time for that fancy ninja fu-fu shit. Frank the freak.

His fists relax.

"I need to know," he says, voice low and quiet. "You promise to show me?"

"I promise. But first you gotta walk."

Cason walks.

THREE BLOCKS UP and one over, they arrive at their destination. It's a single house with white siding, sandwiched between two sets of brown townhomes—the world's ugliest ice cream sandwich. The siding on the house is green with striations of mold and mildew. Gutters hang, broken. Latticework under the front porch reveals gleaming eyes: cats or raccoons or possums, Cason doesn't know.

Broken walkway stones lead to the front steps, which are themselves just cinder blocks with boards laid across them.

The wind shifts and a smell comes from the house. Something wild and gamy. Olfactory memory is strange—Cason knows it reminds him of something, but he's not sure what. He knows he remembers it, but he can't put his finger on the memory itself.

"Go up and knock," Frank says.

"Whose house is this?"

"I *said* go up and go knock. Unless you want me to knock you on the head with the butt of this .45, pal."

"I'd like to see you try."

"*I'd like to see you try*," Frank mimics, his voice a nasally, raspy whine. "You want in on this adventure, then you gotta knock to be let in."

Cason hesitates, but finally walks up on the wobbly two-by-fours across the cinderblocks and steps up to the porch. Beneath the creaking wood, he hears the animals shuffle and skitter. Again that smell hits him: musky, earthy, wild.

It's then he realizes what it reminds him of.

The primate house. At the zoo.

Sweat and fur and piss and shit. All wrapped up in a blanket of animal musk.

Cason walks up. Sees a mailbox stuffed with mail. Number on the box and a name: ARTHUR MESSING. The mail is piled up and tumbling over the edge. Junk, mostly—coupons and menus and other mailers. Some bills, by the look of it. All cascading from the box to the porch floor like a paper waterfall interrupted.

"Knock."

Cason sighs. Lifts his hand, raps on the door.

The house shudders with approaching footsteps.

foom

foom

foom

FOOM

FOOM

The door opens.

That heady monkey smell really hits Cason now, a punch to the nose as a massive dude answers the door—giant, not like Tundu, who's big all around, but giant in the way a cave troll is giant. Long legs, long arms, but a short torso and a head the size and shape of a small watermelon. The man's hair is a wild thatch of brown and gray, his mouth a mess of crooked teeth, the nose a smushed piggy snout. Dirt on his cheeks, under his nails, across his yellow chompers.

The guy starts to ask "Who the hell are—"

But he doesn't get to finish the question.

Cason's head explodes—or at least that's how it feels. Frank sticks the gun up over Cason's shoulder and pulls the trigger. The gunshot is everything: noise and fury and stink, and the massive man's head snaps back and his body topples backward like a redwood felled with dynamite. The floor shakes as he hits.

Fuck, Cason thinks. He can't hear anything. Only the pulsating shriek in his ear. He staggers forward into the house, shoved by Frank.

Cason didn't ask for this. Didn't ask to be in on a *murder*. Bad enough what happened to his boss—but he thought today would give him context, not just another dead body to deal with.

He snaps. Yanks Frank into the house by his gun-hand. Slams him into a wall lined with ugly mural wallpaper meant to look like a pine forest—a framed painting, of a couple of deer sipping lake water in the shadow of mountains, tumbles off the wall and shatters. Frank yelps—the gun goes off again, this time the bullet whining against an old iron heating grate—Cason pulls his arm taut and kicks hard up into Frank's solar plexus.

The freak *ooomphs* as Cason twists the gun out.

Then brings the flat of the gun hard against the bastard's head.

The Cicatrix goes down—a still, unmoving, scar-flesh lump. The bag under his arm now a crumpled-up package smashed beneath his hip.

"Jesus," Cason says, panting. In his ear: the deafening whine.

He thinks: *just leave, just go—run—you were never here.*

But the guy could be okay. Well—not *okay*. Nobody's okay after getting shot in the head. But some people survive it, right? The head's made of harder stuff than people realize. Bullet maybe rides the skull to the back. Or shoots a part-the-seas path through the two halves of the brain and goes clear out the back without blowing out any vital circuitry.

Cason kneels over the giant.

Oh, shit.

Multiple problems strike Cason as notable.

First, the bullet. It's half-flattened against the wrinkled flesh of the man's brow—a squashed mushroom of lead.

Second, the man's eyes are open. And blinking. And looking at Cason.

Third, and most troubling: the man is not a man.

He's changed.

His piggish snout is now an actual pig snout. His mouth is a thresher bar of crooked needle tusks sticking out over the top and bottom lip, criss-crossing like briar barbs. His face is a pelt of hair to match the snarl upon his head.

Yellow eyes.

Leathery flesh.

Breath that'd make a vulture choke on its own puke.

A low rumble rises in the beast-man's chest. Cason can't hear it but he can feel it. The creature says something—the words lost to the roar in Cason's ears—just before the monster lifts Cason up like he's the father and Cason's a newborn baby.

Of course, this father doesn't mind throwing his infant into the ceiling.

Cason slams into popcorn ceiling—then the floor rushes up to greet him and punch the air clean out of his lungs. The monster man is already up, standing over Cason.

Again he's trying to say something—foul mouth moving, teeth gnashing together, but Cason can't hear it.

And *again* the monster tosses Cason like he's a ragdoll. Into one wall. Then the other. Then the door. Then back to the floor.

The giant beast-man—fur now bristling through his greasy gray shirt and around the margins of his baggy shorts—squats over Cason like an animal squatting over his kill. He roars words, this time words that Cason can hear as they barrel through his temporary deafness:

"—he should have never created man. Man ruins everything. Have you seen? Have you looked outside? You spread your filth everywhere you go. All that you touch is poison and sickness. Kishelemùkonk moved mountains to prove you should exist, but he was wrong. The Great Spirit was wrong!"

The monster forms a wrecking ball with both his hands and raises them high above Cason's head—

But then pauses.

Draws a long, deep, snorting *sniff*.

The beast-man's yellow eyes narrow.

"But you are not all-man, are you? You are a child of the Beast, too."

Cason tries to say something—*anything*—but his words come out a breathless squeak. Then, from behind the giant, a voice.

"Hey, skunk-ape."

The beast wheels.

Cason catches sight of Frank standing there, facing down the monster. Frank lobs something—the brown bag—toward the giant.

The giant, reflexively, catches it.

The bomb goes off.

CHAPTER ELEVEN
Monster Mash

NUMB, WEARY, EYES red, ears buzzing.

A little while later, after Cason makes sure he's not dead, Frank says the show-and-tell must continue.

They leave the hallway where the walls are cratered (in Cason-sized cavities) and worse, peppered with bits of black ichor and stuck fur and splinters of—Cason blinks, sees that it's wood. Sees that the splinters are in his hands, too. His foot nudges something: a tiny wooden doll head. Before he can look too long, Frank is pulling him upstairs.

The smell is strong up here. Coppery, greasy. Wild, too—gamey, untamed. They pass by a bathroom which is covered in mold—not black mold or pink mold like you'd find in a shower, but green *fuzzy* mold. The kind you find on an old loaf of bread. Cason staggers through the tour, not sure what he's supposed to see or why he's even here at all. His body hurts. Like he's been hit by a garbage truck, then thrown into the *back* of said garbage truck, then crushed and pulped with the rest of the waste.

They pass a bedroom. Just a mat on the floor and some pillows. It's like a greenhouse in there—not just because of the heat, but because the room is all tables and potted plants. Most of them huge. Red roses, red not like blood but like globs of bright paint on dark stems. Plants with leaves like floppy elephant ears. Ivy and clematis vines climbing well beyond their latticework mooring and up the walls and to the ceiling and into the vents.

And still Frank waves Cason on.

To the attic. No steps for the attic—just a pull-down ladder. Cason grits his teeth as he climbs, trying not to drive the splinters further into his palms. He uses his wrists to stabilize and hauls his body up into the dark space.

The smell. This is the dark heart of the awful smell. It hits Cason the way the monster-man hit him—his stomach shudders and he wonders if he's going to throw up.

Click. Darkness banished by a bare bulb hanging from a brown wire.

Cason throws up. Head turned aside. Eyes closed because he doesn't want to see.

Frank just nods. "I figured you'd wanna see that."

FLASHES OF THE attic: *blood and bones and pelts and child's toys piled in heaping, steaming mounds; abattoir, slaughterhouse, feeding ground, bear cave.*

Cason sits in the beast-man's kitchen, picking splinters from his hands with his teeth. It's hard work, because his hands are slick with his blood—and the blood of the beast-man who disintegrated before his eyes in an exhalation of fur and red mist.

He spits each splinter onto the dirty tablecloth. Trying not to throw up each time he does it. But it gives him something to do. Something to think about other than—

Well.

Frank steps into the kitchen, his freakish near-lipless grin calling to mind a cackling skeleton one might put outside the house for Halloween.

He tosses something onto the table:

A charred wooden head of a little girl doll. Yarn hair. Triangle eyes and smiling mouth forming the face, with no nose to speak of. The doll head hits the table, rolls to the edge, then goes over onto the floor.

"I have no idea what the fuck is going on," Cason says. He bites on another splinter, spits it onto the table. Still dozens more to go. "Time to start telling. The showing part is over. Because, I have to tell you, Frank, whatever you just showed me didn't help me understand the situation any better, you feel me?"

Frank chuckles. "Ehhh-yeah, now that I think about it, I guess maybe that didn't really answer *all* your questions."

"It didn't answer any of them. And now I've got about a hundred more."

Frank sits on the edge of a cracked formica counter. "We just killed a monster."

"What kind of monster?"

"Kind that eats raccoons and possums. And stray cats and lost dogs. And... once in a while, a little kid or three." Frank shrugs like it's no big deal. Snaps his fingers, slaps them on his knee in a jerky drum-beat. "The, ahh, this area was once settled by some Indians. Lenni-Lenape. They venerated this spirit, this creature called 'Meesink' who was said to keep the balance between the world of man and the world of nature. All the stories and paintings have him looking like a big, y'know, a Bigfoot—which, as you can see, turned out pretty goddamn accurate."

Cason's head spins. His entire reality does. "Is this real? Is this a real thing? Am I just... dead? Sick? High on something?"

"It's the real deal, dude."

"Monsters are real."

"Not just monsters."

Cason's eyes narrow. "What else?"

"The gods."

"Gods. Plural. Not God."

"He's real, too. He's just one among many."

Cason stands. Almost falls. "You know what? I'm outta here."

Frank hops down, stands in Cason's way.

"Whoa, whoa, whoa. Slow your roll, stud. How do you think this whole thing works? You think your wife and kid want to murder you because that's just how they feel? Or you think it's because someone's pulling their strings? It's time to open your eyes—really *open* them, now—and look around. There's magic in this life, and it ain't ours to play with. It's *theirs*. The gods are the ones with all the tricks. We're just their playthings. They're the kid with the magnifying glass and we're the burning ants."

Gods. Monsters. Impossible. And yet—not really, not at all. Women with wings, man-boys with unholy magnetism, and that little business about his wife and son burning alive in a car but now, miraculously, being alive as if it never happened.

His legs almost give out, but Frank steadies him.

"But they have a saying," Frank continues. "The ants weigh more than the elephants. You know that saying?"

The smallest head shake. *No.*

"The ants weigh more than the elephants. Doesn't seem true, because a teeny tiny ant is just a squirming black bug in a big-ass elephant's butthole. But that's not what the saying says, the saying says *ants* and *elephants*, plural. Because all the ants together weigh more than all the elephants together. And that's how we are. Gods and man. We don't outweigh them one to one, but together, boy. There's a lot more of us than them."

The questions—his mind is like a bucket that just overturned and now he can't stop the questions. "Who are they? How did they get here? Why me?"

Frank chuckles. "The easy answer? *They were pushed.* The longer, crazier answer is—"

His already bulging bug-eyes seem to go wider as the skin around them pulls back—Frank's look of perpetual surprise is suddenly magnified.

"Someone's here," Frank says.

A knock at the door.

Not a friendly knock, either. *Wham wham wham wham.*

The hairs on Cason's neck stand. Arms, too. Straight and tall like soldiers.

"One of *them*," Frank says. "How the fuck—" He hurries over to the window over the sink, pulls back a filmy curtain, quickly lets it fall back in place. "We gotta go."

"I want to see," Cason says, moving toward the sink.

Frank stands in his way. "No time. We have to go."

"Move."

"Case, the longer we wait—"

Frank's not a big man. Cason shoves him aside.

And then he sees. The window overlooks the porch. It takes a second to click, but the wild hair gives it away. It's the woman from the woods: the one bound in golden chains. The one with wings— wings that are, at present, nowhere to be seen.

Someone else is there, too—

The other person takes a step back.

Alison.

Alison.

Her eyes, empty. Mouth slack, with saliva moistening her lips. Her head has this gentle swaying, like a boat on the ocean lost to the waves. She's holding a gun. A gun he bought her to defend herself—at the time she was working at the Children's Hospital of Philadelphia in the telemetry unit (he remembers the way she answered the phone there: *Alison Cole, 2B Telemetry*), and she sometimes walked a long way to work and he wanted her to have a gun. She never took it. Never used it. And now here she is with it.

Suddenly, a feeling in his mind—different from when he was around E. but the same, too. Like an invasion. Like someone cupping his consciousness in a pair of cold hands. Probing. Looking for something.

"Alison," he says. He has to get to her. Save her from this.

He turns.

There stands Frank. Gun in one hand, a steak knife in the other, with a silverware drawer open behind him. The gun is leveled at Cason's head.

"Don't," Frank says. "You can't help her. Not today."

"That's my wife."

"Trust me, I know. And I get it; I do. But this isn't the day." Frank takes the hand with the knife and pulls down on the collar of his filthy white t-shirt. Turning it into a v-neck before finally the fabric starts to rip.

A symbol reveals itself. A symbol in scar tissue. Three lines crossing one another, forming a kind of asterisk. Smaller symbols at the six points, dead-ending each line: they look almost like letters (N, M, U), but they're not quite.

"I gotta carve this into your chest," Frank says.

"Fuck you. I want my wife."

"And you'll get her back. With my help. Not by running off half-cocked."

Outside, more knocking: *wham wham wham*. A voice calling:

"I know you're in there. Your wife and I would like to talk to you."

The invisible hands cupping Cason's mind start to squeeze. The urge rises in him, hot and white, to go to the front door. To kneel there. To let his wife put that gun into his mouth so that he may embrace oblivion.

Frank seethes: "She's in your head already." He smacks Cason across the face—not with the gun, but with the back of his gun-hand.

Reaction. Cason has Frank's hand in his own. One twist and the man yelps: the gun drops into Cason's hand. "I'm not letting you carve that into my chest."

Frank's eyes dart around the room. Sees a cup of pens and markers next to a dented toaster and a pile of fraying napkins littered with mouse turds. "Then we'll do something more temporary."

HE'S THERE, AND then he's gone.

Psyche stands on the decrepit porch, feeling tight and tense and *unclean,* and one second she feels Cason's mind in the house like a mouse in a maze, and then there's the light of pain and he's gone. Not fading like a ghost, but rather as if he was never there in the first place. How dearly, deeply disappointing.

She searches, of course. She pulls Alison along—not by her hand, but by a leash wound around the woman's mind—and stalks around the outside of the house. The alleys between this house and the row-homes. Past barrels filled with rainwater and thousands of mosquito larvae twisting in the murk. To the house's back door, long boarded up, beneath eaves thick with wasp combs. No one. Nothing. No trace of human life.

Worse, she can't feel him *at all*. It took her a while to find him at first—she had to probe the holes in Alison's mind, creating an image out of negative space, the Cason Cole-shaped *cut-out* in her memories, an elegant act of psychic surgery with the fingerprints of Psyche's husband all over them (incurring in her no small swell of pride). Once she had him, she had him, and it was time to hunt. But now: nothing. Gone again. As if he never existed.

She goes inside the house, of course—no stone left unturned and all that. She finds the splintery wooden dolls in the walls. She sees and smells the residue of the creature that lived here: some foul skunk-ape from the local pantheon, nobody of any consequence, but worryingly dead just the same. She finds the plants. The bones. The blood. The mold. A wild-man with a wild-house, all *wildly* out of control. Ugh. So unpleasant.

It takes her far too long to find the passageway.

It's more *cellar* than *basement*—dirt floor instead of concrete, rock walls. A great many bugs. Cockroaches and crickets and pill-bugs. Spiders, too—thin-bodied, diaphanous spiders with long, wispy limbs hiding in the nooks and crannies.

Behind a water heater is a hole.

She smells Cole's scent: his blood, his sweat. His fear and uncertainty.

But there's someone else, too. The smell of blistery skin. Lotion and eyedrops. Fear, too—but more overpowering is the hatred lurking there. It's a smell she knows. One she hasn't caught scent of in quite a while, now. Decades.

The smells are fading. The breath from the tunnel is old, stale, carries only meager strands of scent. Still. It's what they have, and the hunt must go on.

CHAPTER TWELVE
The Ants And The Elephants

THE COLD CONDENSATION on the outside of the pint glass feels good against Cason's palms. The splinters are all gone, now: picked out in the bar bathroom and dumped in the toilet before a flush. He knows he should be afraid of infection, but right now he's afraid of *so much more*. Afraid for his wife and son. Afraid for himself. Afraid for the world, and most of all, afraid for his own sanity; because none of this can be real.

Except it sure feels real.

The symbol on his chest is a reminder of that. Drawn there by Frank with a permanent marker. Frank snorted as he drew it, muttering, "Bullshit it's permanent, you'll *wish* it was permanent, shoulda let me use the knife." The symbol only added to Cason's fear and frustration—it offered him little psychic solace.

Now: the two of them sit in a red leather booth not far from Citizens Bank park, where the Phillies play. Frank totters back over, drops a wooden bowl of peanuts on the table. The floor is littered with peanut shells: everywhere you walk, *crunch crunch crunch*.

"I like to make bombs," Frank says, out of nowhere.

"That one I already figured out."

"My bombs are special. Different."

"Yeah, they're different all right. That last one was filled with dolls."

"Ohtas. Little wooden ceremonial dolls made by the Lenni-Lenape."

"The bomb that killed E.—"

"Eros."

"That wasn't filled with little dollies."

Frank shakes his head. "Nah. Arrowheads. Specifically bronze arrowheads. Paid a pretty penny to have those made. I mean, I guess I coulda just robbed a bunch from the Art Museum—they got a whole collection and I know a guy—but it felt wrong somehow."

"You seem like a guy who's real concerned about right and wrong."

"You'd be surprised."

Cason sips the beer. Dark. Bitter. Cold. Good.

"Can I tell you a story?" Frank says.

"Can I stop you?"

"It's an important story."

"They have my wife. And probably my son. Nothing's more important than that, Frank. You understand?"

"I do, and that's exactly why you need to hear this story."

He shifts uncomfortably in his seat. Fingertips with too-long nails—each overhanging a half-moon of filth—pull tight across the table.

Then he tells it.

"YOU KNOW HOW, in the 1980s, the 1950s were big again? *Peggy Sue Got Married* and *Back to the Future* and Oldies Stations and all that garbage. I was young, twenty-two at the time, and a buddy of mine convinced me to go to this... sock-hop. A dance, a fake high school dance where they played Chubby Checker and 'Johnny B. Goode' and you danced for hours—but you had to take your shoes off, like in the original sock-hops, so your shoes didn't screw up the floor varnish."

It must be hard for him to talk this long. As he speaks, he dips a paper napkin into a glass of water, wets his lips with it. A little tub of petroleum jelly comes out of his pocket, too, and occasionally he dabs a blob onto a pinky finger and smears it around his mouth—not just on the scar tissue that forms his false lips, but a good half-inch radius in every direction. His crater mouth shines in the light.

"I didn't know what I was doing at this thing. I couldn't dance worth a good goddamn. I was like a bug trying not to burn his feet on a hot plate. Better than how people really danced in the '80s, I guess, but I didn't have a lick of rhythm.

"Good thing is, while I may have danced like a drunken orangutan, I still looked damn good. I know, you're sitting there thinking—*but how could he look sexier than he does now?*—but trust me, I did. I wasn't just handsome. I was what you might call a 'pretty boy.' Hell, that's what my friends actually called me. Pretty Boy. Frankie 'Pretty Boy' Polcyn."

The words are made imperfect by ruined lips. Consonants are breathy and ill-formed; the 'p's don't pop, the 'b's buzz unnaturally, the 'm's are a whisper that never quite connect. His s-sounds are sometimes mushy and slurred (*thatsh what my friendsh actually called ffffee*).

His eyes glisten. They stop watching Cason and drift toward the dim bar lights hanging from the ceiling.

"So I attracted the eyes of an equally pretty lady. Hair the color of straw. Freckles all up and down her cheeks. Some girls there did the Pink Lady *Grease* thing, but not her—she was all sweetness and light and twirling seafoam poodle skirt. And *she* came up to *me*. That's how she was. Forward but not forward, you know? Still made you feel like you had to work for it. She didn't come up and ask me to dance. She hovered. Acted all coy. She still made me do the work, right? I still got to feel like a man. She gave that to me."

He draws a deep breath.

"Sally. That was her name. Sally Delacroix. Sweetness and light and seafoam. Did I say that already? Whatever. We danced. Danced for hours until the music wound down and the lights came on and for a second I thought the dream was over. Dead and done. The lights killed it—bright, harsh, hot. But then she asked if I wanted to go out and get a drink, and at first I thought maybe she meant a milkshake or something—keepin' in the spirit of things—but she said no, a proper drink, and we did. We went to a bar not unlike this one. The Buttonwood. I remember I had a beer. She had a gin and tonic.

"We made love that night. Yeah, yeah, yeah, it's easier just to say that we fucked like two ferrets in a tube sock—but this was something different. It wasn't just the in-and-out of the thing, it was the way we moved together. Way I felt nervous. Way she..." He pauses. "I remember she shook, you know? Trembled. And I could smell her deodorant, a powdery smell, light and airy, but I could smell *her* beneath it. Could smell her sweat and her body and then her hair would fall across my nose and I'd smell strawberries and cream because that's how her shampoo smelled. She was soft and long and moved against me like a pillow stuffed with angel feathers (and just so we're clear the air on this, angels are real, don't you dare think they're not—scary motherfuckers each and every one of 'em)."

He sips his beer. A long slow pull.

"We got married a week later. I know, right? Fuckin' bad idea, and maybe it was, but nothing in my life has ever felt smarter than that one decision. We went to Las Vegas. At the time I lived out on the West Coast, so driving to Vegas was a thing you did; and so we did it. We did the whole Elvis schtick. I guess continuing that whole 1950s vibe. We did the Elvis chapel where you get married by him—though not the young jailhouse Elvis, nah, they stick you with the bloated toilet-clogger Elvis all stuffed in his sequined jumpsuit, like some kind of fat-ass Evel Knievel. But it felt great just the same. We loved our Fat Elvis. We hugged him and laughed and he watched us kiss.

"So began the honeymoon. We didn't have a lot of money—she answered phones for a local construction company and I drove a schoolbus—so we ended up at this little motel way off the Strip. But it was nice. Pink flamingos. Palm trees. A kidney-shaped pool that had waters so green it glittered like emeralds—though thinking back it was probably just the tile they had at the bottom of the pool, but fuck it, the illusion was the illusion and was good enough for me.

"First couple nights we did our thing—*that's* when we fucked like ferrets, boy. We did it up-down-left-right-sideways. We were like deep sea divers, having to come up for air from time to time. Towel off. Drink some water. Get back into it. The room was like our womb. I'd filled it with flowers, you know, like, tropical flowers. Not roses, but—well, I don't know my flowers, but the kind you'd find strung on a hula girl's necklace. It was perfect. Best days of my life.

"But on the third day... that's when we had our first 'marital disagreement.'"

It's here that Frank lifts a finger to call over a waitress. The one who comes over is different from the one that brought them their beer—this one's older, more haggard, stringy red hair hanging in front of deep-set eyes. She stares at Frank like he's a pile of roadkill, but Frank's expression says it's a look he's used to. He just mumbles an order for a shot of Dewar's. Gets one for Cason, too. Cason tells him no, it's too early, but Frank just tells the waitress to bring both shots and they'll figure it out.

"Sally wanted to sit by the pool for the day. Maybe go get a drink at the little cocktail lounge down the block. Tiki bar, I remember. Tiki Tom's? Something. But I said, shit, we're in *Vegas*. And we hadn't done any gambling yet and I just wanted my one day to play the blackjack tables. She said pool-and-lounge, I said gambling, and in the end it wasn't a fight—nobody raised their voice, everybody stayed smiling. We just decided to each do our own thing that day and we'd meet back up at night at Tiki Tom's."

Shots arrive. Frank pincers his with thumb and forefinger, then lifts his craggy chin toward Cason. "Go on. Drink."

"Seriously?" Cason says. "It's early."

"You're already drinking beer. Go harder, boy. You're gonna need it. Or *I'm* gonna need you to need it. Or something." Frank's jawline tightens, and when his face tightens, you can really see it—all the scar-lines tug and pull like a net with a fish thrashing in it. Cason shakes his head and figures, *what the hell*, it's been that kind of morning. Both men tip their heads back—the amber liquid disappears. Frank coughs, tinks the two glasses together, and continues.

"So. She stays poolside. I go to the casinos. I started at the Circus Circus because it was closest, but what a mistake. Clowns are bad luck. I lost a couple bucks. Moved onto the Harrah's. Lost a couple more bucks there. I was starting to feel shitty, like I was being punished for leaving Sally behind. So I'm there at the third casino—the Mirage—and a little voice like a little bird starts pecking at me. Asking, what if something happens to Sally? While I'm gone? I don't know Vegas. I don't know what can happen. And there I sat, thinking I should leave, and so I plopped down the rest of my chips just to get rid of 'em, and what happens? I won. Boom. Big money.

"The rush hit me. Like a warm wave. And I kept playing. And I kept winning. Each win quieted that voice a little more until I couldn't hear it at all, and I was up $1200 by the end of the night. I looked at my watch and saw that it was 8pm—and I was supposed to meet Sally at the lounge at 7. And it wasn't a short walk off the strip, either."

Eyedrops, now. He fishes them from a pocket, squeezes a few into each eye. Cason finds it hard to watch. The man can't blink. You put eyedrops in your eyes, that's the first thing everybody does is blink. But Frank's big bloodshot eyes remain open as the drops slide across them—water running off a blister. Cason's own eyes feel suddenly dry and he finds himself blinking a whole bunch without meaning to.

"I go to the lounge. Gaudy, kitschy old Hawaii. Makes me think of the flowers in our room. But Sally's not there. I ask the bartender if he's seen her and he doesn't know shit from shinola. Now I'm getting worried. Anxiety starts to crawl in my gut like a big fat hairy spider and that voice is back, loud now, real loud, *what if something happened to her*—? So I get up and I hoof it back to the motel. And I go to our room and I remember fumbling with the fuckin' keys and I drop them—and I hear a cry from inside the door, a cry of what sounded like someone in pain. Sally. I finally get the keys in the lock and throw open the door."

He hisses air through his teeth.

"And I find her there on the bed. She's face-down between the legs of some broad. Straw-colored hair sliding against this other woman's milky thighs. They're both naked as they were born. Making sounds. Sally's moaning like she never moaned for me. The woman's fingers are in Sally's hair—gentle one minute, tightening her grip the next, then back to gentle. Sally's fingers are curled up under this woman's knees, with her elbows out. All around them are flower petals. Petals from the flowers I bought. Torn up and sprinkled around the room and on the bed.

"The strange woman gives me this look. She just... smiles. Like she doesn't give a fuck." Frank's tongue slides out. Snakes along his non-lips, leaving a slug's trail of spitty slime. "I know what you're thinking. You're thinking, *way to go, Frank, lucky fuckin' ducky, every man's fantasy right there—you shoulda just hiked down your dungarees and got into the mix because one day the honeymoon'll really be over and shit like that won't happen anymore.* But that's not what I was thinking. I was mad. And sad. And this deep well of jealousy started burning me up from the inside like I just poured boiling water down my throat.

"I start yelling. Try to pull Sally out from between this bitch's legs, and Sally just looks up at me—eyes unfocused, mouth all sloppy with juices and lipstick. It's like she doesn't even know me. That just makes me madder, so I really pull this time and yank her ass off the bed—not to hurt her, but just to break apart this—this horror show that's playing out in my motel room, on my goddamn honeymoon.

"I pull her off and she rolls and cracks her head into the set of drawers. You're thinking that this is where she dies or I kill her, but that's not it—she's fine. It's just a bump on the noggin, no blood or brain scrambling or anything, but before I know what's happening, the strange woman is up and standing on the bed like the fuckin' Queen of Sheba, and she's got me by the throat..."

He rubs his face. Dry hands scrub across hard scars. He leans in suddenly like he's sharing a secret. Voice low and slow.

"Listen. This was the most beautiful woman I'd ever seen. Green eyes, red lips, hair wild and blonde like a fire-flare coming off the sun. Curvy, too—not like the twigs they call women these days. A chest you could sleep on. Hips you could build a home on. And she smelled like—like the beach. Not like the nasty beach, not like dead fish, but like sand and salt air and the perfume of tropical flowers."

Cason's innards twist.

The Lexus. The forest. The apple.

He sits up straight. Suddenly tense.

"Next thing I know, she's got me outside. Carrying me by the neck like I'm nothing. And..." He swallows hard. "You won't believe this part; or maybe you will, I dunno. But she whispers in my ear, *Sorry, Pretty Boy*, and then she tosses me into the pool. But the pool isn't just the pool anymore. It's like a... a hand, a cradle, the water catching me in a geyser. For a moment I bob there and then I feel the pain. Water forming whips—sharp like razors, like needles—and cutting across me. Lashing my face and arms and fuckin' everywhere. My lips and couple toes and ears and—"

Here he stops. Crossing his legs under the table. Nervously he fumbles with the eyedrops and plops a few more upon his peepers.

"The water was hot. Burned me, too. When I awoke I was in a hospital. Cops said it must've been some kind of gang thing. Initiation, maybe. Nobody saw anything. And I never saw my bride again.

"That was love, what we had.

"And love... love dies."

So ends Frank's tale.

OUTSIDE THE BAR, Frank smokes a cigarette that he bums off the haggard waitress. She probably doesn't want to give it to him, but he leers and sneers and she's likely afraid to do any differently, so there he stands, puffing comically on a Virginia Slim.

Cason doesn't tell him about his own meeting with the pretty, pretty lady. The lady of the sea. The lady of wrath.

Instead he changes the subject.

"This thing. That you drew on my chest—?"

"Mm," Frank says, exhaling smoke, not by blowing it out, but just by letting his mouth hang open like a door—the smoke tumbles out of his maw. "Sigil. A symbol of protection. One of Solomon's seals.

See, the Old Testament still admitted that other gods and demons and monsters and all that shit were real. Yahweh's the One True God in that book, but only by comparison to all the gods that are considered His lessers. New Testament rolls around and all those other gods are gone—just false idols that never existed. But Solomon knew his shit. Knew how to keep those assholes away from his door. This seal *hides* us from them. They can't just... smell the air and find us by our stink."

"Oh." Cason doesn't know what else to say. This is all a bit much. He pats his chest.

"You're gonna want to get that branded. Or inked. Because it won't last."

"Yeah. Sure." He looks at his watch. It's only noon. "Listen, I'm gonna get out of here. This has been a long, fucked-up day."

"I'll be in touch."

"I think we're done here."

"Listen. The gods? I told you that there were gods, and there were monsters. That's a bit of bullshit right there, because you wanna know the real truth? Truth is, the gods *are* monsters. They're not like you and me, Case. They play at being human, but they're made of ideas and emotions and they're far fucking weirder and meaner than anything we could ever hope to be. You feel me? They've got your wife and your kid twisted around their fingers. Which means they still have *you* wound up, too. I want to cut you free. I want to cut us *all* free. I want payback. We're the fuckin' *resistance*, you and me."

"I dunno, Frank." Cason can't deny it: his heart is pounding, an angry, excited gallop. Get his wife back. Get his *son* back. Rip the scales from his eyes and start paying back those cosmic, celestial sonofabitches who thought they could fuck with him and his.

"Like I said, I'll be in touch."

"How will you know where to find me?"

"Truth-telling time. Your brother sold you up the river."

"What?"

"Uh-huh. Called a guy I knew who called me. Said you were poking around looking for me. So I looked back and... he set you up."

Conny. That prick.

"So," Frank continues, "I know how to get in touch."

Cason says nothing. He's too outraged. He just nods. And that's that.

FRANK WATCHES CASON go. A big African dude picks him up in a yellow cab.

He pitches the cigarette into a puddle. It fizzles.

A voice whispers in his ear—a voice that has no body, that stinks of burning rock and makes the air in front of Frank's face warp and shift like heat coming off the hood of a hot car. The voice says:

Is he with us?

Frank grumbles in assent.

How much does he know?

"Enough. But not everything."

As is the plan.

Frank shakes his head. Cason, that poor fuck.

PART TWO
THE DIVINE
RIGHT OF KINGS

CHAPTER THIRTEEN
The Whispered Missives
Of Secret Gods

CASON RUNS.

Dark trees against a moonless night turn the forest into a labyrinth and Cason into a blind man—branches whip against his face, cutting his cheeks. Thorns catch at his fingers and palms. But the Antlered God is coming.

His coming is heralded by the crashing of brush, the angry snorts, the occasional howls that turn Cason's blood and bowels to cold milk. He looks up. Tries to think of how he could guide himself by the stars, but it's a fool's endeavor—he knows nothing of the stars and the broken ceiling of trees above does little to afford him a proper view. And so he does the only thing he can—

Run, rabbit, run. He lets his head fall forward and works his legs to catch up—a terrified, inelegant flight.

The Antlered God laying on the forest floor, the dark woman with devil horns straddling him, pinning him to the earth with hands like bird-claws—moving against his bristled hips, his hooves digging ditches in the mossy loam. Beast mouth raised to the sky, tongue playing across white fangs, antlers tangled in brush and vine. The dark woman laughs—her breasts are small and sharp, nipples tilted upwards like the beaks of curious birds, and as she laughs, real birds settle in the eaves of the trees above, dark birds, black crows with blood-red eyes. Cason sees, but he's not supposed to see—he knows this, knows intimately that he's just seen something that human eyes are not meant to witness, and before he knows what's happening, the woman is shrieking as she's thrown into the brush and the Antlered God is up and charging and—

Cason runs. But the forest is deep and dark; the maze seems forever. Where is Tundu? And Frank? In the distance, he hears Alison: sobbing, sobbing his name.

He passes a tree. On it, a yellow sign, rusted: the three-bladed nuclear trefoil, round in the center of a triangle, hanging half-obscured by an old twisted vine climbing up the tree-trunk—

A root snarls his foot, and he goes down, face first into a flat stone. Moss cushions the blow, but still he's left reeling.

Up on his hands.

Ahead, he sees:

A shaft of light from above—no moon, and yet there it is, a perfect beam coming through a break in the trees. Crystalline and blue—wavering and shifting as if through water. And in that beam sits a throne.

A throne made of bones and glass. Each skull, each femur and finger and spinal column, encased in bubbles of clear glass—jagged edges made smooth by the encasement.

The throne is empty.

Cason reaches for it—

It remains empty no longer.

A man sits on the throne. He's reedy and lean, chest bare, the flesh there marked with fresh cuts but the rest of his skin smooth as marble—

"Devil's in the details," the man whispers.

The ground shakes again—

The Antlered God is coming.

Suddenly—

Cason shudders. Coughs. Tastes blood.

Cason looks down. Sees the sharp antlers already jutting out from the middle of his chest—feels his own heart go faster and faster until it stops, and it's then he realizes that the Antlered God is already here.

CASON GASPS. JERKS his head up, sucks in a string of drool, chokes on it, coughs, blinks, looks around.

Books beneath him, a dim desk lamp shining down from above.

The sky beyond the hotel window is dark.

He groans, checks his phone: just past 2:00AM.

The dream again. Same as always. A few details different—last time the Antlered God was giving it to the horned woman against a tree. Cason hit his head on a rock in this dream, but a few nights ago it was a stump. But the gist is the same: the maze-like forest, the Antlered God in pursuit, the dark woman, the ruby-eyed crows, the empty throne, awaiting... something. The man on the throne. Means nothing. Nothing but anxiety.

Thanks to it, Cason's got a belly full of acid.

It's been a month since E. blew up. Since Cason met Frank.

Alison and Barney are still at home. So Frank says. But he says the other woman is there, too—though, not really a woman at all, is she? Psyche. That's what Frank calls her. Apparently she was the wife of a god whose name everybody knows: Cupid. And another name—the Roman name, or maybe it's the Greek, Cason can't keep all this shit straight—is Eros. (*E. Rose.*) Eros got dead, blown to bits by one of Frank's crazy bombs, and now the wife is pissed. Wants revenge. Great.

Thing is, Cason's been doing some reading. He was never a strong contender in school—he survived okay, did the bare minimum and wasn't a dummy about it and so he floated by on a string of C-grades. Reading and research back then didn't do anything for him. None of it seemed relevant. All ideas and problems for adults who had... well, other ideas and other problems. Cason's problems were how to get to second base with his Homecoming date. Or how to get his Pop's old Caddy up and running. Or how to not get his ass kicked by one of the gangs who hovered around Kenzo like yellowjackets around a trashcan. Math didn't help. English didn't help. Science didn't help.

None of it had any bearing to his problems at hand.

That is no longer the case.

Now, reading takes on a terrible urgency. He's poring through myths and legends like a starving man in search of food. What's doubly troubling is how this stuff no longer sounds like stories from a dead religion. These stories are alive; the gods are real. First he started to look only through the stories of the Greek and Roman pantheons, but Frank told him it goes bigger than that. Way, way bigger. Zeus and Hera. Heaven and Hell. Shiva and Vishnu. All of it.

When he explained it, Frank stood in his hovel apartment, standing on his tippy-toes to pin a printout from the Internet onto the wall—some fuzzy pixelated image of a man whose head was that of a howling monkey, jumping between rooftops somewhere in Bangladesh—and he said to Cason: "No, no, no, you're thinking too small, Case-o Fresco. It ain't just Greek and Roman assholes. It's all of them." He thumbtacked the printout to the drywall, then got back down to face Cason. "*All of them.* Every scary deity from every freaky myth is here. On Earth. With us, among us, upon us. Like a plague we choose not to see. Hidden in plain sight, if you will. I mean, that bigfoot in Eastwick? He's not from any Homeric epic I've read. He's a local boy. Lenni-Lenape, like I said."

At the time, Cason asked, "How is that even possible? That it's all... true?"

Frank just shrugged. "You'll have to ask one of them that. Sometimes they stick together—you know, within the same, ehhh, pantheon and all. Other times they mix it up and mingle. City to city. Country to country. Some like to hang out with the people that once worshipped them. Others don't give a thimble full of rat turds. Some are content to toy with just a few of us at a time and build up little cults of personality. Others like it big. They tank economies. They wipe out crops. They elevate bad men with little mustaches to positions of great prominence and help men fly planes into buildings."

"You're saying—"

"That Hitler and Osama bin Fuckhead are pawns in a much greater game? Hitler's a little outside the range—the gods only came to earth a half-a-century ago. But Osama? Or any of the other human monsters? I dunno, Casey Jones. I'm just talking shit over here. *Speculating.* Human evil's still a thing, don't get me wrong. The gods are not responsible for the bad things we do, just like a vulture ain't at fault for running over the deer. But the vulture's gonna feed on the fresh carcass just the same."

So, after Frank told him that, Cason's been looking deeper.

But sometimes he flips back to one of the books on Greek mythology—it's a big encyclopedia on myth and religion. Illustrated. He got it out of the library.

Page 14.

Aphrodite.

The art doesn't do her justice. It's beautiful, of course—delicate lines, pastel colors. The artist got the blonde hair right. The eyes here are blue, not green. And she's too thin. She's rising up out of the ocean, the froth of the sea clinging to her feet.

Mother to Eros. Though the book notes that she's not his mother in every myth—some have him as a god without parents, a 'primordial.'

Just proves that the myths don't have all the facts.

He runs his fingers along the page without meaning to.

The apple—red and lush with its dark twisted stem—sits nearby.

Part of him thinks to walk into the bathroom and conjure her. He thinks about it every night. He could send her to Frank and demand—well, *ask*, probably with weepy eyes and lust-slick mouth—for recompense in the form of his family's return.

But then...

He thinks about Frank's story. What she did to him. Did to his *wife.*

The gods are cruel. Men are nothing but their little dollies.

That thought is what stops him from going to the mirror. Because he doesn't know what the goddess did to him. And he doesn't want to feel that way again—standing in her presence felt like being on some kind of drug. He's never done heroin, but after fight injuries (which blessedly never lasted long with him) they gave him the

standard regimen of good meds—Percocet, Darvocet, Oxy, Vikes—
and he saw how easy it would be to just... keep... taking them. So
it is with the gods. All too easy to keep warming your face in their
glow.

Aphrodite could gut him like a hog and he'd thank her as she
spilled his bowels on the floor.

His phone—sitting near to the lamp atop a stack of dusty books
on religion—buzzes and lights up with a text:

WHERE YOU AT MAN – T

Tundu.

Cason's own personal savior. Not just for rescuing him from the
bad situation with Alison and Barney, but rescuing his sanity from all
this... insanity. (Was there any other word for it?) Over the last few
weeks he's needed to escape from the madness, decompress, wrench
himself loose from Frank's eye-bulging intensity. Tundu's been the
release valve for that head of steam. And he doesn't ask shit for it.
Cason tried to pay him but Tundu wouldn't take it. Said Cason was
his friend, now. Cason's never really had many friends, at least not in
his adult life—is this how friendships are made? Randomly between
two people who just plain get along?

He texts back: *At the hotel.*

SHIFT OVER COMIN UP

"I LOVE THIS room, man," Tundu says later, relaxing in one of the
hotel room's armchairs. "You got the microwave. You got the little
tiny fridge. I bet the shower's nice." A big smile crosses his face.
"One of those showerheads like it's raining on you?"

Cason laughs. "Yeah. It's all right. Water pressure isn't so hot—
less like raining on me and more like an old diabetic man peeing on
me—but everything else is aces." Over the last several years he'd
been working for E., he'd been collecting a paycheck—he just never
had much to do with it. He stayed at the brownstone. Didn't have a

car. Any expenses were paid for—and he didn't have many of those to begin with. Life was boring, and the house had all the amenities he needed. The money accumulated. Time, he figured, to spend it. And so now, here it is. In a suite at the Omni. Nice. Not top-shelf, but nice.

"So, whatchoo got here? Homework?" Tundu indicates the spread of books with a sweep of his arm. "You taking night classes?"

"Something like that." Cason's still not told Tundu about... well, any of it. From the bomb at E.'s brownstone to everything that followed.

Tundu picks up a book on symbolism, then another book on Native American mythology. "This some heavy shit, man."

You have no idea, T.

"It's not worth talking about. Hey, you want to get—"

He's about to say *breakfast*, but there's a knock on the door.

These days, a knock on the door makes him clench up. But this time it's just Frank. Voice on the other side: "Open up, Cason. I got a lead."

Tundu raises his eyebrows.

Shit. Two worlds about to collide. Cason doesn't want this. But what choice does he have? Send Frank packing? Can't kick Tundu out—the door is the door.

Reluctantly, he goes, opens the door. Frank barrels in like a hard desert wind.

"All right! I figured it out," he says, "I have the first target—"

Frank stops, mid-room. Frozen like a deer in the lights of an oncoming pickup.

"Psst," he whispers to Cason, comically loud. "Did you know there's a big giant black guy sitting by your window?"

"Tundu," Cason says by way of introduction, "meet Frank. Frank, Tundu."

"You're big," Frank says.

"You ugly," Tundu says. But then T. stands and offers a hand.

Frank winces as he takes the offered hand. "Eesh, got quite a grip there, Kong."

"Hey. That's racist, man."

"That's not racist. You're big and black, King Kong was big and—oh, for Chrissakes, I'm not comparing black people to monkeys."

"King Kong was an ape."

"I don't study primates, and I'm not racist, either. It was like, a, a, you know, a metaphor for—"

"Frank," Cason interrupts, poorly stifling a yawn. "What do you want?"

"I, ehhh, I got something to show you. About our thing." His mutilated face gestures unsubtly toward the pile of books on the hotel desk.

Tundu steps forward, towering over Frank—a small frail man in the shadow of a human obelisk. "You in Case's class?"

"Class?" Frank coughs a laugh. "I'm the teacher."

"Frank—"

"Cason. C'mon. We gotta hit the bricks. Let's go grab a cab."

Cason shrugs. "T., maybe take a raincheck on the breakfast—"

"I drive a cab," Tundu says specifically to Frank, his mouth a grim, suspicious line. "I'll take you wherever you want to go. No cost. For free. Free is good, yes?"

"Free *is* good," Frank says with a whoop. "Free is the best thing since salt and vinegar potato chips." As an aside, he says, "What? They feel good on my fucked-up lips. C'mon, Casey and the Sunshine Band, let's take a drive."

CHAPTER FOURTEEN
Eye Of The Beholder

THE WOMAN CRIES. Sometimes softly, a sound that Alison can hear like a drip in the pipes or a mouse in the walls. Sometimes the cries are loud, her shrill wails echoing through the house, her broken voice like a yowling animal as it tries desperately to claw its way free from its cage. Always in the bathroom. She goes into the room, looks into the mirror, and gently closes the door.

That's when the weeping begins.

And that's when Alison gets a small part of herself back.

Psyche's control is a one-way street. Usually. But when she cries, it's as if her concentration is shaken, and in those moments the invisible leash and collar around Alison's neck do more than tug and pull—she feels in them how the woman feels. She feels her grief and rage. She feels her narcissism and her fear. It's a steady stream of whispers: *love is dead my beauty is fading she was right the bitch was right what am I who am I worthless worthless worm crying weeping look at me listen to me what good am I love is dead my beauty is fading...* and on and on.

When that happens, Alison feels herself. She's suddenly more aware of existing inside her own body. When Psyche takes control—which is now most times—Alison is a small mind in the vast darkness, all the strings to her limbs cut. She still has her senses and witnesses all that goes on around her—but her body is not hers. Her mind is not her own, either, not really. It's like she's on some kind of psychic Novocain, numbing her feelings and fears and even her desires.

All except the desire to find and kill a man named Cason Cole.

A man Alison Cole does not know, but for whom, even now, in thinking of him fleetingly, she feels such a hot surge of hate and fury and *kill kill kill* that she has to tamp it down; it's like covering a boiling pot with your bare hands.

Cason Cole. (*kill*)

She does not know him.

And yet, she does. Somehow. She must.

He shares her last name.

He looks like Barney.

She does not know him and yet she feels that she must to have such hatred toward him (*kill gut stab burn him cut his heels crush his throat*)—the signs are clear. He's either her brother or her husband. Both impossible, because wouldn't she remember? How could she not? And yet here she is, bearing the yoke of a madwoman named Psyche.

In times like this, when she has control, she goes upstairs. Creeping quietly on the balls of her feet, stepping where the boards don't squeak.

She eases past the symbols scrawled everywhere with Barney's markers—hundreds of them line the walls and halls. Upstairs. Downstairs. Symbols of circles and stars and strange baroque lines. Greek letters merging with words in languages she's never before seen. Sometimes, out of the corner of her eye, Alison is convinced that the symbols *move*, twitching and shifting as if they were made of snakes instead of scrawled in ink. Psyche said, "We need these sigils. Just as our enemies hide from us, we must hide from other enemies." Someone she refers to as the 'driver.' Whatever that means.

For now, she continues forth.

She goes into Barney's room—usually to watch him sleep, but now, for another reason.

He's been asleep for weeks now. He has not thinned or lost any weight at all, as Psyche said. He appears to be in some kind of coma. His face is a mask of peace.

But it's also ashen. Gray like old rotten cloth. His hair, too, seems to be losing its luster—in fact, all the color seems to be draining out of him.

Normally, when she comes up here, she sneaks weapons. Knives from the kitchen that won't be missed. Barbecue skewers. A corkscrew. She kisses her son's cheek and strokes his face and then hides the weapons between the mattress and the box spring.

Today, she is not hiding weapons.

She is reclaiming them.

Or one, at least.

She reaches under the mattress and pulls out the revolver.

Psyche is still sobbing softly.

Then: the squeak of faucets. Splash of water.

A sign that today's time of sorrow draws to a close.

Have to move fast.

Alison kisses Barney on the forehead. Whispers to him that she loves him, that Mommy will be back in just a moment.

She quietly slides along the margins of the hallway. Toward the bathroom door.

Hand on the knob. Gently turning.

When it opens, Psyche is startled. Face puffy and red from crying. She's doing like she does every night—leaning forward on the sink, staring into the mirror.

She jerks her head toward Alison. Her face is a conflicted mess of rage and confusion. The leash snakes out, winds around Alison's mind. A python, swiftly tightening.

"What are you doing?" Psyche asks.

Only.

One.

Shot.

Alison cries out, muscling past the psychic lockdown, and raises the gun and fires.

Psyche's head snaps back and she staggers. Alison keeps firing.

One, two, three—the gunshots are everything, noise and wrath and stink. The hammer suddenly falls dry as the cylinder empties—*click click click click*. The madwoman lays over the toilet, back arched like a bridge, hands scrabbling on the linoleum but finding no purchase.

The psychic leash unspools—a thread pulled from a sweater until it unravels.

Alison is free.

She knows she doesn't have long.

Move fast, then. Gun on the floor with a clatter. Into Barney's room. Scoop up his comatose frame—he's still not waking, she hoped he would wake, *damnit*—and hurry down the hall, down the steps.

Psyche makes a sound from the bathroom, a kind of *"Gggggh!"*—a garbled, pissed-off gargle that precedes her screaming Alison's name.

But by the time Alison hears it, she's snatching the car keys off the hook by the front door and then she's outside.

Air. And the sound of birds. And traffic, somewhere.

Everything feels crisp, like hotel linens. Hyper-alert like she's just had a whole pot of coffee. She smells herself: a whiff of sweat. Has she showered? She doesn't even know.

People are coming out of their houses, now—a gunshot in Philly means everyone turtles, ducking into their homes and turning up their televisions, but here in Doylestown it's a different affair. Faces poke out of windows. Doors open. Half a dozen people will already be on the phone. Good. Fine. It doesn't matter.

To the car. The red Toyota. Its inside scrawled with symbols like those in the house. Inked on the windows, carved into the dash. Psyche put them there. For protection against her 'enemies.'

Alison fumbles with the keys.

Psyche screams.

She's at the front door.

Unbloodied. Untouched by bullets.

She's out. Running across the lawn. Alison feels her fingers sinking deep into her mind like jagged spears—but then she slips into the car, falling forward over Barney, and it's like a big iron door slams down, cutting off Psyche's invisible fingers.

The symbols.

It has to be the symbols.

No time to think about that now. Psyche slams up against the glass as Alison locks the door. The madwoman begins punching the glass. First hit: nothing. Second hit: the glass of the driver side window spider-webs with a crunch.

Alison turns the key, and the engine starts.

She guns it forward. Clips another car's bumper—whatever.

She sobs and screams as she leaves Psyche in a cloud of exhaust.

No no no *no you stupid woman no no no*—

Psyche stands in the middle of the street. The car speeds away, tires shrieking as it rounds a tight corner and then is gone.

She reaches out with everything she has to find Alison's mind, but the very sigils of protection she placed inside the car to keep the Driver from finding them work on her, too, when she's out of the car.

Her body is electric with anger, and with a deep and vibrant channel of potent self-loathing. Faces peer out of windows and doors open; Psyche plants her feet on the earth and screams to the heavens, and the faces snap backward, noses squirting blood. Doors slam on bodies and fingers.

She needs her. Needs Alison. She's a channel to her husband's killer. And better—she's the perfect instrument of revenge. To have the man murdered by his own wife would be exquisite—such an eloquent orchestration of justice. It must happen that way. *It must.*

But now—sirens.

Not *that* kind, but the human kind. The 'authorities' will be here, soon.

And now that she's outside of the house, one of the *inhuman* authorities will be here, soon, too. Psyche's done so well at staying hidden, and now here she is—ripping off scabs and letting her mindsblood flow. The shark will have her scent.

She's lost everything.

She hates herself.

She goes inside the house to wait. And weep. And break mirrors. She could run. But what's the point?

Eventually they come. The police. In their crisp blue uniforms. Two at the door, another two at the sidewalk talking to neighbors—neighbors with bruised faces and broken noses, by now trying to explain to these very nice officers exactly what happened (Psyche can hear their confusion like a scratchy radio frequency: *looked out the window crazy woman on the street car driving away and then next thing I know it was like someone hit me in the face and Merle was knocked out cold and—*).

The cop's knocking gets louder and louder. More insistent. Eventually he kicks down the door, and Psyche is there.

It takes little effort, really—just a twinge of her own mind and the cop takes his own gun, shoots his red-haired partner in the throat, then steps out onto the lawn to the screams and whoops of neighbors. He shoots the other two cops—one doughy man, one mannish woman. Then he starts shooting at neighbors as they flee.

It doesn't take long. A minute, maybe. The lawn and street are littered with the dead.

When the cop is done he turns the pistol on himself and blows out the ceiling of his own skull. He pops like a bottle of champagne and that's it.

THE DRIVER DOES not drive. The stakes are too high; the car, too slow. And driving is so... *human.* She despises humans. Weak, mewling, pealing little grubs. Pale and pink, and filled with blood that comes out so easily.

In fact, the Driver despises that she is named for such a human act.

Sometimes she pretends it's for something else. Driving her prey beneath her. Driving mortal men to entreaties, blubbering, and eventually madness. The driving flap of her gristly wings.

For now, the Driver flies.

She'd been standing in the back as Sister was doing her thing—the warehouse of men and women, rising and falling together. Humans standing, kneeling, sitting, prostrating themselves, then back to standing, all moaning and singing hymns to Sister as they rose and sank, rose and sank, eyes blank and mouths open and tongues ululating lost paeans. Disgusting. Why some of their kind demanded such worship still was beyond her.

The Driver did not demand worship.

She was Erinyes. She was a Fury. She did not want worship—she sought its opposite. Fear. Disgust. Uncertainty. Nobody prayed to her for anything. They prayed to every other god that *she*—or one of her two sisters—would never come. A prayer never to meet the woman with the teeth of a dog, the eyes of blood, the hungry serpents coiled about her waist with fangs that ever drip with venom.

For Psyche, that prayer was a useful one. Because as the Driver stood in the shadows of the warehouse corner, she felt the signal flare of Psyche's presence—red and fierce, sparking madly—rise in the deep of her mind.

Psyche was back on the tapestry. Her image seen.

Sister knew it, too. Her eyes opened, met the Driver's.

A subtle nod told her all she needed.

Go.

She drops out of the morning sky and onto the street with nary a sound. All around her, bodies, still warm. Few flies. Sirens in the distance (but not *that* kind).

Psyche has been busy.

There. In the doorway of a small house, Psyche sits.

Weepy thing. Too human. Because she was once human.

The Driver represses a shudder, then approaches in long strides, her black wings tucked back and disappearing beneath her chauffeur's suit with a flutter of fabric.

"You've come to take me back," Psyche says. Voice small and sad.

"If it were up to me, I'd have my serpents bite you a thousand times over. The venom coursing through your body for not years, nor decades, but for centuries."

"Tisiphone. If only you lived up to your name."

Her name: *avenging murder*.

"Don't taunt me. And stay out of my head."

Psyche hisses: "I can't get *in* your head, you foul thing. But I know your heart just the same. How low you are, these days. Once a creature of wrath and vengeance—punishing brothers who murder brothers, husbands who end the lives of their wives, mothers who drown their children in rivers. But now look at you: upholding meager oaths at the behest of your prettier sister."

"Perspective. I do not find her beautiful. I and my two true sisters were born of blood. Venus was born of semen and sea-froth; Cronus' foul ejaculate and the foam of dead fish. I find none of the beauty there that I find in blood."

"And you're still Aphrodite's gopher. Fascinating."

"Will you come? Or must I make you?"

Psyche stares at the bodies on the street. "No. I've done awful things here; because I am awful..." Her words trail. "I'll come home."

"Not home. Not this time. The Farm."

"Ah. The Farm."

The Driver extends a hand tipped with the milky talons of a diseased bird.

Psyche takes the claw. And away they go.

CHAPTER FIFTEEN
Welcome To The Death Factory

THE CAB SITS double-parked outside the hotel.

Frank raps on the Plexiglas divider separating the front and back seats. He opens the little drawer and yells through it to give his voice some volume.

"Hey! Cason. The hell are you doing up there?"

Tundu turns up the radio: classic rock, Led Zeppelin's *Whole Lotta Love*. Then he changes the speaker balance so it plays louder in back, quieter up front.

"I no like this guy, man," Tundu says, indicating the backseat with a dismissive jerk of his thumb.

"Is it because he looks like someone threw him in a wood chipper?"

"No!" Tundu's face scrunches up. "Well. A little. But he has shifty eyes!"

"Anybody without eyelids ends up having shifty eyes."

"I do not trust him. Something else is... off. Like a smell in the refrigerator, you know? You look and look but cannot find it until later and you one day see a tiny little nugget of spoiled food making a very bad, very big smell. That's him."

"He's a nugget of spoiled food?"

"Right, man. Right."

"He's... okay. Frank's been through some stuff."

"You vouch?"

"I vouch."

Again the little drawer pops. Frank's voice: "We gonna go or what?"

Tundu drums prodigious fingers on the steering wheel.

Finally, he asks: "Where to, Mister Ugly?"

Frank grins a devil's grin and gives him the address.

"WELCOME TO THE death factory," Frank hisses, sweeping his arms across a derelict factory—a block-long complex of soot-black buildings and smoke stacks all ringed in a circumference of warped chain-link fence. Everything is broken windows, rusted pipes, and very long shadows.

They're not far from the river. The road—Unruh—dead-ends here, with the waters of the Delaware just behind. A red light blinks and bobs out on the water.

Frank had Tundu drive 95 north, to Frankford Avenue, then into Tacony. Not a part of town Cason knows well. Like everywhere else, it's a depressed area—the mighty thumb of economic erosion pushing down hard on the blue collar neighborhood. As they drove, it was hard not to see the many yellow Sheriff Sale signs on doorways—the symbols of a foreclosed home.

Frank had Tundu drive down toward the river. Past an all-nude strip club.

Then past a graveyard. A big one, too—big as a city block. None of the antiquity or historical value of some of the cemeteries toward the Philly center; just a flat plain of scrubby grass, row upon row of unexceptional headstones. A graveyard of the common man. No founding fathers here. Just cops and plumbers and shopkeepers.

They drove past the graveyard and then—

There, the factory complex.

Longshore Wire Company.

Shut up and closed off for a long time.

"What the hell is this place, chief?" Tundu asks. "Why must we come here?"

Frank holds up a finger. "All will be revealed, my giant cab-driving friend."

"We are not friends."

"That hurts my feelings. I was just about to order you one of those bouquets where instead of flowers, it's all those little pieces of fruit. So yummy."

Tundu's about to say something else, but Cason steps in, pulls Frank aside.

"What's your game, here? T.'s not involved in any of this and wouldn't believe it if he was."

"Why not tell him? Hell, we can *show* him."

"Like you showed me?"

"It worked, didn't it? Listen, Case-a-dillas. I said the ants weigh more than the elephants and I meant it. And your cabbie friend over there is a *very big ant*. Let him decide what he wants to believe." Frank pauses. "Oh, I get it. You're afraid he won't be your buddy anymore, that it? Listen. Come out of the closet. Put your balls on the table and slap them like bongos. Guy deserves to know what kind of crazy whackaloon shit you're up to, just in case the cops come to knock on his door and ask him questions about you."

"Not a fan of plausible deniability, are you?"

"Not so much, no."

Cason leans in close. "Just keep the... gods and magic bullshit out of it, okay? I don't care how. Just do it."

Another demon smile from Frank.

He wanders back to Tundu. Sweeping his arms in a showman's gesture, he says, "Welcome to the site of one of America's first mass murders."

"Ah, man," Tundu says, shaking his head.

Frank continues. "Fella worked here by the name of Theodore Stapleton. Teddy. Oh, by the way, this is the late 1940s we're talking, here. Old Teddy, he was a vet of World War II, but not a soldier—he was a, I dunno, a typist or something. And that's what he did here. He typed. Kept books. He didn't work the line. Didn't make the wire, test the wire, fix the machines, none of that. White collar job in a blue collar environment."

"Just get to the part where he kills people," Cason says. "It's late. Or early."

"Not a fan of stories, are you?" Frank asks, following up with a quick wink.

Cason frowns, and mocks Frank: "Not so much, no."

"Fine. Teddy was gay. Or people said he was gay, I dunno. Guys on the floor made fun of him night and day, merciless bullying. Called him names, played pranks, whatever. And this was an everyday thing. For Teddy to get to his desk, he had to cross the factory floor—the longest walk of poor Teddy's life, I bet. Well, Teddy may not have been in the shit during the war, but he still had a few keepsakes. Like, say, a P38 pistol reclaimed from a factory in Spreewerke. Sides all pitted like acne scars from the explosion. Never used to kill a man—but looking like it'd been though hell, right? So Teddy takes this pistol. Loads it up with 9mm ammo. And goes to work one day; but he doesn't head upstairs, and instead just marches down the line and starts shooting." Frank mimics the movement, taking measured steps—*one, two, three*—then fake-shooting with a finger pistol. "Bang. Bang. Bang. Seventeen men dead. Another six wounded. First official mass murder in American history." Frank lowers his voice: "Not counting those on behalf of our own government, of course."

"Great story," Tundu says, obviously unimpressed. He brings his big hands together in a booming clap. "I tell it to my nieces and nephews at bedtime."

"You could've told us this in the hotel room," Cason says.

Frank licks a too-white canine. "Story's not over, *compadres.* This isn't the factory's final brush with death. In 1957? Smallpox outbreak. Just here. *Only here.* Another seven dead, a dozen more disfigured and disabled by the disease. In 1969, one of the wire spoolers goes nutso, breaks off its mooring, the wire lashing about like a horse's tail trying to chase away a fly. Result? Three dead. Two of them cut in half, the third left without a head. Then, 1980: suicide of factory foreman Ray Redman. Wrote a note, said he saw ghosts and that they wouldn't leave him alone, so he jumped into the wire-cutting machine and chop-chop-chop, diced him like a salad. Come 1995, explosion on the floor of Factory Building B. Big boom. Ten men dead. Another ten wounded. Press got hold of it. Enough was enough. They shut the place down."

Tundu throws up his arms. "What's the point, Mister Ugly? Why you gotta tell us all this nasty business?"

"Because," Frank says, moving fast, coming up on Tundu like a barracuda. "Because I think a god of death lives here, and I not only aim to prove it—"

"Frank!" Cason yells, incredulous.

"—but I aim to kill the sonofabitch. Kill death. Ain't that a peach?"

Cason's about to do some explaining, maybe try to spin this into some kind of juke, but he notices that Tundu doesn't seem to care. The cabbie isn't even looking at Frank anymore. He's staring at up at the factory.

Frank turns, follows his gaze. Cason, too. They see the building with a thousand eyes, all of them blind and dark—broken glass and framed squares of shadow.

"I saw someone," Tundu says.

"Huh?" Frank asks. "Who?"

"I dunno, I dunno. I just looked up and in one of the windows, a... shadow was there. A man. I could see his eyes. Watching. I... dunno."

Cason looks. Doesn't see anything. But a shudder runs across his arms, leaving the flesh looking like plucked chicken-skin.

THEY STAND CLOSER to the river. Just Cason and Frank. Tundu's back at the cab. Sitting there, staring out, watching the factory from behind the windshield.

The sun's not up, not yet, but the horizon's edge is starting to show that creamsicle glow. One thing Cason can say for the sunrise and sunset in Philadelphia—all the chemical plumes make for a spectacular sky-show, day in and day out.

The river itself is quiet. Couple gulls at the edges. Couple more dogfighting out on the water, over what, Cason doesn't know.

"Way to go, Frank," Cason says. "Now you got him seeing goblins."

"Goblins aren't real," Frank says. Matter-of-factly.

"I'm just saying, he's seeing—"

"He saw *something*, not *nothing*. And that's good. That means he's in. He may not realize it yet, but he's been touched. It doesn't take much. You knew it the first time you met Eros. Don't lie."

"Maybe." Cason clears his throat and Frank gives him a look. "Okay, *yeah*. I knew it. He was different. It wasn't just what he did—which was unbelievable in and of itself. Stopping time. Bringing my wife and son back from death. E.—Eros—was on a whole other level."

"That's the thing, Case. Eros may be, er, *have been* on a whole other level, but these gods, they got rules. Things they can do, things they can't. Like, a god of war can't make you fall in love with him. A god of the sea doesn't fuck with earth or air or fire. The Humbaba only knows the forest, the minotaur only knows the maze. Eros was a... a love god, a deity of *sex* and *beauty* and, and—and *hedonism*."

"The hell are you saying?"

"I'm saying he didn't resurrect your wife and kids. He didn't stop time. He didn't program their heads to hate you. He could've done the opposite. He could've made them love you forever and ever, regardless of what you did or what you wanted."

"If he didn't do it, then..."

"Other gods, Case. Other gods. This wasn't just a one god thing. Many hands built the trap that snared you. And, oh, what a trap it was."

"Trap. What the fuck do you mean, a trap?"

"The SUV that hit you. They ever find the driver?"

"No. They said... whoever he was, he fled the scene."

"They didn't even have the right name for him, did they? Car was registered under somebody else. And no fingerprints, either."

"That's what they said, yeah."

"I don't think anyone was driving, Case. I think it was a setup from the get-go. A conspiracy. The gods had their sights on you and they spun this all out for a reason. No one god can make time stop and people rise from the dead with new brains. Even beyond that boy-slut Eros, you got... three, maybe four others involved."

Cason feels suddenly hot, though the wind coming off the river is cool. He grinds his back teeth. Anger and confusion spar with one another in his head.

"Why?" A croak. Almost like he doesn't want to ask.

Worse, he doesn't want to hear the answer, which is:

"I don't know." Frank offers a shrug. "I don't. But I'm here to help you find out, and I figure that getting your cabbie buddy there in on the parade is a good fucking idea. We need whoever we can get. Especially for this next part. Because I'm not kidding when I say I think a god of death lives in this place. First I thought maybe it was Ereshkigal; I knew she was... up and down the East Coast."

Cason's brows scrunch up. The name's familiar from his reading— but retention isn't his strong suit. "She's not Greek pantheon. She's... Middle Eastern."

"Old, old Middle Eastern. Sumerian. Real wicked chicky. Likes to trap people down in the dark with her. And that's the thing, here— the death factory isn't underground. And then there's the smallpox thing? Came out of *nowhere*. So I got the idea that it might be her boyfriend, Nergal. Another god of death—he got kinda trapped into it by her way back when, and he's got a real boner for pestilence and what-not. So I'm thinkin' that's him up there in the factory."

"A death god." Cason chews on that. Tastes bitter. "Why do we need to go up against him? Seems..."

"Dangerous? Like a bad idea? Yes and yes. But someone had to bring your wife and kid back to life, and I want to know whose hand was the one that pulled those particular puppet strings. Only someone with command over life and death could've pulled them out of the fire—not just alive but unharmed."

"Aren't there gods of... life? The books said there were."

"Sure. Dumuzi. Osiris. Ehh, Demeter, kinda. But none of them are around. That doesn't necessarily preclude them, mind you. But I'd rather look local, first. Gods tend to shit where they eat. So. Here we are. God of death."

"Nergal."
"Mmyep."
"Shit."

"SO WHAT NOW?"

Tundu asks the question. Frank's gone. Dropped off at his apartment above the falafel joint on South Street. It's morning, now, officially. The streets filling with people walking to work—bankers, fry-cooks, baristas, black, white, immigrant.

"Go home," Cason says. "Have a nice life."

"So. Leave you to this, then."

"Sounds about right, T."

"Okay. Okay. I do that. I go home. I forget about all this."

"Probably wise."

"You be safe."

Not likely. "I will. Thanks."

Tundu goes to shake his hand, but then holsters the gesture and goes in for a big hug instead. Cason feels like his bones are being pulverized in the bag that is his skin. The guy hugs like a bear trying to break a tree to get at the honey inside of it.

And that's that. He drops Cason off there on South Street. The cab drives away and Cason fights the crowd coming out of the subway to head back to the hotel.

CHAPTER SIXTEEN
The Director Of Traffic

AH. THERE SHE IS.

She sits inside the hospital room, the blinds half-turned so that she is hard to see, but not impossible. A child lays on the bed. Asleep. No—something else. Something beyond sleep. The woman is talking to someone: hard to see now, but when she moves, he sees that it's another, different woman. Oh, but not so different. Same look. Heavier. Older. But same look. The woman's mother.

As the little man watches, his smile is tight and pained. He does not want to intrude upon the conversation. Time is on his side, and the tumblers in the lock have not yet fallen into place. That's okay. He chuckles, does a little dance over to a set of chairs near to the nurse's station, and sits.

For a while he contemplates the many doors and hallways of a hospital. So many junctures and apertures. As many crossroads here as in a small city. Deeper, stranger junctures lurk, too—many roads crossing. Sickness and health. Strength and frailty. Hope and loss. Life and death.

He lets his mind wander through the many permutations.

Just to see.

While he waits, he pulls a few dried chili peppers from within his pocket—little red things, dry and crooked like the walking stick of an old, destitute man—and chews on them. The heat fills his mouth and he laughs quietly to himself.

An hour later, the child's mother emerges from the room.

As she passes him, the little man gets up, totters after. Others watch him, suspiciously. They are right to be suspicious, but for all the wrong reasons. They think the color of his skin is worrisome. They think it strange that he's so small, and that he's smiling like he is. They may not like the red and black beads clacking together around his neck, or the way he walks with such a light touch that none can hear, or the way that he sat there eating hot peppers, one after the other, seemingly produced from nowhere.

They are right to think him strange, yes. Even dangerous.

But not for those reasons.

The woman turns the corner. Choices, choices, always choices. So many hallways, so many doors. She could choose to leave the hospital and never return. Could steal medications and use them to push away the pain and sadness that flicker like the light of a lightning bug. She could fuck a doctor, overdose on pills, jump off the roof, run screaming through the halls.

But instead she goes to the snack machines. A cup of coffee from one. A baggy of Ritz crackers from the other.

Humans always make such boring choices.

That's okay. That's why he's here. Eshu Elegba. Master of the crossroads.

She goes and sits, and he totters over, settles next to her.

He introduces himself.

"I am Shu," he says. A nickname he likes.

She seems startled. As if he jostled her free from some reverie—or whatever reverie's grim opposite shall be. She blinks, then forces a smile. "I'm... Alison."

"Hospitals," he says, shaking his head, clucking his tongue, but never losing his smile or the brightness in his eyes. "Difficult places."

"Yes. They are." She pops the tab on her coffee lid, blows in through the hole to cool the drink, with a thin whistle. "Are you here visiting a patient?"

"Visiting," he says. "But not a patient."

"Oh. A doctor?"

"No."

"Do you work here...?"

"Yes," he says, deciding to lie. Lies are good sometimes to get what you want, equal to truth in that way. Neither better nor worse than the other. Both a tool, each with different purpose, each a different weight in the hand. Lies are light and effortless—a scalpel. The truth is heavy, hard to lift—a mighty hammer.

A scalpel is necessary. For the moment.

"Oh." She laughs, light, airy, but awkward. "I'm here for a patient. My son. He's... in a coma. There was... an accident."

So she knows the power of the scalpel, too. Though her deception is not as far from the truth as she thinks.

"I'm very sorry to hear that," he says, never losing his smile. He can't lose the smile. Well. He *can*. But it takes an effort equal to moving a mountain with a single finger—his smile is affixed to his face like paint on a wall, like skin on a skull. It's because he's so happy, of course. So happy just to be here. To be the cause of strife. And chaos. To be the rock in the stream that diverts the waters— diverts them always in an unexpected way. Waters run to strange places. If all of life did as you chose, if everything fell to a plan, what fun would that be? It would be no fun at all, and then his smile would truly go.

"The doctors don't know what's wrong." Her voice creaks here like an old door. This was truth. Not a lie.

"You love him."

"Of course." Incredulous. "*Of course*. He's my son."

"Do not assume that all mothers love their sons. Yours is real. I can see that."

"Oh. Well." She sips the coffee. Wince. Still too hot. Steam rises from the cup, curling in the air like a winged sky-serpent twisting. "I just want him to be okay."

"Yes. Absolutely. But something here is troubling you."

She says nothing. Which is just another way of saying *yes*.

He continues: "His condition is a mystery and that concerns you. I see that. But I also see that you are troubled by other things. Events have lined up, one after the other, and too few of them make sense to you. Is that right?" He gives her no time to answer, allowing only for a tiny, fearful nod. His smile broadens as he speaks. "Things don't seem to add up anymore. As if you glimpsed a world that, had anybody else told you existed, you would say they were mad. You would ease away from them, trying to be subtle but failing, thinking them dangerous or deluded.

"And now you worry it is you who has become dangerous or deluded, and yet, there, in that room, is your son. A son who won't wake up. Who seems healthy except for the fact he is not precisely *with us*, either. You haven't told the doctors the things you know yet, and part of you wonders if you should—maybe it'll help, you tell yourself, but in your heart you know it cannot. How could it? They haven't seen what you have seen. They don't have a specialist for the problems you and your son are facing. And so you sit quietly hoping it was all a dream, even though hope does little to erase the truth from your mind, for hope is a dangerous thing. Hope, a mirage in the desert, a curtain of vapor forming for us an image of that which we most sincerely desire. Hope is not an oasis but rather, a trap.

"So let us instead look at the truth, heavy as it may fall upon us. The truth is that you have seen things you do not understand. The truth is that you have holes in your mind—memories cut from you like a child cut from a womb and kept from you, alive but somewhere far away. The truth is that your own child lies still, caught in a trap of magic that you have no way of defeating."

She's crying, now, tears running soft and silent down her cheeks. This is pain. This is truth. Gone is the scalpel. Time for the hammer-blow. His smile tightens, lips pinched together. Eyes, too. The face of a little old grandfather offering platitudes and comfort. But it is not comfort his words offer. Not yet.

"I have something for you. I don't know how it helps you, but it does." He unfolds a little piece of paper—hardly bigger than the fortune in a fortune cookie—and he presses it into her cold and clammy hand. "On that paper is an address. It is far from here. But if you drive there—begin your journey now, not later, but now— then you will begin to solve the problem you face, and you will find answers to your questions. Most importantly of all, you will fill those cavities inside your mind, and your memories will again return." His smile widens—comically, impossibly, stretching almost ear to ear as his eyes pucker to the point of disappearing, as his ears grow and his chin lengthens and all his features seem to stretch out of proportion. "But you must go now. Leave your son and go."

The woman holds the paper and unfurls it like a little banner, pinched between the thumb and forefinger of each hand. Her hands shake. Her lips, too. She sniffles. Blinks back tears. Sees an address handwritten there.

And then she stands, pockets the slip of paper. Picks up her coffee and crackers.

"I... have to go back to my son."

"He will never wake up if you do. Go now. The door is closing."

More tears.

With trembling hand, she gives him the coffee and the crackers.

Then she turns and goes down the hallway.

Not toward her son's room, but away from it, keys jangling in her hands.

Oh, humans.

Once in a while they *do* make interesting choices.

Eshu Elegba chuckles and opens the crackers, happily munching between sips of too-hot coffee.

CHAPTER SEVENTEEN
How Death May Die

NERGAL.

Nirgali. Ner-uru-gal. The raging king. The furious one.

God of fire and storms and destruction.

God of death.

Not by choice, it seems.

Stories say that Nergal didn't play well with others. When other gods were asked to kneel before the Skyfather, he did no such thing. He stood, defiant.

The punishment for the transgression? Death. He managed to escape the sentencing with the help of his demons—creatures of plague and lightning!—but the bounty was on his head and if the gods caught him, he would die.

Normally, the gods of the above could not descend into the underworld, and the opposite was true, too. But as Nergal was marked, he carried with him the stink of death and thus was allowed to descend into the Underworld to meet with its queen, Ereshkigal, in order to plead for his life and to have his coming death undone.

Before going, the god Ea instructed Nergal not to partake of any hospitality—no food, no drink. Don't even sit in a *chair*. Just ask for the pardon and go.

But Nergal cared little for rules. His stubbornness was profound; an unending well of resistance. When someone told him to do something, he did its opposite, and so when Ereshkigal offered him her hospitality, he took it.

Hospitality is a tricky thing in the land of the gods. Eat of a place and it binds you to that place. Drink its water, sleep in its beds, it gets its claws into you.

That's how Nergal became bound to the Underworld.

He went to escape death, and joined it instead.

It was then that Ereshkigal forced him to marry her. He was made to rule the place whose dominion was the very thing he hoped to elude.

At least, that's how one story goes.

"FIND ANYTHING?"

Frank hovers. He smells of eucalyptus lip balm. His whole scarred-up face is greasy with the stuff. He says it "helps with the tightness," which it very well may. It also makes him shine in the lights of the university library like a suckling pig hot out of the BBQ pit.

And he smells like an old woman.

Cason sits at the table, a kink in his neck ratcheting tension between his shoulders and head, sending a hard shiv into his brain. Before him, an advanced version of what he has back at the hotel room: books upon books upon books.

"No," Cason says. Yawning. Rubbing his eyes. Needs more coffee. "I don't even know what the hell we're looking for. These books are all filled with... conflicting stories and academic write-ups. Half of them are translations. It makes my damn eyes bleed."

This really isn't his... thing. Frankly, Cason just wants to go out and punch something. Anything. He's starting to feel those old urges— urges that got pushed down during his years with Eros, hidden in such a way that wonders now if it was supernatural. Now he's starting to feel like a fighter again. Doesn't hurt that this morning, peeping at himself in the mirror, he looked like he'd lost a stone. Still nowhere near fighting shape—but some of the blubber is gone. Muscle tone isn't back, not like it used to be, but this morning he took a jog and did a workout in the hotel gym. He'll get there. One way or another. The Beast, resurgent.

"We're looking for a way to kill this motherfucker."

"Yeah. I get that. I just... I don't know what *that* is."

"They all have weaknesses. Like Superman has his—"

"Kryptonite. I know. You told me." Cason's head lolls back on his shoulders. He stares up into the lights of the university library. Shelves and shelves of books in his periphery. "That officially falls into an *easier-said-than-done* category. Eros was, what? Arrowheads. And the Sasquatch Man was—"

"Ohtas. Little Lenii-Lenape dolls."

"How the hell did you know that it was arrowheads with Eros and dolls for the Sasquatch Man?"

"Meesink. His name was Meesink." Frank pulls up a chair, drops his cut-up scarecrow's body upon it and starts poking through books. "I dunno how I knew, I just knew. I mean, Eros was easy. Honestly, seriously easy. His whole schtick is making people love him or love somebody else, and the way he does that in the stories is with a scratch from an arrow. As for your so-called 'Sasquatch Man,' well—"

"No, no, hold up one minute. You used bronze arrowheads. Specifically bronze. Why? Why not obsidian or iron or something you bought from Wal-Mart?"

Frank shrugs. "It seemed right. Your old boss is out of the Greek pantheon. Bronze Age stuff. So. Bronze arrows. Seemed stupid to just pick up a six pack of the things from Wal-Mart. You're gonna murder a god, I figure, you gotta do it up right. A plus for effort." The man known as Cicatrix scratches his hairless, scar-laced scalp. "Plus, seemed disrespectful, somehow."

Disrespectful. Irony is alive and well, even if Eros isn't.

"And the ohtas. Sasquatch Man."

"Meesink was a, uhh, whaddya call it. A spirit. A Lenape life-spirit. A..." He snaps both his fingers. "A manitowak! Or manitou.

And the way the Lenape venerated the manitou was with those little wooden dollies."

"But how did you *know*?"

"Oh, I didn't. With Eros, I was pretty confident. This time, not so much."

"That's real comforting."

Frank cackles. "We're hunting and killing gods and goddesses, Casey-at-the-Bat, not baking brownies. There's no recipe. This is jazz, not Beethoven. It's all improv." He stabs down with a lobster-red finger onto one of the books. "And this is where we find out how to kill Nergal. It's always in the myths. The legends. The history. *The stories*. The stories have secrets. They tell the truth, even when it's a lie."

"So, what you're saying is..."

"Keep reading, buddy. The stories shall lead the way."

THE HOUSE HAS gone to hell since Mom died. A herd of beer bottles on the coffee table. A spill of something—wine, gravy, who knows—on the living room carpet. Cobwebs in the room corners, and everything else covered with a thick rime of cakey dust.

Plus, Pop's done up his own décor—like, now that she's dead, it's time to make it look less like her and more like him. Ratty taxidermy fox on the mantle—one eye cracked and a little wobbly. Mom's old knick-knacks are gone, replaced with gaudy tavern junk-and-jumble: beer steins and beer signs, corks and caps, coasters and posters.

Pop sits in the recliner, feet up, bowl and spoon on his belly holding the last melted remnants of chocolate ice cream. Cason sits there for a while as Pop watches a Phillies game.

"You goin' to church?" Pop asks, breaking the silence between them.

"Not really. You?"

"Nah. That was your mother's thing."

And back to silence. The air filled with the sounds of the game. Cracks of the bat and cheers of the crowd and long lulls of nothing because for Cason, that's baseball—sharp moments of action punctuated by a whole lot of nothing. Pop loves baseball. Pop would kill for the Phils.

Time to get to it, then. Cason says:

"Something I gotta tell you, Pop."

"Nngh. What's that?"

"I'm getting married."

That raises Pop's flag. He grunts, leans forward in the chair, spoon rattling in the bowl. His legs kick inward, pop the recliner shut. The old man scratches a bristly eyebrow, cocks his head. "Married, you say."

"Married."

"Soon, I'm guessing?"

"In the fall. September, we're thinking."

"Awful fast."

"I'd like you to meet her before then."

Pop picks something off the end of his nose. "Mm-hmm. Mm. Let me ask: she got one in the oven for you?"

On the TV: base hit. Crowd cheers.

"She's pregnant, yeah."

"Right. Had to figure."

Cason sighs. "Pop, it's not like that."

"It's always like that with men and women."

Pop turns back to the TV, eases back into the recliner—feet up, hands steepled on his belly. He smiles at the game, but Pop's got this way of scowling at the same time he's smiling. Something to do with the eyes. And he's doing it now.

"Like I said, I hope you'll meet her. Before the wedding."

The old man doesn't look at his son when he says, "I won't be meeting this one."

"What?"

"You heard me fine, unless one of those thugs in the ring punched your eardrums out. I'm not meeting your bride—now, soon, later, or ever."

Cason doesn't know what to say. "You're going to have a grandson."

"I'm not gonna have shit. Not unless your brother has a kid."

"A grandson is a grandson, whether you like it or not. It's a technical term, not a fucking honorary. Since I'm your son, any child I have will be—"

"Who said you're my son?"

A cold slush in Cason's heart.

"What?"

"You're not my son. You're not your mother's son. You're fucking adopted. About time you knew. I wanted to tell you years ago, but your mother—well."

"Pop—"

"I put up with you because she loved you. Make no mistake about that—your mother cared for you very much. I always thought you were a fuckin' weak-kneed little gobbler, honestly. A goody-two-shoes. A taker, not a maker, clinging to your mother's pockets like a baby squirrel. I never liked you. Now, Conny, he's my son. You're somebody else's son that just happened to live at my house."

"You sonofabitch."

"Go on, get angry. I'll allow you that. But for Chrissakes, do it somewhere else, will you? The game's on."

CASON WAKES UP that night. Sheets drenched. Heart pounding.

Couldn't be a nightmare about Aphrodite twisting his head off his shoulders like a petulant little girl destroying a dolly. Couldn't be about Sasquatch Man pulling his stuffing out. Has to be his father that runs him through the wringer?

He thinks, that's just how we are, isn't it? Nothing scarier in our own lives than our own lives. No monster is mean enough to beat our own inner demons. Humans, more vulnerable to their own past than to anything—

He gets up out of bed, and a gear turns inside his mind. As one turns, others turn with it, faster and faster. Click, click, click.

To the phone, then. Two calls.

The first, to Frank. Frank's up. It's past midnight and of course he's up. Cason tells him to get over here. "I think I have it figured out."

The second call, downstairs. To find out if the hotel has a copy machine.

Cason grabs a book and his room key (both near to a bright red apple sitting all proud and shiny on the hotel desk), then heads to the elevator.

CASON STANDS INSIDE the hotel lobby. The guy at the front desk—a small, feminine man with dusky skin and dark eyes—watches Cason without trying to hide his suspicion. It's then that Cason realizes he came down here in a t-shirt and boxer shorts. It's not like he didn't realize it, what with the fact his hotel keycard is tucked in the hem of his underwear. But he didn't *think* about it. Not really. And now the front desk guy is staring at him like he's a mental patient on the loose.

Too late now. The show's about to get far more interesting, anyway.

Frank walks in the door. Dude at the front desk hasn't seen Frank before, it seems—he's physically taken aback, as if a hard wind just gave him a little shove. The guy's eyes go wide as Frank comes toodling through the lobby with his jigsaw-puzzle skin, unafraid of being seen.

So much so that Frank makes a face for the front desk guy: a leering, toothy, bug-eyed boogeyman stare. He yells: "Booga booga booga!"

The man swiftly turns back to his computer screen. Probably playing solitaire or watching cat videos on the Internet.

"People are so rude," Frank growls. "Hey, nice boxers, Case-of-the-Mondays. Pinstripe. Simple. Elegant. Understated. You're about to poke out of them, though." Frank points toward Cason's crotch, then whistles.

"Please don't look at my dick, Frank." Cason shakes it off. "Here, check this out." He shakes a paper—a copy of a two-page spread out of a book.

"What's this?"

"A photocopy. I was thinking. Nergal, right? This god's got a... history. A complex. He was this one god, and then he fucks up, and suddenly he's forced to become a different god entirely. And there's this one passage that keeps coming back again and again..." He didn't have a highlighter, just a pen, and so he circled a line on the paper.

Frank mumble-reads it aloud. "An adab to Nergal for Shu-ilishu. Lessee. Uhhh. *Lord, mighty storm, raging with your great powers, Nergal, who smites the enemy whom he has cursed. Exalted lord, strong one with powerful wrist, whom no one can withstand. Nergal, rising broadly, full of furious might, great one praised for his accomplishment, pre-eminent among the youthful gods. Nergal, angry sea, inspiring fearsome terror, who no one knows how to confront, youth whose advance is a hurricane and a flood battering the lands. Nergal, dragon covered in gore, drinking the blood of living creatures.*" Frank sniffs. "He sounds like a peach. The hell's your point? You dragged me over here for this?"

"There's a clue in here somewhere. I can feel it."

"You can *feel* it? Show me on the doll where the Adab-to-Nergal touched you."

"At the library, you said you just *knew*. You follow your gut with stuff like this, and Frank, I'm following my gut, here. Listen. Look at Nergal like a regular person. He's a guy with a former glory that lost everything. He's an all-star quarterback taken out of the game with a leg injury and made to coach from the sidelines. He's a top-shelf detective who gets chained to desk duty for the rest of his cop career. He's an aging pop-star, a brash young prince made into an ugly old king—"

"Okay, okay. Onward and upward to an actual goddamn *point*, please."

"Who he was *haunts* him. This adab—it's like a prayer, by the way, a hymn from the original Sumerian—it glorifies who he *was*, not who he *is*. This is the yearbook of that old quarterback, the case-notes of the old detective. There's something here. I can taste it. It doesn't call to mind any one object, but..."

Frank's face lights up. Which is not a pretty picture—it looks like a lobster flushing red after getting dunked in boiling water. Still. He gets excited.

"We don't need an object," Frank says, his voice a breathy hiss of mad glee.

"What?"

"This!" He shakes the paper. "This *is* our object. The past is our friend's weakness, and this adab is his past."

Cason still isn't getting it. "A photocopy isn't a weapon."

Frank chuckles.

"You ever get a papercut, Cole?"

CHAPTER EIGHTEEN
Death By A Thousand Cuts

IT'S A FORTUNE cookie from Hell.

Frank's bomb. A satchel bomb—just a ratty backpack stuffed with screws, nails, thumbtacks, glass shards, and about a hundred little pieces of paper. Each one containing a line from Nergal's hymns. They found plenty more than the ones Cason had discovered. Songs sung to Nergal at his temples, when he was still a rage-fueled storm-god, when they called him both *lion* and *dragon* in the same breath. Prayers to a god before he got whipped and shackled to the Underworld like a once-scrappy beagle chained to the porch.

Frank finishes the bomb by adding a hunk of homemade plastic explosive. It stinks like someone chucked rotten eggs into a too-clean chlorinated pool. Dueling stenches. Cason blanches.

"The smell," Frank says. "Yeah. Doesn't bother me too much. It's the potassium chlorate. It's not real stable, so I had to make a fresh batch last night. And it ain't like baking cookies." He pauses, shrugs. "Though it is a little like making coffee. High-test horse-kick coffee."

They stand in Frank's apartment. Cason still doesn't see a cat, but smells the animal just the same. Frank explained earlier: "She likes her privacy. She's around here somewhere. Under the sink. In a toilet. Out in the hallway eating rats."

"So this'll work?" Cason asks, tossing a thumb at the bomb.

Frank rolls his eyes—and given the lack of eyelids, it's a far more profound gesture when he does it. "Will it work? Are you seriously asking me if it'll work? Please. Case-of-beer, c'mon. You're talking to the Wolfgang Puck of god-killing bombs."

"And yet I'm the one carrying the thing. So I want to know." That was what they agreed upon: Cason doing the deed. "Why am I the one bringing the bomb, again?"

"Revenge. You got a right to it."

"I'm happy however he gets blown to shit. Whether you're holding it or I am."

"Fine. Take a good look at me, then take a good look at you. I'm like a... man made out of tinker-toys and naugahyde. I'm not exactly an all-star athlete. You, though..."

"I'm nowhere near what I was."

"C'mon. Even over the last couple days you're looking tighter. Leaner. Meaner than a starving monkey." Frank's right. Cason *is* looking different. Better. He's barely had time to work out, but it's like his body remembers the way he used to be. He still needs to tighten up the loose skin, but the flab beneath it has started to disintegrate, as if it was never there in the first place. "See, you got the physicality I don't. Easy for you to chuck the bomb and run. Me, I'll trip on a loose wire."

"You've taken out others just fine."

"Just three. Your boss. The Sasquatch Man. And..." His eyes lose focus. "That's a story for another time."

"But you have a reputation. As some kind of bomb-making genius."

"Your brother may have inflated that story a little."

Cason cocks an eyebrow. "You said my brother sold me out."

"Still true."

"But that means you talked to him before I did."

"So?"

"You were looking for me."

"Kinda. I was hoping *you'd* come looking for *me*. I wanted to work with you. Like I said, ants, elephants. I didn't want to do this alone. I figured we were kin."

"I don't like people keeping secrets."

"I'm not! I'm not. I should've said something. I'm sorry." Frank opens his hands and shows his scarred palms in a mea culpa. "Seriously. I'm sorry."

Cason leans back. Beholds the madness of Frank's apartment— dusty strings connecting photos to articles to sketches and back to photos. A flow-chart for the insane.

"You really think this'll work?" he asks Frank. "The bomb."

"I do. I feel it in my guts."

"And Nergal. He was involved. In the thing with Alison and Barney."

"Had to be. He's local. This is his bag of tricks. It's him."

"Is it time?"

"Soon. Nighttime. So nobody sees."

THE DEATH FACTORY looms. The wind blows and Cason catches a scent that at first he thinks must just be his mind playing tricks on him—the sour pickled smell of something dead. But then as he stalks along the fence, he sees: a rat, dead. Big as a poodle. Ripped into thirds, the red parts almost artificial looking, like a spilled cherry slushie. In the moonlight, he sees the rat's coat ripple. Maggots beneath the fur?

Frank's hand falls on his shoulder and jostles him.

"Stinks," Frank says.

"Yeah."

"You ready?"

"I dunno. Nergal, he..." His jaw tightens.

"Hey, you can say it. You're scared."

"I'm not scared." But he is. He really is. It's like from the old days—about to get into the ring with a fighter twice his size and with a helluva lot more skill. Like when he fought Manny Corrado. Or Paul Kevitts. Or Udo, that rabid German who went by one name like he was Madonna or some shit. Stepping into the ring with those guys was like diving into an ocean teeming with sharks. Sharks you could see. Sharks you *knew* were there, *knew* were hungry, who saw you like one big bag of frothy chum.

Of course, he beat those guys. Each one of them.

Cason Cole. *The Beast.*

This time, versus Nergal. The God of Death. The Lion. The Dragon.

Ding. The fight bell ringing. Cason's body tenses.

"How do we get in?" he asks. Fists balled at his side. By the looks of the place, it's pretty well bound up in chain-link fence. Barbed wire atop it. And, peering through the darkness, he sees another fence, deeper in, by thirty feet or so.

Frank answers by pointing down.

Cason gives him a look.

"Sewer. We go down, then we pop up like gophers at the hole."

Above their heads, thunder tumbles across the sky—a steady clamor of rumbling boulders behind phlegmy clouds.

That's not a great sign.

Frank just laughs, and heads to a manhole in the middle of the street. He twirls a small blue crowbar pulled from his backpack. "Once more into the breach!" he hoots.

THE POP-HISS OF a signal flare, and the sewer tunnel is lit by crimson fire, the blood-red torch carried tight in Frank's scar-knuckled grip.

It stinks down here, but not like Cason thought—sewer to him means human waste, but this is mostly just street run-off. Oily water. Condoms and condom wrappers. Big cups from 7-11. Mysteriously, a one-eyed teddy bear snarled up in a tangle of wire.

They move through the tunnel. Elbows rubbing against old stone.

Cason hears scratching ahead. Like rat claws on porous brick. *Scritch-scritch. Skitter-skitter.* Water dripping, too.

And, sometimes, a breath of damp hot air moves down the tunnel. Through them, over them. It smells of rainwater. It carries a sound like someone moaning, then someone laughing. Then it's gone again.

Frank doesn't acknowledge it.

So Cason decides to ignore it, too.

"There," Frank whispers—the whisper a loud susurration crawling along the tunnel on the back of an echo. He points ahead—a small rusty ladder climbs to another manhole cover.

Cason heads over. Tests it with a boot. It squeaks, shifts with a complaining groan—it's only a ten foot climb, but he doesn't feel like falling down into filthy city water. The tunnel keeps going. "Go deeper?" he asks.

"Nah," Frank says. "Take this one."

"Not too stable."

"It's a ladder. If you can't handle a ladder, I'm not real sold on our chances with the Sumerian god of death. Grow a pair and climb, big guy."

Frank's a real asshole sometimes.

Cason climbs. The ladder sways like a homeless drunk, the satchel bomb on his shoulder swaying with him—a tiny spark of fear alight that the whole thing will go off suddenly, that the bomb is unstable and the swaying will blow it to hell and then he'll never see his wife or son ever again. But then a rain of rust flakes falls and interrupts his thought—Cason coughs, spits, blinks them out of his eye. He hears Frank grumbling beneath him, so he climbs faster. He presses his head and shoulder snug against the manhole cover and grunts as he presses his boots hard against the ladder rung.

The cover shifts, starts to rise. Clanging. Scraping.

Cason plants one hand, opens it up, climbs out.

He tilts the lid back like the head of a Pez dispenser, holds it there as Frank drops the flare and starts to ascend. The ladder again shaking beneath his feet.

"Case-of-herpes," Frank calls, "gimme your hand, this damn ladder—"

The bolts holding the ladder in place shear, and it drops. With Frank on it.

At the same time—

Thunder booms above. Vibration in the ground.

The edge of the manhole cover beneath Cason's palm suddenly

bites—a sharp electric sting—and before Cason can do differently, he yanks his hand away.

The manhole falls back into place with a reverberating *bang*.

"Fuck!" Cason says, shaking his hand like he just palmed an angry hornet.

From beneath the manhole cover, a muffled "ow."

Cason kneels down, gets his hands in the thumbholes on the metal disc, tries to lift.

Nothing. Doesn't budge.

And Frank has the crowbar.

"Frank," Cason yells. "Can you hear me?"

Another muffled: "Ow." Then: "Yeah. Yes. Fuck."

"I need the crowbar."

"And how'm I supposed to get it to you?" Frank coughs. "I'm not magic."

"I'll see if I can find something."

"I'll head down the tunnel. You got the satchel charge?"

Cason yells down an affirmative.

"And the trigger?"

In his pocket, the trigger mechanism—a radio transmitter built off a small remote control once used to steer a toy speedboat. It's just a green box with a black dial on it. Frank showed him—turn the dial hard from 0 to 10 and bomb go *boom*.

"Yeah. Yeah, I got it."

"Good. Then go meet me at the next manhole."

Another growl of thunder.

A greasy, cold rain starts to fall.

Shit.

CHAPTER NINETEEN
The Seven

THE RAIN PICKS up—a hard knife-slash of water that falls at an angle, needles of rain lit bright by pulses of lightning. Cason hurries along, the factory grounds rising up around him in black shapes darker than the backdrop of night; he tries to keep to a straight line, hoping he knows where the next manhole cover might pop up.

The sudden storm isn't helping.

And something gnaws at him, too. *Nergal was once a storm god, wasn't he?*

Is this just a storm?

Or is this *him*?

Cason tries to remember whether or not he checked the weather today. Was it supposed to rain? He doesn't know.

Doesn't matter. Onward. Find Frank.

Ten yards. Twenty. Fifty. A hundred. Boots splashing in swiftly-formed puddles. Cason thinks he sees something along the roof-line of one of the buildings—a rusted hulk with a hundred shattered windows, each a broken eye—but when he follows his gaze upward he sees nothing. Just shadow against shadow, just the lightning and the rain.

And what *doesn't* he see down here? Another manhole cover. Damnit.

The rain picks up. Cason can't see. Can't hear. The downpour sounds like the pounding surf; white noise drowning everything out.

He pulls the satchel charge tight against his shoulder, ducks left and darts under a concrete overhang whose pillars are crumbling—each with big hunks taken out of them, like something bit through the cement, exposing rusted rebar bones.

Then—

A scuff of a boot behind him.

Cason wheels, body tensing to a defensive stance—

"Dude, whoa."

It's just a kid. Some teenage wasteoid—his ratty blond curls sticking out from under a red-and-white trucker hat that says FUCK YOU. Thin frame beneath a tattered Operation Ivy t-shirt and stuffed into a pair of slashed jeans hanging too low on the kid's knobby hipbones. He's got his hands up, mouth in a surprised O, backpedaling.

Cason asks: "The hell are you doing here? You scared the piss outta me."

Thunder booms. The ground shudders.

"Dude, yo, are you here to see him, too?"

"Who? See who?"

The kid smiles a snaggle-toothed grin. "The Tacony Hermit, yo."

Cason wants to look around. See if someone's playing a prank on him. Half-expects Frank to be hiding behind that snarled tangle of wire over there—it's all a joke, all of it, the gods and goddesses, the freaks and the monsters, there is no Sasquatch Man, no beautiful Aphrodite, no Nergal and no bombs that blow these divinities back to whatever cosmic seed-bed they came from—but then Cason hears the sound of his wife screaming inside a burning car, hears hands slapping against window glass and against a melting dashboard, and knows that this isn't a joke. It's all too real. And all too horrible.

"What hermit?" he asks.

The kid laughs. Waves him on. "Come on. We got a bead on him. I'll show you."

* * *

THE KID TALKS as he walks.

"So, there's this fuckin' homeless guy, right? He lives here. He *lives* here. He lives *here!* Fucked. Up. He's got this, like, huge beard and these wild eyes and he's got all these blankets and rags wrapped around him. Sometimes you can find him by the smell 'cause, like, he smells *so bad*—I mean, I guess the only showers this nutball gets is when it rains like this, right? Hey, dude—if you're not here for the Hermit, what *are* you doing here?"

They dart into the nearest building and cross an old factory floor: defunct extruders and wire-cutting machines rear up to the left and right, massive metal skeletons, all spider-like, as if they might come alive at any moment—hungry for a meal of flesh. Far above them hang catwalks that sway and squeak. In here the rain is a dull, distant roar.

"I'm a..." Cason thinks. "An urban explorer."

"Dude. That's awesome. Like those spelunker guys from Detroit. Fuck yeah."

"Hey, what's your name?" Cason asks.

But the kid doesn't seem to hear him. He hangs a sharp left through the machines, keeps blathering. "So this Hermit, right? Some people say he's like, not even alive. That he's just a ghost, but that's bullshit because we've seen him. We've *talked* to him. Other people say like, he's the last of the wire factory workers. Like, they closed up shop and he didn't have anything or anyone and he fuckin', you know, he just fuckin' *stayed*. But the weirdest story says that he's a mass murderer and shit. Like, he killed a bunch of people and this is where he hides out—his mind couldn't handle it and even *he* doesn't remember who he is or where he came from. Fucked up, right? Fucked. *Up*."

Fucked up, indeed.

At first, Cason thought—maybe this so-called 'Tacony Hermit' can lead him to Nergal. If this derelict factory is his home, well, maybe he could point the way. But now, a new theory: the Tacony Hermit *is* the god of death. Lost. Insane. Like the way the Sasquatch Man became polluted by the area around him. Turned into a shut-in.

That sends a chill scrabbling up Cason's spine.

"This way," the kid says, taking another hard right toward a door. "My buddies are over here. We'll take you to see the Hermit. I think we know where he is."

The kid throws open the door with two hands. The sound echoes: *kachoom*.

Inside, a room lit by a barrel fire. All around, the ghosts of big aluminum bins and rack upon rack of rusted, coiled chain-link fence. Storage area. Once upon a time, the wire came off the line, got bundled by one of the machines, then hauled in here—Cason sees a break in the wall above their heads, where a hanging track carried wire spools between rooms. Now the track—and the catwalk above it—has buckled, kinked like a garden hose.

Gathered around the barrel fire are two other kids. Late teens, by the look of them, their faces lit from underneath by the flickering orange glow. One kid's got straight brown hair framing a long lean face, and is wearing a Cannibal Corpse shirt. The other kid's shorter, fatter, showing off a shorn scalp and a blank white t-shirt.

Embers swirl around them—fiery snow turning swiftly to ash as it disappears. Holes in the barrel show off the molten light of burning wood.

"Dudes!" Operation Ivy yells. "This is—" He turns. "Who are you again?"

"Cason."

"Cool name, cool name." He turns back to his buddies as they approach. "This is Cason! He's like, a fuckin' urban spelunker and shit."

Cannibal Corpse offers a fist to pound. "Cool. 'Sup."

Shorn Scalp smirks, offers not a fist to bump but a hand to shake. His voice is high-pitched yet gravelly, too, like he's a smoker—a fact fast confirmed as he precariously lights a cigarette off the barrel fire. "That's pretty rad. You here to see the Hermit?"

Cason shrugs. "I am now."

"Cool, man, cool." Shorn Scalp puffs on the cigarette like he's mad at it.

Cannibal Corpse pokes at the fire with a hunk of rebar. Cinders belch forth.

"Where you kids from?" Cason asks.

"Around," Cannibal Corpse says.

Shorn Scalp chuckles. Raspy. Like a saw cutting rough wood.

Then nobody says anything. Or makes any other move.

"I'm ready to roll," Cason says, interrupting the silence. "We good to go?"

He feels Operation Ivy come up on his side, close enough for their elbows to touch. Cason pulls away. Shorn Scalp gives him an irritated look.

"I dunno," he says. "You *ready* to see the Hermit?"

"What is he, the Wizard of Oz? I'm ready."

Cannibal Corpse shakes his head. "I'm not sure you are." *Poke, poke.* The barrel coughs fireflies of ash. "You a religious guy?"

"What's that have to do with anything?" Unease crawls under Cason's skin.

"The Hermit," Shorn Scalp says, "is special."

"*Real* special," Op Ivy says.

Suddenly, something Frank said rears its head: how some gods are content to toy with just a few of us at a time and build up little cults of personality...

Little cults of personality.

Cason fakes a laugh. "You guys are creeping me out a little."

"Hermit ain't like you or me," Shorn Scalp says.

"Yeah," Op Ivy says. "Fuckin' *yeah.*"

Cannibal Corpse chimes in. "He's got flies in his beard. Lightning in his eyes. Disease on his breath." With each word, the kid taps the barrel with the piece of rebar. *Whong. Whong. Whong.* Whorls of hot ash rise with each hit. Shorn Scalp bends over, fakes playing the guitar. Op Ivy gnaws on a thumbnail and giggles like a girl.

Cason feels his teeth hum, mouth slick with spit. Pulse beats in his neck. "You guys know the Hermit's name?"

"Ner-uru-gal," Op Ivy says between giggles.

"*Nirgali,*" Shorn Scalp says, letting smoke drift from his mouth and nose-holes.

Cannibal Corpse nods. "Lion. Dragon. Storm lord. Dead king."

From behind Cason, another voice, a girl's voice: "Lord of the Great City."

Another voice from the shadows, this one a boy's: "Lord of Cutha."

Cason turns. Sees more of them coming. The girl in a too-long Hello Kitty shirt, punky pink hair in a single side ponytail. Next to her, a boy—shirtless, scrawny, ribs showing, khaki shorts bulging at the pockets. Two more behind them—Cason sees a girl with a Superman shirt and a mini-skirt, and behind her, a boy with a blaze-orange vest.

They begin to chant. All of them.

Ner-uru-gal.

Dan-nu-um

i-na ili ga-ba-al

la ma-ha-ar.

Again and again. From hissing whispers to speaking voices to an angry, belligerent mantra. Drowning out the sound of distant rain, hiding Cason's own drumming heartbeat.

They encircle the burn barrel.

Cason, his back against it. The heat licking his neck, fire between his shoulder blades. Sweat dribbles down his back.

Then the chants end suddenly. Cut short, as if with a blade.

Cannibal Corpse clucks his tongue. "You shouldn't have come, human."

Cason turns. Is about to say something.

But then Cannibal Corpse cracks the barrel with the rebar—a cloud of hot bright ash rises, and from the boy's mouth keens a loud howl, a hard wind of breath—

Cason's vision is all embers, all fire, his hand up, his eyes blinking away ash—

Hands shove him.

Someone pulls at his hair. Blind, he stabs out with a fist, finds nothing there.

A foot kicks against the back of his leg. His hip drops; he almost falls.

His vision clears—

This is no cult.

Cannibal Corpse has the face of a lion.

Shorn Scalp puffs on a cigarette pinched between bird-like talons—his mouth still human, his hands most certainly not.

Op Ivy has pig tusks and all-white eyes.

Hello Kitty has a tiger's head, its muzzle flecked with red.

Shirtless has a pair of insectile mandibles. *Click, click, click.*

Supergirl has glossy black crow's eyes and feathers tufting over her ears.

Blaze-Orange has cracked hooves and lobster-claw hands. *Snap, snap, snap.*

They begin to circle. Like sharks swimming clockwise around a sinking boat. Cason feels his face stinging from where little motes of burning residue marked him. Orbs of light bob before his eyes. Shorn Scalp swipes at him with a claw—not to connect, just to threaten. Cason backs away, almost hits Op Ivy, who snorts and giggles.

Cannibal Corpse speaks—the lion mouth moving, but human words coming out.

"We are the Sebittu. We are the Seven."

"*Dude,*" Op Ivy says, slick tusks pushing at his upper lip.

Shorn Scalp flicks away the cigarette.

"You want to see Ner-uru-gal," Cannibal Corpse says. "You have to go through us."

The lion-face roars, and they advance.

CHAPTER TWENTY
Stuck Pig

THE TOYOTA HISSES. Above it, a whisper of steam from under the hood. Below it, a spreading pool of neon green—like the blood spilled from a gut-shot alien.

Alison sobs.

She had just passed Dayton, Ohio, headed toward the Indiana border, when all *this* happened. The car overheated. Needle into the red. All the vehicle warning lights going off at once—moments later, the engine started to gutter. And now, here she sits. The Toyota just a lump of dead metal on the side of the highway.

So, she cries.

A hard, heavy cry, like rain on a metal roof, like hail against the side of a house. She misses her son. She feels the hole in her mind. Everything seems impossible and out of control—a windmill spinning faster and faster until the slats and blades start to squeak and complain and break off, falling toward the earth. Her hands grip the wheel. Her forehead presses against her knuckles.

She hits the dashboard with the heel of her hand. Once, twice, thrice. A tiny childish hope inside her that she, like the Fonz, has the ability to make things work just by hitting them. It used to work on

Nintendos and VCRs.

It does not work on the Toyota.

She keeps crying.

Eventually, the sobbing tapers. The tears dry up. She blows her nose.

Then she calls Triple-A.

THE MECHANIC LEANS over the desk. The minty tobacco stink of chaw rises up off him, mixes with his cheap cologne, does little to settle Alison's already agitated stomach.

"Distributor's busted," he says.

She knows that. The other mechanic two hours ago said as much.

"How long?" she asks.

"That's the thing. We don't carry the part."

"It's not an uncommon car."

"No, but it *is* four years old and that part..." He licks along the inside of his gums. "It breaks a lot."

"So you should have ordered a lot."

"Lady, we *did*," he says, starting to look irritated. "But the part's back-ordered. That's not us, you understand. That's them. The manufacturer."

"Fine." *It's not fine.* "How long?"

"A day. Maybe two. We checked with the local dealers, with a couple other garages and—no go. But we got a guy out in Scottsdale who has the part, so he'll send it up. Just depends on if UPS plays nice or not, getting it here."

"Arizona? That'll take..." *Forever.* "I can't be here. I have somewhere to be." *Somewhere insane. Somewhere that doesn't make any sense. An address in the middle of Kansas.*

"Well, you're not getting there in your car. Not today, at least." He looks out the window, points. "There's a Red Roof Inn across the highway. I can have one of my guys drive you over there."

"But..." Her voice trails off. She doesn't have the energy for it. "Fine. That'll be fine." Suddenly she remembers her manners. "Thank you."

*   *   *

THE RED ROOF Inn. Night. The room is loud. Ice maker in the hallway humming. The susurration of traffic from the highway nearby. Through the wall, a couple yelling at one another, then screwing hard against the wall, then yelling at one another again.

Doesn't matter. Alison can't sleep. Doesn't even bother trying.

She paces the room like an agitated zoo panther.

This is all a mistake.

She should be back at the hospital. With her son. Everything that happened has been a delusion. Alison is sure of that, now. She's suffered a... what's it called? A psychotic break. A couple days where she and reality are broken apart like a boat drifting away from the dock, but now she's feeling like it's time to drop anchor, throw rope, go back to shore.

What was she thinking? Out here on this crazy trip. Following the words of... some tiny little madman? Probably some homeless guy, wandering in off the street. Spins for her a tale and shoves an address in her hand...

She pulls the address out again. Just to see if it's real.

It's real. The paper slip crinkled. The edges sharp enough to cut.

The address: 5456 E. Atlas. Russell, Kansas. No zipcode.

The GPS knew where to take her. Twenty-some hour trip west.

Until the car died. Until the part was back-ordered. Until here: the motel. Or hotel. Or whatever it is that marks the difference between the two.

She picks up the remote control, thinks to turn it on, doesn't. Tosses it back on the pillow, where it kicks up dust. Wonderful. Another good reason not to sleep.

"I need a cigarette," she says to nobody.

Hasn't smoked since before Barney was born.

Hasn't been away from Barney since then, either.

Her heart twists in her chest like a fish on the line.

*   *   *

CIGARETTE MACHINE. SHE didn't even know they still had those, but they do, at least here at the Red Roof Inn just outside Dayton, Ohio. She puts her money in—*so* much money, smoking is more expensive now than ever—and a pack of Parliaments drops into the tray with a clunk and a bang.

She taps the pack against the heel of her hand.

Pulls a cigarette out with trembling fingers.

In between her lips. The taste—old, familiar, shameful, wonderful.

She pats her pockets, an old habit that will now go unfulfilled.

Lighter. She doesn't have a lighter.

Hasn't carried a lighter in years.

Crap crap crap.

And it's again that the seawall that protects her crumbles down and she thinks to turn around, sit on the curb, and cry. Because she's spent up. Run ragged. *E for Empty*.

But then a hand taps her gently on the shoulder.

She turns, and finds that the hand is holding a Zippo lighter.

And the hand is attached to a tall, lanky man. Dusky skinned. Latino, maybe, or Native American. Long dark hair pulled back in a pony tail. Nose like a falcon's beak.

The thumb strikes a flame.

Hesitantly, Alison lets him light the cigarette. Her lungs fill with nicotine. Smoothest poison on the planet. It brings a sudden bloom of clarity as the stress retreats once more out to sea.

"You look like you needed that," he says. Mouth a flat line, but eyes smiling.

"I did. I do." Again, her manners. "Thank you."

"A pleasure. You traveling?"

"No. Well. Yes, in the sense that we're all traveling. But right now... stuck here."

"We all get stuck sometimes."

"I guess. Doesn't make it any less frustrating."

He leans back against a post. Pulls out his own smoke—a small cigarillo. Swisher Sweets, cherry-tip. Fire at the end, a plume of pungent, scented smoke as he takes it in, puffs it out. Watching her like a fox the whole time.

"Where you headed?" he asks.

She thinks, *where I was headed and where I am headed aren't necessarily the same thing.* And so her answer is: "Home. Pennsylvania. Philly-area."

"Thought you might've been heading West."

A grin tugs at the corners of his mouth.

"Why?"

"You just have that look. The West has power the East does not. It has a... gravity. That's why men and women have been compelled to go that direction. They begin in the East and move to the West. You can see it in the sun—the way it's pulled across the sky, born in the East, dragged to the West, until it slides behind the horizon and"—he blows a trio of smoke rings—"then it's gone. Light to dark. Life and death. East to West. You looked like someone making that trip."

She takes another drag. Then a step back. The little hairs on her arms and neck tingle and stand. "Thanks for the light. I better be going."

"To Philadelphia."

"To my room. I'm stuck."

"You don't have to be stuck."

She takes another step backward.

Just as he takes a step forward.

"I don't... know..."

He pulls a key fob from his shirt pocket, jangles the keys. "I've a horse to ride just over there." She doesn't know what he means—a horse?—but then she sees a cherry-red Mustang at the end of the row. "If you're up for the trip."

"I don't know you."

"What does that matter? I don't know you either. Nobody knows anybody." He laughs around the little cigar. "We barely even know ourselves."

"I have things in my room."

"You have your purse here."

"I have luggage."

"Luggage is just baggage. I say we get rid of all baggage."

Another drag. Each puff keeping her from freaking out and bolting like a spooked nag. "I have maps."

"We don't need maps. I know where we're going."

She swallows. "Do you?"

"We're going to Kansas."

That's it. Done. No way. She hears herself gasp, and before he can say anything else, she's turning tail, flicking the cigarette to the ground, and hurrying away. Back toward the lobby entrance, hand fishing around her pocket for the room key—

The doors ahead of her open. Double doors. Automatic.

And the man with the cigarillo steps out of them.

He was behind her.

Now he's ahead of her.

Again he dangles the keys.

"Last chance. I'm told you need a ride."

She folds her arms in a defensive posture. Feeling suddenly cold, too.

He continues: "Life is a series of choices, Alison. We don't change our lives by making safe choices; we change our lives by making the crazy choices. By taking risks. By throwing ourselves off cliffs. Learn to love the fall. Fall with me. Drive with me. To Kansas. If not for you, then for your son."

His hand jerks. The keys fling toward her and she catches them in her cupped hands—her palms sting from the hit.

Again he tilts his head toward the parking lot. "I'll let you drive. Let's go."

Alison makes her choice.

Her teeth bite the inside of her cheek as she follows after the man, wreathed in serpents of cherry-touched cigar smoke.

CHAPTER TWENTY-ONE
Circle Of Beasts

CASON BLEEDS. HE had to duck a swipe from the lion-head in the Cannibal Corpse t-shirt, and as he did, a lobster claw snipped the skin at his elbow, and now blood runs down to his wrist, his hand, his fingers.

Supergirl shrieks—the raucous caw of a crow whose meal was interrupted—and he hears a flutter of feathers and then she's in front of him. Mouth open—toothless, gums hard like a beak, and she snaps at the air in front of him—

And then it's on. Cason reacts. His head whips forward, connects with her nose, feels a crunch that isn't altogether human, like the feel of a beach shell under a bare foot—she squawks, blood squirting in twin streams, arms pinwheeling as she backs away. It's a dirty move, the headbutt. Would never fly in the octagon.

But this isn't that.

Nobody sanctioned this fight; and it's seven on one, a fight Cason can't win. His only goal here is to break a hole in the seven and to run.

If that means fighting dirty, then so be it.

Shorn Scalp rakes the air with his raptor claws, but Cason sidesteps it, brings a knee up into baldie's gut, then fishhooks his mouth with a hard finger and drags him along like a whipped puppy. Just as Blaze-Orange comes at Cason with the clacking lobster hands, he whips Shorn Scalp at him—the two bowl into one another and hit the ground.

A snort in his ear—

Op Ivy is there. A kick to Cason's knee. He takes it—it's a shitty kick, kid doesn't know how to fight. Cason jams the sole of his boot into Op Ivy's own leg, and the kid howls in guttural rage—but before the tusked freak can drop, Cason has a fistful of the kid's hair (another no-no in the ring) and brings his head up just in time to catch a swing of Cannibal Corpse's rebar.

Op Ivy's tusks shatter. His mouth is blood. Cason throws him away like an empty food wrapper—

Cannibal Corpse cares little for his pal; he steps over Op Ivy's writhing frame and swings the rebar again. And again. Each time, Cason steps just out of range.

He smells the lion's breath. Rank. Like hot, raw meat.

Then—

Hands from behind.

The sound of an insect's mouth chittering.

The scent of raw meat, not from the front now, but from behind.

Shirtless and Hello Kitty.

They grab under his arms, hold him tight as lion-head raises the rebar like it's fucking Excalibur—

Cason stomps a foot. Not sure who's, but fuck it, doesn't matter—then he twists, gets under someone, lifts someone across his shoulders just as the rebar cracks down across that someone's back. Turns out, it's Shirtless—his mandibles part and sing a wretched insect song, the screams of cicadas in a forest fire, the hum of a thousand locust wings descending on this dark earth—

The sound gets into his head. Drilling deep. He flips Shirtless, drops him—

He stands, staggers back—

The tiger's maw snaps the air behind him. He jerks—

Lurches forward—

Catches the rebar across the shoulder—

Then the back—

Cason falls, chin hitting the earth. Teeth biting his tongue. Greasy copper on his mouth, lips wet with his own blood. Hands find him, flip him over like he's nothing. Shirtless the Bug-Man pins him. Mouth-parts twitching with excitement—

Lobster claws get under Bug-Man's skinny arms, throw him aside—

Here comes Blaze-Orange—kid cackling, eyes bright with a flash nothing short of total psychosis. Cason throws a punch, but the kid tilts left, lets it miss him, uses his claw to capture the wrist—

Cason feels the serrated edge bite flesh. Feels it start to close. The pain is white hot, an electric bolt running to the tips of his fingers and down to his elbows—

He screams—

But then Lobster Boy is gone. Thrown aside.

A roar parts the air.

Cannibal Corpse replaces him. Standing, not pinning.

He pokes Cason hard in the breastbone with the rebar.

"You're not gonna see the Storm Lord," he growls. "Like Gandalf said in that movie: *You Shall Not Pass.*"

All the freaks chuckle. Start quoting lines from the movie.

Hello Kitty, her tiger's growl: "Fat hobbit."

Shorn Scalp: "One does not simply walk into Mordor."

Op Ivy, through broken teeth and shattered mouth: "*Preshusss.*"

Then they start kicking him. And beating him with fists. A fist knocks the air out of him, a boot connects with his head, the rebar against his leg—

THE PANIC OF a beat-down, revealed:

The body on full-alert. The pain of the assault. The senses light up like a paparazzi parade watching the celebrity du jour doing the walk of shame—the anguished darkness cut by constant flashbulbs, pop, pop, pop. Everything is fear and trauma, mind and body a squirrel with its back broken. Wants to stand, run, flee, fly, but the only option is to lay there and take it, because the body doesn't move fast enough, the body isn't strong enough, the attackers are too many.

Soon the pain becomes dull—the edge of the blade chipped and rounded as it hacks away, as dull as the roar of rain hammering on the factory roof, and it isn't long before the body starts to shut down. Disconnect from it all. The mind retreating deeper inside the shell as the shell is destroyed, conscious thoughts fleeing like rats pouring off a sinking ship.

Eventually the trauma is complete. The mind hides. The body is just meat.

But that's not what happens to Cason Cole.

Just as the mind starts to pull away—as the fists rain down, as the kicks get harder and faster—the darkness inside him blooms with a curtain of red fire. He hears the crackle of brush, the thunder of earth beneath crushing hooves. He feels a pair of searing charcoal briquettes at his brow and his heart comes alive, screaming like the primate house at the Philadelphia Zoo—the smell of the forest fills him, his mind a maze, his body a weapon.

On his hands and knees—

Head forward, legs beneath him—

He lurches forward, bowling someone over, not sure who, doesn't matter.

Tucked shoulder. Body rolling, feet beneath him, suddenly standing—

It's like they're traveling in slow motion.

He, far faster, far more aware, every second sliced into its composite moments—

He howls, louder than they—

A lobster claw snapping at his face. Cason takes it, twists it, cracks the shell, pink and bloody meat sliding to the floor and plopping wet against the concrete—

Hands around bug parts, yanking down, uprooting the mandibles the way you'd rip a fist of weedy taproots from the earth, wet rip, sound of celery broken, hornet wings and panicked crickets—

The rebar comes—foot out, hand up, catches the rusted metal bar, pulls it, crashes it against a tiger's head, feels the bone give way—

Breaks the bird fingers at the end of Shorn Scalp's leathery hand—

Collapses Op Ivy's pale throat, the monster choking on his own tusk bits—

Rebar forward, thrusting through a crow-eye, into the brain, won't come back out—throws her and it to the ground—

Cannibal Corpse sees what Cason has wrought.

The lion turns tail and runs.

Everything slow, languid, time trapped in cold honey as the final monster flees, each foot falling slow against the concrete, the sluggish pivot of his leonine features as he turns to see if Cason is following—

All is slow until the lightning.

A scorching white lance of electricity comes from above.

The lion is just shadow and X-ray and then a cooling pile of charred skin. The smell of burnt hair fills the air.

A man stands over the body of Cannibal Corpse.

The tall shadow says: "Bow before the Lord of Cutha."

Cason bows. Because he can do nothing else.

CHAPTER TWENTY-TWO
The Center Of The Circle

NERGAL.

The tall, broad-shouldered man steps forward. Long wild beard hanging down to his bare, muscled chest. Flies nest in the kinks and curls, fat black bodies catching what little light there is to catch. His own scalp is bare—his legs swaddled in leather strips and torn rags. Bare feet slap against the concrete as they approach.

And all around are the bodies of dead teenagers. *Children*. No longer wearing the features of animals. All human. All dead.

"Worry not," Nergal says, his voice deep, crisp, but there lurks an almost regal trill to the words he speaks. "They were dead long before you came. I just borrowed their bodies to house my Sebittu. My seven protectors. I will have to find new... volunteers."

Cason cannot stand. Not yet. But he forces his hand to the pocket. Where the trigger for the bomb waits. He slumps a shoulder, lets the pack slide off.

"You bested them all," Nergal says, now standing tall over Cason. The man—*the god*—smells of ozone, of streets after a rain, of an infected wound, of musk and flesh and electricity and death. Flywings buzz. "You have the beast in you. Wants to rise to the surface, doesn't he?" Nergal runs a callused thumb over Cason's brow. "Here. And here. The marks of that beast. Fading. But they'll come again."

Cason has no idea what the man is talking about.

Doesn't much care, either.

Frank's gonna miss the show.

"You brought my wife and son back to life," Cason says.

"Did I?" The god seems bewildered. "Oh. Good."

"I want to thank you."

"Of course you would."

"I got you this." Cason shifts a shoulder—lets the bag hang off his forearm.

Nergal stares at it like it's naught but a fossilized turd, as if to say, *this is my gift?* He sneers and scratches the beard—flies take flight before roosting once more in the dark twisted folds of hair. Cason thinks, *he's not going to take it*, but then, sure enough, Nergal— the god of storms, the Lord of Cutha, the inadvertent king of the underworld—reaches down with a hand and haughtily raises the bag in front of his face to give it a long sniff.

Cason grits his teeth, breaks free from his subservient position, and leans backward—

Just as his hand spins the dial on the remote control in his pocket. *Boom.*

The air pops—a brief wind shoves Cason back—and there's a flash and a bang. His ears ring and a stray thought flits through his mind: *blowing up gods is getting to be a real habit*—and then he's crab-walking backwards and scrambling to stand.

When the white smoke clears and the middling darkness resumes, lit only by the faltering barrel fire, he sees the broad-shouldered shadow of Nergal the Storm Lord standing there. Silent. Trembling.

All around, little white pieces of burning paper float to the ground.

What Cason expects: Nergal slides into component pieces, like a cartoon knight sliced into chunks by a swift-cutting sword.

What Cason does not expect: Nergal brushing himself off as if nothing happened.

The latter is what happens.

"That was no gift," Nergal's voice booms. A voice that seems genuinely surprised, as if incredulous that any would dare give him anything less than a chest of the richest gold, the finest silver, the rarest gems. It was an attitude Cason remembers in Eros—his boss always seemed to expect the world to bend to his will. And it almost always did.

Little pieces of paper smolder in Nergal's beard. Flies gather to extinguish the cinders of the smoking adabs.

The bomb didn't work.

That's not good.

"You made a terrible error," Nergal says.

And before Cason can do anything else, the Lord of Storms is standing before him. From ten feet away to ten inches, in the space of a single heartbeat.

Cason does what Cason does. He fights. Throws a punch. Connects with Nergal's face—the god's head snaps back and a cloud of flies coughs into the air. Gut punch. Knee-kick. Elbow to the throat. Nergal stands there. Takes each blow the same way a building takes a bird flying into its side: with complete and utter disinterest.

One more, for good measure—a deal-closer in the ring, when he was afforded the rare chance to pull it off. Cason snaps a high kick to the side of Nergal's head.

The god stops it.

He reaches up like a lord waving to his serfs and catches Cason's ankle. Balance gone, Cason's other foot skids out from under him—

Nergal reaches with his other hand, grabs Cason's knee. Then, one hand low and one higher up, he twists.

The bone snaps.

He drops Cason like a sack of potatoes.

Then Nergal steps on the other leg. Lends it his full weight—an inhuman weight, the weight of a horse, a truck, a mountain.

The bone creaks. Grinds. Then snaps.

Cason screams like he's never screamed before. Not in the ring. Not ever.

Nergal grabs him by the scruff of his neck and carries him like a mother cat carries an impudent kitten.

CHAPTER TWENTY-THREE
Broken Legs

BARNEY RUNS AROUND, *whacking the remote control against everything: window sill, chair tops, heating vents. Cason catches up with him, gently plucks the remote from the one-year-old's hand.*

Of course, the kid cries.

Alison, in the kitchen washing dishes, looks out—the apartment is all pretty open, so it's not hard for her to see. "I swear, he's only one and we're already into the terrible twos."

Barney does this foot-stompy, hand-wavey angry baby thing when something he wants is taken away. And that's what he's doing now.

But Cason has a trick. He takes Barney, spins him around once, twice, then a third time, and when he's finally done spinning, Cason gives Barney a favorite toy: a little wobbly plastic police car with one rolly ball in the center instead of four functional tires.

All the tension in the boy's face melts away. He smiles—showing off his two goofy looking teeth jutting up out of his lower jaw like a pair of tiny white stones—then grabs the toy and toddles off like a drunken robot.

Cason heads into the kitchen, comes up behind Alison. Hands around her middle. The flats of his palms under her shirt, across her stomach.

He kisses her neck.

"*That was a smooth move back there,*" *she says, leaning back into the kiss.*

"*It's aikido.*"

"*I don't think I saw you karate kick our son.*"

He laughs. "*Aikido isn't karate, Al. It's a different martial art. Means the 'Way of Harmony.' It's all about redirecting energy, right? Attack comes in, you move them a different way—redirect their energy, leave them vulnerable to attack. That's all I did. Redirected his energy a little.*"

"*Well, you're good at it.*"

His hands travel lower, sliding past the hem of her jeans.

"*I'm good at a lot of things,*" *he says. She moans.*

Then: fump fump fump fump.

Cason feels arms wrap around his knee. Then a string of babbled gobbledygook rises up from behind him. Barney's at that stage now where he doesn't say words so much as he fountains forth whole paragraphs of complete and total nonsense.

"*Hey, Barn,*" *Cason says with a sigh.* "*You're kind of c-blocking Daddy over here.*"

Alison twists her neck, plants a kiss on his chin. "*The joys of parenthood.*"

"*Nobody told me celibacy was one of them.*"

"*Do you regret it? Being a Daddy?*"

"*Not one bit.*"

"*Your Daddy did.*"

He lowers his voice, grumbling. "*Well, my Daddy can go to hell. Besides, he's not even my real Daddy, anyway.*"

"*Maybe you should try to find your real Daddy.*"

He ducks down, grabs Barney, flies him around the kitchen before plopping the kid's diaper-clad butt down on the kitchen counter—an act that earns him a cockeyed look from Alison, who likes to keep the counters clean. Cason ignores the look and says, "*I don't need any more family than what I have in this room, right now.*" *He kisses the top of Barney's head, who squirms and giggles. "All right. The fighter fights. Back to training, babe."*

CASON AWAKENS WITH a gasp—pain jumps between both legs, zig-zagging between them. His eyes cross, everything blurry until they start to adjust—

A room lit by fire. Torches bolted into the wall, giving the industrial space a gloss of the medieval.

Old red brick. Flies buzzing.

A metal desk turned on its side in the corner. A few framed photos hanging on the wall—dusty, the glass cracked, pictures of men from decades past.

A few papers slide around the room on unseen currents of air.

Then there's him.

The Storm Lord. Nergal sitting on a throne made of white wood— each piece carved and sculpted, the wood smooth as untouched snow, gleaming like polished bone. And that's what it's made to look like: bones. Skulls and femurs and rib-bones—and many other bones that don't seem human, don't even seem *mammalian*, giving the throne less the look of a chair one sits in and more the look of a dead steed one rides into the thick of battle.

Nergal slouches in the chair. Gut out. Beard of black hair and blacker flies draped across his chest. Every time he shifts, the delicate chair shifts with him. "You are awake."

Cason pants, tries to see past the pain—looks to his legs, which lay in front of him, useless, bent at wrong angles like the legs of a dead puppet. He grits his teeth. Tries to sit. Fails. Lays there instead, sweating.

"Go to hell," Cason says, the words a misery even to say. It's not just his legs; his whole body feels like it's been run through a gauntlet of the world's top fighters.

"Hell." Nergal says the word like it's foreign. "One realm of many. One for which I care little. The Devil's domain. And he has not been seen in years. It is a realm that is closed to us, so your wish cannot be granted."

"Fuck you."

"You do not want that either, weakling. I'd split you open like a pomegranate. Your insides spilling out all over the floor like red arils." Nergal sits up straight, his back stiffening. "Besides. I am taken."

"You're pussy-whipped," Cason says. A laugh—a crazy one, at that—bubbles up out of him. Part of him hopes to enrage this fly-bearded fuck. Maybe then Cason can be put down like a dying dog; some small mercy to help end the misery. But then, in the dark of his mind, Cason hears Barney's voice—a giggle from many years ago...

"Do you mean her womanhood? That I am tamed by it?" Nergal stands, suddenly, and Cason thinks it's in anger, but then the god begins to pace, staring off at some place beyond the brick, beyond this moment. "I *was* tamed by it. I was tamed like a temple dog, for it was glorious. Soft and deep. Infinite folds. And when it needed to, it would breathe fire. It could strip flesh from bone with its bitter secretions. Serpents would crawl from her inner channel, serpents with many heads and venom so potent that even a drop of it could slay the Mighty Humbaba." His voice gets small, speaks with love, lust, reverence: "Her womanhood was beautiful. I bowed before it. I worshiped at it as if it was a fount of sacred water. My tongue, my mouth, my teeth, my fingers, I would sometimes crawl deep within that charnel space and let her give birth—I would be born upon the cold floor of her palace, wet and squalling, and she would pick me up and kiss me and I would be... complete."

"Ereshkigal," Cason says.

"Yes. Ereshkigal. My only love." Nergal sighs. Then, a spike of anger: "You are not fit to say her name. Do not say it again, or I shall have you eat the meat of your own shattered legs."

"I thought she had you trapped there. You... partook of her food and drink and then couldn't leave. A trick. A ruse."

Nergal smiles. Yellow teeth past the buggy beard. "I did not merely partake of her food and drink. She bedded me. For seven days and seven nights, we stayed in her bedchamber. Her palace shook. The seven gates swayed as the fifty lesser gods howled for us to quit our lusty clamor. All the monsters of Kur tore at their eyes and ears so that they could not behold our love-making. She trapped me. Yes. And I loved it."

"And you loved her."

"I did." A pause. "I do."

Pain in that voice. A pain altogether different from Cason's own—deeper. The pain of loss. Come to think of it, Cason knows that pain quite well; his mind travels to Alison and Barney. Today is not a day he can die. Not until he finishes this. Not until he can be back in her arms and hold his son once more.

It's time to mine the stone of the Storm God's misery.

"You've lost her."

Nergal winds his way back to the throne of white wood, and slumps into it. "I have. Again."

"She left you."

The god's lip curls into a sneer. He rakes his beard with dirty fingernails, and the flies move to let his digits pass and comb. "She's... off again. To see the world, she says. So much death. That's how she put it. This modern age lets us die in myriad ways, ways she has not seen—train crashes and building collapses. Diseases that cause you to vacate your bowels from your body. Men killing men with weapons undreamt by us. Humans have become masters of death, she said. Masters of avoiding it. Masters of creating it. *I want to reclaim my mantle*, she said. She said, she said, she said."

"But you don't believe her."

Nergal growls: "She's off with *him* again."

"Another man."

"Another *god*. She'd not dally with a man." Nergal's voice again softens. No less bitter, but now a quiet wind, if still an ill one. Mocking, too. Petulant. "*The Bull of Heaven*. Gugalanna. She chases him. He chases her. He should have died when those two heroes slew him and cut off all his limbs, but no. She had to breathe life into the sagging leather carcass." Nergal rubs his eyes. "I like to think she loves me and only... lusts after him. But now I fear differently."

Cason's not sure what his play is, here. But he's onto something. He remembers what Frank told him: *...this is where we find out how to kill Nergal. It's always in the myths. The legends. The history.*

The stories. The stories have secrets. They tell the truth even when it's a lie. Except here, Cason doesn't want the lie. Fuck the legend. Because he's getting the tale right from the monster's mouth.

Which means: keep him talking.

"Tell me more."

Again Nergal stands. "You don't command me."

"I'm not commanding. Just saying. You seem to like talking about her."

Nergal steps closer, coming between Cason and the torchlight. His long shadow like a cold night. "You know nothing."

"I know what it's like to... lose someone you love."

Nergal kneels next to Cason. Cason's not a small guy, not by any means, but here he feels tiny—a mouse in the shade of a lion. "The way you say that, it sounds like you think we are equal. What I feel is love. All you can feel is some crass facsimile of it. Yours is a dog's love for a dish of water, or for licking his own privates. Mine is a true thing. A beast of many faces, a gem of many facets. Deep as the primal ocean, tall as the roof of Heaven."

You're losing the thread... "I'm sorry, I—"

Nergal squats closer, leaning in. The flies hum and buzz. Lightning flashes in the dark of the god's eye. "Do you know what I have planned for you?"

He doesn't wait for Cason to answer.

"I'm going to keep you alive. I will take your body, and I will break it into its component pieces. I will make out of your bones and tendons and bleats and screams a brand new throne for the Mistress of Kur, for the Lady of Death, for my one true love. A throne that, this time, she will not choose to abandon."

His hand closes around Cason's throat.

Cason says, "That's... her... throne there?"

His eyes darting to the pale throne of white wood.

Nergal loosens his grip.

"Yes. That is her throne."

"She..." Cason coughs. "She must have been happy to have it. Once."

"Once. I made it for her before the gates closed. Carved it from bone-wood before the doors of our world shut and we were all exiled to this..."—Nergal makes a face like he's got something foul in his mouth—"ugly place. I was able to bring it with us. I moved mountains, quite literally, to bring it here before my power diminished with that of all the others. A reminder of that other place. A *memento mori* from the throne room of the palace of Kur."

Nergal stares at it longingly.

Cason knows this next part is going to hurt.

But he doesn't see any other way.

Cason sniffs, and says: "Looks like a piece of shit to me."

Nergal sits still for a time. Then slowly turns his head toward Cason, nostrils flaring, teeth grinding in a way that sounds like stone sliding against stone.

"You compare my handiwork to a nugget of dung?"

Cason swallows a hard, fearful knot, then shrugs. "No wonder she left."

The god strikes like a thunderclap.

THE RAIN FEELS good on Frank's scalp. For him, his skin is always hot—hot like a griddle is hot, always ready to cook a couple eggs. The rain is cool.

The buildings of the wire factory rise up around him. Offices, factory floors, warehouses, all defunct, *all dead*, empty brick and boneyards of rusted wire.

He doesn't know where Cason is.

That's not good. The sewer tunnel kept going and going—next two manhole covers down were sealed up, covered over. Had to hit the third one down, and by then it was well over a hundred feet, and by the time Frank popped his head up like a prairie dog, he was alone. No Cason to greet him.

Then, not long after, he heard the calls: jeers and cheers and chanting and—the roar of a big cat? What the fuck?

By the time Frank tracks down the source of the noises, all he finds is a scattered contingent of bodies united in death. They're already rotting. Flies feasting, maggots munching. Teenagers, by the looks of them. Long dead. Seven of them.

Seven. He's read the myths. Hell, he and Cason have been pickling in the old stories. The Sebittu? Nergal must've found a way to give life to his demons. Seven protectors. Fierce warriors, by the stories. Though these looked like the farthest thing from fierce fucking warriors, but what does it matter?

What mattered was, no Cason.

And, worse: Frank saw the little burned papery bits. Each with a charred adab to Nergal. It was wrong. The bomb didn't work.

Uh-oh.

So now here stands Frank, back outside under the downpour, trying to figure out where the hell to go next.

That's when the shit hits the fan.

First, Frank hears Cason. A cry carries across the factory grounds—a cry of pain, without a doubt, coming from the old offices dead ahead. From up above, too—top floor. Where the owners and managers used to sit, watching their little workers work.

But only moments later—

A shape above in the sky. A dark shape, with long wings.

Like a bat. But *human*-shaped and, worse, human-*sized*.

Then, the snapping and popping of metal—sparks from the far end of the complex, as something shears through the chain-link.

Headlights cut through the night.

One car. Two. Then a third.

Frank feels his skin crawl.

They're here.

It's too early. They shouldn't be clued in this soon. Not yet. Not now.

Frank looks toward the office building, then toward the approaching cars, rain disappearing in the headlights.

He makes his choice. Frank darts back to the open manhole cover just as light sweeps over the space where he just stood. He knows he should go save Cason—Cason's all part of the big plan, part of what the boss has in store—but whoever's coming, Frank's not ready to deal with them.

Sorry, Cason. Can't help you with this one. Not now. Not yet.

And Frank hurries through the tunnels, away, away, the scurrying rat.

CASON HURTLES ACROSS the room. Thrown like an errant dish.

He crashes against the throne. It creaks as he slams against it, as he rolls to the floor. By now the pain is almost meaningless—so much noise the new pain is lost among the old and vice versa, and all Cason has is a pile of dead limbs to call his own.

Again Nergal kneels. Presses Cason's face hard against the white wood. Cason's eye focuses in and out—sees how intricately carved it is, a filigree of bones within bones, of skeletons and skulls carved within the osseous wood, of cities and palms and footprints in sand and for a moment Cason wants to be lost there, wants to crawl within the open spaces and be one with the precious wood, just as Nergal desires—

But then Nergal presses his face harder—Cason's own vision distorts, washed out by the pressure and the pain.

"Look at it," the Storm Lord seethes. "Behold my handiwork. Admire its beauty. *Absorb the art.* I worked on this chair for an epoch. I separated myself from the flow of time and the river of life so that I could complete this for my bride. Who are you to tell me that it is as dung? You know nothing, half-breed."

"I know—" Nergal mashes Cason's face harder. "I know you put yourself into this chair."

"It is the only way for one to create."

"I agree," Cason says.

And then he grabs one of the delicate throne legs—just enough of a leg to get his hand around—and yanks.

It shouldn't work.

He knows this.

And yet, something courses through him. Something wild and mad, something dark and light, something that accelerates and outruns the pain and fills him with a giddy inhuman vigor (*you know nothing, half-breed*), and the strength that blooms within him lets him snap the chair leg off its base—

The crack of the wood is the same crack his own leg bones made.

He'd take a moment to appreciate that, but there's just no time.

Nergal is taken aback. The Lord of Cutha jerks his head back. Gasps.

"My lady's throne," is all he says.

Then Cason jams the chair leg into the god's flinty eye.

Nergal stands, staggers backward. Fingers feeling along the dagger-like splinter of white wood sticking out of his face. He whimpers, then growls. Then fixes his one good eye on Cason. And that's when Cason's resolve breaks apart like a sand castle under an ocean wave—

This was supposed to work.

This was Nergal's vulnerability. Arrowheads for Eros. Ohta dollies for the Sasquatch Man. And this chair—not the adabs, not the prayers—was what would lay the Storm God to rest. It had to be. *It had to be.*

And yet, there stands Nergal.

Now marching toward Cason.

Now reaching down with a trembling hand and lifting Cason high.

Now staring an infinite beam of hate straight through to Cason's soul.

The man's mouth opens. Blue threads of electricity snap between his teeth. The flies take flight, and now Cason sees that each fly has a man's face, caught in a perpetual scream. His hiss brings waves of sickness that pour over Cason like a bucket of brackish water: the smell of cancer, of roadkill, of every hospital and funeral home and mass grave and—

Nergal's eye pops like a grape under a boot.

His head follows suit, deflates like a punctured basketball.

And suddenly Cason drops to the floor as Nergal's body folds into itself and collapses like a skinsuit without a hanger—all his bones turned to air.

The last flies circle, then drop to the floor.

Cason laughs.

It worked.

It worked.

The God of Storms, and Death, and whatever else fell under the madman's aegis, was now gone from this world, *this world of men*, and there's a moment as Cason lays there like a broken doll that he feels a sense of elation, a kind of deep self-satisfaction he hasn't felt in a very long time. This god was complicit in the conspiracy against him and his family, a conspiracy he has yet to understand.

His elation is woefully short-lived.

Something punches through the wooden floor beneath him. Like zombie arms rising from the grave, hands encircle Cason's midsection and pull him down through the shattering wood and throw him to another floor below.

He crashes into the darkness. Smelling dust. Rust. Wood. And...

The sea.

Brine and salt and sand.

Aphrodite stands over him. Even in the darkness, her beauty radiates off her in waves Cason can almost see—like ripples in water, shimmering and silver.

"You had a chance to save yourself," the goddess says.

Cason tries to answer, but finds his words are only a whimper.

She shrugs at his attempt. "Pity you did not take me up on my offer."

"To the Farm, then?" comes another voice behind him. A woman's voice.

"Yes, Driver. To the Farm."

Hands grab Cason. Leathery wings envelop his face, cover his mouth—*can't breathe, can't breathe*—and claws dig into the meat of his back. Then, suddenly, rain and wind and the sense of falling, and Cason's whimper turns into yet another scream.

CHAPTER TWENTY-FOUR
Horse Thief

THE WOMAN IS off doing her... well, he doesn't know? She hasn't smoked another cigarette, so it's probably not that. It's likely some woman thing. She's got to, and this is all just a guess, fix her makeup, pee for the hundredth time, adjust her bra, have her period, milk her bosoms, or maybe just sit on the toilet and cry.

Of course, Coyote—'Kai,' he told her his name was—isn't very good with women.

He's made love to thousands of women. Most of them human. All of them acquiesced to his charms, his wiles—it's not magic. He *has* magic, yes, but that's not what brings them to his bed (or to a patch of field, or to a rock in the middle of the woods, or to an ice floe, or to a... well, where hasn't he done it? A gazebo. He's never made love in a gazebo. He makes a mental note: *have wild rumpus in gazebo*). The women come to him because they want to ride the Ki-yote Express. They want to feel his howls reverberate down through their lady parts and up through their teeth. They want to *trap* him, make him theirs. Ha, ha, ha, ladies. Good try. Good try.

Everybody wants to trap the Coyote. But nobody can.

Ah-ha-ha. So many women.

And he still understands them not one fiddly whit.

He wants to make love to this one, too. She's a bit older, but certainly pretty. Her skin is like milk. Her hair is like fire. Primal and comforting, in equal measure.

In his pocket, his member twitches.

But that's not why he's here.

At present, Coyote stands in the parking lot of a Conoco gas station in Missouri, the morning sun coming up over a flat blasted brown nowhere nothing patch of dirt that surrounds him and stretches off in all directions. The highway a pale ribbon cutting through it all. Tractor trailer grumbling by.

He waits for the woman.

Coyote leans back against the Mustang and pulls out his phone. He sends a text to someone in his address book listed only as 'E.E.'

The text: *The golden thread is unbroken.*

The thread. Sometimes: the chain, the rope, the ladder. He's even heard it spoken of as a frequency, as a *signal*, but to him it's always been the golden thread. A thread is delicate. Easy to tear a thread in twain, and yet, the golden thread always remains, strung between all the gods of his ilk. They never know what will come down the thread or what the instructions will be when it comes to them. They never know the outcome or even the *why*. They only know that they do what they must because the golden chain must remain unbroken and what it demands must be done lest the whole thing come falling down.

The world. Suspended by a thread.

A beautiful image.

It almost gives him a boner, honestly.

Then again, a spring breeze gives him a boner. See also: a car honking, the smell of coffee, the stink of beaver pelts (not a metaphor, except when it is), a sneeze, a cough, a hiccup, a cricket chirping, peyote buttons, scorpion venom, the sound of flip-flops on a heavy woman walking along the boardwalk next to the beach...

It *all* gives him a boner. He has a boner for this entire world and its contents.

Other deities seem to hate this place. Those mopes. They dismiss it. They treat it like it's a... a *prison*. Exiled here, thrown down (or in some cases, dragged up) from their places of import. Each seeing themselves as a pretty necklace around a beautiful woman's neck that was suddenly yanked from her neck and thrown into the gutter forever.

But Coyote likes the gutter. He likes *this* gutter, *this* world, most of all.

It has hamburgers! And pornography. And remote control cars and Swisher Sweets cigarillos and cat videos and fast cars and loud noises and gazebos and lust and love and charity and books and soft human women with imperfect, asymmetrical breasts.

Oh! And phones with the ability to text message.

This, Coyote decides, is what Prometheus stole from the gods.

A text comes in, *bing-bing*:

DO NOT LOSE THE THREAD

Ahh, Old Man Shu. For such a tiny fellow, he's always so *loud* in his text messages. Time and again Coyote has told him: "You don't have to type in all caps," but Shu just shrugs and smiles that pinched little smile like he knows something nobody else knows (which is kind of their gig, isn't it?). Coyote figures he should just be happy, since some of the others don't tweet at all. Like that asshole Monkey King. What a sonofabitch.

As Alison comes back out of the gas station, Coyote texts back: *Not going to lose the thread shut up.*

Reply:

GOOD

Are you sure I can't bed this one?

Reply:

YES

Well, fuck-buckets.

Alison eyes him warily. She has the keys; he's been letting her drive.

"I didn't know if you'd be here," she says.

"Why wouldn't I be?"

"You seem like that type. I don't know."

He just laughs and hops in the car.

WEST. LIKE THE strange man—'Kai'—said.

The sun comes up. Orange like an egg-yolk, then a bleached yellow like the pith of a lemon beneath the zested rind.

They don't talk much. The man whistles. Fiddles with the radio now and again—often singing along, smoking out the window and laughing at jokes apparently only he can hear. For now the radio is just static warbling between fundamentalist Christian stations and country music. He spins the dial, catches some hellfire-and-brimstone snippet—

"*Oh, how miserable your pleasures will be, when you must crawl through hellfire for an age...*"

Kai snorts. Shakes his head.

"Not a church-goer?" Alison says.

Another snort. He sweeps his arms. "This is my church."

"The inside of a Mustang?"

He laughs. "The whole world."

"Oh. Cool."

"You people think you know God. Or the Devil. That amuses me."

"You people?"

"Americans. White people. Same thing."

"You're not American?"

"I'm a bit older than that."

"You're Native American, then."

To this, he says nothing. Offers her only a wink.

"Don't judge us too harshly," she says. "We try to do okay. And we're not all like that. Just the loudest among us."

"Then you shouldn't let the loudest speak. You should get louder!" He shrugs. "Or shut them up with duct tape."

"Maybe. But we are who we are."

He smiles. "Good thing, too."

It's then she asks, because she must.

"Are you human?"

Another wink.

"Okay, seriously," she says, "no coy winking, I want to know. Are you human? Is this real? Is this *really happening*? Who are you?"

"I told you. I am Kai. Beyond that: what does it matter? This word, 'human.' It's not a meaningful word. I've known some humans who were less than human. Sub-human. I've known humans that were better than the angels, stronger and smarter than all the gods in all the heavens. I've known some animals that were the nicest people I've ever met, and I've known some gods that were more human than human. Human is just a sack of skin. It's just the flavor of your meat, like pork or beef. Don't worry about that word. Human."

Her hands tighten around the steering wheel. "You didn't answer the question."

"I often don't."

"Oh."

He clears his throat, flicks his cigarillo out the window. "Hey. Don't suppose you want to have a quickie?"

She's about to be appalled, to refuse and say *no, double no, hell no—*

But before she can:

Woop-woop.

Strobing cop lights. Red, blue, back and forth. The wail of sirens.

"Oh, what the hell? I was doing the speed limit. I'm in the right lane." She flicks on her turn signal. Kai gives her a quizzical look.

"What are you doing?"

"Pulling over."

He flips the turn signal back off. "Just gun it."

"What?"

"This car has pep. It's like if a horse had sex with a rocketship and this is its baby!"

"I'm not outracing the police."

He sighs. "We'll be *fine*. Vertical pedal on the right. Come on. Chop chop, vroom vroom."

"Wait. Why are they pulling me over? Do you have outstanding tickets or something?"

"I don't know. I don't care."

"What are they going to see when they pull your license plate?"

"License plate? That's not my license plate." He shrugs. "This isn't even my car."

"*What?*"

"Oh. Yeah. We stole it. Did I not explain that?"

"We?"

"You're driving. Actually, I'm not even in the books. So, legally speaking, it's pretty much *you*, not *we*."

"Oh." She feels the blood drain from her face. "Oh, no. I'm not a car thief. I don't... I don't do this." It's like her whole life is a train on a rickety trestle that's creaking and swaying, the tracks starting to fall apart beneath her.

She again puts on her signal and this time lets the car drift over to the shoulder. As the car slows, her heart races.

Kai just shakes his head, clucks his tongue.

The cop pulls in behind her. The sirens no longer wail, but the strobe continues. Red, blue, red, blue, sweeping over the car.

Cars pass on the highway. Alison can feel the eyes of rubbernecker drivers watching her, in the same way she's watched dozens of others get pulled over.

Shame sends blooms to her cheeks.

"Okay," Kai says. "I didn't think it would come to this but... you never know, so." He goes rustling in his pocket, pulls out something that looks like a foot-long desiccated strip of beef jerky. Like something a dog would chew on. He hands it to her.

"What is this?"

"It's my penis."

She doesn't drop it so much as fling it at him.

He bats it back at her like it's an errant volleyball.

"You're going to need that," he says, frowning. "Take it. It has powers."

"This is all some kind of strange joke." She feels queasy. "I'm not taking it."

In the rearview, she sees the cop step out of the car.

She turns back to Kai, starts to say, "You have to explain to him—"

But nobody is there.

Alison is alone in the car.

Knock, knock, knock.

The cop. Military-looking type. Aviator sunglasses. Stubble.

She rolls down the window.

She sees the crooked strip of jerky sitting on the passenger seat. The cop is speaking to her, but she can barely hear him. All she hears is the whoosh of traffic, the rush of blood in her ears, the sound of her own breath—tight, shallow, fast, panicked.

Alison closes her eyes.

Then she knows what she has to do.

COYOTE SITS ON his haunches and watches as the cop loads her into the back of the cruiser. She didn't use the weapon he gave her. It would've been so easy. It would've done all the work for her. Sprayed him with blinding coyote urine. Animated and beaten the cop about the head and neck. Then slithered away like a snake while they made their getaway.

Coyote's got a great penis. It always gets him out of trouble.

Of course, half the time, it's the thing that got him *into* trouble, but whatever.

For a while she sits in the back seat. The cop roves back and forth on his radio. In the car. Then out of the car. Does a walk around the Mustang, checking it for... well, whatever it is that a cop would look for in a stolen car.

Alison stares forward until, finally, she lifts her head and looks out the window.

She sees him out there. Their eyes meet. He wonders how puzzled she must be, seeing not the man, but the animal. A ragged, skinny coyote with tortoiseshell fur. And a cigarillo sticking out of its muzzle. Recognition flares in her eyes.

He really thought she had it in her to make the brave choice. The *interesting* choice. She's made so many before now, he just figured...

It was the penis, wasn't it? That took it one inch too far.

Coyote pads away. Stalking the margins of the highway for a while until he's out of sight and can hide behind a berm of earth covered in dead grass.

There he becomes human again and pulls out his phone.

To Old Man Shu he texts:

I think I lost the thread.

Shu texts back:

IS IT BROKEN?

I don't know.

THEN FIND OUT.

Coyote figured that would be the answer.

Besides, the cops have his penis, so he's going to need to get that back.

CHAPTER TWENTY-FIVE
The Farm

THE GODDESS PACES the floor. Her feet make no sound on the polished wood of the farmhouse. She pauses by the great stone fireplace, in which burns a primal flame that needs no kindling and gives off a gauzy greenish glow. Aphrodite flicks a small piece of black lint off the fabric of her white dress. Imperfections will not do.

This, the gathering room. Exposed beams two stories up, the second floor overlooking the first. A cursory glance makes it look like a farmhouse renovated by the rich—and that's true, to a point. Artifacts and animal rugs, Brazilian hardwood floors and crossbeams, smells of lavender and spice. But a deeper glance shows things that don't add up—the green fire; soft violin music that plays, not from speakers, but from a Stradivarius violin on the wall; a Grecian urn that whispers blasphemies as one walks past.

No one god or goddess owns the Farm. This is where they meet.

Usually to discuss problems.

Such as this newest: Cason Cole. Now truly a murderer of the gods.

"I know what we do with him," says a pale, wormy man sitting in a wicker chair by the corner. His long, oily limbs are pulled up around his body. Slogutis. Of the Lithuanian pantheon. His mouth pulls back into a wretched half-smile, half-sneer, gray-pink tongue sliding over nicotine teeth. "I just need five minutes."

Pain and misery. Always his solution.

Aphrodite sniffs dismissively. "To a hammer, every problem looks like a nail. No. This will take something else. He's a... special case."

Movement from above.

Dana, once more at the railing overhead. The older goddess's hands sway back and forth like the tides, appropriately passing a thread of salt water between them—it floats from one hand to the other like a serpent made of the sea. *That's my trick*, Aphrodite thinks.

"We must do something," Dana says. Voice commanding. Irish bitch. Aphrodite is tired of her. Acting like the mother of all, the voice of reason—it's a power-play. Of course it is. She's tired of playing second fiddle to Aphrodite, the Deity Regent of the City of Brotherly Love. Dana continues: "We cannot sit idly by as this... interloper runs amok, murdering our kind. Who even knew we could be so dispatched?"

Aphrodite tries to maintain calm and clarity in her voice, but even as she speaks, she hears how each word has sharp teeth: "We are *not* sitting idly by. We have him in our custody. He's chained in the barn, his body broken. We're not feeding him tea and cookies, are we?"

"Yes, but he should be made an example of. We should take him and crucify him. Flay his body and animate the parts in the skies above the city so that all know it is unwise to move against us, the Exiled—"

"*This* again," Aphrodite says, voice carrying. "We have rules. We have *laws*—"

"Laws that come to us from above, not from within!" Dana twists her hands, and the sea-made snake between her hands turns to mist and is gone. "It is time we go against the Ways once more, and show the Great Usurper that we will not be bound, that we seek our rightful place in the tapestry—"

From the leather couch by the fire, a man with skin like dark chocolate barks an incredulous laugh. His suit—a blue the color of slate, so blue it's almost black—fits him like a shadow. "All this over Nergal? He was barely one of us."

"But he was one of us!" Dana cries.

"He was a lunatic," the black man—Shango—says. "An exile among Exiles. He did nothing. He *was* nothing. To him, good riddance."

Slogutis hacks, coughs in his hand. "You're just happy to see the world with one less storm god. Maybe you want to see them all dead, yeah? Who you want to go next? Lei Gong? Thunderbird? Oh, fuck, Thor?" The god of pain and misery cackles. "Thor. I'd like to see you two mix it up."

"I could take Thor," Shango says, nodding with some certainty. "He needs his hammer. I only need my fists."

A sylph-like Chinese woman from across the room scoffs: Long Mu, mother of dragons, the tattoos of five colored dragons rising up each arm and crossing each shoulder to meet in the center of her back and her chest. "Thor," she sneers. "Lei Gong is the only true thunder god *I* know. You could not take *him*."

Shango stands, chest puffed out—the air around him warping, stinking suddenly of ozone, the ground trembling *just slightly*, as if a distant herd of bison came tumbling across the plains. Aphrodite claps her hands.

"Nobody is *taking* anybody else," Aphrodite hisses. "*Especially* not here. This is neutral ground. None shall violate its sanctity; unless anyone wishes to spend time in the Barn?" Nobody moves. Nobody wants to back down. That's how they are, gods. Ego-driven. Megalomaniacal. How could they not be? "Well?"

Long Mu sniffs, and breaks the tension with, "Has anyone told Nergal's consort?"

"Ereshkigal?" Shango asks, moving over to the sidebar. He begins fixing himself a drink—golden nectar and a splash of 151 rum, stirred with a cinnamon stick. "No. I won't go near that one."

"I'll tell her," Dana says. "If I can find her, I'll tell her."

"She is not the order of our business. She chose to once again leave the embrace of our protectorate—she refuses to participate in our society."

"Good for her," Slogutis mumbles, offering a crooked thumbs-up.

"Our business tonight is what to do about Nergal's killer?"

"We need justice," Dana says. Again conjuring water from her hands—this time in two threads that she braids and unbraids.

"Before justice, we need answers," Long Mu says. "We must interrogate."

"I concur," Aphrodite says.

"As do I," Shango says.

Dana says nothing, chin aloft, nose in the air.

Slogutis chuckles, claps his hands like a child eager to pluck the legs off a beetle. "Then let's go have ourselves a conversation!"

HIS MEMORIES LIKE pages, flipping faster and faster.

His first car: Chevy Camaro, early 80s, white, dirty, pink dice hanging from the rearview.

His first fight: not MMA, but behind the green wall outside the high school, near the alley where all the cats lived. Eddie Pistone said that Cason had a 'queer's name,' then 'accidentally' poured hairspray all over the Camaro's windshield, shellacking it good. The fight was longer than most of the MMA bouts Cason ever had—two untrained idiots pawing at each other like drunken orangutans. Eddie got Cason in the nuts with a kick. Cason headbutted Eddie in the teeth. Cut up Cason's head (he still has little scars), but Eddie's front teeth were knocked down his throat. Cason knew then that he liked fighting. Made him feel good, strong; like it was something he could do. Like an animal lived inside of him and wanted to come out.

His mother's funeral. Gray day, pissing rain. Father drunk. Conny late.

Wedding. Church ceremony, fire hall reception. Kerry Coogan got drunk as a snake, knocked over the punch. Everybody laughed and danced. Alison looked beautiful in the dress—the baby bump added to the beauty, made everything feel more complete. Conny came by after it was all done. Handed Cason a check for twenty-five dollars. Tried to sell him some weed. Week later, check bounced. He heard later the weed was oregano. Asshole.

Barney's first birthday. Cookie Monster cake. Nuclear blue icing. Barney got his hands in it. Then on Alison's shirt. And the wall. And the white tablecloth. Hardly any in his mouth.

First MMA fight. Versus Muay Thai fighter Pedro Santiago. Over in five minutes. Cason, beaten blue. But one reversal, he got Pedro down, head smashed against the mat. Submission, tap out. Game over. Next day, Cason felt like he'd been wrung out like a washcloth. It's when he learned that pain felt like victory.

The memories flip faster. Back and forth. Not always in order. Losing his virginity to Missy Calhoun—condom on wrong, came off inside her, a whole month worrying about her being pregnant. First taste of liquor: blackberry schnapps. First baseball game: Phils versus Mets, pulled it out in the seventh, Mike Schmidt grand-slam.

Fast forward to present, *flip flip flip flip.* Car burning, Alison screaming. Barney just a shadow in the back. Time still. Eros there. Cason weeping on his knees. Weeks, months, Eros bringing lover after lover back to the brownstone—liquor flowing, every kind of drug available, cameras, sex toys, all the moaning and screaming and sounds of bodies on beds and slammed against walls; his memories pause here, flip back and forth over the faces of lovers, men, women, younger, older. Dark hair, freckles, long hair, bald, blue eyes, green eyes, collagen lips, thin smile, scars, pockmarks, perfect skin— hovering over each face like a snapshot held in the hand—then back to Cason, sitting bored in the hallway, body-guarding the boss against a threat that would never come—

Until one day it did. RC car. Bomb. Boom. Arrowheads.

Eros falling apart like a doll. Feathers rising, falling, ears ringing.

Flip back. Eros' face. One last look in his chambers. After the bomb went off.

Then—

Two thoughts hit Cason, and they're not his own.

You didn't kill my husband.

Followed by:

You're not human.

He's wrenched up from the darkness.

He smells hay.

And the musk of barn animals.

And old wood.

Cason's eyes open.

Sure enough, he's curled up on his side on a wooden floor strewn with hay. Above him, the eaves and lofts of a red barn. Spiders weaving webs in the cracks and corners. Moths circling what few electric lights brighten the place.

He sits. Pain wracks his body. He stops sitting.

Your body is broken. But it's fixing itself.

"Who are you?" he says, aloud.

He blinks. Looks around. He's in a stall. Wooden walls. Rusted metal gate. All of it wound with glittering gold chain—thin chain, not thin as a necklace, but the kind from which a pocketwatch might dangle.

And he's alone.

I'm in your head. Not in your stall.

The words inside his head have a voice.

He pats his chest—but the sigil drawn and redrawn there is long gone, isn't it?

Here, now, in Cason's mind—there behind his eyes—that lightshow forms a face.

The woman from the woods.

The woman from Sasquatch-Man's front porch.

The woman who stole his wife, his son.

He feels his blood rush to his limbs, carrying the blue blazes of a raw red rage—he lurches forth, standing on broken legs, the pain lost in the white wall of fury. "My wife," he growls. "*My son.* Where are my wife and my son?" He staggers over to the metal door, legs barely supporting him—he grips it rattles it, tries to climb over it—

A shock goes through his body. Liquid lightning, burnished gold.

He finds himself lying on his back once more. In the hay. Light smoke drifting from his palms and the center of his chest. The anger robbed from him by the surprise.

Unbreakable golden chain, says the voice. *Forged by Hephaestus. It traps even the gods.*

"But I saw you break it."

No. You saw it fall away. Aphrodite was controlling the chain with her mind. You distracted her and that was my moment. We won't be so fortunate again.

"Alison. Barney. What have you done with them?"

I let them go. They escaped me.

"Good for them." In this, a spike of anger. "Because fuck you."

I made an error.

"Damn right you did."

I thought... I thought you'd killed my husband.

"I didn't. He was my boss. He..." Cason grits his teeth, uses the flats of his hands to push his body backward until he's sitting up against the back stall wall. "You know, fuck him, too. It's because of him I'm even here. That any of this is *happening.*"

You're right, of course. To a point. But I've seen inside your head. I moved through your memories and beliefs as if they were my own. Please believe me when I tell you: you're mistaken about a few things. A few very important things. May I have a few minutes to talk?

"Do I have any choice?"

In this, you do. I'll be quiet if that's what you'd prefer. I owe you that much.

He sneers. The skin of his legs itches something fierce. His toes twitch without him asking them to. "Fine. Talk. Anything to get my mind off the pain."

CHAPTER TWENTY-SIX
Truth And Consequence

I AM A *girl who appreciates determination.*

A little about me, then.

Aphrodite despised my beauty. She sent her son, Eros, to me, in the hopes that he would scratch me with one of his arrows when I slept so that when I awoke, I would fall in love with the first horrible creature she placed before my eyes—toad, snake, minotaur, who can say? But the plan failed. Eros accidentally scratched himself with the arrow and fell in love with me.

That was the start of my troubles.

I was just a mortal girl, then. Just a fool in love with a god, a god who was the son of a jealous, overprotective mother who decided she would do anything to keep us apart. She moved hell and earth— separating us time and again, cursing the both of us, ensuring that we could not be together. Illusions and lies. And yet we persisted, and then came the day that I was done with illusions and lies, so I went to Aphrodite in her temple and asked her what I must do to earn her favor.

She set before me task after task, all meant to be impossible. I had to separate grains by hand—thousands upon thousands of them, each impossible to distinguish from the other with the human eye, and so it was that the ants took pity on me and helped me (earning the goddess's ire in the process). Seeing that I had completed that task, she had me bring to her a snippet of golden wool—another impossible chore given the fact that these sheep were thrice the size of what you and I know, and would crush you against the rocks or buck you off the cliff. And so I waited for them to sleep and instead plucked the snippets of wool from the thorny trees against which they slept.

She had me collect water from a forbidden river.

She had me stalk and behead seven lamia.

She had me bottle the tears of the sea serpent, Scylla.

She had me pluck out the eyes of the one-eyed men and bring them to her.

Those, not in the myths. But true just the same.

Then came the day when she said that the stress of having me in her life had caused her beauty to spoil—"curdled like sour milk," she said. And so she sent me to the Underworld to reclaim some of her beauty. The only way to the unloving depths was to kill myself, so I leapt off a cliff and died. That allowed me to enter the Underworld and navigate its catacombs, hiding from Cerberus and eating nothing but moldy bread so that I would not be bound to that place. Finally I found Persephone and asked her to gift me with a bit of her beauty.

She complied, and sent me on my way.

That last thing, a trap for my own vanity. I thought to open the box just to see—but contained within was not beauty, but sleep. Endless sleep that consumed me.

But then my husband came. He came to save me. He wiped the sleep from my eyes and took me to a safe place, while he traveled to the Mount to ask Zeus to intervene on our behalf—and the Father God did indeed intervene, and declared that we could be married. To protect me from Aphrodite, he poured for me a draught of nectar and fixed a meal of ambrosia and it changed my humanity to divinity. And, for a time, Aphrodite and I shared a grudging peace.

The point of all this is to say that, to dispel illusions and lies, I had help. I had help from my husband. I had help from the ants. An eagle helped me get the water from the river. Hercules helped me slay the lamia. Glorious Zeus, my father figure among the gods who has now gone from us, helped me marry. Sometimes we require assistance in our quest.

And so I'm here to aid you, by telling you the truth about you, your family, and your so-called 'friend,' Frank Polcyn.

A SOUND INTERRUPTS the story.

A snort.

The floorboards of the barn tremble.

Then: the acrid smell of piss.

Cason shifts, tries to stand, fails. Tries again—gets a leg beneath him, finds that it supports his weight, if barely.

Hobbles over to the metal gate. Doesn't touch it, as getting another shock from the golden chain isn't a particularly endearing notion.

But he looks.

The barn is huge. Stall after stall. Dimly lit. Cast mostly in shadow. And up above, in the lofts, he sees hay bales and small wire cages. Can't see what's in them, if anything at all.

Another snort. And a stomp. Cason feels the vibration in his ribs.

Down the way and across, he sees something shift in a stall. A glimpse of fiery eyes—like drips of molten iron, glowing in the darkness.

He smells a stink like rotten eggs.

"The hell...?"

It's a unicorn.

He almost laughs. "Okay, really, though. What is that thing?"

I'm not joking. It's a unicorn.

Then: a whinny. Buried in the cry is the sound of children screaming.

"I thought unicorns were nice and sweet. Little girls love 'em."

They were once creatures of rare purity and innocence. But this is not an innocent time. Purity is a legend. Unicorns are... different, now. The Barn is a place where things are kept so they don't... escape. Like me. Like you. Like the—

The animal slams itself against the stall door, then bleats in pain—Cason imagines the thing just shocked itself, just as he had done before.

Like that unicorn.

"Jesus." Cason retreats back into the stall, weary and scared.

Jesus has no part of this. May I continue?

"Go for it."

THE FIRST THING *you need to know:*

Frank Polcyn is not your friend.

He is not who you think he is.

I see the story he tells you: his wife taken by Aphrodite. He, a man going against the gods to save his wife, but tortured and tormented in the process.

I know Aphrodite. She is my mother-in-law. Since the Exile, she has taken it upon herself to act outside of Zeus' purview and keep me away from my own husband, so that, in her words, "he may be happy." And so she kept me like a pet, and as a pet, I saw things.

I saw what happened to Frank Polcyn.

He was a handsome man. Beautiful, even. A shining example of just how perfect humanity could be, given the right random combination of DNA.

Aphrodite wanted him *in her collection. Not Frank's wife.*

He didn't even fight it. I've seen true love, and I've seen how potent it can be. One will move mountains for love. One will deny the gods for love. I did.

Frank did not.

Frank gave in without a peep or a whimper. His wife, left out in the cold. It was him in that motel room, his wife that went to the bar to wait for him. He never went gambling. He stayed there all day long. Praying at Aphrodite's temple, so to speak.

I know. I watched. Chained up in the corner.

He bent over backwards to pleasure her. He was like a pig at a trough. This beautiful specimen of man—made to beg and grunt and lap like a beast.

Aphrodite loved it. She loves to subvert man. Loves to subvert love. Her beauty is what matters to her, and she believes it is the pivot on which all the world turns—whenever she can prove it, she will. She had another chance to prove it when Sally Delacroix— now, Sally Polcyn—came back to the motel and found her husband doing things she didn't even know could be done between two people. Sally sobbed. Begged him. Tried to pull him away.

She tried to get me to help her. But what was I going to do? The chain bound me.

Sally wept and pleaded, and the goddess just laughed.

Aphrodite told Frank: "Take care of her."

And he did. He carried Sally outside. Kicking and screaming.

He told her how much he hated her. How ugly she was. How this was all just a game, a scam, a con, how he had found true love. He shoved his wedding ring in her mouth. Made her swallow it. Then he picked her up and threw her in the pool.

The humiliation, all a show for Aphrodite.

A week later, Sally killed herself. Wandered the city, tattered and bedraggled before finally stepping in front of a bus.

When Frank heard, he just shrugged. Then he went back to licking Aphrodite's body clean.

Ah, but then came the day, as it always does, as you saw with my own husband, when the cat is done playing with the mouse, and so eats it or bats it away.

Aphrodite was done with Frank. She'd had her fill. On to the next.

She threw him away. She disappeared.

But Frank was diligent. And obsessed. As they all are, really— but when most are abandoned by the gods, they live out their lives as empty husks. Not Frank. In Frank's belly grew a terrible fire, and it took him the better part of a year to find her again.

And he did. He came here.

He found her. Begged to be taken back. Threw himself at her mercy.

His pleas turned grim. He threatened to burn the place down. To tell the world who she really was. He was enraged. Insane.

Desperate for her love—the wild-eyed aggression born of rejection and obsession.

But you don't threaten the gods.

As you'll learn.

She took this handsome man and she made him ugly.

She did to him as he did to his wife: threw him in the pool, and here his story meets the reality—she churned the waters and made them come alive and had them cut him, flay him, excise lips and nose and fingers and toes, flesh carved away until he was vented like fish gills, bleeding everywhere, made hideous by her affections.

And then she threw him away.

As he did with Sally.

But it did not cow him. It did not send him to die. It filled all his empty spaces with even greater rage. That, then, is what his purpose is, to—

A SUDDEN FRESH flurry of gate rattling, snorting, neighing, stomping—

The unicorn is pissed.

Cason is, too. Pissed that Frank lied to him. He tries to find a way around it, wonders if maybe the so-called goddess is deceiving him, just to get in his head. But if it's true... if Frank put his own wife through hell like that and didn't care... Cason can't ever imagine doing that to Alison. Alison could try to kill him ten times a day and he'd never treat her that way.

The Barn shakes as the unicorn stomps around.

No beast likes to be caged.

"Tell me about it."

I can see this one. She's across from me. Red eyes glowing. Plumes of hot sulfur from her nose. She'd much rather be out there than in here.

"And what is it a unicorn wants to do?"

I don't know. I don't know her mind, can't get into it. Fighting? Fornicating? Running free? When they find a wild monster and cage it here, it's not because it wants to frolic about and drink tea with little girls. We've had all manner of creature here. Ghouls. Glaistigs.

Anthropophagi. Bishop Fish in the lake. Dybbuk boxes in the loft. Not all the creatures of the infinite bestiary are dangerous—I've met Feng Huang, for instance, and found him cordial, if a little insane— but many are, and when the gods of the respective protectorates track down such a creature they contain it. First in places like this, later in... deeper, darker prisons.

"Who the hell are you people?"

That's just it. We're not people. We're gods, once of spirit, recently of flesh. Thrown from the firmament to the fundament. I was human, once, but that's over and done. I barely understand humans anymore. I did something before they reclaimed me, brought me to the Barn. I killed... well. I killed a number of policemen. And I felt no remorse. The only remorse I felt was at feeling no remorse, isn't that strange?

"Sounds pretty awful to me."

It is. I'm awful. My beauty is fading, and I'm becoming less like me and more like them. Which is, I suppose, what we should talk about next, because you're more like them than you know, Cason Cole.

RIGHT NOW, YOUR *body is broken. But it's healing. All bodies would be—but you stood up just minutes ago. On legs that were snapped like a piece of peanut brittle, only hours ago. All after sustaining attacks that would've killed anybody else. You should've died battling Meesink, that poor dumb wilderness spirit—were you anybody else, your body would've been pulverized. Look back over all your fights. Look how many injuries you sustained. Look at how hard they had to hit you just to make a bruise.*

Lesser men would've brain-bled. Never to fight again.

You are not lesser men.

You are barely a 'man' at all, Cason.

You are human. If a little. I see that spark inside you—bright like a torch on the beach, the human soul in all its glittering, shimmery unpredictability.

But the rest of you is divine.

It's how you survived this long; it's how you're healing even now. And it's why the gods wanted to control you.

There was a conspiracy against you.

A car comes out of nowhere. Strikes your own. Your wife and child burn.

That, the province of a god named Slogutis. A god of pain and misery—pain is a channel for him, a doorway. He can open up a body, cut into it with invisible knives, and step in through the unseen wound to puppet the body. He wore the driver's skin. The driver of the white SUV.

Then: time stops. The fire frozen. Your wife and son, rescued from certain death, resurrected—both these things the responsibility of the Ollathir, Dagda, an old mad god who is father to Dana and also her son. And also, her lover. Such is the nature of time gods; they are able to be their own parents. (It unsettles me still.)

Then my husband—though I suppose with a heavy heart I should acquiesce to calling him my 'late husband,' should I not?—Eros steps in and makes the offer. Your eternal service for their lives. A trade you easily made. Why wouldn't you? You know love. I see that. Sometimes love in humans isn't really love, but something else: lust, need, hate turned on its ear. But for you it's pure, uncut love. And so you said yes. Of course you did.

And with it, the noose tightened. They wanted you in their pocket. For reasons I cannot comprehend; I can see inside the minds of gods as I can humans, but with others of my kind the trip is short-lived, as they sense me probing. I'm always on a time limit and so my discoveries remain incomplete. There remains one more piece of the puzzle missing, another divine hand at work—a long reach with fingers deep in the mud, but I do not know who. I can see the trail—

CASON CAN'T HACK it anymore. Again he stands on legs less wobbly than before, legs that she's right about—he has no right to be standing on these damn things, and yet here he is, up and marching toward the gate again, fury twisting fast through his arteries like a bullet down a rifle barrel. He marches to the gate, growls, delivers a hard kick—

And shock lances through him.

He's blown back against the stall wall, where the golden chain dangles on the other side—delivering a second shock. *Boom.* He falls forward on his hands and knees. Gasping for air and finding little.

You cannot break the chain. You cannot move the chain.

"You..." *Gasp.* "You did it."

You helped me do it.

"Fuck."

Sorry.

"Nergal." Cason almost weeps with the pain. "You didn't mention Nergal."

I did not, no.

"What"—he swallows hard—"What role did he play?"

He played no role at all.

"Don't fuckin' lie to me. Don't! Not now."

I'm not lying. I'm sorry. He was the wrong target. Dagda stopped time. Dagda revivified your wife and child. And you don't want to fight him.

He presses his forehead against the wood. Hay prickles the skin. Guilt goes through him. Nergal wasn't innocent. He animated the bodies of dead teenagers—teenagers he probably killed himself—to serve as his 'bodyguards.' He was a fucking nutball. Death and storms and flies and...

And yet, Cason feels shame over the act. His own divine heritage shouting out for justice? Is he really not altogether human?

"My parents," he says, his words more a desperate bleat than anything else. "Who were my parents?"

But no answer is forthcoming.

"Hey. You. *I'm talking to you.*"

Nothing still.

"Psyche, if you're there, I swear to God—"

God cares little for what you swear. Hush now. Someone is coming.

CHAPTER TWENTY-SEVEN
The Ugly Little Nightmare Man

SLOGUTIS DRIVES THE golf-cart, whistling a jaunty tune. He's not sure what it is, at first—just an earworm that crawled into his head and laid eggs. Something from an American television show from days past. *I Dream of Jeannie*? No. *Bewitched*! That's the one. *Bewitched*. Not entirely inappropriate, really.

The golf-cart bounds through the night, away from the farmhouse and toward the distant Barn—a Barn that sits a quarter-mile *thattaway*, kept separate from the house just in case one of the, erm, 'residents' should somehow get free.

Sprinklers wet the grass.

To his left: a lovely pond, the dock painted brick red.

To his right: a springhouse lovingly put together with rocks.

Beneath him, beneath the ground itself and so not visible to the eyes: the temple-mazes, where the gods of the protectorate gather for rituals and where they bring their most beloved cultists for hymns, paeans, chants, odes, invocations, evocations, summonings, banishings, pleasure orgies, mating orgies, blood orgies, birth rites, death rites, first rites, last rites, parties, food, drink, and assorted magic miscellany.

Slogutis hasn't been down there in a while.

Slogutis isn't very important.

After all, not all gods are created equal. And the Exile didn't help matters—it just shook up all the pieces, and now the gameboard looks like a hundred chess sets (and checkers, and Battleship and Scrabble) all smashed together.

Slogutis has always been something of a pawn in this game. He knows it. He's not particularly *happy* about it, but he's found comfort—a cold and slimy comfort, yes, but comfort just the same.

Some gods are primal. They've been here since the beginning, or close enough to it—as mankind was born, so too were the gods. No god *predates* humanity, of course, but fuck, don't remind them of that. Most of them... ennnh, not a fan of the idea, and many have convinced themselves otherwise.

At the other end of the spectrum are the half-gods, the demi-gods, gods that were once human, or at least, didn't start out divine.

Beneath them: all the monsters, creatures, slaves, spirits, demons, half-breeds, automatons. Plus your heroes, your avatars, your what-have-yous.

Slogutis isn't any of those.

He's firmly fixed in the mushy, gooshy middle—the hazy gauzy nowheresville belonging to the largest bulk of *deitydom*, the 'lesser gods.' They're gods. Proper gods. But nobody really gives much of a shit about them. Hanuman? Eh. Monkeys; so what. Oh, you're the god of a tiny island in the Pacific? Well, bully for you, you big fat fish in a tiny fucking pond—don't swim up-river, or the big gods will eat you. Is the Pacific a pond or a river? Slogutis isn't sure, and doesn't much care. Gods of, what, of trees and breezes, of words and friezes, of rainbows and spring flowers and spiders and blah-blah-blah.

Slogutis knew this one old broad—Ament. 'Greeter of the Dead,' that was her gig in the old life. The spirits of the dead came to her, and before they officially passed on to their respective Otherworlds, she handed them, like, a piece of bread, a couple coins, and a map. You know what she does now? Same thing, basically. Attendant at Disneyland. Or Disneyworld, whatever. She doesn't hand out bread, but she gives out tickets and tokens and, sure enough, a stupid fucking map.

Ament really *owns* the 'lesser god' thing.

Thing is, Slogutis shouldn't really be a lesser god. His dominion isn't puppy tails or squirrel turds or some obscure emotion like *ennui*. It's pain! Anguish! *Misery*. Core components of the essential human experience. In fact, if you ask him, Slogutis will tell you that they are in fact the *very keystone* of what it means to be human. Outside birth and death, the only thing a human is guaranteed to experience is pain. Pleasure, maybe. Pain, *certainly*. Hell, it's not like he's got much competition. You're a storm god, like Shango, you're in a pretty crowded elevator—explains why he was slinging arrows earlier, talking trash. There's a lot of sour grapes within given dominions. But who's Slogutis shouldering out? A few pain spirits? A couple avatars of misery? Or there's Acheron, who swears he's a god of pain but *really*, let's be honest, he's the god of the *river* of pain (uh, big difference).

All that should bump him up the ladder, shouldn't it?

But it doesn't. He's not from a primary pantheon, they say. Nobody worships pain and misery, they claim. Oh, and he's unpleasant. "Like a tree grub," that's how Aphrodite referred to him *just last week*.

So he's a nobody.

Except when they need him. Like now.

They shoved him in a golf-cart, told him to bring Cason Cole up to the house. Oh, and, as Aphrodite herself said: "Make him feel it."

In other words: hurt him. Deep hurt. Pain of many flavors.

Which brings Slogutis happiness, if temporary. Any chance to do what he does best shines a light in an otherwise foggy, depressing existence.

Up ahead, then: the Barn. It's a big building. Old, technically, though refinished to the point where the only original wood is the floor. The whole thing the color of blood, which Slogutis figured was because... well, blood wouldn't show, then, would it? But when he suggested that, the other gods just looked at him (again) like he was some kind of freak. "No," Aphrodite explained, "it's because American barns are traditionally *red*."

Fine. Whatever. She's so unpleasant. Beautiful, sure, but it's like putting a dress on a badger. Pretty dress. Nice face. Still a badger.

Right now, the Barn's pretty empty of residents. Got the crazy bitch—Aphrodite's own daughter-in-law, used to live with Aphrodite north of the city, but now given a stall. The unicorn (that awful thing). Last week they had a couple Eloko up in the loft cages—horrible little dwarves, pale and hairless, covered in a coat of grassy sprouts. Got tiny little mouths, but their jaws unhinge and open wide enough to gulp down an entire human being. They're bound and gagged and, blessedly, weren't allowed to keep their little bells. Love to ring those things. Ting-a-ling, ting-a-ling; they ring the bell, someone comes looking. Someone gets eaten.

Slogutis parks the golf cart. He glances in the back, sees another pile of glimmering golden chain. Walks away without it. *Pfeh. I don't need those*, he thinks. *Human suffering is chain enough for me.*

As he heads toward the Barn, he feels her—Psyche. At first it's just a gentle sweep, an intrusion that's equivalent to a glance and then, a stare. But then her invisible fingers try to plunge into his pie and he has to quickly slam the psychic doors to keep her out. He lets her have this thought before he does: *You can get in those human heads, lady, but you're not allowed inside* this *god-mind, thank you very much.*

He unlocks the Barn's side door. Walks into the stable.

He whistles as he works. He can't whistle very well. Slogutis carries a tune the way a rust-eaten pail carries water. Still, it brings him pleasure.

Ah. There. The... well, he's not all human, is he? No, no, he's not. Frightening parentage, that one. He's already up on his broken legs, standing there, shaking, swaying, sweating. Eyes rimmed in dark circles, lip sniveling. Got his arms wrapped right around his midsection as if he's cold, and the way he's shivering, he might be. Feverish.

"You look like a hot mug of puke," Slogutis says, his own oily arms folding up into one another. "You're lucky ol' Nergal didn't tear off your head and piss into your neckhole, then animate your headless-puppet-piss-soaked body."

"Go fuck yourself."

"What an attitude. Listen, I'm not the one who thinks he can go around willy-nilly, killing gods like he's mopping a floor. Actions have consequences."

"Go fuck yours—"

"Self, yeah, okay. Conversation over, then." Slogutis affects a haughty tone, and while bowing, says: "*Let us begin the delicious torment.*"

He reaches into Cason Cole's body. Finds all the bundles of nerves, then grabs them hard. In Slogutis' mind, he braids those pain channels together and sends a searing spike of straight-up agony through the braid to every part of Cole's body. From the tip of his nose to the tip of his dick. Heart probably feels like it's exploding. Toes probably feel like they're being eaten by rats.

It shows, too. The poor sumbitch drops like somebody kicked his legs right out from under him. Lands on the side of his hip. He makes this sound through his teeth—a sound Slogutis is pretty familiar with, actually—that goes a little something like this: *Nnnnggghhhhhuuuhhh*—and then it kind of... *melts* into a scream.

He hopes Psyche is enjoying the show. He can feel her there, hovering in his mind.

With the prisoner out of action, Slogutis begins undoing the chain.

Whistling again. Doo-doo-dee-doo.

He throws the chain to the floor, opens the stall.

Grabs Cason by the scruff of his shirt, drags him out.

In the back of the Barn, the unicorn stomps and whinnies. Slogutis hears a pile of somethings rattle against the floor, like someone just dumped a bag of rocks on the ground. Given the sudden burning stink, he's pretty sure the unicorn just voided his—er, her—unicorn bowels. These days the thing shits coal. Literally shits hunks of shiny anthracite. Smells like charred sulfur.

It's then that Slogutis realizes something, and as it often is with him, by the time he realizes it, it's far too late. He realizes:

He doesn't feel Psyche anymore.

Huh.

And then, just as abruptly, his connection with the prisoner is gone. Cut off. Sheared like a piece of rope in a slamming door.

Cason grunts, rolls over.

Starts to stand.

Still shivery, still shaky. And super-pissed.

It times out so, when Cason's fist clocks Slogutis in his pale, thin-lipped mouth, the minor god of pain and misery figures it out:

Psyche's not in his head anymore because she's back in Cason's.

She's the slamming door that sheared his rope.

Suddenly he's being thrown around like a dance partner, and Cason Cole has taken the lead—Slogutis slams into a post, then a stall gate, then another post. Fist breaks his teeth. Slams into the side of his head. His gut. His nuts.

A tiny thought strikes him: *The Beast has awakened.* If only for a moment.

As Cason picks him and hurls him ten feet toward the back of the Barn, Slogutis reaches out wildly, blindly, a pair of lashing mental ropes that—as he slams against the wooden floor and bowls over, rolling another ten feet—fail to find purchase.

At first.

But then, as Slogutis lays flat, his head smacking dully against the old wood, his psychic lassos seize a pair of minds.

Cason's.

And Psyche's.

It's not easy. It is, in fact, a challenge that requires the uttermost concentration. Slogutis stands, a seed of bitterness blooming fast in his stomach, because once upon a time, this would be a task equivalent to blinking both eyes at the same time—totally natural, without issue. He could let a wave of torture roll over entire *armies* if he so chose. His power, the power of all the gods, was once nearly infinite. But now, since the Great Usurper seized the throne...

He can't think about that now. Or he'll lose at least one, maybe both, of his victims.

Slogutis stands. Sees the wild-haired looney-bird Psyche in her stall. This time, nobody swaddled her in a straitjacket—the Driver said it'd be better if the chain was wound directly around her, and that's what it is, here. A golden chain wrapped around her body again and again and again. A body now seizing in abject anguish.

The pain god chuckles.

"You... think... you... can stop... *me*." He shakes his head. Sweat beads on his grimy brow, his ink-black hair stuck to his forehead. "You're... *less* than... me."

Then he hears something behind him.

The rattle of a chain.

He turns. Sees Cason on the ground, body wracked with spasms.

But he's got something in one of his hands—a golden chain, death-gripped like an eagle talon holding a serpent.

Where the hell did he get it?

"You... don't... need *that*."

Slogutis twists, sends a psychic knife through the bones of Cason's wrist: his fingers jerk open, and the chain drops.

And then the floorboards vibrate.

There's a snort, and—

Something very sharp punches through Slogutis' chest. Something quite visible, in fact: a unicorn horn. Twisted and black with his own heart's ichor. The unicorn stomps a hoof, shattering wood.

Then it screams in victory.

CHAPTER TWENTY-EIGHT
Goodnight, Moon

IF AT ANY point in Cason's life one were to ask him, *What is the strangest thing you think you'll ever see?* who knows how he'd answer? The Internet. Life on Mars. Hell, one time, he saw a tiger piss on a little girl at the Philadelphia Zoo. That was pretty strange.

But he never figured he'd answer: *I'll see a unicorn impale a lesser pain-god through the heart with its horn, rear back in victory, scream like a demon, then turn around and punch a hole in the barn door and run off—oh, with the pain-god still impaled on the horn.*

And yet that's exactly what happens. Cason, in the middle of an excruciating paroxysm, expended all his effort to reach up, grab the chain binding the unicorn's stall door, and pull it off.

The stall door drifted open, and the unicorn stepped out.

It was a ragged, tattered thing—a froth-slick coat, eyes like burning cigar-tips, nostrils flaring and cracked teeth showing.

The only thing about it that looked at all pure and innocent was its horn: it was like a perfect spiral of polished ocean shell, glimmering with an iridescent shimmer.

Then it stabbed that horn through Slogutis' chest. His blood blackened the horn, and the shimmer was lost.

It rose up on its back legs. Keened like a banshee.

Before Cason even knew what was happening, the thing burst free of the back wall, blowing it open in a rain of splinters. The one-horned hell-horse galloped away, Slogutis' own screams trailing away with it.

There comes a sound like a gasp and then a whooping, raspy laugh, and it takes a few seconds before Cason realizes it's his own damn self making that sound.

He stands, again on wobbly legs.

Looks over. Sees Psyche. Slumped against the back corner of the stall, legs folded beneath her. She says, her voice cracking, "I suppose I don't need to talk into your mind anymore."

"Guess not."

"That was spectacular. Although a unicorn on the loose..."

"Will that be okay?"

She manages a shrug.

"Do you think I'm pretty?" she asks.

"What?"

"Am I beautiful?"

She is. Or was. Her hair's a hot mess. Looks like she French-kissed a wall socket. Her cheeks are tear-stained. She's pale, frail. This is not the pinnacle of beauty deserving Aphrodite's jealousy-fueled scorn. Maybe once, but not anymore.

Still, he nods. "You are."

Psyche offers a small smile.

"We just made a great deal of noise. They'll come for you, sooner rather than later. I don't know where you'll go, but head the same direction as the unicorn—there are woods at the far side. You might be able to lose them there. If you—"

She pauses as he heads inside the stall, grabs a fistful of golden chain, and yanks it free before tossing it into the corner, sending up a cough of hay dust.

Psyche looks confused. "What just happened?"

"I freed you."

"Why?"

"I'm not going out there alone."

"I hurt people. I hurt your wife and son."

"All the more reason for you to come with me and help fix all that."

Hesitantly, she stands.

"Besides," he says. "We were having a conversation and I suspect you weren't done talking. Am I right?"

She nods and is about to say something—

But then her eyes roll back in her head for a moment.

When she returns her gaze to Cason, she says:

"Someone else is coming."

WAY HE SAYS it, all the words run together so they sound like some kind of heretic prayer, some madman's mantra: "This is a bad idea, this is a bad idea, *thisisabadidea thisisabadidea thissabaddea thissabaddea*—"

The bad idea in question is driving a yellow cab full throttle down the long-ass driveway leading to a house filled with—if Tundu was to understand this correctly—an unholy host of gods and monsters. The ranking gods and monsters of the region, in fact.

But that's what he's doing.

Giant foot mashed against the pedal.

Car rocketing down the paved drive.

Past a gazebo.

Past a terrace.

Past a succession of marble fountains and statuaries—a woman rising out of a clamshell spewing water from her mouth, a different woman rising out of a bubbling cauldron, a man standing with palms out and stone lightning rising from his hands.

And straight toward a massive farmhouse. The kind with an east wing and a west wing and made of gray stone *and filled with angry deities*.

Tundu can't help it. He screams.

So loud he can barely hear the radio.

Crackle-hiss. "—left turn left *turn left you big ape*—"

This is a bad idea.

This is a bad idea.

Tundu sees where the asphalt becomes gravel and he cuts the wheel left—the tires squeal just as something flies overhead, something human-shaped but with very big bat-like wings. Gravel kicks from under the wheels and he guns it again.

In the distance, a big barn.

That's where Frank said to go.

That's where Frank said they'd have taken Cason.

So, that's where Tundu's going.

Screaming all the way.

AND LIKE THAT, boom, powder keg. Frank's been sitting in a distant tree for the better part of a day, rifle scope (*sans* rifle) in his hand, peering out at the Barn for some sign, *any* sign, that it would be safe to mount a rescue effort—okay, a totally insane super-psycho-batshit effort—to nab Cason. Tundu asked how the hell this place wasn't a crazy over-protected compound and the answer there was simple: the gods never expect anyone to actually assault this place. They're gods. They've got it covered.

Frank chuckles. Arrogant assholes, this group.

Then, it all went down. Someone in a golf cart. Shrieks of pain from within the big red barn. The wall blew out and a—a unicorn? Christ, an actual *unicorn*—fled, galloping forth with something, or rather, *someone*, impaled upon its horn.

Frank likes chaos. It is optimal operating conditions for him.

And that, down below, looked like chaos. He gave Tundu the signal over the walkie and, sure enough—

A yellow cab bounding toward the pastoral prison.

The voice, suddenly in his ear. Disembodied.

Are we almost back on track?

The air shimmers when it speaks. He smells a whiff of char.

"Almost."

Go to it, then.

Frank climbs down out of the tree and runs toward the barn, grinning like a fool.

* * *

CASON WANTS TO kiss him. So he does just that. He hobbles over to Tundu fast as his rickety legs will carry him, throws his arms around the massive human-shaped redwood tree, and gives him a big kiss on his cheek. Tundu laughs, nervous.

"Whoa, man. Prison changed you."

"I can't believe you're here," Cason says. "Is this a dream?"

"No dream, chief. No dream."

Then Psyche steps out of the shattered barn-hole. She says: "No dream, but it'll be a nightmare soon enough. We have to go."

"Look," Tundu says, pointing over the roof of the cab toward the distant treeline. Sure enough, Frank is bounding toward the car, cackling like a mad crow.

Psyche bristles. Cason holds out a hand, says, "This gonna be a problem?"

She scowls. Before she can answer—in the distance, back toward the farmhouse, a shriek. An inhuman, impossible shriek.

Psyche stiffens. "The Driver. We have to go."

Into the car. Tundu behind the wheel. Cason up front. Psyche in back.

Tundu takes a deep breath. Blinks. Cason sees he's scared. Which has a right amount of sense to it—because Cason's scared, too. Terrified not just of this moment, not just of the escape, but what happens after. *You're not human*, a little voice reminds him. *Is that really true?* No time to think about it now.

Because Tundu guns it.

First, toward Frank.

Cason's knee knocks against something. A shotgun rattles.

Window down. Shotgun up. Pump-action. Stock sawed off, barrel shortened. He jacks a shell into the chamber, checks the safety, hopes he's remembering how the hell to do this—

Tundu gets the car close to Frank, then pulls the emergency brake and cuts the wheel—the cab's back end slides around like a pad of butter drifting across a hot skillet, turning the taillights toward Frank.

Frank whoops like a war chief, throws open the door. He's saying something, clapping Cason on the shoulders—

But Cason can't hear him.

All he can hear is his own heartbeat as something slams down onto the grass about fifty feet in front of them, the headlights capturing the horror.

It wears a chauffeur's uniform.

But it has long wings—no feathers, only black skin shining red where the flesh thins around the margins of fat veins.

It has a human face, a *woman's* face, but then the jaw opens wide and razor teeth glint. Arms grow long. Legs, too. Fabric ribs. White claws—white like pus, not white like ivory—thrust out from the tips of fingers and poke through black boots.

She shrieks. Long whip-like tongue flicking the air, throat ululating.

"Tisiphone," Psyche hisses.

"Hey!" Frank barks. "What the hell is *this broad* doing here—"

Cason growls. "Shut up, Frank."

The Driver begins stalking toward the car.

"Oh, shit, shit, shit, shit," Tundu says, leaning back in his seat like somehow he can avoid what's coming.

But he can't. None of them can.

Cason tells him: "Gun it."

Tundu doesn't hesitate. He punches the accelerator. The back tires spin on dew-slick grass. The cab's back-end wobbles and shifts left and right—but it doesn't move forward.

"No, no, no, no!" Tundu cries. "Go-go-go-go-go, you piece of shit!"

Cason grabs the shotty, pops the door, leans out over it—

He jerks the trigger.

Buckshot sprays the Driver in the face. It's like throwing M&M's at a wall. The shot just bounces off and she shakes her head.

The car lurches forward—

The passenger side door closes on Cason's torso and he winces—

The Driver leaps up onto the hood of the car, howling—

A claw swipes through the air just as Cason slides his body back into the car, the door clicking closed behind him.

The windshield of the car is filled with the beast.

"I can't see! I can't see!" Tundu's driving blind, jerking the wheel left and right, trying to shake the monster—

The Driver's mouth opens, wide, too wide, her mouth a black abyss, and from that abyss rises a wretched song that causes the entire car to hum and vibrate, pieces rattling against other pieces—Cason can feel it in his teeth, just as all the glass in the car spider-webs, cracks spreading, windows and windshields still in their frames.

Tundu screams.

Cason raises the shotgun, winces—

Feels a hand in his mind. Psyche. Her voice: *I can only get away with this once, before she puts up all her walls*—

Psyche reaches out with a hand, a real hand—and points all her fingers toward the monster on the hood of the car. She gives her wrist a twist.

With the turning of Psyche's wrist, the Driver's own head wrenches left. Tongue out, eyes bulging, howl cut short. The Driver tumbles off the hood. Just in time to see the Barn zooming up into view.

Tundu cries out, cuts the wheel—

The cab misses the corner of the Barn by inches.

A rain barrel is not so lucky. It explodes, pieces flying up over the top of the cab, murky water sloshing down over everything, again distorting their view.

But the sound beneath the cab's tires changes from soft to hard. Asphalt, not grass. The water recedes from the windshield.

Ahead, several figures exit the farmhouse, stepping into the driveway.

And it's then that Cason knows they're fucked.

The beauty of Aphrodite shines brighter than the moon, and Cason has to steel himself so as not to just open the door and tumble out before her and beg for mercy. A tall man next to her holds his hands by his side, and lightning snaps from his fingertips, licking the ground at his feet. An Asian woman, tall and thin like a wind-blown reed, extends her arms, and even from here Cason can see the tattoos on her arms flickering, growing brighter, colors like running paint. An older woman steps next to her, long red hair in a braid over her shoulder. Her hands pull at a long thread of water like it's taffy.

The gods have gathered.

Everything seems to slow—

Tundu jerks the wheel right, away from the farmhouse—again the tires bound off the asphalt and onto grass, and again the car slides across the green. The cab blasts through a barberry hedge, cutting a car-shaped swath through it.

The gods stir. They move. They *come*.

The cab leaps back up onto the driveway, and Tundu straightens the wheel. They run the gauntlet of fountains, statues, and trees. The driveway is long. Escape is ahead—it's night and Cason can't make out where the road is, but he knows it must be there, must be coming up on them soon—right?

It may not matter.

The gods are coming.

Across the moon, a winged shape flies.

The man with the lightning rises up off the ground, the crackling fingers of lightning carrying him forward faster and faster, his body tilted forward at a lean, mean angle.

The woman with the water flows forward just as swiftly, standing tall on her tip-toes, cresting a small froth-churned wave.

And then come the dragons.

Five of them—red, blue, green, white, black. Small at first, no bigger than dogs, but then growing, swelling, heads soon as big as wheelbarrows, their tails tied together like the flags on a pinwheel, anchored as they are to the Asian woman's arms. They pull her along like huskies drawing a sled.

He can't see Aphrodite. But Cason's sure she's coming. They're all coming.

It's then that it all starts to come crumbling down: his hopes of escaping, of seeing Alison and Barney again, are as tangible as a fog, as real as a dream. He has no means of fighting these monsters. Whether he's human, part-human, or some secret monster in a man's costume doesn't matter. He can't stop what's coming.

The car barrels forward.

Thunder crackles. Rain begins to patter the back windshield.

Dragons roar as a jet of flame crackles above the roof of the car, brightening the dark, turning rain to steam.

The car gauges begin to spin and flicker. The LCD clock shifts, blinks, and the numbers turn to letters that spell DOOM.

"What the hell do I do?" Tundu asks, panicked.

"I dunno," Cason says. "Lemme think."

"Fuck 'em!" Frank hollers. "Just keep driving!"

Then he starts humming *Ride of the Valkyries*. Dun-dudun-dahn-dahn...

"Shut the fuck up, Frank!" Tundu says.

It's then that Cason knows what to do.

He focuses a thought toward Psyche—he doesn't know how this works, doesn't know if she's still in his head or somewhere else entirely, but he reaches out and finds her reaching back. Her awareness, a snarled ink-scribble at the back of his mind.

He tells her what to do.

His stomach feels like it's going to drop out of him. Like a rock dropped through a piece of tissue paper.

Cason turns around in his seat. Meets Frank's lidless eyes. Frank's grinning like a kid on a roller coaster. Licking his teeth.

"Almost there, Casey Kasem!"

"Is it true?" Cason asks Frank.

"Is what true?"

"Sally. You abandoned her. And now she's dead."

A flicker of guilt and recognition across Frank's face. That's all Cason needs to know.

"I'm sorry, Frank."

"Sorry? Sorry for wh—"

But he doesn't get to finish the question.

His jaw locks. Neck tendons snap tight. His eyes follow Psyche as she leans over him, pops the door handle. Frank starts making a wordless noise: "Nnngh. *Nnngh!*"

Tundu looks back, raising an eyebrow. "Hey, what the hell?"

Psyche shoves Frank out the door.

* * *

FRANK'S HEAD CRACKS against the driveway—skin scrapes from his scalp as his body tumbles like a discarded crash-test dummy.

It's not the pain that gets him. It's the betrayal. It's the fear that the plan is falling apart.

As control of his body returns to him, he scrambles to his feet, panic at what's coming shooting through every nook and cranny of his being.

Rain falls upon him as the gods come.

He looks toward the road, sees the cab fishtail, tires screeching. Then taillights, as the car rockets away down the road.

They slow upon seeing him.

Shango, the Thunder God, drifts back to earth—from floating to walking without missing a step. The Dragon Lady, Long Mu, settles in alongside him, the dragons shrinking and yowling and once more returning to bright ink on her pale arms. Then water like a slow tide splashes up, and on it rides Dana, the Mother Goddess.

Behind him drops the Driver. Claws out. Teeth bared. Talons clicking as she paces.

Then: her.

The one he loves. The one he despises. The one he needs. The one he needs gone.

Venus. Cytherea. Aphrodite.

Shango asks her: "Do we go after the others?"

"No." Aphrodite shakes her head. "Let them go."

"But," Dana protests, "Cole is dangerous, and he's with your daughter-in-law—"

She cuts him short. "We'll see where they go and it'll tell us more. Relax. We have the true terrorist in our midst right now. Don't we?"

Frank's skin feels hot. Tight. Dried out. "Hey, babe," he says.

"Hello, Francis."

"Been a long time."

"Not that long. I thought my warning was enough to keep you away."

"What can I say?" He shrugs. "I'm like a dog with a bone. I just keep coming back for a lick."

Aphrodite steps closer. "I can give you a taste."

"Not how I want it."

"Maybe. You still love me, don't you?"

He pauses. Hands flex in and out of fists. "You don't own me anymore."

"That's not what I asked."

"You're all going down," he hisses. "There's gonna be a reckoning, you know that? You thought the Exile was bad? You have no fucking idea. You're going to pay for the way you treat people. Like this place is your playground and we're all your toys."

"You are our toys," Shango says, voice booming. He, too, takes a step closer.

"You'll pay for Nergal," Long Mu says, her voice barely above a whisper. A green dragon lunges from her arm, breathing a cloudy ochre vapor before she reels it back to her flesh. "You cannot do what you do and escape justice."

"We'll see," he says.

Shango sucks in a deep breath.

The ground begins to rumble. Overhead: thunder.

In Dana's hand, a lash made of water grows. She cracks the air—mist flecks Frank's face.

And once again the dragons begin to emerge from Long Mu's arms. Small, now, small as rats, but growing bigger.

Aphrodite nods. Gives them the signal.

They attack at once.

A jagged knife of lightning strikes from above—

A red dragon grows ten sizes and belches a plume of flame—

The tip of the water whip sails toward Frank's head—

Movement behind him, too, as the Driver pounces from the dark—

And all of it stops. The lighting crackles above his head. The fire parts in front of him as if it's a river and he's a stone in the water. The water whip dissipates. And the winged Fury is bowled backward, ass over teakettle.

In front of him he holds a severed hand.

Gray-green flesh. Nails craggy, broken. On each fingertip burns a small blood-red flame, flickering in the night. The palm is marked with a sigil carved into the wrinkled palm: several upside-down triangles merging into a flourish, crossed with what looks to be the letter 'V.'

Aphrodite gasps. A pleasing sound. Frank says, "I like that I can still surprise you."

"A Hand of Glory," she says. Straightening and scowling as she says it.

"Ayup. This old baby's my Get Out of Jail Free card, innit?"

Long Mu weeps. "He cannot escape us! Murderer! Murderer!"

Frank chuckles. Starts to back away.

They try to follow. But can't.

Even the Driver squirms out of his way.

Frank waves goodbye with the Hand. "See you later, cats and kittens."

Then he turns tail and runs like he's never run before.

CHAPTER TWENTY-NINE
Lineage

HE'S STARVING. HIS body feels like a hollow shell of itself, waiting to be filled up with—well, not guts or lungs or blood, but potato chips and slushies and those little doughy-chewy pretzel bites dipped in the nuclear-yellow probably-plastic cheese. It was like this after a fight, too—the worse the fight, the more ravenous Cason felt.

He's never before felt this hungry.

He comes out of the convenience store with both arms loaded. One bag looped around the crook of his elbow while his hand shoves a super-size Snickers bar into his maw.

Back in the cab.

Psyche still in the back. Tundu outside the car, pacing, using his cell. Talking to his family.

"*Ahm sho hungry*," Cason gurgles, finishing off the Snickers and dipping back into the bag for a sack of Bugles. Little crispy horn-shaped corn snacks. *Crunch, crunch, crunch.*

"It's your body repairing itself," Psyche says from the back. "The human part of you needs it. To replenish. To rebuild."

"Oh," Cason says, gob-flecks of corn chip peppering the dash. He wipes them away with the back of his hand. He *does* feel better. Not perfect. Not all the way back up to speed. But good. And he feels thin, too. Ropy. Strong. Like he's back in old fighting shape. All the lumps and mush have burned away. Tightened up. "Okay."

"I sense you're feeling guilty about Frank."

Dry swallow. "I don't want to talk about this." He pops the cap on a Dr. Pepper. Guzzles it. Burns his throat as it charges toward his guts.

"You shouldn't feel bad. He was leading you astray."

"Please."

"He lied to you. He knew that you weren't human. Did you know that? He knew."

"I'm not talking about this. We just left him—no. We're *really* not talking about this." He finishes the Dr. Pepper, gasps for breath, then shifts his torso so he's staring back at the pale, wild-haired girl in the back of the cab. "What I want to talk about is: who the hell am I? We didn't finish that part of our conversation. I want to know who I am. I know I'm adopted. And now you're telling me I'm... I'm not human. And shit, who knows? Maybe you're right. I just broke my legs and now I'm up and walking around. I got the shit kicked out of me and while I do in fact feel like I was hit by a dumptruck, I should be in traction for the next six months. So, you're telling me I have divine parentage? Then I need to know who. Who are my parents, Psyche?"

"I don't know. I've been trying to figure that out since I met you."

That's not what he wants to hear. He tells her as much.

"I know. But it's true. The others, at the farmhouse. I think some of them knew. They must've. They targeted you for a reason. But I wasn't privy to that. Aphrodite didn't even know. Not all of it, at least. I think the others did this to you without... without her involvement. If she was involved, I'd know. I was her shadow for a very long time." She sighs. Under her breath: "My mother-in-law. Ugh."

Outside, Tundu paces, gesticulating as he talks into the phone. Trying to explain to his family where he was all night. Tundu said that Frank called him, told him the story—or most of it—and that Tundu didn't hesitate. Cason, he said, was his friend. And he said the last few nights he went to bed feeling helpless, a small man in the face of very real gods. He doesn't want to feel helpless, he said. So, here he is.

"Can't you..." Cason gesticulates around his brow. "Get into my head, figure it out?"

"I do see someone. I see your mother, I think. A woman. Dark hair. Dark eyes. Humming a song. The song about the mockingbird and the diamond ring. And I smell the city and I hear cars honking and—that's all I see. It's buried deep. From a long, long time ago." She pauses. "But there is something else."

She hands him a road atlas.

On the cover is an icon of a man holding up a globe. She taps the man on the cover. "Atlas. I know him. Well. I've met him. Dumb as a sack of amaranth. Couldn't find his own tiny shorts with all the maps in the world, so I don't know why he's on the cover of this one."

"What's your point?"

Psyche flips to the middle of the book.

Hands it to him.

It's open to the state of Kansas.

"I see a crimson thread," she says. "A literal bloodline. Faint. Like someone is trying to hide it. But it's there. It starts with you, and connects here."

She taps the map.

"Concordia, Kansas," he says.

"Yes. Something is there. Something bound to you."

"Then that's where I'm going."

"Are you sure? There's no promises that this harvest will yield fruit. We could find your wife and son. I could... try to quell their... feelings about you. I'll do it. To make up for my... transgressions."

"No. I have big question mark-shaped holes inside me, and I need answers to fill them. Somebody's messing with me. And worse, they're messing with my wife and my kid. I still don't know why or who I even am, so..." He trails off. "Concordia, Kansas, here I come."

PART THREE
TO THE HEART
OF THE MAZE

CHAPTER THIRTY
This Tenuous Thread

THE PLAN IS simple.

Well. No. It's not really *simple*. It's actually quite complex.

But it's simple in theory. Coyote finds elegance in complexity.

The woman, Alison, is inside this police station. In a holding cell. Awaiting—well, whatever it is you await when the police think you stole a car.

Coyote will crawl through the air ducts.

He'll use his nose to scent his penis, which gives off a piquant, ermine-y odor that the ladies cannot resist. This will likely lead him to the evidence room, where he will find within the full-figured, robust-shouldered, ginger-topped Officer Bonita Squire, and he will then cast into the ducts his Bonafide Penis Returning Powder, a fine concoction made of lavender, sage, beaver pelt, and the dried, pulverized shame of an ugly swan.

Then, he will descend into the evidence room.

As his penis stirs to life and seeks to return to him, he will begin to seduce the lovely Officer Squire, and just as he has disrobed her and laid her on a cardboard pallet, his penis will burst through the wire cage and reattach to his pelvis and he shall fornicate with her until she achieves the mighty gush of a well-satisfied woman. That will, of course, put her to sleep. From there he will steal her outfit, paint his hair orange, fill the outfit with whatever he can find nearby to pad the uniform, then wander into the small police building while masquerading as the beautiful, thick-bodied Officer Squire.

Then, blah-blah-blah, down to the basement, unlock the door, open the holding cells, free Alison, and once more find and follow the golden thread to its natural and necessary conclusion. Whatever that may be.

Excellent.

Coyote stands out back of the police department, hunkered down behind a few scrubby shrubs. He crawls over to the vent. Rattles it. Plucks numbly at the four screws with his hands.

"I should really have a screwdriver," he says.

It's then that a big fat horsefly lands on his shoulder. *Zzzzzvvvpppt.* He flicks it away.

It returns. This time, to the other shoulder.

He swats at it. It takes flight.

Then: on the bridge of his prodigious nose.

Oh, no.

He can barely make it out, but it's there—the horsefly has a human-looking face. Green fly eyes, but the rest is all tiny human.

It all happens so fast.

There comes a *whumpf* of air, a reverse imploding thunderclap—

There stands a tall, lithe man with dancing green eyes and long greasy hair draped around sharp-angled shoulders, ill-contained in a v-neck black t-shirt.

The man snaps his fingers, and in his hands a serpent appears. Black skin, green eyes, long fangs.

"You sonofab—" But Coyote can't finish the statement. The snake stabs out with its triangular head and bites him right on the cheek.

The venom is quick like a jackrabbit chased by a hawk—

Lickety-split, it's through Coyote. The world tilts. His chest tightens.

He's hit in the face with a tidal wave made of his own unconsciousness.

Boom.

*   *   *

LOKI STANDS OVER Coyote's body. Not corpse, of course—the mangy trickster isn't dead, just resting. Gods don't like to kill gods when they can help it. Put them out of commission for ten minutes, ten years, ten glacial epochs, fine. Death, though, is so permanent. Rude, too, though Loki has little concern about violating social norms.

Time is running out. The thread fraying, ready to snap.

Coyote would've taken too long. He always takes too long.

Loki pulls out his iPhone. Texts to Eshu: *In progress.*

Then he enters the police station, whistling.

ALISON SITS. THE jail cell is cleaner than she anticipated; some part of her figured this place would smell like body odor and other... fluids. But it doesn't. It is, in fact, only one of three cells, and now she knows the difference between holding cells ('drunk tanks') and a full-bore penitentiary. This is the former, and thankfully not at all the latter.

Just the same, it does little to quiet her slow-simmering panic and despair.

Because the penitentiary—jail, prison, the Big House, the Hoosegow—is where she'll be headed. She committed Grand Theft Auto. She stole a car, with the help of a man who was probably not at all a man, because he was, at least in part, some kind of rangy, mangy wolf-dog-dingo thing. She didn't even bother telling the police what's really going on. What's the point? She's already starting to wonder if this is the result of a complete and total breakdown of reality. Why chase the rabbit down its hole?

They offered her a phone call, but she didn't know who to call. So she called her mother at the hospital. Her mother started crying. Said Barney still hadn't woken up. Alison started to cry, too, told her where she was. Her mother said she'd get a lawyer. They'd figure this out. Mom says what Alison is thinking: "You just... had a nervous breakdown, is all."

And now she sits. Empty of tears. Empty of most everything, it seems. A tray of fast food nearby that she hasn't touched. The cops here have been very nice. Which she doesn't deserve, but it is what it is.

It's then that she hears someone yelling. Above her. In the station. Muffled, because, well, she's in the basement surrounded by a whole lot of concrete.

Then: she's pretty sure she hears goats.

Outside the cells, there sits a cop—in this case, Officer Masterson, a small, older fellow with a big gut hanging over his belt and holster. Bald on top, and a fuzzy red mustache, hanging on an outthrust lip.

She sees him peer in through the door window. Just a spot check.

He meets her eyes. She gives a little wave. He nods.

Then his eyes go wide. Like he's in shock, or in pain.

Then, he's gone. Just like that.

And just outside the door she hears the bleats of a goat.

The door drifts open. Sure enough, a goat comes tottering in. Head stuck up through a cop shirt. Back legs kicking off the uniform pants, replete with belt and holster. The goat's belly hangs low. Fat.

The goat is Masterson.

Masterson is a goat.

It's then another man walks through the door. Sharp boomerang smile. Glittery emerald eyes. Scruffy stubble, long hair, v-neck t-shirt.

He dangles a set of keys.

"Alison," he says in a sing-song voice (*Aaa-leee-sooon*). "It's time to go, doll. Your ride has arrived."

The keys jingle.

CHAPTER THIRTY-ONE
Flight Plan

ANY LIQUOR YOU want. Complimentary hot towels. A lunch of Maryland crabcakes, steamed broccoli, a small tray of moist, homemade cookies. And it's quiet here. Like someone put a gentle pillow over the engines and hushed them to sleep.

Cason's never flown first class before.

He looks over, sees across the aisle that Tundu seems to be enjoying it. Digging into the crabcake with abandon, forkfuls into his smiling mouth, his head bobbing to some kind of music piping into headphones.

Psyche, on the other side, looks like she's going to be sick.

"I hate flying," she says.

"But you—" Cason suddenly lowers his voice. "But *you* fly. Like, with wings."

"That's different."

"How is it different?"

"There I'm in control. And I don't fly ten miles up into the atmosphere."

"We're not ten miles up. Five, maybe."

She blanches. "I don't fly that high, either."

"It's not like if we crash, you'll die."

"No. But it'll be terrifying all the way down."

It's then on cue that the plane hits a pocket of turbulence. It rattles Cason. Then: another hit—*whuh-bump*. The luggage racks overhead shudder. Turbulence doesn't really bother him in theory—he just tells himself it's the equivalent of a pothole in the airstream. And it's not like people *die* from turbulence—its bark is worse than its bite.

But then the plane hits another pocket. Not a pothole but a ditch, a pit—and Cason's body lurches upward, straining against the seatbelt as his head hits the side of the luggage bin—

And he's about to say something, about to try to laugh it off at just how spookily *well-timed* all of this is, what with him and Psyche talking about plane crashes—

That's when the roof above his head rips off.

Peels back like the tab on a soda can. Suddenly it's bright light. Clouds above, blue sky, screaming winds, screaming *passengers*, and the glint of the sun on the side of shredded metal and—

Nothing.

The roof is still there.

No sound of shearing metal or panicking passengers.

The plane glides along like the puck on an air hockey table.

"See?" she asks.

"What? Did you—did you just *put* that scene into my head?"

She shrugs, looking a little guilty.

"You're sick," he says.

"And you're not worried enough."

He pauses. Scowls. Lunch no longer looks very good, so he idly picks at a cookie, just pulling it apart and smooshing the moist bits back together. "Hey. So if I'm not, uh, human, exactly? What happens if we crash? To me."

"You probably die."

"But gods don't... die very easily, and—"

"You're not a god. Not all god, anyway. Divine parentage does not make you functionally immortal. It does, however, make you preternaturally tough. At least in your case. You can't shrug off a bullet, but you can probably push past the pain and heal up. But if someone takes out your heart or your head, you're still deader than a pocket of dust."

"Oh," he says. "Good to know. I probably shouldn't let that happen, then."

She shrugs. Chews a fingernail.

"Why are you doing this for me?" he asks her.

Distracted, she gives him a look. "Hm?"

"Helping me. I don't entirely get it. You wanted me dead."

"I thought you killed my husband. You didn't. You served him faithfully for years. And then I took your wife and your son and..." She shakes her head. "I owe you. Besides, I'm not much of a fan of the gods, either. You deserve truth. And I'm a very curious creature." She sighs. "Did you call her? Alison?"

"Tried her house. Just went to voicemail. Tried her cell phone, but that goes to voicemail, too. Tells me her inbox is full." He shrugs. "Not that it matters much, I guess. She still wants me dead."

"Maybe we can change that."

"I hope so. Because I don't know what I'll do if we can't."

CHAPTER THIRTY-TWO
Off To See The Wizard

THAT LINE KEEPS going through Cason's head: *Toto, I've a feeling we're not in Kansas anymore.* Except that the opposite is true—Kansas is exactly where they are.

He loved and hated that movie as a kid. Something about it always felt off-kilter—men made of metal or stuffed with hay, monkeys with fangs and wings, evil witches, lying wizards, a cold city made of emerald. It never surprised him that all Dorothy wanted to do was go home. Other kids said, *why does she want to leave? She just wants to go back to boring old black-and-white Kansas.* But boring old black-and-white Kansas at least made sense. Home was where you came from. It had rules. *Sanity.* But Oz was a place of madness. Of dreams and nightmares, where impossible things were possible.

Even driving through the flat-plane empty-plain nowhere of Kansas in a rental Dodge SUV, Cason can't help but feel unpinned and lost, like Dorothy—swept up by a funnel cloud, thrown into a land where the impossible was suddenly all-too-terrifyingly-possible. Gods and monsters, good and evil.

Like Dorothy, Cason just wants to go home.

Wants to find out this was all a dream.

He's not sure he'll be afforded that luxury.

"It's empty, man," Tundu says. "This place is dead nothin'."

He's right. It's flat as a sheet of paper. Cason never much thought of Pennsylvania as having a real intense topography, but compared to Kansas, Pennsylvania's the Rocky-fucking-Mountains. Some of it is green—corn or wheat, soybeans or sorghum. Some of it is blasted and brown: giant squares of dry, tilled earth growing nothing, not even weeds.

Couple barns and silos, here and there. Some of them run-down, rust-chewed, slowly sinking back to the earth. Sometimes they see a real big operation—metal buildings one after the next, big green tractors and threshers and other farm equipment churning along, leaving a line of black smoke in the air.

And then back to nothing again.

"It's sort of peaceful," Psyche says from the back of the car. "It's like the end of the Earth. Perhaps somewhere ahead we'll find the horizon line and drop off into nothing."

Cason thinks but does not say: *That's what I'm afraid of.*

The GPS they rented dings, calls out a new direction.

And they turn off the highway.

THE WIND WHIPS across the tall grass, hissing and shaking. Clouds like tufts of fur from a car-struck deer drift across the pale blue sky.

Beneath them, a concrete circle in the earth. Footprint bigger than a barn silo. Diameter of five cars lined up bumper to bumper.

About ten feet past the circle, a small red shack with a padlocked door.

Psyche's eyes roll around behind her eyelids, like a jawbreaker pressing against the inside of a child's cheek. They suddenly snap open.

"Something is trying to keep me out."

"So, this is the address?" Cason asks, slinging his pack over his shoulder. It's filled with a few provisions from Philly: food, water, a bit of rope, a telescoping baton, and a few other... mementos. "There's nothing here."

"Something is down there," Psyche says, pointing to the concrete. "Down deep. That red thread, that bloodline—it ties you to this place."

She shudders.

"I don't like this," Tundu says. "I think we should go. Maybe get a... a motel room. Think this through."

Cason sighs. He knows his friend is right, but...

The Wizard of Oz again. *What makes a king out of a slave? Courage!*

He shakes his head. "No. I need to do this. You guys can go on ahead, though. Get the hell out of here. You got me this far, and I appreciate the company, but I don't want to put either of you at needless risk. Go home. Or go get a steak somewhere. I'm good."

Tundu laughs. "That's some action movie bullshit, man. No way. I'm staying."

"And like I said," Psyche explains. "I'm a very curious girl."

Cason stares at them. Finally, he nods. "All right, then. Let's figure out how to crack this nut. This is an old missile silo, am I right?"

Tundu gives Psyche a look. Psyche just shrugs.

"I don't know nothing about missile silos," Tundu says.

Psyche agrees. "I don't even know what that is—" But then Cason feels fingers plunging into his mind—a cold mental saline rush—and then she blinks. "Oh. *That's* what a missile silo is. Yes, this looks like one. By the way, the human race is sort of terrible. Trying to explode each other with weapons of that scale?"

Cason frowns at her. "Don't do that again without asking."

"Yes, sir." A twinkle of mischief in her otherwise icy eyes.

"Try that shack," Tundu says.

The shack has paint peeling off in big leprous strips. The padlock isn't particularly impressive, but it's enough to keep them from opening the door. Cason rattles the door. Shoulders into it. Nothing.

"I didn't bring bolt cutters," Cason says. "*Shit.* We're gonna have to find a... hardware store or a Home Depot or something." *In the middle of wide open nowhere.*

"Back in the car?" Tundu asks.

Psyche touches Cason. "You've got godsblood in you. Maybe it's

245

time to start acting like it." He feels her inside his head again, this time giving something a little push, like nudging a coffee mug off the edge of a table—

A blush of power blooms within him.

It channels to his limbs. He feels a rush, a steroidal high.

One hard kick shatters the door inward. The padlock thuds, unbroken, against the ground. Cason laughs, and Tundu just looks amazed.

"That was some shit, man." Tundu nods. "Respect."

Into the shack, then.

The shack is shoddy wood, but the ground inside is hard, clean concrete.

And in the center, a hatch. Cason kneels down, tries to turn it. It won't budge. But he takes Psyche's words to heart—he wraps his arms around it, puts his shoulder into it like he's not just trying to choke out a human opponent, but trying to pop the head off a pissed-off grizzly bear. Sweat pops up on his brow, his bones and muscles cry out in pain—

The wheel barks, groans, then turns.

Cason spins it. The hatch opens.

A stainless steel stair twists down into the darkness. A breeze breathes up through the passage. Cason detects smells that don't make much sense: musty mold, fine, but he also smells the scent of cut mushrooms, of dried leaves, and of a bestial musk like he smelled back in the house of the Sasquatch Man.

"I guess it's time," he says. "Into the belly of the beast."

"I'm ready," Tundu says.

"No. No way. You're staying up here." Tundu starts to protest, but Cason holds up a finger. "I appreciate it. I appreciate like hell you coming out here to help me. But I can't have you going down there with me. Besides, I need someone up here. To watch our back while we're down there and to get ready to drive us far, far away from here." Cason grins. "And I figure you're too damn big to fit down the tunnel, anyway."

Tundu chuckles. "Yeah. Yeah, okay, man. I stay up top. You got it."

Cason looks to Psyche, eyebrows raised.

"Ready?" he asks.

"Half-gods first," she says, gesturing to the hole.

Down, then, into the dark.

CHAPTER THIRTY-THREE
The Spiral Forest

BOOTS ON METAL steps as they sink into darkness, *clunnnng, clunnng, clunnng*. The stairs are a tight spiral, so that Cason's elbows and shoulders are always colliding with the sides and the railing. He smells the must, the dust, the distant acrid tang of metal, but then sometimes that other breath rises from below—cold-yet-humid, carrying with it a pungent, musky smell. Of animal glands and human sweat. Of cut grass and pulped wood. Of life in its myriad forms. It's dizzying.

Down, down they go. Cason first, Psyche second.

Ten steps. Then twenty. Thirty, forty.

The steps stop making the *clunnng* sound when they step upon them. Instead, Cason's boots step on something soft. Spongy and almost slippery. He reaches into his bag, pulls out a small flashlight.

Click.

Each step, a green brighter than he's ever seen—a carpet of thick moss. The walls, too, are striated with moss and black mold, and lined with the occasional woody vine.

"I'm guessing this isn't what the missile silo used to look like," he says.

"A terrarium of atomic death?" Psyche says, voice echoing from above. "Certainly not, no."

"Keep going?"

"I do not think we have a choice."

"What? Why not?"

"Shine the light up."

He does. Sees her staring down with her frizzled hair and pursed lips—

But above her. *The steps are gone.* The center pole to which they are attached remains, rising into shadow, but ten feet above her, the stairs just... end. Or, rather, begin.

Fear crawls into his heart, nests there. Has babies.

"I... guess we keep going."

"I concur," she says.

And they continue their descent.

ANOTHER FIFTY STEPS down.

Here, the stairs really do end. The last step hangs loose like a busted piano key, dangling into what appears to be a bottomless pit.

A pattern of orange mold clings to the wall near Cason's head: a clumsy, crooked spiral, glistening in the torchlight.

He shines the beam dead ahead. Here is where their ride officially ends. A round metal hallway waits ahead, the floor a metal grate tented and dented by the intrusion of pushy thick roots growing from underneath.

The metal hallway emits a faint, eerie luminescence, like the light reflecting off a long-disused swimming pool—swimmy, sickly, shifting. Born of a chain of mushrooms growing up out of the walls like steps, or rungs.

"This is us," he says.

He hops down. Careful not to, well, go falling into eternal darkness.

There's a flutter of wings and Psyche stands next to him.

He sighs. "You can fly."

"We already knew this."

"The steps end, but we could've just... flown back up."

"That is true. Would you have?"

"No."

"Then this is all magnificently irrelevant. Shall we?"

He nods, at least comfortable that they have a way back up.

Except, as they step forward, he shines the light back one more time—

And the steps—*and* the pit—are gone. Sealed over by a white concrete wall lined with a tangle-snare of thin, green vines like veins.

"This place isn't right," he says.

"Just figuring that out?"

"Don't be a smartass."

"I wasn't trying to be. To be clear, no, this place is not normal. The shell was built by humans, but has since been... repurposed. This is a creation of the divine. It sings of impossibility. It throbs with life. My mind can't probe it, but I feel it there. Waiting all around us. *Pulsing.*"

They walk. First, through the metal tube—and, nestled in amongst the glowing fungi, Cason sees another nuclear trefoil sign hanging on the wall. As if those who worked down here could possibly have forgotten that they were doing their job within spitting distance of a world-ending missile. What a fear that must've been; to know that one day the klaxons would sound and the lights would flash red, and up out of the fields the American missiles would fire and, not long after, the Russian missiles would fall. And the world would be obliterated, bombed into an irradiated nuclear-winter wonderland.

Cason shudders at the thought. He remembers as a kid being afraid of nuclear war. His father didn't help, telling him the Russkies were coming.

I survived the imaginary nuclear war. But can I survive this?

Metal gives way to concrete—bunker-like, the paint an olive drab. The walls are cracked; branches and vines grow out of each breach. The floor is again spongy with moss, and now with leaves—leaves that occasionally drift down from broken panels where the boughs of underworld trees hang low.

The remnants of the silo—of humanity—linger, too. A corkboard once on the wall, now hanging cockeyed off a furry, coiled vine.

Down the hall sits a metal water fountain—that by itself a scary idea, for who would want to drink the water that passed this close to a nuclear missile? But here the fountain has been disassembled, articulated into pieces by impertinent, invasive branches. Cason sees black thorns dripping tarry red goo, each big as his thumb.

"Those don't look like something I want to touch," he says, shining the light. Not that he really needs the flashlight—all around, the mold and the mushrooms are glowing. The beam serves more as a pointer than anything else, and now they point out the barbed thorns.

Psyche steps over and bends down, smells them.

"Godsblood," she says.

"What?"

"Ichor. The gods are filled with it. It's blood, like a human's, but thicker. More sap-like. Yours is probably ichor-ish. Which rhymes with 'licorice,'" she adds, not at all playfully.

"My blood isn't entirely human." A statement, meant as a question.

"No, probably not."

"*I'm* not entirely human."

"We've been over this."

"I'm still getting used to the idea."

"I suppose that's fair. It took me a while to find comfort in the idea when I fed on the food of the gods and become one of them, thanks to Zeus."

They continue to walk. Stepping over knobby roots that look like knees, ducking under broken ceiling tiles or bundles of dead wire hanging down.

"Zeus. I can't believe he's real. I read about him in school. Everybody did, I guess. Everybody's first taste of mythology. I hated most of my classes, but reading those stories... it's like comic books, you know? Heroes and monsters, gods and goddesses. Turns out it's all real. What's Zeus... you know, *do*?"

"Zeus hasn't been seen in the half-a-century since we were Exiled to this place. The last someone saw him, he had taken command of a derelict boat—an old oil tanker beached somewhere off the Mumbai coast. The *Pavit*, I think it was. He got onboard, called lightning to his scepter. The boat shuddered, slipped back into the sea, and he sailed away. Nobody's seen him since. The boat washed up on shore again a year later. Hera went and looked; he wasn't on it. Not that she could ever find him when Zeus went wayward."

Cason tilts an ear. Thinks he hears something—a rustle, a rasp of something rough—but then it's gone.

"Exiled," Cason says. "You keep using that word. Why are you here?"

He feels Psyche in his mind.

He sees. He *feels*. The Exile. Fifty years ago. All the doors and portals closing. Gateways slamming shut. Gods speared with white fire, thrown down from the myriad heavens to earth, or pierced by swords of light and slammed up through the world's crust—infinite dimensions folded against one another like playing cards, a single hole, as though from a bullet, punched through all of them, gods with bull-heads, goddesses with chameleon skin, demons and goblins and creatures of light and monsters of shadow all dragged through the hole just before it closes. Drawn forth by winged, sexless humanoids with golden skin and gemstone eyes. Ejected here. Closed off. Together.

It's then Cason sees.

"God," he says. "The... our God, the..."

"His proper name is Yahweh. Jehovah." Said with ill-concealed disdain: "*The Lord*. We simply call Him—"

"The Great Usurper."

"Correct."

"So. He just... took over Heaven."

"All the heavens, all the worlds and overworlds and underworlds. Uniformity, He said. Sanctity. *Stability*. We were not a part of that. The world was increasingly smaller, more connected, and we were chaos when He wanted order. He had the power to do it. The belief. The angels. We were already marginalized. And so He cast us out and cut our power to a fraction of what it was. So now He sits on the throne at the top of the heavenly Spire, this world and the many universes His, all His."

"Sounds pretty shitty."

"A bold understatement. For us it was like being locked out of our homes and forced to wander the trackless wastes, cold and hungry. It was jarring, to say the least. But maybe it was for the best."

He turns around, gives her a quizzical look.

"Well," she continues. "The gods, as we've learned, are fickle, dramatic, sometimes even insane. With all that 'endless divine power,' we represented a true danger to the world. Perhaps the Usurper had it right to lock us out. Cut us down at the knees. Not better for *us*, of course. But better for this place and its people."

Cason's about to say something else, but whatever it is goes out of his mind—ahead, at a T-intersection, he sees an image carved in stone, easily as tall as him. "Take a look at this." He waves her on.

The image is carved out of the cement, the contours lined with lichen and fringed with moss.

Cason can barely catch his breath while looking at it.

It's the Antlered God from his dream. Lean, long face—a stag's face, but human. Black almond eyes. Antlers not like that of a deer or an elk, but almost like trees formed of pointed bone, trees whose snarled branches grow and twist to the heavens. The Horned Beast has a broad, bare chest, narrow hips, and a studded, thorned phallus hanging between a pair of furry thighs.

All around the Antlered God are the beasts of the forest—but mutated, like creatures born of a disturbed child's mind. Wolves with tusks. Pigs with snake-tails. Owls with human faces roost in the antlers, while long-legged razor-mouthed rats stalk the ground.

The ground itself is a twisting knot—like they're all standing on a maze carved out of the very earth, a twisting double-back labyrinth that spirals in on itself.

"I dreamed of this," he says in a voice barely above a whisper.

Psyche says nothing.

He turns to ask her if she knows the figure in the carving—

But she's not there.

And the walls of the hallway are gone. Stretched out before him is a forest. Like from his dream. No walls, no more missile silo. No boundaries at all. Twisted black trees grow together above his head like intertwined witch-fingers. The ground is lumpy, mossy, littered with twigs and leaves. No sky can be seen, but moonlight shines through branches.

Some of the signs of the missile silo remain. He sees the corkboard, the water fountain, the nuclear sign. But they hang from trees, or sit on the ground.

No walls. No structure at all.

And no Psyche.

Then—somewhere—he hears leaves rustling. Twigs snapping.

Something moves—a lean, rangy shadow—between two distant trees.

Behind him, something chuffs, snorts. Cason turns and sees nothing there.

For a few moments, all is quiet.

Then: shapes emerge from all sides, blasting out of the brush, shouldering between tall trees and bent saplings—dark shadows with yellow eyes and white teeth, coming for him, hissing and howling and spitting.

Cason turns to run, but a tree branch snarls around his foot, and the forest tilts as he tumbles, the flashlight spinning away, the light dim, then dark.

The ground shakes.

The creatures pounce.

CHAPTER THIRTY-FOUR
Children Of The Antlered God

JAWS SNAP CLOSED in front of his face—wolf jaws that hang not on a wolf at all, but thrust from the face of a boar, spit-slathered tusks gleaming. Cason grabs those tusks, twists, throws the beast off him—the creature rolls away as two more dash forward from the shadow. One a skinny fox with a spiral of goat horns and paws like a human child's hands, the other a chimera of indistinct origins: rat's head on a long, leathery neck, the body a hairless pock-marked tube of sagging skin, its six limbs more like spider's legs than anything else.

Other beasts dance in the margins—yellow eyes, white teeth, growling, hissing, circling, circling. Cason tries to stand, but the rat-chimera pounces, knocks him flat to the ground. The horned fox pounces at his front, little needle teeth coming right for his face—eyes, nose, all the soft bits. He grabs its head, holds it as the teeth *tick* and *tack* in front of him.

The rat-thing bites the back of his neck.

Pain shoots up into his head, across his shoulders and into his arms.

He tries to stay calm, tries to think, *Okay, I'm a tougher guy than*

I ever figured, I'm not even a guy so much as I am—Well, he doesn't know *what* he is. But he can't worry about that now. Point is, he can survive this. Bloodied and beaten, but alive.

Cason rolls, crushing the rat-thing beneath his back while hoisting the horned fox into the air—it writhes and yowls, bushy fox tail whipping the air.

He hurls it hard against a tree, hears its back break. It lays, twitching.

Up, up, up, go! Cason lurches, but it feels like his legs want to go out of him, like they're made of rubber bands dangling from his hip sockets—he feels suddenly sluggish, slushy like a winter puddle, and it's then the thought strikes him:

The bite was venomous.

Down, down on his hands and knees. He reaches for his bag, but it seems miles away, now. The world slides into deeper darkness. All around him, shadows encroach. A black blob with a crocodile's maw. A falcon's beak with human eyes set above it. A mangy dog with feathers instead of fur. The beasts creep forward. A new wretched thought strikes him—*Nergal. These are Nergal's pets. Like his seven warriors, his guardians, they are*—

But his thoughts die incomplete. They're suddenly a jumble as the venom seizes, wracking his body with spasms.

He collapses. Hears the ginger tread of the approaching monsters.

His fingers sink into the forest floor. Deep through moss and leaf layer, down through dark earth and into the domain of the earthworms.

And suddenly: a terrifying bloom of awareness. A feeling like falling.

The forest is alive. He can see it. He can see the roots and shoots, the runners and briars, can feel every stone, every mote of dirt. He can feel the beasts, too—he doesn't see them so much as *discern their shape* in the deep of his mind, and there he sees the crocodile maw drawing open on its leathery hinge, opening wide around his skull, ready to snap closed and take his head clean off its shoulders.

Panic causes his mind to lash out.

He seizes the beast's jaws, not with his hands but with his mind.

He wrenches the jaw wider, wider, until the bones creak and the tendons snap and suddenly the monster's head rips in half.

Cason signals to the others: *run.*

And they do. They do just as he asks. They turn tail and flee, whimpering into the shadows as if castigated by their master's hand.

Their master, Cason thinks.

They ran like he commanded them.

That's not normal.

It's lights out. He lets the venom take him. Into sleep or death, he's not sure.

But something stops his descent.

Out there. In the forest. There's a mind—it evades him like a firefly ducking a child's swooping jar. He reaches for it, and it moves. A blue mote, flashing, flickering. He expands his mind like a net, drops it down—

Cason.

A small voice, a scared voice.

Alison.

Alison is here in the missile silo. In the forest maze.

Alison. His wife. His love.

Cason growls. Feels his forehead burn like two cigars are pressing into his flesh. He growls and shakes his head like a wolf tearing meat off a carcass—the venom inside is part of the beasts, and the beasts are part of the forest, and that means it does what he commands. He screams inward at the poison lancing through his body and suddenly it lurches up out of his mouth and nose in a black, tarry stream.

Clarity rings like a glass bell.

Cason stands. Head no longer burning.

He hears Alison's voice, now—small, but real. Not in his head.

"Cason..."

He runs. Ducking branches. Leaping roots. Tearing through coils and tangles of pricker bush. Ahead, two of the shadow-beasts gather, but when they see him coming they yelp and whine and flee in opposite directions.

A sign to his left, hanging from a twisting branch. AUTHORIZED PERSONNEL ONLY: *It is unlawful to enter this area without permission of the Installation Commander.* Next to it, a desk ripped almost in half by a boulder.

"Cason!"

Her voice—calling through the woods. *Echo, echo, echo.*

He finds what might be a deer path. Or, at least, the path that the beasts wander—a muddy rut carved through the forest floor. His feet pound, pinwheeling out of control, boots almost slipping time and again on the greasy earth—

The path turns inward, and inward again, tighter and tighter, a terrible spiral—

Another sign. A nuclear trefoil.

A water fountain.

A stone frieze of the Antlered God.

I'm traveling in circles.

Cason leaps the path, runs straight toward the voice without care for the obstacles in his way. Cracked boulder, fallen tree, a rocky furrow—

A broken desk. An AUTHORIZED PERSONNEL ONLY sign.

He growls. Kicks the desk. His boot *gongs* against the metal.

Alison's voice—indistinct, this time, a cry of pain—

He feels the pain. He feels her out there.

And that's the secret. Isn't it? This forest. He's part of it. Somehow. Or it's part of him. He reaches down, pulls a clod of earth, and again the awareness rises inside him, like a blush of food coloring inside a glass of water. He can undercut the maze. He can *cheat.*

He feels her out there.

Cason closes his eyes and walks forward.

CHAPTER THIRTY-FIVE
The Root Cage

HIS HEART BREAKS and reforms all in a single moment: there stands Alison. Contained within the exposed roots of a tree, the twisted bark tendrils forming the bars of her cage. The tree itself is a blasted dead thing, rising into the forest ceiling, the bark stripped away and bitten into as if lightning has clawed its way through. The ground inside the cage is an ankle-deep pool of brackish, dirt-flecked water.

Alison is beaten and bloodied—eyes ringed in puffy purple bruises, capillaries burst in her eyes and her cheeks, bottom lip split, the chin crusted with black blood. Someone hurt her, and when he sees that he wants to find whoever that is and break their bones inch by inch until their skin is just a sack for a shattered skeleton.

But then she smiles and it washes away the anger. Like an antiseptic poured on a wound to clean away the infection.

"Al," he says, almost crying. Cason drops the bag he's been carrying, slams himself up against the root cage. He reaches through, touches her hand—she pulls herself toward him and touches her forehead to his.

"I... I don't know how long I've been here," she says. "It feels like forever."

"I'll get you out of here." He draws a deep breath. "I love you."

"I love you too." She blinks back tears. "Someone brought me here and... please get me out. Please."

He grabs at the roots, pulls with all his might. Agony assails the muscles of his arms, his back, his hips and legs—and still the roots remain.

Again, it strikes him, the realization coming faster than before.

You control this place.

The roots are just part of the forest.

He calms his heart, stills the flutter inside his chest and gut. Zeroes out any of the noise in his mind as he leans up against the cage, feels the craggy dry bark scraping the calluses on his palm and fingers, feels the faint throb of life still living inside this tree.

Then he grabs that tiny pulse and pulls it like a fishing rod.

The bark cracks, splits—

And two of the tendrils pull free of the earth, dirt raining from fine roots at the base. Then those two tendrils curl up into tight spirals, opening the way for Alison's escape. She gasps, weeping—

Cason feels her wrap her arms around him. It all feels right.

But something smells wrong. Literally. A stink crawls into his nose.

The smell of smoke and burning. Lit match-tips. Charred leaves and ashen bog.

There's a flash of light—

Cut to his retinas, imprinting a silhouette on the backs of his eyes—

Cason is thrown backward, into the root cage.

The tendrils drop, uncurling and thrusting down deep into the earth. Alison no longer stands outside the cage.

Instead: it's a man. Tall, lean, bare-chested, the chest laced with a network of dark scars. Head a mane of salt-and-pepper hair. At a distance he looks older, but his skin is smoother than plastic. Untouched, unmarred. No lines at all.

Cason's seen him. In his dream. On the glass throne.

The man grins. Cinches up a pair of dirty jeans. Dries his toes on the mossy ground.

"Freedom," the man says, sucking air between his teeth. He stretches out his arms, spins around in a giddy circle. "Sweet, glorious freedom. I have to tell you, that cage? Not pleasant. I don't recommend it. And yet—there you are. You'll see. Sometimes, these bugs come? Chew your skin off? And then other times, it rains, but the rain—you can't drink it. You're thirsty, so you'll try, but it's bitter as anything and it'll strip the meat right from your throat-hole." The man waves a hand. "Ooh, sorry. I'm over here ruining all the good surprises."

Cason stands. Dusts himself off. "I don't know who you are, but you just made one hell of a mistake."

"Hell of a mistake. That's funny."

"This forest is mine."

"Is it, now?"

"That's how I found you. Because I control this place."

Cason stalks forward. Puts his hands on the roots. Feels for that pulse and again pulls it taut.

The roots don't move. Not a quiver. Nary a tremble nor a twitch.

He growls, tries again—reaches deeper, feels his eyes rolling back in his head—

Nothing.

"Now, think about it," the man says. "What kind of cage would it be if the person inside could get out? You *had* the key. You were the keykeeper, one might say. But not anymore, Cason. This cage is built right. I should know. I've been in it for..." He checks his wrist, where no watch exists. "About fifty years, now? Feels like an eternity. And I should know eternity."

"Who are you?"

The man grins ear-to-ear. "Shoot, you know me, hoss. I'm the Devil. Satan. Lucifer. Sammael, the Thorn of God. But you might want to call me..." He lets that dramatic pause hang in the air like a sword dangling from a tiny string. "*Daddy.*"

The Devil brays with laughter.

Tundu sits.

It's been about five hours now.

He sits there in the Dodge, drumming his fingers. He wants to listen to the radio, but doesn't want to burn out the battery. Thing is, it's quiet out here. Freaky quiet. It's not like the city. The city is—well, the city *is* noise. Honking, tires, construction work, yelling, laughing, crying, music. Even if you turned all that off there'd still be the sound of the city itself: the wall of white noise. In the ground, in the buildings. The hum of every traffic light, the thrum of subways and sewer gases.

Out here, though, it's dead still, and that drives Tundu crazy. Makes him feel itchy, like he's got ants between his ears.

His mind wanders into bad spaces. Spaces where he feels worry and fear over this new world he's discovered: a world of beings well above the station of man. It makes him feel small, and it makes him worry about his family. He wanted to have kids someday of his own, too—his nieces and nephews are a real pain in the ass, sure, but he still wanted to have a couple himself, raise them up *right*. Now he's not so sure. What would it be to bring kids into a world like this? A world where he knows that the nightmares really exist?

It's then he hears a sound.

A scuff of a shoe.

Then—

At the window. A face. Lidless eyes, lipless mouth.

Frank.

He waves, waggling his bright red lobster fingers, and then mimes rolling a window down. Nobody 'rolls' them down anymore, but the gesture is universal. Tundu complies.

"What the hell, Frank?" Tundu asks. "How'd you get here?"

Frank just shakes his head, then shows his other hand.

In it, he holds a stubby-barreled nickel-plated revolver.

He thrusts it in through the window and shoots Tundu twice in the chest. Tundu feels his body shudder with each hit. He tries to say something, but it comes out a whistling squeak. The back of his tongue tastes blood. He coughs.

"Sorry, T.," Frank says.

Then he walks away.

*   *   *

"YOU," CASON SAYS. "You're my divine parent."

It starts to add up.

He's adopted.

They used to call him The Beast.

The gods wanted him out of the way, so they arranged for the accident and the subsequent indentured servitude to Eros.

The Devil laughs again. "You ass. I'm not really your Daddy. Relax."

"What? But—"

"I'm your grandfather."

Cason presses his face against the roots. Shows his teeth. "Now you're just playing with my head. Who the hell—"

"I told you for real this time. I'm the Devil. I'm your granddaddy."

"Go fuck yourself."

"What's that, you said? You'd like me to tell you a story, young whippersnapper?" Lucifer stoops, snaps up a thin green tendril up off the ground, uses it to tie back his hair. "I guess I got the time. My coming out party can wait another five, ten minutes—besides, isn't that the thing? To be fashionably late?"

"I don't want to hear the story of some two-bit angel—"

The Devil scowls. Kicks the roots. "Angel? Fuck you. *Angel*. I'm no angel. I'm the real deal, kiddo; a certified god. When the Big Boss with the Heavenly Hot Sauce kicked my can out of His little sky-country, I plunged through the worlds and into my very own special Hell—and there I became its King. *Angel*." He spits on the ground, and it sizzles. "I'm no angel. I have a whole *religion* around me. I'm in movies. Comic books. More stories are written about *me* then they are *Him*. So don't you sell me short, you little pissant. You give your elder the respect he deserves."

"I don't want to hear any story you want to tell me."

"Too fucking bad, kid. I want you to see just where you come from, because it'll burn your ass real good. Mmkay? Mmkay. Now. About your mother? Lydia, *oh, Lydia. Say, have you met*—? No, I guess you haven't. Gods, what a crazy, sexy bitch your mother was. Like, genuine nuts, you know? Her head was a can of broken cashews. Well, *as I mentioned*, I had quite the following—still do, but it really peaked in the 1970s, you know? Great time to be the Devil. Fond memories. Whatever. Point is, Lydia was a beloved proselyte of mine. I heard her prayers and felt her energy from across the miles—the praises of the most devoted, I could hear all the way down here in the dark. Like I was a radio and they were the only frequency I could get."

The Devil leans back against the cage. Relaxing. Looking up, wistfully remembering. "Well. Lydia was one of the strongest signals to hit my antenna, right? And I thought, hey, I'll try to talk back to her. So I tried and tried and squeezed all my evil muscles together and one day—*pop!*—I got through. And I told her my situation, I said, honey, this is the Devil hisownself, and I'm trapped down in a prison made just for me by a bunch of petulant snot-nosed tricky-dicked deities—right? Bunch of bullies who think that *just because* I'm the Devil, *just because* I've got some of the same 'divine matter' as that giant celestial jerk who locked them out of their own homes, that was a good enough reason to lock me away in this place until the sun and stars flicker to ash.

"But I'm a guy with a long view of things. And a way to see through it all, to see how the dominoes tumble into one another, again and again. So I said to her, to Lydia, I need your help. And I told her what to do."

Here the Devil chuckles, shakes his head like he's real pleased about what's coming. Still facing away from the bars, all the while.

Cason inches closer. Hands flexing.

"She did just as I asked. She came out here. Found her way into the installation, down through the forest, and all the way to me. We kissed—just once through the cage roots, and it's then I tasted it. She was my own daughter!" He claps his hands. "You believe that? I mean, once upon a time I got around here on Earth, but really, most of the time my diabolical seed didn't take. It's why there aren't a lot of half-god hybrid babies running around—it's rare that our divine swimmers or little demon eggies manage to sync up with the oh-so-very-vulnerable human body. Hell, most times it's just a miscarriage—and usually one that splits the mother like a tomato. Ugh. But I guess at one point my goo found a home and... well, ta-da. Lydia Cranston."

Cason lunges.

Hands around the Devil's neck. He gets his arm through, wraps it around Lucifer's neck, starts to squeeze. Choke him out the way he'd choke out an opponent on the mat.

Cason grits his teeth. Puts his back into it.

The Devil cranes his head back and cocks an eyebrow.

"You finished?" Lucifer gurgles.

Cason gives it a couple-few more hard shakes. Then quits.

The Devil says, "I don't really *breathe*, you know."

"I'll kill you somehow," Cason says.

"Unlikely, kid. You don't know what'll do me in and even if you did, you won't get access to it. Tough titty, said the kitty. Now, back to the story—so, Lydia leaves my company and meets, as you did, the sentinels of this place. Ugly little chimerae. And with them comes Mister Antlers, the Lord of the Hunt, the Keeper of the Forest Maze, Cernunnos. Big dick swinging. He's the Green Man. Hard as a knob of cypress wood, and she, fertile as a verdant island valley. She offered herself to him. On my command. And he, being the horny old stag that he is, took her right there."

He smiles a sweet smile. Like he's remembering the perfume of a first date.

"And then, she did as I asked. She left. Fled her new lover. Gone, gone, and nine months later, you plopped out, and she was of course a total fuck-up—like I said, crazy—and she gave you up for adoption not knowing what kind of creature she gave birth to and... well, fast-forward a bit to the part where the gods eventually suss out that someone with my diabolical heritage is wandering around the country punching people in the head and choking them out on mats inside octagons and they figured it was high-time to corral that unruly horse. So, they arranged for your little... situation. Ah, but one thing they did not arrange for—and here is where I stepped in again—I tweaked their magic just a touch. I'm the one who made it so your wife and son hated you, wanted you dead. That wasn't them. That was all me, kiddo. Because I needed you mad. Mad enough at them to think about revenge." He sighs. "And that took longer than I thought. You got fat. Complacent. So I sent my man along—good ol' Frank—to tweak the equation a little."

"Why? Why have me kill those other gods?"

Lucifer shrugged. "That was mostly an *added value* for me. I'm not a fan of theirs and I'm happy to get rid of the competition, so. And Frank really wanted it, and if that's what hooked him... hey, I figured I could let that go as long as it needed to. Long as the road led you here to let me out. Because you're the key, kiddo. Your Daddy is the one who made this prison, so that means you could open the door. And you got my blood, too, which means the cage thinks it has the right prisoner and nobody knows different."

"So you're the one who broke my family apart."

"Guilty! Of this and so many other things." Lucifer winks. "Anyway. I gotta hoof it—although your Daddy's the one with the hooves, I guess. Point is, I've got a Heaven to overtake with my charm and might."

Cason sneers. "I thought God kicked all of you out."

"Oh, he did. But I know a little secret: God's gone. Packed up His shit and high-tailed it out of Heaven. Same time that a host of the father gods left—Zeus on his boat, Odin on that horse made of fire, Ahura-Mazda in that Casa Luz pit. He's gone. And the throne is open. So, since I'm kinda next in line for the job, I'm pretty much gonna kick open the door and take it while nobody else knows the position is open."

"I won't let that happen."

The Devil shrugs.

"I don't think you have much choice, kid. Sorry we couldn't have had dinner. Played a little catch, maybe."

"We still can."

Lucifer smirks. "Oh?"

"There's an apple. In my bag. Last thing I'll get to eat in a long while. You throw it to me and I eat it. Two birds with one stone: dinner and a round of catch with my grandpappy."

Lucifer eyes up the bag. Picks it up, empties it out. The apple drops on the ground with a *thud*. The Devil rolls his eyes. "Oh, *fine*. Anything for my dear old grandson. I do spoil you, sometimes."

Then he kicks the apple in through the cage bars and walks away, laughing.

CHAPTER THIRTY-SIX
Bearing Fruit

PSYCHE CAN FEEL Cason. His mind is there, inside the image of the Antlered God—which, if she has it right, is the Horned Lord of the Hunt himself, Cernunnos. Not a friendly one, that god. A lot of the gods are human-seeming—they act like people, more or less. Not him. He acts like the offspring of an animal and an alien, as implacable as the forest, as sensible as a Martian.

And one minute Cason was there, staring at the carving.

The next, gone.

She runs her hands along the stone. It's cold. Feels wet.

The air in front of it starts to shimmer and warp, as if seen through melting glass.

Psyche steps back just in time—

A man steps through the empty space.

At first she thinks—*it's Cason*, but it's not; his mind remains distant. But she spies a familiarity there.

It's then she recognizes him.

"You," she says.

"Me," the Devil says, smiling.

It's then she figures it out. "This... is your prison." She's heard the stories. The Devil. Trapped and jailed. Kept away from the world, for he was a danger to it, and to all the gods.

He winks. "*Was* my prison."

"You look like him. Like Cason. A little."

"Blood is blood, though his is not all mine. He's more Old Antlerface over there."

They share an uncomfortable moment. Two gods standing before one another. Her shifting nervously from foot to foot. Him standing tall and grinning ear-to-ear.

"You should come with me," Lucifer says. "I could use someone like you. I like your skill-set, honey. And for once I think I'd like a queen by my side. Wouldn't that be something? The Devil and his beautiful bride."

"You..." Her soul flutters. "You think I'm beautiful?"

"I sure do."

"I..." Part of her wants to go with him. She doesn't know him. She's heard the stories, though. His betrayal of Shaitan. What he did to Eris. And yet, the twinkle in his eyes when he tells her she's beautiful. The way he stands there, smirking, hips cocked. Finally, she says, "I can't."

"Shame," he says, clicking his tongue.

Then he thrusts his hands up and a blade of blue glass cuts through her heart. He holds it there for a second, the glass flickering and shifting like there's fire inside it. Then he slides it free, and with a flourish of his wrist, the sword is gone again.

"Guess that still works," he says. "Cool."

Psyche gasps and gapes. She tries to flail out with her mind to seize his, but she feels the strength of his will batting her away like she's a bee and he's a tiger.

"Oh no, no, no," he says and taps his head. "No getting into *this* vault, honey. So sorry." He lifts a bare foot, plants it against her chest and shoves her down to the floor. Black blood smears the earthen ground beneath her. "That won't kill you, I suspect. But it's going to hurt for a long, long while. That sword's a mean old tooth. It really is a tooth, by the way; when I first fell to Hell, see, the space was already taken over by a mighty dragon, and—" He waves dismissively. "See? Your pretty face has me in the mood for stories and I've told enough of those today."

She coughs. Tastes her own godsblood. "You don't *really* think I'm pretty, do you?"

"Not particularly."

"Liar." She spits blood at him.

He wipes it from his face, then shrugs.

"We all have a role to play."

Lucifer steps over her body, and walks off, whistling.

CASON DROPS TO his knees, apple in hand. *Splash*. The water is brown, murky, cloudy as a sinner's heart—he waits for the waters to still, for the ripples to quit, and the waiting is interminable, it goes on and on to the point where he almost runs out of patience and once more breaks the water with his hand.

But he doesn't.

He waits. Calms his breath. Looks down.

He can see himself. Reflected in the turbid broth.

Barely. But he's there.

He gently brings the apple to his mouth—

Crisp apple skin crackles as teeth puncture into the fruit's flesh. A taste both sweet and bitter fills his mouth, and suddenly there comes the sound of the ocean surf crashing against craggy rocks and his nose fills with salt air.

And there stands Aphrodite.

He wants to lay before her, pressing his face into the muck until he drowns—

But he controls it.

He can. He must.

"I didn't expect *you* to call," she says. Gliding over to him atop the water, never once disturbing the murk. "If there is one thing you have proven to me, Cason Cole, it's that I still retain the capacity for surprise."

"The Devil is free," he says, the words hurrying out of him. "Lucifer. This was his prison and now I'm here in his place. He's responsible for my wife and son wanting to murder me, and I'm responsible for setting him free." He begs: "I want out of here. I want to make things right. *All of it.* I want it over. I want to end it." He finally adds, with a ragged gasp: "I want to be with my wife and son again."

Aphrodite sighs. "You've made a mess of things."

"I know."

"I can't help you."

"What? But... I called you. And I gave you Frank—"

"My old toy *escaped*. Given what you've just told me, and the infernal sigil carved across his chest, it's safe to surmise he's on the Devil's payroll, now."

"You don't have him."

"I don't."

"Then I can help you get him. I'll do anything. Please, just get me—"

"You're not understanding me. I *can't*. This is a prison. A cage. If anybody could just hop in and hop out, it wouldn't be particularly secure, would it? But I'll give you a hint, Cason. You belong to this place. It belongs to you, in return."

He barks at her: "I already know that! That's *not new information*."

"Then you're not *thinking* hard enough," she barks back. "But I can't help you. I want to. I really do. There's a part of me that feels for you. That cries out for your plight. And I'll confess I wonder what you'd be like as a lover. You're visceral. Passionate. The lengths you go to for the ones you love is..." She shudders in a wave of imagined pleasure. "There's nothing I can do for you."

"Wait—"

"Goodbye, Cason."

And then she's gone.

Psyche lies bleeding.

The pain is like nothing she's ever felt. It wracks her body again and again—like someone pouring fresh gasoline on a wound. Once the throb dulls, more gas. *Pssshh.* Then someone lights it on fire and the cycle begins anew.

The Devil was right. She won't die by this wound, but it'll mark her. It'll cripple her for a long time. Centuries. Maybe longer. The weapons of the gods are like that—and Lightbringer, Satan's infamous sword, is just such a maker-of-misery.

She's in such agony that when she sees Aphrodite appear, she thinks she must be dreaming. Or hallucinating. But she knows her own mind; such self-deception is rare, if not impossible. Which leaves the unlikeliest choice: this is really happening.

Aphrodite stands over her. Arms crossed.

"Come to see me suffer?" Psyche says, her voice a shuddering whisper.

"No."

"Then why?"

"I was called. Now I'm here."

"Go on. Gloat. Kick me while I'm down."

Aphrodite sniffs, then stoops and offers a hand.

Psyche stares at it like it's a venomous snake.

"Take it," Aphrodite insists. "I'll... help you."

"Why? After all this time, why?"

"You were my son's wife. And you're all I have left of him. We will never be friends, but we will always be family."

"Family." The word tastes strange on Psyche's tongue.

"Will you take my hand?"

Psyche nods, reaches for her. Aphrodite helps her stand, then places the flat of her palm against Psyche's chest. A warmth radiates out, and sheer bliss rises and thrives in her mind. When Aphrodite takes her hand away, the shirt is still torn, but the wound between her breasts is healed over—a scar like a toothy mouth in its place. The pain is still in there, too; an ache, with dull teeth. But it's manageable.

"Let's go," Aphrodite says. "We have something to do."

HE FELT SO clever. Get the Devil to throw him an apple. Find his reflection. Conjure Aphrodite from across the miles to free him. But then she told him no. Can't help. Sorry.

Now she's gone, leaving him only with the tidbit of information that somehow, someway, he can do this himself.

Cason wracks his brain. Tries to feel the forest through the mess beneath his fingers, then at the roots themselves. The forest is there, all bright shadow and tangled vine, all of it reachable in the front of his mind, and yet no amount of effort will make the roots part. They don't even twitch.

He snaps. He can't hack it anymore. Anger burns in his mind—a sunflare. He channels it into the forest all around; the trees shudder, and black leaves fall. The ground rumbles and growls. He hears the beasts whimpering in the distance and—

Something is beneath him.

Suddenly. Something massive. He can't see it, can't feel it, but he *senses* it. A presence like a blue whale rising to the surface.

Then he *does* feel it. Outside the cage, the ground cracks. From the dirt, steam rises. A mound forms. Starts to break apart. At Cason's feet, the water ripples.

Beyond the roots, two bone spires rise from the earth. Then four. Then eight. Bony tips, woven together like the roots of an upturned tree.

Antlers. Massive antlers.

The Huntsman rises. Clods of dirt and moss-rugs cling to his leathery shoulders before finally tumbling to the earth.

In the distance, the beasts howl and wail and gibber at the arrival of their master.

The man—no, the *god*—stands twice as tall as Cason.

He sniffs the air. Nostrils flaring.

Black almond eyes blink, then turn toward Cason.

Cernunnos growls, and the sound vibrates Cason's bones. He can feel it in his organs, his ribs, his teeth. The god lifts a hand—a human hand, though his feet are massive oxblood hooves—and angrily swipes it across the root cage.

They shatter like splinters, like toys thrown from the table by a petulant toddler.

The monster picks up Cason like he's nothing. Bares teeth that are not sharp, but blunt—like flat pieces of slate shoved up into red, red gums.

Cason knows he's dead.

But then the god drops him to the dirt. Leans down, his lean face pressed tight against Cason's. The Huntsman's lips peel back and he utters—in a human tongue that seems a chore to produce: "*Child*."

Then he lifts his head, turns, and stomps away.

BOOM, BOOM, Boom, Boom, boom, boom

That's it.

The root cage is destroyed.

Cason is alone.

And he's pretty sure he just met his father.

Holy shit.

THE DEVIL THROWS open the shack door, saunters out across the concrete top of the silo. The sun shines down on his face, warming his cheeks. It's almost like the light pulls his face into a big, shit-eating grin.

He's happy.

Excuse the saying, but, he's happy as *Hell*. Not that Hell was all that happy. It was for him, once upon a time. Though boredom set in and—

That's really not what matters right now.

What matters is: happy.

He waves to Frank, who stands there next to a white Dodge rental, gun hanging from his hand. Frank nods.

"When the Devil's happy, the world should fret," Lucifer boasts, clacking his teeth like he's taking bites out of the blue sky above. "I feel good, Comrade Polcyn."

"Cason. He still..." Frank points to the ground.

"As was the plan."

"I feel bad about that."

"You should. You betrayed someone who considered you a friend. And now he's in an eternal prison, likely never to escape. Way to be a pal, Frank."

"Look who's talking. You're the guy's *family*."

"Only in blood. I don't know him. You do. Or did."

"You're not helping!"

The Devil shrugs, the grin never wavering. "This your ride?"

"What? No. It's—it was Cason's. Had a guy with him. I shot the motherfucker."

"He had someone down there with him, too. The girl. The one with the frizzy hair? A goddess. Whatever. I stabbed her."

"Oh. Good."

Lucifer shrugs. "You bring the boy?"

"He's at the car about a quarter mile back."

"So, we have to walk?"

"We have to walk."

"Yuck. Well, it's a nice enough day, at least. And the church is nearby?"

"Not even five miles away."

The Devil snaps his fingers, forms them into guns and fake-shoots Frank. "Super. Let's take a stroll, Frank."

CHAPTER THIRTY-SEVEN
Collision

ALISON SITS NEXT to the man with the long, greasy hair. She grips the seat belt like it's a safety line, like if she clutches it tight enough the strange man will stop driving down these narrow Kansas backroads at a hundred miles per hour, slicing a scissor-line through corn and wheat and other grains.

The man hums. *Mmm-mm-mmmm...*

"Who are you?" she finally asks after ten minutes of driving.

"Hm? Oh. Just a friend."

"A friend. My friend."

"Didn't say *your* friend. Just *a* friend. Friend to the world. Trickster extraordinaire. Defender of the golden thread. Which is, I think, close to snapping..." He looks down at the dashboard, then presses on the accelerator. The car whips forward. Rows of cornstalks fly past, blurring into an indefinable green smear.

"Please. Don't kill me."

"Kill you? I would do no such thing. Oh, that reminds me—" He holds the wheel with one hand, reaches across her lap and wrenches open the glove compartment. Inside, a knife rests on the maps and old receipts. He snaps his fingers and the knife rolls out, bounces off the lid, and lands in her lap.

She yelps.

Quickly she fumbles with the knife, picks it up, and holds it to his throat.

"Really?" he asks.

"You stop this car."

"Not yet."

"Stop the car!"

"I just *gave* you that knife. And now you're threatening me with it?"

"Stop the car!" she screams.

He slams on the brakes. Tires squeal. Smoke from burning rubber rises up on both sides of the car. Her own head smacks against the dashboard, and she almost loses the blade.

Before she knows what's happening, he's snapping his fingers again and her car door flings open from invisible hands.

He waves at her. "Bubbye, now. Nice to see you. Keep the thread intact."

Then he pushes her out and accelerates away.

A CADILLAC SITS on the side of the road. A few bumblebees buzz between white wildflowers as the wind shakes the corn. The Devil peers into the back seat of the car. There lies the boy—his great-grandson.

"Barney?" he says to Frank. "*Ugh.* That's his name. Barney?"

"Mm," Frank says. "Short for... I dunno. Barnabas or something. Wasn't easy sneaking that kid here, by the way. Thank God for your guy with the plane—"

Lucifer wheels on him. "Did you just say, *Thank God?*"

"I—wait—"

"I'm sure you didn't. Because the 'guy with the plane' was *my guy*. He was a *Devil worshipper*. He's in my pocket. God had nothing to do with this. Nothing."

"I'm sorry, I'm sorry—it's just a saying. Everybody says it."

Lucifer's scowl turned back to a smile. "Well, soon they'll be saying

Thank Satan when anything good happens. Or anything bad. Or anything *at all*, because I'll be the one turning the clockwork gears that make the whole universe go." Again he peers back in through the window. "Barney. What a horrible name. It just... falls off the tongue. Like a bridge jumper plummeting to his death. Remind me to think up a new name for our young Prince, here. Something *infernal*. You know? In the tongue of my corrupt angels."

"Sure. Whatever. Why you need the kid, anyway?"

"Like I said, I need a prince. The throne has rules, Frank. God had one of His blood with Him ruling Heaven—nobody's seen Jesus yet, have they?"

"Nope. It was like he didn't come to earth with the rest of the... the rest of you."

"Mmm." The Devil pulls himself away from the window, opens the passenger side door. "Well, whatever. I need someone with me on the throne. Someone who has my blood. Plus, that way I can leave the little prince behind as I go do... you know. Whatever it is I do. I don't want to be shackled to that fuckin' chair all the time, do I? No, I do not. Kid's my proxy, he's my blooded regent on the divine—oh, shit."

Frank turns.

A white Dodge SUV appears down the road.

Barreling down the asphalt toward them. Erratic. Swerving like a drunk is driving.

And it's headed right for them.

Frank cries out. He's got the gun up. Firing shots into the car. Three bullets drive into the grille. Two more punch uneven holes in the windshield.

Lucifer growls. Mercy is not a thing he particularly enjoys—it's a fucking *chore* is what it is, but sometimes you have to do what you have to do, so he whips open the Caddy's back door, grabs the kid, and backpedals away—

Just as the SUV plows into the Cadillac.

The two cars, like crumpled soda cans, do a funny cockeyed waltz further down the road before both slide off and into the corn. Both cars honk—a droning horn that keeps going and going, as if each is trying to drown out the other.

The Devil sets Barney down in the weeds just as Frank stalks past him.

Frank roars, gun up. Fires another round into the SUV—the back window shatters.

The front door of the Dodge pops open.

And out comes a big sonofabitch. Black as the tar-pits of Hell itself. His gut a blood-soaked mess, the blood already turning brown and black.

The Devil stands back, decides to watch.

Frank breaks into a run, the revolver raised—

He's pulling the trigger but it's almost like he doesn't realize it's not firing. The cylinder is turning with every pull, the hammer clicking, but no bullets are coming out.

The black fellow, well, he's got a tire iron in his hand, which he brings down hard against Frank's skull.

Frank drops like a sack of rocks.

His body is still.

Ooooh. Ouch.

Now the big bastard has turned his attention toward the Devil. His face a contorted mask of pain and rage, he stalks toward Lucifer, the tire iron again raised.

"No," the Devil says, then points at the man with an index finger. The SUV's driver stops, frozen and in considerable agony. "Nuh-uh. Sorry. I've got plans and now you've gone and slowed the proceedings down. The church is five miles away, which is perfectly fast *by car*, but now I'm going to have to walk. And I'm not carrying the kid. What am I, a common mule? So, here's what I'm offering you"—he searches the man's mind—"Tundu? Is that your name? Loyal to my grandson, I see. Yes. Gods, even half-gods like Cason, tend to draw devotees, and I can see the connection. So that means you won't mind helping Cason's boy, right? Carrying him for me? Good. Great. Whatever."

He reaches into Tundu's mind, flips all the right switches and pulls all the wrong levers. The man is his. At least, for a time. He'll die soon: that gut shot is pretty bad. But for now, he'll serve. Penance for his crime.

Nearby, Frank twitches. Moans. Still alive, then.

Lucifer walks over. Kneels down in the gravel. "Your job is done, Frank. You're fired. Pink slip. Do they still give out pink slips? Mm. Disappointing that our journey together comes to this end." Blood pools beneath Frank's head. "Bye now, Frank."

He points at Tundu. "Grab the boy. Let's walk."

CASON OPENS THE shack door, stumbles out into the light. He's not sure what's real anymore. He knows this is the reality, but down there in the forest maze everything felt crisper, more real than this— that tiny fracture in his expectations troubles him.

But he can't stop to think about that, now. He's tired. Bedraggled. Muddy.

The Devil is free, and it's all his fault. Before he entered the missile silo, that wasn't even an option—it wasn't a problem he could've possibly imagined. And now it's real. And the Devil is his grandfather. He has no time to ruminate on how fucked up that is.

Down there in the silo, he didn't see Psyche.

And up here, he doesn't see her, either.

Or the Dodge rental.

That's a problem.

Cason cups his hands, yells out. His voice echoes over the corn.

He yells again—for Tundu, for Psyche, for anybody.

No sign. No Devil. Nothing.

He feels alarmingly alone. A tiny seed inside sprouts a germ of fear—the Devil is free and he's already gone and ruined the world, and this is Cason stepping out into *that* world, not the world he remembers. Or maybe he's been down there for hundreds of years and all that he knows has passed him by.

What he knows is that he's worried about Psyche and Tundu.

Which means it's time to walk.

ALISON DROPS THE knife. It sticks in the dirt past the road's shoulder. She looks around like this is some kind of joke.

She's alone. The road stretches in both directions, an asphalt ribbon parting the seas of wheat and corn.

Everything about her feels like a raw nerve exposed to the air. Alive, but stinging.

Then she picks the knife back up. And puts it back down again. A fear fantasy plays out in her mind where the cops—the *real* cops—show up and see her carrying a knife and suddenly everything goes bullet-shaped as they fill her full of lead.

But then she's afraid that the *other* guy, the fake cop, will come back.

Him, or the Indian.

Or the strange little man.

Or the horrible narcissistic woman with the mad mane of hair and the ability to crawl inside her mind like a mouse.

She picks up the knife again.

And it's then a voice echoes out over the corn—

Indistinct at first, but louder the next time:

"*Tundu. Psyche! Hello?*"

The voice. Familiar. All her senses awaken. It's an overwhelming rush, a powerful flashbulb inside her head—

Rage rising—

Blood in her vision, red haze, red rage—

Cason.

Alison clutches the knife and heads toward the voice.

CASON STAGGERS UP the drive and toward the road. Sees tracks on the ground—car tracks. Looks like a second set. From the Dodge, maybe. They swerve. With each turn, the rubber gets a workout—black track-streaks. If Tundu was driving, he got out of here in a hurry. What happened?

He gets to the road. Looks right. Nothing. Left? Nothing.

Knows there's a crossroads back the way they came. Not far. So he heads that way.

Crows fly overhead, chased by a pair of smaller birds. Swifts or sparrows or swallows, he doesn't know. They dog-fight above his head, and as he walks, he looks up and watches.

His heart jumps in his chest.

It can't be.

Another illusion.

It's Alison.

Dead ahead. A hundred feet before the intersection. Marching toward him with eerie purpose and grim determination.

"Al," he says. Again not sure if this is a trick. "Alison. Is that really you?"

She just stares. Continuing her dread march.

Something glints in her hand.

A knife. It's a knife.

Cason's not sure what to do. Run? Hug her? Try to dispel the illusion somehow?

He stands at the ready. Defensive position. Hands up, palms out. "Alison, stop right there. Okay? I'm going to need you to—"

He feels it even before he registers what happens. Her hand moves, and with a flick of her wrist the knife leaves her grip and... he paws at his throat, finds the hilt sticking out. His words dissolve into a gassy gurgle.

She picks up speed. Crashes into him.

Alison wrenches the knife free and brings it down again. And again. And again. The blade perforating his chest. Lungs. Heart. Everything else.

Something Psyche said scratches at his mind:

But if someone takes out your heart or your head, you're still deader than a pocket of dust...

Heart or head.

Pocket of dust.

All goes black.

CHAPTER THIRTY-EIGHT
Eschatology

CASON FINDS HIMSELF standing in a dimly lit tunnel. Walls of wet rock. Flickering green torchlight. He gasps. Feels his chest. His face. His throat.

No wounds. No injuries.

Ahead—the tunnel splits into two. The right tunnel heads up, the left down. A swimmy orange glow pulses in the left-most tunnel, like someone way down there is tending a forge. The right path offers a bright light—like looking into the spotlight from a helicopter flying overhead, a winking starburst of white.

A man sits between the two.

No. Not a man.

Men don't have wings.

This man is naked. Though, given the appearance of what's between his legs, he might not be a man at all—it's a puckered, leathery pouch, a ruined coinpurse of flesh

The wings are white of feather, but patchy. Feathers gone, showing empty circles of gooseflesh skin—the skin white. Not Caucasian, but white. Like alabaster.

The man's shriveled face looks up.

"How... interesting," he says.

"Interesting. I don't understand."

"No. I suppose you wouldn't." The winged man's voice is almost monotone. Little inflection. "I am the Archangel Michael."

Blink, blink.

"Oh," Cason says. He's not really sure what else to say. "I'm Cason."

"Are you." The angel stands. Bones creaking and popping. He looks Cason up and down at a distance. "You're blooded." Suddenly, the angel's lip twists into a sneer. "You have *his* blood. The Betrayer. The Thorn."

Lucifer. The Devil.

"I do. But I'm not... him."

"You'll be wanting the Hell path, then." The angel cocks his head toward the leftmost tunnel. "Though you won't find much down there anymore. An empty palace. Dead furnaces. Forgotten pits and eyeless worms squirming in the deep dark, hungry for something—souls, company, amusement, but nothing there for them, nothing at all." The angel squints. "Unless you've come to take the throne. One supposes that is an option."

"The throne. Heaven's throne."

"Yes. Is that why you're here? I knew someone would come eventually. It's empty up there, too. The angels are still home, but we shrivel without our maker. We're nothing without the Master. We're like dried bugs now—curled up on our backs, feathers fallen, our swords gone dark. Kick one and he'll crumble to ash. I'm the only one left standing, and I don't know how long I've got left." The angel watches Cason. "You're still shocked from the passing. You have died. You see that, don't you? You're dead."

"I can't be dead."

"You can, and are." Michael waves him on. "Come. Let's go see the chair."

THERE COMES A noise inside her head like a hard burst of radio static—a sharp dagger of noise. And then it all comes flooding back.

Her husband. His face. Their wedding. Their honeymoon. Their fights. *Their* son—not her son, but *theirs.*

She remembers burning alive in a car.

Then, once it all snaps in place, she sees.

The knife in her hand. So wet. So red.

It clatters to the ground.

Her husband is beneath her. Bloodslick. Empty eyes. Mouth open in frozen horror.

She wails and falls upon him, sobbing.

Coyote watches her from the corn. Bending over the corpse, blubbering and shrieking. Grief makes him uncomfortable. It's so real, so strong. And such a boner-killer.

He's not sure if the golden thread is still intact. He has no sense of it. It's so thin, so frail—it may have already snapped. And if it did, this world is in dire straits.

At least he's got his penis back.

He whispers "sorry," because he knows he helped bring this moment to bear, whatever it means. Then he turns around and pads away on his four paws.

There. The Church.

The steeple rises out of the corn like a stalk taller than the rest.

Tundu, blank-eyed and shuffle-footed, carries the boy while the Devil saunters ahead. He's close, now. It took him too long to walk here—five miles, what a bear—but the delay will be for naught. Because what could've happened in that time?

It matters little.

Hopefully Frank did his one last job and called ahead.

Because the Devil needs a Holy Man if he's to enter Heaven.

Frank rolls over.

The clouds above him shift and part. One cloud is three clouds.

His vision, ruined. He's got a concussion. He knows that. Doesn't know what it means, but he knows he's got one.

Skull, dented like a can. Cracked like an egg.

Should've made sure the big fucker was dead. He didn't.

And now here he is.

He can barely feel his legs. His heels scratch the ground, mostly for naught.

Then the smell reaches him, and it's here he *knows* he's going crazy. Because he's in the middle of Kansas, not the beach, and he's smelling beach sands and ocean wind and—

Oh. *Oh*.

Aphrodite appears above him.

He smiles. Laughs. "I love you," he tells her.

"I know you do."

"It's why I did it all. To get close to you. To get away from you. To spite you. All out of love. Love I can't control. You made me love you."

"I did. But you are who you are and were who you were, even before I got to you."

"Can you make me handsome again? The Devil said he'd make me handsome again. Please. *Please*."

She sighs. He hears the ocean surf coming on, fading out.

Her hand waves over his face.

Then she moves her face closer.

Her eyes, like pools of water. Green, blue, shimmering. He can see himself in that gaze. He's beautiful. It's returned to him. The scars are gone. His heart dances. He blinks. *He blinks*. He can blink!

"Goodbye, Frank," she says.

Then she closes her eyes.

His skin splits, like a sausage casing too long on the grill. Like window blinds retracted. Everything is hot. All is pain. He feels like a boiled lobster.

Frank Polcyn dies.

THE SKINLESS MAN writhes once, yelps like a kicked puppy, then expires.

Psyche finds it all rather grotesque. Her mother-in-law is cruel. She knows that. And her last kindness to him somehow makes it all the crueler.

But he deserved it. She takes no joy in what happened, but she finds no grief for him, either. What she *did* find, however, was in his mind. In his last hour.

She sees what happened to Tundu.

Sees the Devil. Sees the boy.

She knows where they're going.

She tells this all to Aphrodite.

"I want to fix things," Psyche says. "I want to go and help."

"We should just go home."

"The Devil is free. Doesn't that concern you?"

"Yes, and that's why I want to stay out of his way. I'll call the others. We'll make a plan. We have time."

Psyche sees what harm the Devil can do. She knows why he's going. It was in Frank's mind and now it's in hers. The Throne of Heaven is empty. Open to be claimed.

Which means there's no time at all.

But she dare not tell Aphrodite.

A world with her as the One True Goddess...

It would be a beautiful world, and so wretched.

"Please. Let me fix this. I'll come home with you then."

Aphrodite seems to ponder, then nods. "Go."

Psyche lets her wings unfurl. She takes flight, catches a heat vector, and moves fast as the wind.

THE MINISTER STAMMERS: "Please, don't hurt me."

He says that because, of course, he's scared. Lucifer can see the fear in the fat man's eyes. Big black dude, gut-shot. Comatose child.

But really, it's his own presence. The presence of the Devil.

God's zealots can smell it on him. They know when they're in the midst of God's Own Scourge. Their stomachs curdle. Their pubes curl. They *know*.

This poor idiot thought he was going to consult on a marriage.

That's what Frank told him. And here he is, swayed by the stupidest of lies so as to meet the shirtless Infernal Lord face-to-face.

"I have to," Lucifer says, shrugging.

Then: Lightbringer's flickering glass blade is in his hand and he beheads the poor fool. The head bounces away like a soccer ball.

The Devil drags the body, one-handed, up onto the dais of this little church. Then he tells Tundu what to do.

The big bastard lays the child down on one of the empty pews, then walks over to the headless, twitching corpse and stomps on it, again and again.

Blood pumping. Squirting, even. Pooling.

It's enough.

The Devil goes and picks up the boy. He steps into the pool of blood, does a little tapdance and says a little evil prayer—Babelian tongue, a string of heretical glossolalia. Then both he and the child sink into the blood and are gone.

Heavenbound, they go.

MICHAEL AND CASON stand on a mirrored black floor, like hematite pounded flat.

All around lie the carcasses of angels.

Hundreds, thousands of them. Desiccated, shriveled. Mouths stretched wide, eyes like raisins placed delicately in puckered sockets. Hands still clutching sword hilts without blades. "My brothers," Michael says. "This way."

He points ahead—the gleaming floor drops off into nothing, down into the infinity of clouds and storms. Ahead, the throne floats.

It's a throne of glass. Like in his dreams, but in the glass he sees no skulls—it's just smooth, no sharp edges, all curves. It shifts. Like it's liquid, almost.

Maybe not glass at all.

The throne rests on a golden disc, and beneath that golden disc are draped thousands upon thousands of wires—golden, gleaming, some red like copper, others burnished like bronze, some thick, others thin, but all some shade of gold. The filaments go as far as the eye can see and then some. They bundle here but then splay out, separating and sinking through a layer of clouds far, far below.

Cason sees no way to reach the throne.

Michael senses his confusion. The angel waves a lazy hand—

And a walkway forms out of smaller golden discs. One after the other.

"Go ahead," Michael says. "It's yours. You merely need to sit upon it."

"I don't want it."

"Why?"

"Because I don't want that kind of power. Or that responsibility."

"But you would become God."

"I don't want that."

Michael looks disappointed. And confused. "Oh."

"I'm... sorry."

"It appears as if I won't have a new M—"

He is split in twain by a glass blade, cutting his sentence short.

The two halves of the Archangel Michael flop to each side. The angel's innards are dry, like burned paper; bits of him flutter up in a non-existent wind.

"I always hated him," the Devil says. "So pompous. So *righteous*. He's the prick who threw me down, down, down. When there wasn't yet a Hell path to walk."

Cason gapes. Staggers backward.

"Hello, *oh, fruit of the fruit of my loins*." The Devil gives a curt wave. "Hey, look. I have something of yours."

From behind him steps Barney.

"Hello, Daddy," Barney says.

Cason can't contain it. He hurries to the child, throws his arms around him. He picks up the boy and backpedals. "Shh, it's okay, Barney. It's okay."

But the boy doesn't hug him back. He hangs there. Almost limp.

Cason rubs the boy's back just the same. To the Devil, he says:

"You shouldn't have taken my son."

"I wanted a prince at my side. He'll do. Unless you want the role?" The Devil slaps a knee. "Hey! I could have my own divine Trinity.

The Devil, the Great-Grandson and the Unholy Ghost. Works for me. You in?"

"Go to Hell."

"Cute. A joke. Though a joke is only a joke if it's funny, and I'm not really all that amused right now. So, if you don't want the job, fine. Stand down and let me have the boy. I'll take good care of him up here. I promise."

"You'll not touch him again."

Lucifer shrugs. "Pity you think so."

Then the glass sword is again in his hand—he crosses the distance in the bat of a fly's wing and there's the blade, and it's coming down on Cason's head.

CHAPTER THIRTY-NINE
Musical Chairs

THE BLADE DOESN'T make it to his skull.

It cracks hard against something.

Lucifer stands there, wincing. "Antlers. Really."

Cason flicks his gaze upward. Sure enough, he sees the shadowy tangle of antlers rising from his brow. His head feels hot. He smells an animal musk.

He growls. With a twist of his head, he sends the blade spiraling away. It falls as just a hilt against the earth.

"A gift from your Daddy," the Devil says with a snort.

Cason lunges forward, impaling the Devil on his antler spires. He roars—a sound in no way human but in all ways his own—and braces himself as he puts his back and neck into it, lifting Lucifer up off the ground.

"You know—" Lucifer says, voice hitching as he sinks down deeper on the horns. "You can't—kill me—*nnngh*—like this."

"I can keep you from the throne," Cason snarls.

"Can you? Have you—*urrrk*—seen your son lately?"

Cason looks.

Barney.

Where is Barney?

Suddenly the child is on him. Crawling up his side like a bear cub scampering up a tree, the Devil's blade in his hand. Cason pivots, tries to grab for his son—the child shrieks, that too an inhuman sound, and above them both the Devil coughs and cackles: "He's my boy now—" *Cough, hack.* "I've got his mind. I've got his soul!"

The glass blade extends, *swipe, swipe*.

Pain lances down through Cason's head like a jet of hot lava.

The Devil tumbles free, the horns still stuck inside him. Barney's cut off the antlers at the base.

The child leaps free of his father.

It's all going sideways.

The Devil laughs, staggers onto the first of the golden discs leading to the throne—

Cason moves to follow, but his own son stands in his way, the glass blade weaving in the air—

He can't attack his own son.

Can't do it.

He does that, the boy will fall. Maybe him, too. Down, down into the emptiness, into the golden wires, through the clouds and—where? Cason doesn't know.

He can do only what he can do. Which is fall to his knees as the Devil takes the throne.

PSYCHE KNEELS IN the blood of the minister and pounds the earth; red flecks her cheeks and shirt as she does so.

Tundu sits against the pew, wheezing, rasping.

"I can't do anything for you now," she tells him.

"Help the boy," he says, then spits blood in his hand.

She presses her forehead against the wet red puddle. Sticky. Warm.

She can feel him out there. Down through the closing channel. She can't make it through, but maybe, just maybe—

Her mind can.

* * *

THE DEVIL SITS.

The glass throne roils. Dark plumes like ink fill the glass. The golden wires dangling beneath the glass throne turn red, then black, as white pulses of light travel their lengths, forming the wisps of glowing skulls. The Devil grins, begins picking antler and bone out of his bare chest.

He sees the boy keeping Cason at bay. Good child. Good little prince.

But then the boy's head snaps up, and he wheels toward the Devil. The young prince walks along the golden discs toward the throne. Cason calls after his son. "*Barney, noooo.*" Bit of a whiner, that one.

Lucifer spins his finger in the air. "Little Prince. Turn back around and go cut off your Daddy's head, will you? I'm tired of hearing his mewling."

But the boy doesn't turn around. He keeps coming.

This is awkward.

"No, no, I don't want to play right now, little boy. Go. *Go.*" He feels power surging through him, suddenly—the divine awareness is electric. His mind leaves this place for just a moment, and he sees everything about all the worlds. The Seven Heavens and the Realms of Hell, Earth and Sky and Ocean, cosmic wormholes and twisting stars, eternal forests and impossible mazes. All the men and the mice, all the falcons and all the fish. All the fallen gods and goddesses, heroes and monsters.

He can change it all. He can remake the world in his image.

There's a sound of a little cough in front of him. A throat clearing.

He opens his eyes, irritated at the interruption. There stands the boy.

He speaks in his voice. But also in another voice. A woman's voice. Cupid's bitch. Psyche.

"The throne is what you always wanted," he/she says.

And he thinks to vaporize the child's body with his mind, but he doesn't get the chance.

The child swings the Devil's own blade upward. Lightbringer cuts through the side of the glass throne and carves off a piece. A very sharp piece.

"What do you think you're—"

The boy plunges the shard into the Devil's throat.

HEAVEN SHUDDERS. THE red wires snap, hiss, shake as if in hurricane winds—all the dead angels suddenly sit up and moan, before again falling back down into torpor. Cason watches the events unfold— his son walking toward the throne, then carving off a piece of it to plunge into the Devil's neck.

The Devil bursts into flames. He shakes and writhes, screaming. Cason runs, feet bounding across the discs as they tremble beneath him. He grabs his son, scoops him up just as the Devil's flesh turns to magma.

It melts into the chair, and becomes part of the glass.

Again the wires go dark. The chair stops pulsing.

And Heaven is still.

"Daddy?" Barney asks.

Cason hugs him. The boy cries. Not a full-on sob: just the quiet whimpering of a very scared, very confused child.

But he sets the boy down. He tells him, "You cross over. You go on back. I'll be right there. I promise. There's... something I have to do first."

Then he takes the sword from the child and gently urges him.

"Daddy, I don't wanna."

"You have to. Hurry. I'll be there."

Barney crosses over, crying. Cason calls for his son to be careful. And not to fall.

He sighs, holding the blade. The glass extends, the edge gleaming as blue fire flickers inside of it. He thinks to sit—knows he could— maybe even *should*. A little voice reminds him that he's dead; genuine dead. This might be the only way to keep on going. And it would always let him stay in touch with his wife, his son. He could give them everything. He could give them the world on a platter.

He raises the blade above his head.

But then he realizes: it would be a gift, wouldn't it? To be God. To have that power. Barney would grow up to be president. Alison would never die unless Cason allowed her to, and then they could rule this place—and all the worlds—together.

A perfect dream.

He's never been a fan of perfect.

He cleaves the throne in twain.

CHAPTER FORTY
Falling

HEAVEN BREAKS APART like a cookie crumbling in a man's grip. Shards and fragments. Golden discs and severed wires.

Cason falls, and so does his son.

They find one another in the whipping winds. Pieces raining down all around them. Angel bodies tumble. Cason holds his child tight as they turn and tilt and rocket downward, the boy wailing, now, sobbing at these moments—Cason doesn't know what's happening, or where they're going, but he knows this isn't good. He thinks, *this must be what it's like to fall out of a plane, to have it break apart and to plummet to the earth below.* A fear that gives way to peace assails him. He whispers in his son's ear, tells him it'll all be fine. Even though he knows that it won't.

Something grabs him, lashes around him.

And pulls him back up.

HE AND THE boy are drawn up through what feels like Hell's asshole. It's soft and hot and burns the skin and—

They both belch up out of a puddle of blood and onto the floor.

Nearby lays a minister's corpse.

Cason gasps, grabs Barney, scoops him up and covers his eyes. All he says is, "We're here. We're home. It's okay. Shh. Shhhh."

There stands Psyche, looking frazzled and freaked out.

And Tundu sits on a nearby pew. Gut-shot. Gray-skinned. Eyes staring ahead, empty. Dead as dead.

"Oh, shit," Cason says, feeling his own tears starting to well up.

Except, then Tundu gasps. His body stiffens. Eyes roll around in his head like loose marbles.

"He's still alive," Psyche says. "I've tried to soothe his mind. Calm his shock. But he needs a hospital soon, or he's going to die."

Cason nods. "I... okay. I don't know how."

"I'll take him," she says. Wings erupt from her back.

"My wife. She's... out there somewhere. I need her."

Psyche touches his brow.

He can see Alison. Out there. In the corn. Sobbing over—

My own corpse.

He knows just where she is. He kisses his son's cheek, tells the boy it's time to go see Mommy, and it's time to go home.

PAT KELLEHER

DRAG HUNT

PROLOGUE
Run to Ground

England, six months ago.

ACHING WITH AGUE, his joints stiff with age, the tramp ran, though he could barely remember how. In desperation, he cast aside the bundle of plastic bags containing all his hoarded worldly possessions, nothing now but ballast. They split as they hit the ground, their contents scattered to the winds as he fled.

He couldn't understand why they were chasing him. He couldn't even remember his name; it had been so long since anyone had used it. But he remembered fear, and he ran.

He darted through the bedraggled copse beyond the abandoned industrial estate, all that remained of the wildwood that once dominated his dreams, now a haunt of underage drinkers and doggers—old rituals turned sour. He loped down old tracks that no longer existed in anything but his threadbare memory. It wasn't even conscious. It was pure instinct.

In the dark, black hounds, eyes glowing as red as torturers' coals, bayed at his heels.

* * *

HE'D SPENT HIS day in the town centre, the kingdom of his prime, reduced to a pile of jealously guarded soggy cardboard boxes and shopping bags, under bowers of concrete blooming with graffiti. In his dreams, people sought him out with offerings, for blessings. Now, invisible, forgotten, he had to beg.

Then *they* showed up.

The silver-haired businessman with the woollen coat had dropped loose change into his broken polystyrene cup.

"I'm sorry," the businessman had said.

The tramp gave him an uncomprehending toothless grin, and watched as the man walked away, taking a small glass tablet from his pocket, and drawing mystical runes on its surface.

"Found him," the businessman said to it. "A genius loci, no doubt."

Spooked, the tramp gathered up his dirty blanket, plastic bags and cardboard, and shuffled off. Maybe he was a council man. He looked the type. It was time to move on, anyhow. The shops were shutting. Their skips would be filling with out-of-date foods. Sandwiches and cakes. Left for him, like the votive offerings of his dreams.

NOW, AIR ESCAPED from his lungs in long, dry rasps. Lank, wet, yellow-grey hair lashed his face as he glanced behind him at the pursuing shadows.

The ground fell away beneath him. He tumbled down the embankment, staggered, dazed and half-blinded, onto the motorway.

He whirled, confused. Around him, rushing lights striated in the hard biting rain. Squeals and screeches filled the night air as metallic monsters roared by. He threw up his arms against the light as cars swerved to avoid him, horns blaring.

He took momentary refuge on the central reservation, before crossing the far lanes in a mad pirouetting dash and scrambling up the embankment on the other side.

Cold, biting rain whipped across the moors above the town. He stumbled over the heather and across the bog that held the bodies of those willingly sacrificed to him, bodies long since drained of any sacred power he might have drawn from them.

They were getting closer.

Why? They didn't need to do this. He was no threat to anyone.

But his pursuers knew the old ways. They had beaten his bounds. They had run him to earth. The boundaries of his dominion had become a cage. Now they were closing in. There was only one place left to run.

The stones rose above him on the brow of Hillstone Howe. Ancient and solitary, the stone circle, known as the Devil's Fingers, had stood there since the town of Bridstowe had been naught but a ford across the river. They had weathered the centuries better than he had. He hobbled in desperation toward its centre, to the tall stone that stood there.

The air burned in his chest as he reached out to touch the greasy wet surface of the menhir, and trace the illegible weathered runes carved into its lichen-poxed surface. He rested his forehead against the soothing cool damp of the stone. In his dreams, this was the seat of his tiny realm. His sacred place. His hearg. The one place he should be safe.

"You gave us good sport!" a voice called through the wind.

The tramp turned his back against the stone.

"Go away! I ain't done nuffin'."

The large black hounds prowled round the edge of the stone circle, low growls issuing from curled black lips. The hound master, a slim man with black hair, jet black eyes and an insolent smile, called out.

"Little god, little god, can we come in?"

A man with auburn hair strode from the shadows and took a defiant step into the stone circle. He looked about, as if expecting something to happen. Nothing did. A grin split his face.

He opened his arms wide. "What, no welcome? Have you forgotten your fridh?"

The tramp dug his heels into the dirt to scrabble backwards, but the stone was hard at his back. There was no further retreat. "What do you want? What do you want from me?"

He saw the well-dressed businessman with his phone, hanging

back. Is that how he got his kicks, having his bullyboys beat up defenceless old men?

"You... you ain't a bunch of them happy slappers, are you?" He'd heard apocryphal tales on the grapevine, of homeless men torched in bus shelters for the entertainment of teenage bastards with nothing better to do.

The auburn haired man shook his head in despair. "That new bypass weakened you, practically drove a stake right through your heart. We're just finishing the job. See it as a mercy killing. You can't survive much longer anyway.

"Look to yourself. Your name is long lost. You are dying, decade by decade. You are tied to this place, to the past, and it is killing you. I can give you a future. Or we can leave you and your eventual death can be meaningless. It is the Wyrd. Your choice here will have consequences. This way, you will live on, become part of something greater." He looked around. The sickly dirty orange glow of the conurbation leeched over the hills. In the distance, the constant rubber rumble of the motorway rushed like a river. He waved a dismissive hand. "This is no place for gods. House god, show him."

Bristling at the name, the businessman in the woollen greatcoat and scarf stepped forward and crouched down on his haunches, pinching and pulling his trousers at the knees fastidiously as he did so. He placed his palms either side of the tramp's head, and searched his rheumy eyes.

"You've lost your memories. I know where they are."

Under his touch, the tramp felt the truth of the words. He remembered now. Those who dwelt around here once worshipped him, they used to seek him out, ask favours and boon. He remembered the offerings, the sacrifices and the fornicating in his honour, but now, all that remained were embers of his greatness and they were fast fading to ashes. He was old and tired, the glories of his youth long behind him. He had been dying for centuries, piece by piece, his spirit necrotising under a creeping industrialisation that spread like a canker across his ward. He was forgetting who he was, what he was. Fading. His end was inevitable.

He drew a great sucking breath, like a drowning man come to air. It was as if he had shed a great burden, although he could no longer say what it was; but the relief was palpable. He relaxed, slumping back against the standing stone. The tramp looked up and smiled, his puffy red eyes welling with tears, nose running with snot. At last, he knew. He remembered. He looked up at the auburn haired man.

"Something greater. You promise?" he asked with a note of desperation, as if this moment of lucidity was only fleeting and would soon be gone again.

The auburn haired man nodded.

The tramp stood up with some measure of pride now in his bearing, an echo of the being he once was. "Then I give it, willingly."

The auburn haired man stood over him and from a sheath at his hip drew a knife, its blade etched with runes.

The man grabbed his hair and pulled his head back, exposing the pale throat, its pores blackened with grime beneath the dirty yellow-grey beard. With a swift movement, he slit the tramp's throat with the knife. Black liquid welled up from the gash.

"Thank... you," said the tramp, his voice a hoarse whisper as his eyes locked with those of his redeemer.

"Quick!" hissed the auburn haired man. "His sacrifice here isn't enough. Catch his ichor. We need his godsblood."

Another man stepped forward with a large ornate two-handled silver phial, catching the vital fluid that issued from the wellspring of the tramp's throat, filling the container and stoppering it.

The tramp's body stiffened. His wretched jumble of clothing appeared to swell, but it was his body shrivelling, the black ichor escaping from his throat now transforming, on contact with the air, into a swirling black vapour, like greasy smoke, that was caught in the rain, dissolved in relentless drops, and pounded back into the earth.

The sodden clothing crumpled, empty, to the ground.

Within moments, the wind began to shriek round the stones, as if the very earth were keening for the loss of its warden.

And in the sodium twilight of the town below, the dogs began to howl.

CHAPTER ONE
Coyote Makes His Mark

THE COYOTE LOPED through the brush of the Mojave desert, toward the heat-rippled vertical smudges of civilisation in the distance.

He loved the rocks, the sand, this shrub here, that abandoned, half-buried shopping trolley over there. He loved it all.

He looked at the sinking sun and grinned. He did that. Him. He gave sunlight to the world. He stole it from right under Owl's wing. Some might consider it a mere etiologic tale, but every word of it was true. It was in books and everything.

And here, in the Mojave desert, mortals had briefly created their own man-made sun. The power of creation and destruction, once held to be the purview of gods. Some gods didn't like that. Not Coyote, though. He admired humans for it. How far they'd come since he stole fire for the People. He found them fascinating.

He raised his nose into the wind catching the scents, searching for something. He found it, stopped, inhaled deeply and licked his chops. Women in ranches. Like hens. Heh. A coyote in the hen house. He tried to smile although he'd never quite got the hang of it. It looked like he was just baring his teeth, but inside... inside he was smiling. Lewdly.

The serenity of the desert evening was shattered by a loud, shrill fart.

"Shut up. Nobody asked you," said the coyote, flicking his tail.

To his left, a cluster of small rocks toppled from an outcrop.

"And the world agrees with me!" the coyote declared with satisfaction.

He sat and watched from a vantage point as the sun set and the lights of the town flickered into life below it. The Sky Beam pierced the evening sky.

The coyote sighed, flicked his tail and headed down into Las Vegas.

EYES OPENED HESITANTLY as he surfaced to consciousness. Reality trickled in. He took in the small environment about him; snapshots of indeterminate ground, like a NASA Mars robot testing its camera. He waited for his focus to adjust, while his senses flooded with data—mostly pain—until he was drowning in it.

He was slumped against the side of a dumpster in a puddle of his own piss. His chinos were wet and cold at the crotch. He put a hand to his head. His fingers came away covered with tiny rust flakes of dried blood. Unable to breathe through his nose, he prised a dried plug of bloodied snot from his nostril with a fingernail and the iron tang caught the back of his throat as he hawked up.

He needed a little help here. He patted himself down. Nothing was broken. Sore, yes. But not broken. No wallet. No ID. No hotel key card. Great.

Something bobbed to the surface. A name. Green. Richard Green. It was quickly followed by the floating memory turds of recent events.

He let out a groan.

No matter how stubbornly he tried to flush them away, the unsavoury facts of his life remained.

A month before, he had had a small but comfortable flat, a safe, if boring, job and a girlfriend, Becky. He'd been happy. Well, not happy exactly, content maybe. But you couldn't be happy all the time. Happiness was moments. Brilliant moments to be sure, but they never lasted. They were the highs, the peak of the wave. Contentment was more of your cruising altitude. Only he'd nosedived from contentment into despair.

Britain had been dogged by outbreaks of misfortune. 'Bad Luck Britain!' the tabloids cawed, gleefully cataloguing the latest misfortunes: a refinery fire in the North East, fourteen dead; three dead from a collapsing church spire in the Midlands.

And six months ago, the tide of bad luck lapped Bridstowe; a multiple pile-up on the bypass, a young kiddy gone missing, the local team on a losing streak that would cost them the final if they couldn't pull their bloody finger out, a swingeing round of cuts from the council. And then, without warning, he was laid off from the electrical chain store where he worked. That was when Becky left him. At least, he had his redundancy pay. That was something.

"You've never done anything with your life. Now's the chance," his mates had said down the Desk and Jockey pub. "Go to Las Vegas, live a little!"

Dave had gone on a stag do. It was proper brilliant, apparently.

It was pointless trying to argue over the blare of the HDTV music channel on the flat screen above their heads, so he'd nodded and grinned, unconvinced at the time, as Dave regaled them with tales of the luck, loot and lewdness to be had. Slightly pissed, a crooked smile slewed across Richard's face as he listened, and the idea grew on him. He staggered back from the pub a little the worse for wear. Before he'd had a chance to sober up and consider the proposition, he'd toggled on his tablet, booked the flights and the hotel.

He'd show Becky.

Oh, yeah. He'd shown her all right. At first Richard didn't realise he could move and, when he did, it hurt. He levered himself upright, leaning heavily on the dumpster, and staggered into the street.

There sidewalk hawkers taunted him with flyers for ranch houses, brothels and escorts. Gaggles of women staggered down the street in impossibly high heels, clutching popcorn-sized buckets full of Margaritas.

Richard glowered at them all right now. He resented Las Vegas with every fibre of his being. He begrudged every cheery raucous shout and smiling face. He hated the gaudy neon lights and huge monumental edifices to greed that rose from every corner.

Las Vegas had shrugged off the resentment of millions of losers; chewed them up, parted them from their cash and their dreams, and spat them out. It didn't notice one more.

Richard Green wandered the Strip in a daze, his mind fixated on the stranger who had got him into this mess in the first place, and his vitriol reserved for the one place that got him into this mess in the first place, the Olympus.

"'Trust me, I have a system...'" he muttered to himself in a mocking whine. He shook his head in disbelief at his own gullibility. "Fuck."

FOR THIRTY YEARS, the Olympus had been the biggest draw in Las Vegas, popular with tourists for its amazing light show. The Bellagio and Luxor both attempted to ape its grandeur and its sheer opulence, but ultimately paled into insignificance. Still, the sympathetic magic worked, up to a point.

Set back from Las Vegas Boulevard, a curved avenue lined with statues of athletically posed Greek heroes led up to it and, nestled within the curve, a full-sized Parthenon sat in front of the hotel complex.

Atop the seventy-floor, white, ancient-Greek-themed building, was a classical Greek temple. This acropolis was as far above the tourists below as the gods were above mortals, and just as unreachable. Each evening, a bank of clouds rolled out from the summit of the Olympus, an ephemeral stage for an aerial Light Spectacular, a show of musical thunder and multicoloured lightning flashing within the clouds, while CGI spectacles were projected up onto the cloud base as Greek myths played out above the tourists' heads.

In the Parthenon, half naked, bronzed and oiled Spartans flexed and posed for the tourists, with refrains of "This. Is. Vegas!" to the squeals of delight from giddy women old enough to know better, but old enough not to care.

It was top of the list for every tourist and Richard had been no exception. It was all part of the genuine Las Vegas experience. The brochures said so. Not that he could afford to stay there. Still, it was something to tick off his list.

Richard pushed through the crowd of tourists, the space filled with the chirps of cameras and smartphones pecking at the sights like ravenous gulls.

The foyer of the hotel complex was the size of an international airport check-in hall, although more opulent and with more Doric columns and marble floors. It could have been the lobby for heaven itself.

At the far end of the foyer, a waterfall dropped several storeys into a river. Bridges led over it to the main complex: the Golden Fleece Casino, the Elysium Lounge and Bar Lethe.

Beyond was a labyrinth of slots, full of Mino-tourists. Row upon row of machines beeping and chirping like one-armed idols as the faithful ploughed offerings into them.

"It's a joyful sound, isn't it?" said a voice at his shoulder. He turned to see a tall, lanky man, dusky skinned with a prominent hawk-like nose and long, black hair pulled back in a ponytail.

Richard frowned. "Pardon?"

The man, who could have been a Native American, cocked his head at the sound. "You're British. Love the accent."

"Uh, thanks."

Richard made to walk away. He didn't really want to get into conversation.

"Your first time in Vegas?"

"That obvious, huh?"

"You look lost." Coyote held out his hand. "They call me Kai." He smiled a self-assured smile. A Danny Ocean smile. It oozed charm and affability. It was the easy smile of an old friend, the older brother Richard never had. The smile washed over him. This was a man he could trust.

Disarmed, Richard took his hand and shook it. "Richard. Richard Green."

Kai's eyes twinkled, lighting up with an easy smile. "So, Richard." A hand dropped on his shoulder as they eyed the slots together. "Want to be a winner?"

"Christ, yes."

They walked though the aisles of slots across plush carpet that did nothing to muffle the electronic beeps, whoops and musical cascades. They passed the Elysium Lounge and headed up the wide stairs that swept toward the Golden Fleece Casino, where a spotlit gold-coloured fleece hung in pride of place on the wall, like a trophy.

Richard hesitated.

So far he had been sensible. Sure, he had his redundancy pay, but he wasn't going to lose it all in Vegas. He wasn't stupid. Gamble only as much as you can afford to lose, he'd heard once. He figured how much of his money he could afford to burn and decided that was his limit. So far, he'd lost a chunk but had managed to make some of it back. He wasn't willing to risk too much more. Safe, dependable, boring old Richard. That, he had decided bitterly, was ultimately what cost him Becky.

Kai winked at Richard and tapped his prominent nose. "Trust me, I have a system," he said. "You'll get your capital back plus a share of the winnings."

Richard found himself at the casino ATM, surprised to realise he'd withdrawn his entire redundancy package. Sod it. He was going to be quids in. Sod Satellite Electricals. Sod Becky. He was a winner and Kai had a system. He couldn't lose. His confidence was unassailable. They made a beeline for the blackjack tables. Some other players nodded as they took their seats.

"Gentlemen," acknowledged the dealer. With a practised hand, he slid them their cards.

Kai, a shit eating grin on his face, glanced at each of the players in turn.

So much for a poker face, thought Richard.

Chips crossed the table, more chips and cards crossed back. They stayed for a few hands. Richard noticed Kai slip his hand into his jeans pocket. What was that, some kind of device, a card counter maybe? Shit. Alarmed, Richard glanced around, hoping no one else had noticed.

Kai caught him in the beam of his smile and everything was all right again.

Richard watched as Kai raked in their winnings and pushed his chair back.

"Thanks, fellas."

They moved on to baccarat. Richard didn't even know what baccarat was. It was just something James Bond played. Was it James Bond? Probably. Strangely, he didn't know much of anything. Couldn't think. It was as if someone had taken his brain out and stuffed it with cotton wool. But that was okay. He had Kai.

Kai, his hand still straying to his trousers, was sufficiently cunning to lose often enough not to arouse suspicion.

Richard remembered the clatter of the roulette ball. The chips stacking up, pile after pile. Kai knew what he was doing.

Then Richard had a sudden attack of lucidity, like a small eddy clearing a patch of fog in his mind. He looked around. Kai was nowhere to be seen. Sod Kai, his money had gone too. Anxiety wringing out his insides like a wet flannel, he prairie dogged, glancing around the casino.

Two well dressed men, casino security, moved towards him like sharks through the sea of gamblers.

"If you'd like to accompany us, sir."

Of course he would. "Thank god, I've been conned. Someone's made off with all my winnings."

"Our footage showed nobody else."

Confusion clouded Richard's face. "What? But he was here. He took all my money. Aren't you going to get my money back?"

One man deftly guided Richard away from the tables and towards the casino entrance. Still, Richard was convinced that they'd soon have this sorted out. After all, they had CCTV. All sorts of security. Bound to.

"Let's take this somewhere else, sir. We don't want to cause a scene."

Scene? Richard blinked. "But surely you don't think—I'm the injured party here. I've been conned in your casino. I demand that you do something about it."

People glanced at the raised voice as they passed various gaming tables.

"We've had a complaint about you slot walking."

"Slot walking? I don't even know what that means."

They escorted him past the golden fleece, out of the casino and through the slots hall. Richard's face flushed with anger and embarrassment. Any attempt to stop or turn was met with a firmer pressure by the hand on his shoulder, steering him as surely as a tiller.

A golden fleece? Yes, it bloody well had been.

KAI WATCHED AS Richard was escorted out, and had a moment's guilt. No, not guilt, indigestion. He looked up at the golden fleece. He wondered what the punters would think if they knew it was the genuine article. He grinned, a coyote in sheep's clothing.

OUTSIDE, RICHARD TURNED and looked back at the hotel entrance. The two security men stood there, eyes fixed on him, as if they were trying to turn him to stone. He took an experimental step towards them. One adjusted his weight marginally—hands held low, palms facing in—and Richard thought better of it.

He wandered down the Avenue of Heroes toward the Strip in shock, past the bars and stores and the street entertainers. The night air cleared his head. It was like a rude awakening, as if someone had just snatched away a warm duvet and a comforting dream. Everything was too loud and bright.

People jostled round him with glances of annoyance as he stood on the sidewalk and looked in despair at his wallet. He stared at the ATM receipt. Everything, his savings, his redundancy. Gone. How was that possible? The bastard had cleaned him out. All he had to his name now was about fifty dollars, cash.

He had hoped that by leaving England the ill fortune that seemed to have dogged his life recently would be left behind. No such luck. So he wasn't entirely surprised when he felt the hard metal in the small of his back, and two men ushered him into the alley.

"Oh, for fuck's—"

A fist slammed into his solar plexus, driving the wind, and any chance at protest, from him. He doubled over and went down, pistol whipped on the back of the head as he crumpled, the jagged pain forking like lightning across his head. He tumbled forward, cracking his forehead on the tarmac, and bit his tongue.

In desperation he scuttled over to a dumpster, his back into the corner, arms over his face to protect himself.

Rough hands went through his pockets. He clawed at the air as they pulled his mobile from his pocket and picked up his wallet from the floor. It earned him a kick to the stomach. His body folded round the boot as it withdrew, only to catch another on his temple. Lights burst behind his eyelids and faded one by one, as darkness washed over him, like the waters of the fabled Lethe.

CHAPTER TWO
Coyote Interruptus

WINNING ALWAYS GAVE Coyote a boner. Putting one over on *anyone* gave him a boner. And there was only one thing you could do with that.

He lay in bed, hands clasped behind his head, his dark hair pooling on the silk pillows. Coyote in the hen house. It had been a good night.

He was in one of the most expensive penthouse suites in the Olympus. It had cost him most of his winnings, but he didn't care. It wasn't his money and he could always get more.

He loved the look on the faces of the other guests as they got into the elevator to see him stood there with five amazingly beautiful women, nymphs all. They didn't know where to look. Well, they did, but they tried desperately not to.

He grinned at the memory and took in a deep, contented breath. The room was heavy with sweat and sex. The women's musk hung in the air, their mascara blotted the pillows and the stains had dried and stiffened the silk sheets. Five nymphs, and none of them had any complaints. His appetites were as prodigious as his member.

He stretched out an arm. The large bed was empty. *Ha!* He wasn't surprised. No woman could trap Coyote, not even the nymphs that had once trapped Hylas.

Just the word 'woman' stirred feelings in him. He smiled and let out a contented sigh as he remembered last night's events.

His forehead creased and he opened his eyes. That wasn't right. That should have roused him. The silk sheet should be rising above him, tented by his tumescence in all its morning glory.

He sat up, arched his back and yawned. The silk sheet slipped down his torso and gathered round his pelvis. He looked around.

"Rise and shine, younger brother!" he said. "The sun is up and so should you be."

He lifted the sheet and looked down his body, over his pecs, to his abdomen where a faint trail of hairs darkened, thickened and curled. He'd lost his boner. Literally. Where his penis should have been, there was nothing.

"Come out, come out wherever you are," he said, looking around the suite.

Nothing.

He leaned over the side of the bed and peered underneath. Nothing there, either.

"Right, come out," he called out. "This isn't funny anymore."

He whistled and clapped his hands as if summoning a wayward terrier. He checked the pockets of his discarded jeans. He checked the pouch he sometimes used to carry it around in. It wasn't there. He scattered his patented Bonafide Penis Returning Powder across the suite. Nothing.

It wasn't the first time his member had gone missing. However, it had always come back before now and he could usually sense it, wherever it was. The disembodied sensations could be *distracting* to say the least, especially if he was trying to concentrate on something else. But now, he could feel nothing. Not a twinge, not a throb, not a pulse. That gave him cause for concern.

He farted.

"And you can bloody well shut up," he told his younger brother, anus. "You had one thing to do, one thing—keep your beady little brown eye on him. I'd punish you but I remember what happened last time."

Still, he wasn't that worried. He should have no problem tracking it down. After all, he had the keenest nose of all the People.

He sniffed the air. There were lingering traces in the room. He went to the door, opened it and sniffed the corridor in both directions. Nothing, no scent of ball sweat, or stale piss. He couldn't even sense its psychic imprint, which was disconcerting. He'd lost any connection he had with it. This, it seemed, was more than just an errant erection.

He went back into the suite and sat down on the bed in disbelief.

Someone had stolen his penis.

Who would want it? That answered itself, really. Who wouldn't? So it was just a process of elimination. He would have to play detective and, he suspected, he would be a brilliant detective.

Then he stopped. "Oh."

This detective lark was easier than he thought. Of course, it was obvious. He knew exactly who had taken his penis. Well, not exactly. But he'd narrowed it down to a few suspects. The usual suspects. Loki. Or the Monkey King. Anansi. Tezcatlipoca. Li-Nezha. Or that Bamapana. Or Ti-Malice. Tricksters, everyone. Bastards, the lot of them. He wouldn't put it past them. If it was him, he wouldn't have put it past himself.

He gathered up his discarded clothes from the floor, pulled on his T-shirt and climbed into his jeans.

He'd see about this. Nobody put one over on Coyote.

He picked up the phone and rang down.

"I want to see the manager," he said. A whiny subservient voice buzzed the earpiece. "No, everything is not all right. I have a complaint." Buzz buzz buzz. "Well see that they do!"

He hung up. It was a small victory. He ran through the evening before, tracing his steps. When did he last remember seeing it? He grinned, distracted by the memory. The look on her face!

There was a knock at the door.

That was quick. But then, the Olympus *was* run by a cartel of gods, so he should have expected it. Vegas had been a prime site for gods to set up house after the Great Usurper exiled them all down here. After all, here superstition still had a strong hold.

At least they were taking him seriously. He drew himself up to his full height and put on a scowl, and went to answer the door.

A tall, lithe bodied man stood in the doorway. Tailored suit. Hands clasped in front of his groin. Gelled blond hair. Expensive wrap-around shades. Behind him were two well-dressed heavyweights. Coyote recognised them as Anemoi or, as he liked to call them, the Breeze Brothers, a pair of minor Greek wind gods.

Blondie's tone was clipped and businesslike. "Coyote."

Coyote regarded the man for a moment. He'd been expecting some flunky he could have bamboozled and charmed, not *him*.

"Hermes."

Son of Zeus. Messenger of the gods. Trickster. Maybe he took it. He was certainly fast enough. A prime suspect if ever there was one. Coyote was curious to see how this one played out.

Hermes stepped into the suite, glancing at the money and chips strewn about the room. The Breeze Brothers stepped in behind him. Hermes turned his head and jerked his chin at the room.

One of the Breeze Brothers raised his hand and a small air current rippled across the floor, gathering up into a small whirlwind in the centre of the room that spun slowly around the suite, ruffling the silk sheets and sucking up Coyote's scattered winnings. It returned them to the wind god, before dissipating gently and depositing the cash and chips into the Anemoi's hands.

"I'm impressed," said Coyote, raising an eyebrow. "In fact, I know someone who'd like to meet you."

"I have a message," said Hermes.

"You would."

"The gods of Vegas are not happy."

"They're not happy? I'm livid."

"They want a word."

"Good, because I've a word or two I want to say to them. This kind of thing gets out and it could ruin reputations."

Hermes jerked his head towards the open door. "They're waiting, and trust me, that's not good."

"Well in that case, lead on."

Coyote allowed them to escort him along the corridor to an elevator. The public didn't ride this one. It was private. It went to the summit of the Olympus, where the gods dwelled.

Once in the elevator, Coyote cocked his head, listening to a voice only he could hear. "No, it's all right. Go on. Say hello. Don't be shy."

Coyote's anus let out a deep, vibrato fart.

"Sorry," he said, giving the Breeze Brothers an embarrassed shrug, and waving a hand under his nose. "What can I say, he's a big fan."

One of the gods scowled, made a small gesture, and a gentle breeze wafted round the elevator herding the noxious expulsion to the floor.

The doors opened and they stepped out onto the sixty-eighth floor, not so much where the gods dwelled, but where the gods did business. It was a large white pillared space, flooded with light, bounded as it was on three sides by floor to ceiling windows that looked out over Las Vegas. The fourth was a frescoed wall, in the middle of which was a set of wooden double doors, in the Grecian style. In the centre was what looked like a marble altar, although the position of a chair behind it and white leather sofa in front suggested it was actually a desk.

The doors swung open and a dwarf walked in with a rolling gait. He had an ugly scrunched face of dusky Hindu complexion, at odds with the immaculately tailored white suit he wore. He had the demeanour of a man who was extremely busy and had little time for all this.

Coyote frowned. "You're not Apollo. I thought he ran this place in his father's stead. Where is the guy with the swan fetish, anyway? I hear no one's seen him in over a decade."

He was looking for weak points, buttons to press.

"Apollo isn't going to trouble himself over an animistic brat like you, trickster," said the dwarf. "I'm Kubera, Treasurer of the Gods. I run the Olympus for the Greek Pantheon, Mr Coyote. Or do you prefer Raven, or perhaps Wakdjunkaga. Heyeohkah, maybe?"

Coyote feigned nonchalance, trailing a finger along the back of the white leather sofa as he walked round it.

"Kai is fine."

The Breeze Brothers placed Coyote's confiscated winnings on the marble desk. An offering, or evidence?

Coyote hadn't been invited to sit, so he sat, arms stretched out along the back of the sofa, his right ankle resting on his left knee, his crotch open and obvious. Despite the rather slack empty feeling in his jeans, and the nagging sense of loss, Coyote was enjoying himself. This had all the hallmarks of a shakedown. And he should know. They probably needed his help and wanted to make sure they got it, that's all. They wanted a little insurance, so they sent Little Miss Fleetfoot here to kidnap his pecker and hold it to ransom. It was classic. Boring, but classic. A bit of praise wouldn't have gone amiss, though. It always oiled the wheels. But, you know, gods. They didn't want to look soft.

"So, is this the point where you tell me I'll get my penis back if I do your dirty work for you?" he asked. "What is it, some inter-pantheon shenanigans? I expect you need Plausible Deniability. And a trickster."

"I'm afraid I have no idea what you're talking about," said Kubera, settling himself awkwardly into the chair behind the desk.

"You *don't* want my help?"

"Whatever for? We have Hermes. He's Pantheon. He knows the meaning of loyalty."

"Then if Hermes didn't take my penis, who did?" Perplexed, Coyote got up and started to pace.

Kubera, watching him like a snake, said nothing.

Coyote stopped and clicked his fingers. "I know. Uranus! He hasn't got his own. Not since his son Cronos castrated him, and mine would make a fine replacement. But, you know, seriously. Eww."

Kubera's faced darkened. "Be warned, trickster, this isn't the Farm. There is no neutrality here. Your calumny may have consequences."

Ignoring him, Coyote waved a finger, his mind racing. "Wait. I know. It's those Fate triplets, isn't it? The Graeae, the ones who have to share the eye. They're sharing my pecker and going all futanari on each other's asses." He fell silent, lost for a moment in a personal reverie.

Kubera fidgeted in his chair with increasing irritation. "I took you to be a more spiritual being."

"Oh, I am, when I'm at one. Unfortunately I'm not. I'm at two, at the very least." Coyote planted his hands on the desk, leaned forward in earnest and cocked his head. "Are you sure you don't have my penis?"

Kubera met his gaze. "I have told you, trickster. We don't have it. That is entirely your own problem. You leave your valuables unattended at your own risk. Besides, if you will carry it around in a pouch, that's your own lookout. No, I called you up here on an entirely different matter."

"Oh," said Coyote. His shoulders slumped under the weight of disappointment.

Kubera leaned forward, one hand patting the untidy pile of money and chips. "You have been using your talents to beat the house down in the casino. If you hadn't spent most of the money on one of our most luxurious suites, and if we hadn't recovered this, then we would have a bigger problem than we do already. Lucky for you there's enough left to cover the bill for the nymphs that you enjoyed last night. You know there are rules here. Gods don't avail themselves of the public casino."

"Odds are stacked, are they? The house always wins."

Kubera shrugged and sat back. "We have oracles, Moirai and Norns on the payroll, so yes, I suppose you could say that. But then gods rarely gamble for money. We have our own private casinos and games rooms, as well you know."

"So what are you going to do, chain me to a rock in the lobby to have my liver repeatedly pecked out on the hour?"

Kubera shook his head slowly. "I think not. Your reputation precedes you, trickster. If you're asking me to do it, I most certainly shan't."

"Spoilsport."

"No, instead we're going to cast you out of yet another heaven. It might hurt a little bit on the way down, but just think of it as a lesson." He nodded to the Breeze Brothers. "Gentlemen, escort Mr Coyote out. No need to be gentle. You're barred, Coyote. I never want to see you in the Olympus again."

Well, that didn't go as planned.

Hermes stood by the desk and watched. A crooked smirk of satisfaction crept across his face as the Breeze Brothers grabbed Coyote by the arms and escorted him towards the elevator.

Humiliated, Coyote found himself thrown ignominiously out of the Olympus with nothing between his legs but his tail.

A GOD STEPPED through the doors, his features lost in the glare of the sun through the glass behind him, his hair shining like a halo. Deities. Always a predilection for the dramatic.

Kubera turned and nodded.

"You heard?"

"I did," the god said, "and I have what I came for."

He patted the ornate silver casket in his hands. It had small crystal windows in its sides, like a reliquary, and through them Kubera could make out a shrivelled portion of flesh within.

"Coyote is going to be trouble," warned Kubera.

"We can deal with it. He's a prankster. Nothing to take seriously."

"Good. And our payment for facilitating this... transaction?"

"Your cooperation is appreciated and your stake in this matter is assured."

Kubera nodded thoughtfully. He hoped it was a wise investment.

CHAPTER THREE
Coyote Gains a Companion

THE SMALL BLACK man wore a cleaner's uniform that was one size too big. His eyes twinkled and he had a smile that never wavered, not the insincere practised mask of the service industry but one of genuine delight, as if he was in on some great cosmic joke.

He pushed the cleaner's trolley down the labyrinthine corridors of the shabby hotel, past door after door, each one a choice, a direction. He loved hotels. Travellers passing through. To and from. Here and there. Lives intersecting. Chance meetings. Illicit liaisons. Anything could happen.

And things were. Things he was not a part of, so of course he wanted to know what. They had led him here. Why, he didn't know. But this was a crossroads. All he had to do was wait and that wasn't a chore, not for Eshu Elegba, God of the Crossroads.

RICHARD GREEN MANAGED to find his hotel eventually. He explained to the desk clerk that he'd lost his key card, but the clerk seemed more interested in the TV show playing on his iPad. Richard gave his name. The bored clerk's fingers clattered across the computer keyboard. His details checked out. He handed Richard a spare key card with complete disinterest and returned his attention to the iPad.

Richard limped along the hushed maze of grubby corridors, past house cleaning trolleys with piles of fresh linen, as staff stripped and prepared rooms for new patrons. He found his room number, swiped the card and pushed the door open.

Someone had trashed his room. *Idiot. Fuck.* They had thrown his clothes everywhere, ripped apart his bags and he couldn't find his passport.

He felt dirty and abused. He winced in pain as he dropped down on the bed and surveyed the wreckage of his life. He wanted to cry, but instead he wiped his eyes roughly, his lips puckered in self-pity. He shucked off his stained clothes, to see bruises blooming on his torso. He walked into the bathroom and turned on the shower, waiting for the steam to build before stepping under the spray. The hot water sluiced down his body, burning the grazes on his hips and elbows. The water stung like hot hail.

How could he have been so stupid? He slumped against the cold tiles of the wall, slick with condensation, the ceramic soothing against his shoulders. He groped for the shower dial, shut the water off and stepped out.

He wiped the steam from the mirror, smearing the side of his fist against the cool glass. The reflection of a face not his own peered over his shoulder, through the condensation.

It smiled at him.

"Jesus!"

"I'm sorry, did I startle you?" Eshu carried on smiling as the young man grabbed a towel and wrapped it round his waist.

"You scared the hell out of me," said the naked man, blinking water out of his eyes, "What the hell are you doing in my room?"

He shrugged, as if it was obvious. "There was no sign on the door."

No signs, no sigils, which was as good a welcome as he ever knew.

"Do you work here?" the wet man asked.

Work here? Yes, in more senses than one. He pointed to his badge. *Hi I'm Eshu.*

"Call me Shu," he said.

"Richard. Sorry, had a shit day. Shit night," said Richard. He saw Eshu's trolley by the door. "Housekeeping, right?"

Eshu was enjoying this. "In a way."

Richard clenched his fists. "I've been bloody robbed."

"Yes, I rather think you have," Shu agreed, but he wasn't talking about material possessions.

"I'm going to go down and report this to reception and they can call the police," Richard was saying as he pulled on a pair of jeans.

"They won't help. You'll be in the system then; organised, ordered. You'll get bogged down in paperwork." He tutted and shook his head. "In triplicate. *Tch.* Thrice named, such a binding."

"What choice do I have?"

Well, not the boring one. That was why Shu was here.

"What brought you to this place?" Shu asked.

"Pardon?"

Shu looked back along the paths that had brought him here and was puzzled. There was a turning in his life that shouldn't have been there. He probed it, examined it, like a tongue in a tooth cavity. What he found was interesting—and disturbing.

"Choices," Shu said. "Choices were made, you were cast adrift on the ripples they caused. They cost you what you have lost long before you came here."

He looked deeper. There, in the tapestry, was a new pattern forming, a pattern he didn't like the look of. It was small so far, but the tiny repeats were indicative of something larger to come, something that wouldn't be seen by others until it was too late. To Shu, it suggested a plan. A plan meant order. Order took time, energy, effort and *coordination*. For which someone somewhere was responsible. Chaos, on the other hand, just took a nudge. The results could be delightfully unpredictable. With the least amount of effort, you could start an avalanche, a hurricane, a tidal wave. All it took was a butterfly's wings. Or a matchbook.

Shu tossed one across the room. Richard reached out on a reflex and caught it. He turned the matchbook over. The Olympus. He glared at it.

"How did you—"

Shu smiled as he watched the myriad paths unfold before him.

"An opportunity," Shu said, "to find what you have lost. Now you have a choice. Make it count."

Richard frowned, pocketed the matchbook and slipped on his trainers.

"Look, I'd better go," he said. "Sorry about the mess. Just leave it. I'll tidy up later."

Shu followed him into the lobby. Richard stopped, took out the matchbook and stared at it, tapping its side with a finger while he pondered. Then he walked past reception and out of the front door and turned towards the Olympus.

Shu smiled and went back to his cart to fetch his phone.

IT WASN'T OFTEN Coyote found himself outfoxed, but it always took him by surprise. Frankly, it was embarrassing. If someone hadn't stolen his pecker, this would never have happened.

The Anemoi escorted him down to the foyer, and took great delight in unceremoniously propelling him though the doors with the aid of well-aimed zephyr. Then, to add insult to injury, the aircon curtain unexpectedly strengthened, preventing him from re-entering. He struggled briefly against it, like a drunken mime artist, until people nearby started laughing and pointing at his performance. Before he knew it, it would be a bloody YouTube clip. Defeated, he gave up and sloped off with what little dignity he had left.

"They won't get away with treating me like that. I'll return and teach them a lesson, but first I shall find out who kidnapped my younger brother." So said Coyote.

His anus farted.

"And a fat lot of good you were."

Coyote straightened his jacket, strode into the Parthenon and walked straight into—

"You!" said Richard.

Coyote looked him up and down and tutted. "I don't have time for this." He side-stepped and carried on walking down the Avenue of Heroes.

Richard called out after him and began following. "Don't you walk away from me. Don't you dare walk away from me!"

Coyote turned on him. "I would be careful right now, little brother." He held up a finger and thumb, their tips barely a centimetre apart. "I am this far from going on the warpath. I am not in the mood for your petty grievances."

"Petty? You gambled away my entire redundancy package. You vanished and left me with nothing, then got me kicked out of the place. That was my life you were playing with. I want it back!"

"I can't give it to you."

"You what?"

"The casino confiscated it. Besides, today I've lost far more than you can imagine."

Richard continued to hound him, like a terrier nipping at his heels. "Well, boo-hoo. I'm not leaving you until you give me back what you owe me."

Coyote looked him up and down. "I can't. Go away. Without my younger brother, I am not whole, my powers are reduced. I cannot help you until I have recovered what *I* have lost. On that day, Richard Green, I swear I will give you your life back. Until then, go away."

Nearby, a fuzzed and distorted heavy metal ringtone rang out across the Parthenon. A metalhead struggled with his pocket to extract his cell phone and answered it.

He looked around, standing on tiptoe, like a meerkat on the lookout for predators. Then he made a beeline for Coyote. His face scrunched in confusion, he handed him the phone.

"It's for you."

Coyote looked at him and took the offered phone.

"Hello?"

"Has he found you?" It was Eshu.

"The Englishman?" He glared over at Richard. "Yes."

"Don't lose him."

"Why now? I don't have time. Someone has stolen my penis. I'm going to find who took it and make them pay."

Silence.

"Then keep the Englishman with you. His name's Dick. He'll do until you find your own. Meet me in the diner. You know the one. Don't forget your Dick."

As Coyote hung up, he could have sworn he heard Old Man Shu laughing.

COYOTE SAT DOWN in the booth next to Richard, who was looking at a large burger, fries and a malt shake that the waitress had just delivered at Shu's request. Richard had been surprised to see Shu, but mollified by the offer of food. He still regarded the two men with suspicion, but he hadn't eaten since yesterday and he was starving.

"What the hell am I doing here?" said Richard. "Who the hell are you people?"

Shu pointed to his plate. "Eat. You will need it. It will anchor you."

Richard found himself tearing into his meal.

Coyote ate nothing. Normally he could be quite a glutton, but he was preoccupied.

"Is this important, or did you just want to stuff your faces?" he asked, arms folded. "I have things to do."

Shu sighed.

SHU LOOKED AT Richard. His old life had been stripped away. He'd unwittingly undergone a symbolic death and now here he was sat before them with nothing. He was ready to be reborn into their world, one that was a shadow of its former self, a twilight world of gods and monsters. Richard now stood on the edge of a precipice—a Fool, with a coyote at his heels. The image amused him.

First, though, Richard needed to experience the shock of a rebirth. There was nothing like being dropped in at the deep end for that.

"Richard?"

"Huh?"

Shu clapped his hands in front of Richard's face.

IN A MOMENT, Richard's world was unmade. The cosy consensual reality that humanity had constructed to protect itself was ripped asunder to reveal the things that circled just beyond its perception. Gripped by a vertiginous terror, Richard experienced the world as it truly was, a place of the unknown and unknowable. There, outside his comprehension, things moved, and an unintelligible roaring filled his ears.

Just as suddenly, the world righted itself. The roar dissolved in a clatter of cutlery and chatter as Richard's default awareness reasserted itself.

"The fuck!"

Richard found he'd scrambled up into the corner of the booth, as if someone had just lit a firecracker under him, his heart pounding against his ribs. Muscles tensed, fight or flight. Fear etched on his face. The rest of the diners were staring at him.

Shu gave him a reassuring smile and coaxed him back down onto the seat. "Sit. Sit down. Eat. The food will ground you."

Hesitantly, Richard slipped down onto the leather bench.

"What... what the fuck did you do? What was that?"

"A metaphysical jolt. I shifted your perceptions momentarily. I showed you a glimpse of our true aspects, our power, of the world as it is. Some call them emanations, others frequencies. I just turned your dial. If it helps, think of it as a weave, a tapestry. Most of the time, mortals just see the pretty picture. I showed you the underside: the stitch work, the knots, the ties that hold it all together. "

Richard clutched the table, his knuckles white. Condiments rattled on the table as he shivered violently. "What... what the fuck are you?"

Coyote cocked his head and looked hurt. "I'm Coyote," he said, as if that explained everything. He sighed. "I'm a being of the creation myths. You call us gods, but I wouldn't know anything about that."

Richard shook his head, not loosening his grip on the table; right now, its solidity anchored him. "I'm an atheist."

"Yet here we are," said Coyote with a grin.

"There are gods," said Shu simply. "You need to know that."

Richard looked at Coyote. Coyote replied with a hapless shrug.

Shu indicated the food. Richard's hand still shook as he picked at the burger, but calmed down as he ate. After a couple of mouthfuls, he had stopped shivering.

"Gods?" he said through a mouth of food. "What, are you for real? Gods?"

Shu shrugged, as if it were no big deal. "Thirty years ago, the Great Usurper cast down all the pantheons, folding the dimensions into each other, trapping us here in yours, our powers diminished. All the gods and monsters of myth forced into this sink estate, this ghetto of a dimension. So many paths crossing. So many crossroads. It keeps me busy."

"Sorry, this is just hard to get my head around. You mean all the gods from all the pantheons are here on Earth? They're real?"

"Well, no one's compiled an exhaustive list, but pretty much I guess," said Coyote. "And yes, we're real. Imagine a downcast diaspora, dispossessed of their respective Valhallas, Nirvanas and celestial manses, licking their wounds and having to make a home here, on a plane that many saw as nothing but sport."

Shu interrupted with a cough as he studied the pair. "You two shouldn't have met," he said, with no small amount of glee.

"I wish we hadn't," said Richard, casting a sideways glance at Coyote. "I wish I hadn't met either of you."

"There is a new pattern forming. Someone is tampering with the tapestry and making a great effort not to be noticed. Why, I have no idea, but there is not a ripple of concern among the bigger pantheons and that worries me. Your meeting would seem to be an unintended consequence of those actions, a loose thread," said Shu, delighted at the prospect. He couldn't have done better if he'd planned it himself. "For better or worse, you are entwined together until you both regain what you have both lost. Follow the thread. East, toward the old lands. East, the direction of paradise. The ripples of consequence that wafted Richard here originated in his country. There is a crossroads approaching and the fate of the world could go either way."

"Right now, your schemes don't interest me," said Coyote. "My only concern is for my younger brother. Get Loki to follow your thread. I will follow mine."

"Your only concern is your wounded pride, Coyote. If you weren't sat here on two legs, I'd take a rolled up newspaper to your nose. This is more important. I still haven't forgotten that Kansas business, or your part in it," said Shu. He smiled, but there was an element of menace to it now, like a mafia boss making an offer you couldn't refuse. "The Earthmaker created you to protect the mortals, pecker or no pecker. Shoot, you might even think better without it for once. It always leads you into trouble anyway."

Coyote fell silent at the mention of his creator. He toyed with a paper napkin, his mouth upturned like a petulant child.

"I'm going to collect my war bundle," said Coyote, getting up to leave. "But only because, when I find out who took my younger brother, I am going on the warpath."

"Don't think you're going anywhere without me," said Richard. "I'm sticking with you until you find him. I want my life back."

Shu, still smiling, sucked on his straw with relish, noisily hoovering up the last of his shake.

CHAPTER FOUR
Coyote Takes a Road Trip

COYOTE, HIS DEERSKIN wrapped war bundle on his back, surveyed the check-in area at McCarran International and picked out his marks as they passed through: the Holden brothers from Chesterfield, those terminals, that TSA official, and those Las Vegas police officers. His plan was simplicity itself, if by simplicity you meant an elegance and intricacy bordering on the fractal. In fact, his plan was nothing more than a delicately localised Rube Goldberg warping of fate and destiny.

"No one will see me. No one will even notice me unless I want them to," said Coyote.

"Oh, well that's great," said Richard. "What about me? I have no money, no boarding pass, and no passport. Do you?"

"I don't need them. I have a plan. Trust me."

"That's what you said last time."

Richard hadn't even had time to salvage his belongings from the hotel.

"Luggage is baggage. A warrior must discard everything that is unnecessary," Coyote had told him.

By the time they got across the main concourse, weaving between the groups of travellers, they had a couple of passports. It didn't matter whose passports. Coyote could make anyone believe they belonged to Richard and him.

They made for the self check-in terminals. A little psychic flexing and the machine spat out a couple of boarding passes, and then off to find their security checkpoint.

They drifted past airport police, to join the queue.

"What are we going to do?" hissed Richard.

"Well, I was rather hoping Dwayne over there was going to do it for us," said Coyote, indicating an overweight TSA agent. "He's got an attitude," he added, tapping the side of his nose.

Besides, they weren't going to stick his war bundle through one of their scanners, or root through it with their unclean hands. That stuff was *sacred*. And they sure as shit weren't going to pat him down and feel around his junk. Not that he had any junk right now, which in itself could cause problems.

The opt-out queue shuffled toward the security checkpoints, the large scanners and the sullen minimum wage stares.

"Don't want the body scan, eh?" said Dwayne with a leer. "What's the matter? Got something to hide? If you wouldn't mind stepping over here—*sir*. And you too, sir," he said to Richard.

"Me?" he protested.

Coyote stepped calmly from the line and followed Dwayne to a clear area nearby. Richard looked like a jackrabbit caught in the headlights.

Passengers watched with morbid curiosity as the pair were ushered to one side for special attention.

"I'm going to have to give you an enhanced pat down, sir," said Dwayne.

He snapped his blue latex gloves for emphasis. "I'm going to run my hands up your thighs, and then feel your buttocks, and then I'm going to reach under you until I meet resistance."

Coyote arched an eyebrow. "I don't think so, Dwayne."

Dwayne's face began to change colour, darkening. "You can't opt out, mister! What are you, unpatriotic? Are you a terrorist? What's in that package you're carrying?" Dwayne demanded, pointing a quivering blue finger at Coyote's war bundle. "Open it up and let me see."

Time to push his button. One little phrase.

Coyote leaned in. "You wouldn't be so tough if you weren't wearing that uniform."

Dwayne blinked. A nerve twitched. The vein at his temple began to throb.

Bullseye. This was too easy.

"Coyote. Kai. What the hell are you doing?" hissed Richard, panic flaring in his eyes.

Dwayne squinted poisonously. "Are you trying to be funny, mister? Are you?" Sweat beaded his upper lip. He licked it away in a manner that was vaguely obscene. "Oh, you're for it now. Tell me you've got a bomb in there. Make my day."

"Okay. You've got a bomb in there," said Coyote, deadpan.

Dwayne's eyes narrowed.

"What?"

"You told me to tell you that you had a bomb."

"No, not, 'you've got a bomb'; 'I've got a bomb'."

"You've got a bomb?" said Coyote, perplexed.

"No! Ya dumb sack of... read my lips," said Dwayne, sweat flying from his face as he spat the words out. "I've got a bomb!"

The screening checkpoint went quiet.

"I've got a bomb!" screamed Dwayne again, panic in his eyes this time. He tried to clamp his jaw shut, but the words spewed out again, because Coyote was making him say the one thing you shouldn't say in an airport. The final taboo, or should that be final taboom. *Ba-dum, tish!* "I've got a bomb!" he screamed.

Chaos erupted. People panicked. Coyote smiled. The area around Dwayne cleared. TSA agents advanced on Dwayne, who thrust his latex gloved hands into the air, the phrase still blurting from his lips. "I've got a bomb." A taser buzzed. "I've gttttaabb..." Dwayne spasmed and fell, before disappearing under a pile of security personnel.

In the commotion, Coyote nodded at Richard. Nobody paid them any attention as they slipped through the security checkpoint to the relative calm of the boarding area, where he gave the patented Coyote Winning Smile to the boarding staff.

"What the hell happened back there?" asked Richard after the commotion died down.

Coyote grinned. "Pronoun trouble."

THEY LANDED AT Manchester Airport fourteen hours later, thanks to the delay caused by Dwayne's bomb scare. Funnelled down a tunnel, with passengers from other flights—boiled red families in shorts and T-shirts, rumpled businessmen, and backpacking students—they emerged in the Arrivals hall.

"So, what do we do now?" Richard asked, tired, stiff, and longing for a proper bed.

A middle-aged man with a Mediterranean complexion, close-cropped white hair and wearing a pastel coloured windcheater and slacks, held up a piece of cardboard that read, 'Mr Coyote.'

Coyote and Richard exchanged a glance.

Coyote's face broke out in a broad smile. He knew a god when he saw one.

"Ask and the world answers," he said, striding off toward the sign. Richard sighed and followed.

"You're expecting me?" said Coyote.

"I think I may have found what you're looking for," said the man.

"And what's that?"

The man glanced at Coyote's crotch. "That which you have lost."

A piercing look. "I have the greatest tracking skills of all the People, even I cannot sense it," said Coyote. "How is it that you can?"

"Though it may be hidden from your senses, its absence leaves a hole in the Tapestry. I am drawn to such negative spaces. It is my nature. I'm Nataero, god of lost things."

"Well, in that case," said Coyote, giving the man a hearty slap on the back, "You're the god's bollocks!"

Nataero caught sight of Richard. "Who's he? I was just expecting you."

"This," Coyote said with delight, "is my change of plan, my temporary Dick. He's with me."

Richard gave Nataero a weary smile.

"Don't you have any luggage?" asked Nataero.

"No," said Richard sullenly. "Apparently, we're warriors."

NATAERO LED THEM out of the building and off toward the long stay car park. He stood for a moment, as if waiting for something to happen. Then, finding his bearings, made a beeline for a two-door silver Nissan and clicked a key fob he'd taken from his pocket. The lights flashed.

"Hey," said Richard, grabbing Coyote's cuff. "I thought we had something else to do first?"

Coyote took him aside, his voice low. "And you want your life back. I can only do that if I'm reunited with my pecker. Nataero here says he can lead us to it. I get my younger brother returned, my power restored, and you get your life back. We're both happy, then I can take care of Shu's task. So, what do you say? Your choice."

To be frank, it sounded like a good deal. The sooner he could leave these people behind the better. He'd had enough madness.

"Well, if you put it like that," said Richard.

NATAERO DROVE THEM from the airport, Coyote in the passenger's seat, Richard in the back. Trees, bushes and lights swiped past in blurs as they headed down the motorway. He knew where he was going, without even having to use the satnav stuck to the windscreen.

Coyote was quiet. The thrum of the engine and the vibration of the road surface should be giving him a boner. It always did. He missed it. He missed its delightfully wilful tumescence and the weight of his balls, he missed those little pulses of pleasure as it strained against the denim. But soon they would be reunited. That gave him a little thrill. It wasn't the same, but it would do for now. He stared out of the rain-streaked windows as drops careened along, colliding and merging, and tried to think of something else.

* * *

"NICE CAR," SAID Richard, trying to make conversation.

"Not mine," said Nataero. "Someone lost their car keys on holiday. They'll find out tomorrow."

"You mean you stole it?"

The man turned his head briefly, flicking a gaze at him in the rear view mirror. "You're not listening. It's not stolen. It's lost."

"Are you a god, too?"

"Of the Roman pantheon. God of lost property. It's what I do, find lost stuff."

Richard smirked. "I guess that explains your taste in clothes then."

Nataero slammed his foot on the brake. The tyres locked, throwing up loose chippings as the car slewed to a halt on the hard shoulder.

The abrupt stop slammed Richard's body forward into the seatbelt.

"I think *you've* lost your manners," said Nataero, his tone hard.

"Sorry," said Richard hurriedly.

"Oh look, there they are." Nataero glared at him in the rear view mirror. "I've found them. Don't lose them again. Not around gods. It's not a wise thing to do."

Staring out of the window, Coyote smiled to himself. Perhaps this Richard had some potential after all.

THE STROBE EFFECT of passing cars and the heat from the air conditioning made Richard feel drowsy. The jet lag rushed in on him and he nodded off; his dreams a kaleidoscopic confection of events from the last few days. Casinos and laughing girls, dirty alleys and diners, and then the sudden rushing and roaring of the world as Shu showed it to him, with things prowling around the edge of his dream, waiting. Once more, the terrifying vertigo seized him, only this time he began to fall...

"Richard!"

... into his body with a jolt.

"Wake up!" yelled Coyote.

"Whathefuck!" Richard yelped in alarm.

His voice was stern. "Dreams have power around gods."

Nataero glanced back over his shoulder. "Oh, yes, you want to watch that."

Coyote turned round in his seat. "Since Shu shifted your point of awareness, it is no longer rooted in the mortal perception of things. It drifted, like a radio dial, further than it should have, lost between stations. If I hadn't woken you when I did, you might never have found your way back and you would have been lost.

"To help protect your newly freed awareness, you will need a new set of personal routines. The only way you can survive is to accumulate personal power. That will help fix your perception to the mortal plane. With enough personal power and practice you might even be able to shift your perception consciously."

Richard's breath came in short, sharp pants. "What the hell have you done to me?"

Coyote threw his hands in the air, declaiming responsibility. "Shu has seen fit to show you an amazing opportunity." There was a long rasp followed by a rotting aroma. "And younger brother anus agrees."

"Jeez!" said Richard, breathing though his mouth.

Afraid of falling asleep again, Richard made them stop for coffee. He also made Nataero drive with the window open, partly to stay awake, but mostly just in case Coyote broke wind again.

"WE'RE CLOSE," SAID Nataero a while later.

A blue motorway junction sign flashed by.

"Hey, Bridstowe. That's where I live," said Richard, swivelling his neck as the sign went by.

Coyote turned and looked at him.

"This is where you live and Shu directed us to begin our search? And this is where my younger brother is hidden?"

He let out a long breath. Old Man Shu was a crafty one.

* * *

NATAERO DROVE THROUGH the town centre. It was late afternoon and in the glow of the street lights, back-lit store signs reflected off wet greasy pavements pocked with the lichen-like blooms of chewing gum. Banks of shops were closed, their graffitied shutters padlocked. After the heat, then bright sunlight, the neon of Vegas, the place seemed dead.

"It was a thriving town a year ago," said Richard.

They passed long avenues of houses, hunkered down against the prevailing wind of the moors; big Victorian houses gave way to smaller thirties homes and, on the outskirts, a few sixties housing estates, open to the elements. Beyond them, the hills rose and the road signs directed them towards the motorway.

Nataero turned off in the opposite direction. A brown heritage sign directed them to Hillstone Howe and the Devil's Fingers.

They pulled into a small municipal car park: puddled potholes, cinder, crushed limestone hardcore and mud. It sat at the foot of a large barren windswept hill that looked out over the town. Apart from their silver Nissan it was empty. They got out.

"This way," said Nataero, pointing to an algae-rimed fingerpost by a stile.

They crossed the stile and started up a path that spiralled round the hill toward the crest.

Coyote, his wrapped war bundle on his back, gazed up at the sodden hill and the gunmetal clouds above and smiled. It was such a contrast to his desert. Even the light here seemed older, more ancient.

"It's up here," said Nataero. He cut an incongruous figure in his windcheater and slacks. His patent leather shoes, not really ideal for the outdoors, were covered with mud, their leather soles sliding on the wet ground, splattering his trousers.

As they came around the far side of the path they were afforded a view over Bridstowe, for what it was worth.

"Always thought Hillstone Howe was a stupid name," said Richard to no one in particular.

"It wasn't 'hill', not originally," said Nataero. "It was 'hel', an Anglo-Saxon word meaning a place of protection. Of sanctuary."

Richard could make out the standing stones as they came up the final rounding of the path. There was a bench nearby, facing out over the town below. It was covered with graffiti, as were the standing stones, decades of crude thin bone-white names scratched into the rock, overlaid with aerosoled tags, defiling them. Empty cans and bottles littered the ground around it, like meagre offerings. If this place was a sanctuary for anything, it was bored youth.

Coyote tilted his head and sniffed, his nostrils flaring. He couldn't detect the piquant scent of his penis. He didn't feel a pulse or a throb in his groin, either, but his penis could have been confined or constrained, which is why it wouldn't answer to his call.

"Where's my penis, Nataero?" said Coyote, his voice low and dangerous.

"It's here. I know it. I can sense it. Perhaps you need to summon it."

Coyote's glower flicked over to a beaming grin. Maybe he had a point.

He took a pouch from around his neck, opened it and took from it a pinch of Bonafide Penis Return powder. He cast it into the damp air and began chanting in a deep sonorous language that Richard felt resonate through his very core.

Coyote threw his arms into the air and began to dance.

At Richard's feet, crushed lager cans and discarded cider bottles began to vibrate and skitter across the threadbare turf as the ground began to shake.

CHAPTER FIVE
Coyote and the Devil's Fingers

THE AIR RESOUNDED with a deep rumble as the earth heaved and bucked. Several stones of the circle slewed and tilted.

"What's happening?" Richard yelped, trying to maintain his balance.

Coyote fancied he felt a stirring in his loins. "It's younger brother," he said, a grin stretched wide across his face. He caught Nataero's hand and gave it a manly shake.

Nataero returned a weak, unctuous smile. "Then my job here is done. What is lost is found."

"Thanks to you," said Coyote, taking a deep breath and readying himself to receive his errant member. "I shan't forget this service."

Then Nataero disappeared.

"Here we go," cried Coyote. "Come, younger brother, I'm waiting for you. I'm here!"

"And your penis is doing all this? Are you sure?" Richard shouted.

Coyote winked at him. "I have often been told that I can make the earth move. And Lo!"

"It just seems a lot of upheaval for a little todger, that's all."

"Not so little, Richard Green," said Coyote with a lecherous wink.

"It can be so large I've had to carry it slung over my shoulder before now. If it has been bound and confined then it will fight to get free. It sounds like a mighty battle!" he said, nodding with approval at his member's efforts. "Do you hear? It comes at my call. Come, my brother. Come."

"I wouldn't put it quite like that if I were you."

The central stone seemed taller now, like a tooth in receding gums, its newly exposed surface wet with moisture and clean of graffiti.

Coyote shucked his war bundle and took a large empty sack from the deerskin wrapping, pulled the drawstrings open and held the neck wide open in expectation. "I've caught and bound great spirits with this sack before now, and contained in it things of great power, but now my younger brother is coming home and he will have need of the sack's chastisement."

"Then I get my life back, right?"

"Yes, Richard, once I am whole again."

There was a creak of soft, damp wood. The park bench came loose as the ground rose about it, toppling the splintered bench and its cracked concrete bed down the hill.

"And does it usually cause such destruction?"

Something priapic headed their way, ploughing through the earth, a red and glistening eyeless head thrusting its way through the soil.

"Jesus, you weren't kidding. When you said big, I just thought you meant, you know King Dong, Dirk Diggler big. This is huge!"

In one fluid movement, the enormous glistening glans burst out of the ground and rose up before him—and kept on rising, rearing over him.

"That's one hell of an erection!"

Coyote's face crumpled.

"That's not my—"

A maw opened in the thing's head as it plunged down on Coyote, swallowing him whole as it dived back into the earth.

"Coyote!" cried Richard in horror.

"That was a close thing," said a quiet voice.

Coyote stood beside him.

Richard stared. "How did you—"

Coyote winked and shoved him on the shoulder.

"Run, Richard Green. This is a trap meant for me. This is no recalcitrant rod, no penitent penis. This is a wyrm. You're mortal. If you stay, it will mean your death."

Richard hesitated. "But what about you?"

"I'm Coyote!" he yelled ecstatically.

The ground shook and the wyrm broke the surface once more, showering Richard with dirt.

"Run, Richard Green, run!"

Richard turned and made for the path. Within seconds of starting along it he had lost sight of the hilltop, but saw the head of the wyrm rear up over the crest and plunge down again, showering him with a spume of earth.

He carried on down the path. Whatever was going on was nothing to do with him, was nothing he knew how to cope with. In a battle between gods and monsters, there was little he could do.

Loose stones skittered away under his feet, his arms flailing as he ran. His heart slammed against his chest, as if it were trying to burst free.

As Richard ran round into the lee of the hill, he heard a raucous caw. A lone raven with burning red eyes swooped down out of the leaden grey clouds that kettled the bleak landscape.

Other caws now answered the first, as shreds of shadow detached themselves from the clouds, taking on form and solidity as they whirled and swooped. A flock of ravens. No, not a flock, an unkindness.

Their harsh calls rent the air as the birds harried him. As he fled down the slope, Richard stumbled away from the path, tripping over tussocks and sods on the steep descent, arms windmilling.

A blood-eyed raven plummeted towards him. Talons sliced. He felt the back of his head open up and put his hand to his scalp. It came away slick and red. He had to keep going. The bottom of the hill wasn't far now. He rounded the corner and saw the silver Nissan in the car park.

Please let it not be locked.

He heard the screeching caws above and chanced a look. Another flight of ravens was sweeping down on him.

He might still make the car.

He turned back to see ravens settling on the Nissan's roof and patrolling the ground. The bastards had herded him down here. They were waiting for him. Cunning little shits.

Richard had run himself ragged, there was nowhere else to run to, and no energy left with which to run there. He spun round in panic and looked up at the hill. From deep within, muffled by rock and earth, came reverberating thuds and impacts, like a pile driver. No help would come from Coyote.

Richard was alone—insignificant and scared. He turned to face the maleficent flock. Fuck English teachers, unkindness was understating it. This was a murder of ravens if he ever saw one. They congregated on the car park walls, watching him with their burning eyes. It was unnerving the way they strengthened and dimmed in time with his breathing, like lit cigarettes. Would they fade to an ashen grey with his death?

He charged towards the car.

They took to the air in a blizzard of wings, wheeling and swooping tighter and tighter until they swirled down around him in a tornado of feathers, claws and beaks, picking and pecking a hundred cuts and scratches. He covered his face with his arms; he squealed as a beak found an exposed rim of ear and bit down. It was like running through a hail of razor blades. He lost sight of the car as the world disappeared in a press of darkness, lit only by cruel constellations of baleful stares.

Richard began to suffocate under the feathers. He reached and felt the car door under his hand, even as the ravens pecked and tore at it. He groped for the handle.

He roared in a primal scream of fury and frustration.

First, his entire world had been stripped away and now to have his very flesh stripped from his bones, a feast for carrion? *Fuck*.

THE WYRM REARED up into the air and bore down into the hill, right where the man had been standing. It swallowed earth and stone and turf, but the man known as Coyote had gone. Stood before the wild wyrm was Coyote the animal, ears flat against its head, tail down, teeth bared.

OLD MAN WYRM bored down into the hill with the ease of a leaping salmon, moving through the earth as easily as Coyote did through the desert.

Old Man Wyrm laughed at him now, mocking him for his lack of manhood. No one laughed at Coyote. And if they did, they wouldn't get away with it.

"Old Man Wyrm, Old Man Wyrm," he cried. "If you want to eat me I am over here!"

Coyote leapt aside as Old Man Wyrm thrust his head up through the spray of loam into the air.

"I may not be able to see you, older brother, but I can smell you and soon I will taste you," he bellowed, plunging down where Coyote stood.

"Oh, I have no doubt of that," said Coyote, pouncing aside. "But I am much better cooked than raw."

Coyote leapt down one of Old Man Wyrm's holes and raced along the dank dark tunnels.

"I can hear the patter of your paws," said Old Man Wyrm burrowing down the tunnel after him.

Coyote came to a large chamber at the heart of the hill, studded with boulders and with tunnels running off it at various angles. "Well this is all very cosy, but I see no cooking pot. How am I going to taste my best if there is no cooking pot?"

Old Man Wyrm's voice echoed down the labyrinthine tunnels. "You can't fool me, trickster. I'm going to eat you raw, swallow you whole. I can't wait, I am hungry now!"

Old Man Wyrm's blind, toothless head protruded into the chamber, glistening and red.

"These are my tunnels and there is nowhere you can hide that I cannot find you."

"How about here?" asked Coyote, dashing off down a tunnel, his paws skittering as he banked up the walls.

Old Man Wyrm's huge bulk slithered after him.

Coyote skittered to a halt and changed direction. Old Man Wyrm was faster than he thought. His mucus-slicked bulk thundered after him, a wake of hot fetid air rushing ahead of it. Coyote switched down another passage barely ahead of the great bulk. He found himself back in the main chamber. Wyrm's length was so long, Coyote saw his great anus disappearing along the passage down which he had just fled.

Then he saw the sigils marked on the walls of the chamber, meant to confuse prey—make it easier for Old Man Wyrm to feed. If he was ever a hunter, he had lost the edge.

Old Man Wyrm's voice echoed round the chamber. "See, little morsel? You can't find your way out and you can't escape your fate."

"You don't mind if I try, do you?" asked Coyote, quick as a flash picking another exit as Old Man Wyrm's head thrust back into the chamber.

"Run all you want. All ways lead back to me!"

The passage led down. Coyote was running so fast he almost missed a turning. He tumbled to a halt and Old Man Wyrm's head was so close behind him he could feel his breath on his tail. He darted down a side passage.

It rose up in a steep incline and he struggled up the slope, the dirt dribbling away beneath his feet as he sought purchase with his claws.

He scrambled his way to the lip of the tunnel and found himself back in the chamber again as Wyrm's middle section rumbled through in continued pursuit of him, just as Wyrm's head barrelled up from below, gaining on him. He pelted across the chamber and over the back of the Wyrm's body and down another tunnel. Wyrm followed him blindly, plunging on like a freight train, into the tunnel after him.

The dark echoed with Old Man Wyrm's voice, its deep vibrato sending down showers of dirt from the tunnel roof.

"Run all you want, older brother. Your sweat will be a fine seasoning!"

Coyote found himself, as he expected, back in the central chamber, along with the bulk of Wyrm's body; twisted under and over and round itself in pursuit of him, tied up and stuck in the chamber.

"You couldn't eat me now if you tried, Old Man Wyrm!" crowed Coyote. "You've a knot in your stomach."

And Coyote laughed all the way along the tunnel to the fresh air.

However, the last laugh was on Coyote. As Old Man Wyrm thrashed about in blind fury, unable to extricate himself, the tunnel collapsed about the trickster. Dirt clogged his nose, stung his eyes and filled his ears.

"Oh what a stupid fellow I have been. I may now be a meal for worms after all," Coyote said.

Then, through the dirt, he saw the faint sickly glow of the town lights beyond. Coyote burst from the hill.

"Ho, but not this day!" he said. The earth was settling now, the sounds of struggle ceased, and the standing stones still stood proud, if a little crooked, atop the hill. Above, the ravens circled, cawing contemptuously.

It was only then that Coyote remembered Richard. Sometimes mortals were such a drag. Did he have to do everything himself?

He bounded down the hill, growling as he leapt over the car park wall toward the scratched and scored car, and the flock of murderous midnight birds that swarmed around it.

He didn't see the heavy chain swing through the air towards him.

CHAPTER SIX
Coyote Finds the Thread

THE IMPACT OF the heavy industrial chain flung Coyote through the car park wall, its dry stone exploding under the impact.

No animal could have wielded that weapon. Nor was it forged by any mortal. The debris clinked and shifted as Coyote rose up from beneath the rubble, fur bristling, teeth bared, a growl of anger building in the back of his throat, ready to face his new opponent.

He was a mountain of a man, by any stretch of the imagination, a broad chest and massive arms barely contained by the oil-smeared mechanic's overall he wore, his long dark hair scraped back in a pony tail, scruffy beard bordering on hobo. He was stood by the car, keeping the ravens at bay. Coyote could smell the fear and piss that was Richard inside the vehicle.

Coyote could also smell the man. No, not a man, this was a god. Under the acrid tang of oil, grease and hot metal was the unmistakable odour of sanctity, the scent of the gods. Coyote wasn't impressed with his physique; after all, gods could change appearances to suit their whim.

The man had his attention focused on the flock about him. He whirled the long chain around his head. Where it whipped into the ravens, it flayed their corporeality from them and they burst into vaporous shadows, dispersing on the wind, the defiant caws dissipating.

Sizing up the battle, Coyote joined the fray, taking out his fury at being duped on the belligerent birds. He leapt up, tearing at necks, legs and wings. He ripped them from the air with teeth and claws until their glowing eyes were snuffed out, and their forms shaken violently into a black mist between his jaws.

He let out a low growl and hunched down on his forepaws ready to pounce again, but there were no ravens left. By the car, the large man, panting heavily with his exertions, turned in a circle, the long chain trailing on the ground, chinking across the surface.

Coyote circled him warily, ears flat, tail down. Meeting new gods could turn into such a pissing contest. *My pantheon's bigger than yours.* Well, bring it on. He'd had a bladder full.

"I meant you no harm," said the man. With a flick of his wrist, he allowed the links coiled round his forearm to drop to the floor. "An accident in the heat of battle."

"Well, why didn't you say," said Coyote, human once more, a smile on his face as he walked toward him, hand extended.

Hands gripped hard as their eyes met, each taking the measure of the other.

Coyote could tell that the man's physique was no illusory glamour, no narcissistic reflection. He had earned those muscles, worked hard for them. That, at least, was deserving of some respect. He also didn't seem to care too much about his appearance. The unkempt beard spoke to that. No huge ego to flatter.

"Coyote. Call me Kai. That's quite a grip you've got there."

"My forge keeps me strong," said the man. White teeth gleamed through his beard.

Coyote raised an eyebrow. A god of the forge, then. But which one? Not Hephaestus.

"Weyland Smith," said the man.

Ah. The Anglo-Saxon.

There was a rattling and a muffled voice from inside the car.

Weyland glanced towards it.

"Yours?" he asked.

Coyote sighed and gave a what-can-you-do shrug. "Yes."

Weyland nodded. "I had one once."

"A car?"

"A mortal."

They walked towards the silver Nissan. It was rocking on its suspension. Inside, Richard sat in the driver's seat shouting and shoving the door.

"What happened?" asked Coyote.

"Flibbertigibbet? He got turned to stone."

Coyote glanced towards the hilltop.

"Oh, not that one."

The car's bodywork was scratched and scored by claws and ectoplasmic bird crap smeared its windows. "You can come out now, Richard."

The car continued to rock. Richard tugged fruitlessly on the door handle.

Weyland took hold of the door handle and wrenched the door open. Richard tumbled out on the ground, his hand crudely bandaged with a handkerchief, his face covered with small cuts, his hair matted with blood.

"They tried to kill me!" He scrambled to his feet. "They tried to kill me. Where the hell were you?"

"You're alive," said Coyote, unconcerned.

"That's not the point."

"Isn't it?"

Weyland coughed.

"That you are, is thanks to Weyland," said Coyote, his voice calm, but insistent. Coyote could tell Richard didn't see the import of it. He leant into Richard's ear and whispered. "Seriously, Richard. Thank Weyland. He saved your life. He has enough power to unmake you at a whim."

"Thank you for saving my life," said Richard.

Weyland grinned with wry amusement. "I hope you're worth the saving, Richard Green." He slapped him heartily between his shoulder blades, making Richard stagger forward unsteadily before he braced his hands on his knees and vomited onto the muddy ground.

Weyland peered over Richard's shoulder.

"Interesting," he said, addressing Coyote. "Is he your emetomancer?"

Coyote shook his head. "Sometimes puke is just puke."

"Too bad. We might have learned something."

"We did. Don't trust Nataero."

Weyland looked puzzled. "That thieving Roman bastard, that jumped up ambitious little house god?"

Richard spat the last lumpy dregs from his mouth, wiped the back of his hand across his lips, and looked from one god to the other.

"Thief?" he said. "I thought he was the Roman god of lost things."

"Only because he's the one who steals them half the time," said Weyland.

Coyote burst out laughing and slapped his thigh until tears rolled down his cheeks. Oh, that was a good one, simple and elegant. He should have thought of it himself. And he could have done, had he wanted. Actually what he wanted now was to find Nataero again. No one got the better of Coyote.

Weyland's face darkened.

"Why are you here, trickster? These aren't your hunting grounds."

"I'm looking for something that was stolen from me. Something of great sentimental value. I was quite attached to it."

"And your search brought you here?"

Coyote looked around, as if this were a trick question.

"Well, yes. Or rather that sonofabitch Nataero brought us here."

"Into a trap it seems. Odd though, Nataero is strictly small fry. He wouldn't have the wit or the skill to arrange an ambush like this. I would warrant there are others involved. Someone isn't keen on you finding your property again, it seems, especially as they're willing to raise a wyrm and bring down a whole flock of ill-omened ravens on your heads."

"I'm lucky like that. And you, what brings you here?"

"Happenstance. I am here on another matter, a matter as close to my heart as I suspect your own is to you. Come, I will show you."

Collecting his chain and looping it over his shoulder and chest,

Weyland led them back up the hill again, his chain *chinking* as he walked.

"I came here investigating the loss of one of my kin and found you two under attack," he told them. "Thinking you might know something, I sought to protect your mortal here."

"I am not his mortal. My name is Richard Green."

"The god of this place has vanished from the Tapestry," Weyland continued.

"I didn't even know we had a god," said Richard, jogging to keep up.

"Few did," said Weyland. "He was an Anglo-Saxon spirit, the guardian of this locality. So old and little worshipped that even he had forgotten his name. But his power was tied to this place and this place alone. His presence protected it, holding back the tides of misfortune. Over the past centuries, his powers were much diminished, so adversity and hardship seeped in slowly, like water lapping under a door rather than a tidal wave. For that, at least you can be thankful. But with his death, the final barrier had gone and everything else with it."

"So you're saying all the bad stuff that's been happening recently—the pile-up, the gas explosion, the businesses closing down, the wyrm—are all down to this local god?" said Richard.

"Amongst other things, although the wyrm was bound. It could not have escaped unless someone released it."

"I lost my job," said Richard, as realisation dawned. Shu had intimated as much.

Weyland nodded. "The result of my kin's disappearance. He was not the first to disappear, either. There have been six others before him over this past year."

"And no one has noticed?" asked Coyote, as they rounded the last stretch up to the hilltop.

There is a new pattern forming, Shu said.

"Why would they? They were minor local gods, long forgotten even by those who dwelt under their protection. Who'd notice the disappearance of those who hadn't been missed? The bigger pantheons would not concern themselves." Weyland scratched his beard. "And that troubles me."

"If, as you say, they have been long forgotten, they could simply have faded from existence. It happens," suggested Coyote.

"I do not believe so. I will show you why."

They reached the top of the hill and Weyland made for the central stone. Two fingertips lightly brushed the menhir's surface.

"See here?" he said, sorrow etched on his face. "It is like the others. All were taken at their place of power."

There, in the rock, a thin horizontal slit.

"A blade."

"A blade that can kill a god and penetrate stone."

"You're talking deicide." What had old man Shu got him into this time?

Weyland circled the stone, inspecting it closely.

"Aye, but what bothers me is the lack of ichor. Here, and at the other places."

"Ichor?" asked Richard.

"Godsblood," said Coyote.

Weyland continued. "If the god was killed here, then the stone should be etched with it. But there is nothing. This is the centre of his power. It shouldn't have been possible to kill him here, but I can sense no sign of a struggle. It's as if he permitted it. Why?" Weyland's brow creased. "Why would he do such a thing?"

He turned in a circle, his arms out, palms down. "And it's twilight. There should be power here, but the hill is cold. Dead. The psychic energy that flows through it has been drained."

"Like the godsblood."

"It's as if the ichor was collected, but for what purpose and by whom, I do not know."

Coyote and Weyland looked at each other, their faces grim.

"A sacrifice?" Coyote said.

"It is more than coincidence that we are here together," said Weyland. "You being lured here to be attacked by the wyrm, freed only because of this local god's death. It would seem our quests have something in common."

"Yes," said Coyote. "How about that?"

*   *   *

IT WAS ALL very interesting, but one thought burned more brightly in Coyote's mind than all others. Nataero claimed to know where his younger brother, penis, was and led him here to be killed, or at least spend a decade or two in the belly of Old Man Wyrm. Why? The Roman knew more than he was telling, but he couldn't sense him. He couldn't smell him. The wily old god had concealed himself with sigils, no doubt. No matter. Nataero wouldn't be able to hide from him for long.

Coyote retrieved his war bundle from where it had fallen when the wyrm attacked.

"You're on the warpath," he said to Weyland. "You seek vengeance for your kin, then?"

"I seek to know who killed them and for what purpose. Then vengeance might follow, yes."

Coyote shouldered his bundle. "My hunt takes me in a different direction. I must find this Roman."

"Very well. There are only so many blades that can kill a god, only so many smiths that can make them, and fewer who would dare. I will turn my attention there. Good luck with your hunt, Coyote. I hope you find what you are looking for."

"You, too."

As Weyland turned to go, he put his hand into the chest pocket of his overalls and pulled out a business card. It was embossed with a rune. "Contact me if you need me. Farewell trickster, and you too, Richard Green."

When Coyote looked up from the card, Weyland had gone.

Coyote pulled out his phone and texted Shu.

I've found the thread.

Within moments, his phone beeped.

Reply: *DON'T LOSE IT.*

"SO, YOU'RE SAYING the god slaying might have been a sacrifice?" said Richard, as they made their way down to the car park.

"Possibly," said Coyote, he looked up at the Devil's Fingers. "The place of power, the ritual nature of the death, the drawing of ichor. It all points to it."

"Yes," said Richard uneasily. "All of which begs the question, who would want to sacrifice a god and, more unnervingly, to what?"

CHAPTER SEVEN
Coyote and the Lost God

RICHARD SAT ON the edge of the driver's seat, feet on the ground, and head in his hands. The feeling of nausea had passed but the overwhelming sense of existential dread still etched away at the pit of his stomach.

Those that had brought him to the brink were gods, or worse than gods, and didn't give a flying fig for him. As flies to wanton boys...

The gods and the monsters were here among them. Only, in his case, *he* was amongst the gods and monsters.

He looked out across the town and thought of Becky. She was somewhere down there among the red brick labyrinth, doing normal things: getting up, going to work, drinking, shagging probably. Oblivious. He envied her. He envied the life he once had.

He looked up at Coyote, facing into the wind, his head tilted back and sniffing the air.

Richard sighed with resignation. "So where do we find a god of lost property?"

Coyote shrugged. "He's vanished. I can't sense him anywhere. He is lost to me."

"So that's it? No matter how hard we look we can't find him?"

"We could search the entire country and not find him. We must wait for him to show himself again."

"Huh," said Richard. "Back when, you know, I *had* a life," he said with bitter emphasis, "I was forever losing stuff: tenners, keys, TV remotes, mobiles, stuff like that. Really pissed Becky off."

"And did you find them, these things?" asked Coyote.

"Yep. Always in the last place I looked."

Richard got into the car and levered the satnav from the windscreen. There was a soft *puck* as its suction cup peeled away. He powered the thing on.

"What do you intend to do?" asked Coyote, his curiosity piqued.

Richard worked his way through the menu. "You like things complicated, don't you? You come right out of left field. Well, this is the most bonkers thing I can think of. I don't even know why it should work, but being around you, heck, I don't know, perhaps you're rubbing off on me." He looked up from the device. "We could spend months, *years*, searching the country from top to bottom, east to west, and not find him, right?"

"Because he'd be in the last place we'd look?"

"Exactly. So why not skip right to the end?"

He toggled through options until he got to 'Set Destination.' He passed it to Coyote.

"I want you to tap in two letters, a number, another number followed by two letters. Any you like."

Coyote tapped his finger on the touch screen, grinned and showed Richard the result.

"And where is this place?"

Richard okayed the code, zoomed out on the map, and turned to look at Coyote in surprise.

"Well, bugger me," he said. "Swindon. A thirties housing estate, judging by the street layout. It's the last place I'd look for a god, anyway. Seems legit."

A grin broke over Coyote's face. "Maybe Old Man Shu was right about you."

"Gee, thanks," said Richard. He gave the satnav suction cup a lick and thumped the thing back against the corner of the windscreen. It stayed. He grunted with satisfaction and went to start the car. Shit, no keys. Nataero had them.

"Looking for this?" said Coyote producing the key fob. "I lifted them from him walking up the hill."

"You didn't trust him!" said Richard in mock shock.

"I don't trust anyone."

"What, not even Shu?"

"Especially not Shu," grinned Coyote.

FOLLOWING THE PASSIVE aggressive directions of the satnav, they drove out of the car park and headed for the motorway.

"Okay," said Richard as they drove south. "I give up. How do you do it, change into a coyote? That was you, wasn't it? How does that even work? What about the extra body mass? It's impossible. It's physics."

Coyote waved a hand airily. "Oh, you don't want to listen to physics. That stuff'll kill you. Even your science says the laws of physics break down the nearer you get to your big bang. Same here. I'm a being of the creation myths. Your laws of physics break down the closer they get to us."

Richard grimaced. "That doesn't even make sense."

"Suit yourself."

IT WAS DAWN as they drove slowly down into Swindon and found a street of identical thirties semis with their bay windows and walled front gardens.

You have reached your destination, the satnav told them.

"But this is just a post code. It could be any one of these," said Richard.

"It's that one," said Coyote, pointing.

Richard leaned forward, and peered over the steering wheel at the unassuming property. "Well it's not the Olympus."

He had at least been expecting something suburban and comfortable. Double-glazing and stone cladding perhaps. The kind of house his grandparents had. Instead, it looked run down. It wore an air of neglect.

Slates were askew on the roof. The window frames were old, with peeling paint and swollen rotten wood. Dirty muslin curtains, yellowed with age and cigarette smoke, hung in the downstairs leaded bay. In the bedroom above, heavy curtains were drawn and looked as if nobody ever opened them. The pointing on the walls was crumbling; a broken downspout bled a damp patch out across the brickwork. Wooden gates barred the path to the door.

The houses either side seemed warm and welcoming by comparison. But this one just seemed to bring down the tone of the neighbourhood. On the other hand, it did have all its original features. Just.

What kind of god lived in a house like this?

Well, he guessed he knew the answer to that one. Nataero probably found the deeds lost down the back of a sofa or something.

They got out of the car and Coyote reached into the back seat to retrieve his deerskin war bundle and slung it over his shoulder.

Richard started to cross the road. Coyote put a hand on his chest, stopping him. His tone was firm and measured, "Let me be clear about this. Be very careful. We're hunting a god. One needs personal power to confront a god. You have precious little. We must proceed strategically."

Richard looked around at the unremarkable suburban street. He still couldn't quite imagine ancient powers slumbering here. Nevertheless, his mouth was dry with fear. Not trusting himself to speak, he nodded in agreement.

Coyote gave him a broad smile.

The next thing he knew Coyote had shoved him hard between the shoulder blades, propelling him into the road.

"That's to anchor your awareness with a little of my personal power, until you acquire your own. You don't want your awareness drifting in Nataero's psychic wash, and believe me he'll try."

Richard opened his mouth to speak but Coyote put a finger to his lips, and jerked his chin towards the rundown house.

He couldn't help feeling a little foolish as they crossed the road.

It didn't seem real. Nevertheless, he felt a knot of fear and a flush of adrenalin as if he were a kid again, playing knock chase on Mrs Battley's front door.

The wooden gate was swollen shut and Richard had to haul it up off the ground to open it. Beyond, the concrete path was cracked, and dead weeds sprouted through it. The terracotta tiles on the doorstep to the porch were cracked and loose. Through the semicircular glass of the door, Richard could see a heavy curtain.

He was about to knock when Coyote grabbed his wrist and shook his head. Perhaps he'd spotted some mystical trap that would have turned him inside out had he triggered it.

"I've got this," he said with a wink. Richard watched Coyote's chest rise as he took a deep breath, as if preparing himself for some physical feat.

Coyote began pounding frantically on the door with both fists, his face contorted with panic.

What the fuck? Richard jumped at the sound. He could almost feel the yell in his chest and he felt briefly nauseous. "What the hell?" said Richard.

"Help!"

Coyote carried on pounding as if his life depended on it. Richard looked around nervously at the neighbours. Net curtains twitched.

"I'm coming!" said an irritable voice from inside. "Hold your horses!"

The door opened.

That was all Coyote needed. He shoved Richard, who stumbled forward in through the door, his boots scuffing over chalk sigil marks on the bare floorboards beyond.

Ooops.

Coyote smiled and followed, slamming the front door behind them.

"You!" Nataero backed away from the door, his eyes wide with alarm. He was no longer snappily dressed. His white hair was unkempt. "You shouldn't be here. You can't be here!"

"We should be dead, you mean?" asked Richard, peering past the man. No, not man. God. He didn't look like a god, with his silver stubble and unkempt hair and the baked bean juice on his dressing gown. But he knew how appearances could be deceptive.

"You, I care not about, but the trickster here? No, not dead. Just out of action."

"In the belly of a wyrm?"

Coyote wheeled round, grabbed Nataero by the lapels of his grubby dressing gown, and hauled him onto his toes until they were nose to nose.

"Yes. Why aren't you there? How... how did you find me?" Nataero said.

Coyote shrugged. He jerked his chin toward Richard. "He wouldn't stop and ask for directions, we got lost—and here we are."

Coyote took in the bare hallway with an appreciative nod.

"Nice place you've got here. Very homely."

The wallpaper was old and peeling. The hallway floorboards were bare, as were the stairs. A single unshaded light bulb hung from the ceiling.

The rest of the house was a museum, a hoarder's paradise. Mounds of papers and books teetered over their heads, their geologies shifting with each creak and movement of the floorboards, their summits swaying precariously. They formed narrow dusty canyons which wound through the rooms, their exposed faces stratified with seams of ancient leather tomes. Elsewhere, there were piles of pens and pen drives, a jumbled heap of government laptops, there were bin liners of stuff, and some things that looked like the mummified bodies of children.

How had he come to have all this here? Richard wouldn't have been surprised to come across the Holy Grail or Excalibur. This man wasn't a god. He was a kleptomaniac.

Coyote sized up the Roman. "Nataero. God of lost things. People pray to you to find belongings and get them back."

Nataero watched them suspiciously. "Sometimes. They used to."

Coyote was dismayed. "Only because you took them in the first place, right? A small god who needed to be noticed, wanted to be noticed, who felt they deserved better."

"They said if I helped them it would be different," said Nataero, his voice weak, but becoming strong and arrogant. "They said that a new future was dawning, and I would be there to see it. And I deserve it. I'm fed up of people treating me as small change. I'm not. I've earned my place."

Coyote shook his head in despair. "So what did you have to do? Steal my younger brother? Find long forgotten gods?"

"Barbarian genius loci. Nobody would miss them."

"And the godsblood? They sacrificed the gods. *Gods*. For what? What would require the sacrifice of gods? Did you try to sacrifice me, too?"

Nataero snorted. "No, they don't want you dead, no. Just out of the way. They need you alive. They're afraid that if you die, your... manhood will die with you."

"What do they want it for?"

"I don't know," he shrugged. "They don't tell me everything. They just engaged me to steal it from you. I don't know why they want it."

Coyote leaned in close. "I'll bet you overheard something. I know how you think. You don't trust them. How do you know they'll keep their word? You know what we're like—fickle, vindictive, and capricious. You've been on the raw end too often not to have something on them, am I right? What did you hear? What is it?"

Nataero pressed his lips together and shook his head. He wasn't telling.

Coyote's eyes narrowed. "Well, I'm still here and free, so they're not going to be too happy, are they? They'll blame you. Do you really think they'll let you take your place after this?"

Nataero chewed his lip, considering, weighing his options which, right now, were pitifully few.

Coyote waited.

"They... they were talking about a birthing—"

Coyote didn't like the sound of that. So that's what they wanted his pecker for, to conceive something? It felt like an assault. They hadn't asked. They hadn't even bought him dinner. Or a turkey baster. Did they have some old Elder god brood hag bound up somewhere? To be fair, his penis would shag anything. It was incorrigible. But there was no way he was going to consent to be a sperm donor to some misbegotten ritual to birth, what, some dark eldritch monstrosity? And if they did, they'd better not come after him for maintenance.

"Who? Who were talking?" asked Coyote, shaking the god by the shoulders.

Nataero shook his head and sneered. "It's too late. They have everything they need. You can't stop them. They'll know you're here. You've cost me everything. It's all lost." There was another silence, then, finally, in a small voice he said, "They mentioned the club."

"A club, which club?"

Nataero looked tired now, beaten. "*The* Club. There's only one. They'll be afraid I talked. I must—"

He stopped when the glass in the front door shattered and the door splintered open, followed by a gust of cold wind that made Richard's eyes sting.

"Christ, where did that come from?" he yelled above the gale.

"Raróg!" wailed Nataero hopelessly. "It is a Raróg!"

The wind whipped around their feet in little eddies, gaining speed and power.

Richard grabbed the Roman god's wrist. "What the hell's going on? Just tell us!"

Nataero snatched his arm back, and looked at him with hatred and disgust. "Why? You have destroyed me. Don't you understand? Just when everything I desired was within my grasp, you fucking mortal! It's over! Over!" He sagged against the wall and looked as if he might weep.

Richard left him there.

The Raróg gathered momentum, building in size, becoming a whirlwind. It weaved unsteadily about the hall, whipping up loose papers and parchment.

Richard and Coyote pushed through the rooms, along the narrow trenches that ran between the high tumbling mounds of other people's belongings. There must be a back door, somewhere.

Around them, objects began shaking and dancing, before taking to the air, caught up in the whirlwind as it began churning up the accumulated lost and stolen ephemera of millennia, and drawing them into itself.

Above the cacophony of wind came a howl of despair.

"No! Please!"

Blinded by dust, Richard and Coyote flung themselves on the floor as the roaring increased and the whirlwind passed over, Coyote hugging his war bundle to him, to prevent the Raróg from consuming that too.

At some point, the sound of the wind lessened and died.

When Richard raised his head, they were lying on the dusty floorboards in the dining room of an old, abandoned house. Of all Nataero's hoarded objects, there was no sign. The house was empty.

"Well, what do you know," said Coyote, dusting himself off. "They *do* want me alive."

"Nataero!" called Richard.

No answer.

They found him, curled in a foetal position against the hall wall; blank eyed, with saliva dribbling from his mouth.

Richard shook him. There was no response. No recognition. He was catatonic.

"There's nothing we can do. His mind has gone," said Coyote.

"How? What the hell happened?"

"Nataero was a god of lost property, a little god, a house god with aspirations. He was defined by what he did. He craved recognition, so he stole things and held them to ransom, basking in the praise of worshippers when he 'found' them. Without his hoard, he was nothing, *is* nothing. That was his weakness. The shock of losing it all has caused him to lose his mind."

"But he's the god of lost things. Surely he can find it again?" Richard said.

"How do you find your mind if you've no mind to find it with? Death is considered to be too quick a punishment by gods. One day he might recover, but the struggle could take decades, centuries. Until then he'll live on like this. You might call it poetic justice. They like a bit of that, gods."

"And what of all the stuff he acquired? Has it all gone back to the rightful places and owners?"

"I doubt it. They are lost again, where even Nataero can't find them. And perhaps that's just as well."

Coyote took a last look at Nataero and patted Richard on the shoulder. "There's nothing we can do here. He made his choice. We, on the other hand, have a trail to follow. We need to visit this Club."

CHAPTER EIGHT
Coyote and the Pissing Contest

THE BUILDING HAD stood off Piccadilly for almost two hundred years, implacable in the face of London's changing fortunes, a neoclassical monolith around which humanity lapped like a feeble tide.

These days nobody gave the old building a second glance. It had built up a grimy countenance, common to big cities, and faded into the background. It was obvious its membership didn't like to advertise. The only indication of its use was a brass plaque by the large black door within the embrace of the Doric portico. It simply read 'The Club'. The place had no need to assume an air of grandeur. The very brevity of its name spoke of entitlement.

"So you're telling me this is an exclusive club for gods only? Doesn't look all that exclusive to me," said Richard, considering the facade.

"Don't let the building fool you," said Coyote. "Even though it's reinforced with wards, sigils and immurements, I can still sense psychic leakage from those inside. Apparently, they take their privacy seriously. I still can't sense my younger brother but, from Nataero's last words, someone here must know of its whereabouts."

"So you can get us in. You're a member, right?"

"Me?" laughed Coyote. "No! Couldn't think of anything worse. Besides, I wouldn't join any club who would have me as a member."

"Ah, Groucho Marx."

"No, actually. Me. I told *him* that."

Richard rolled his eyes. "So, is this wise, then?"

Coyote said nothing. He watched. He waited, glowering at the building across the road. Richard sighed and gazed longingly at a nearby coffee shop. Coyote looked up at the upper floors. The silhouette of a bird caught his attention as it disappeared over the roof.

It was an omen.

On the street, a car backfired. An agreement.

Coyote cocked an eyebrow and grinned. "Wise? Seriously? You're asking me?"

Coyote pushed himself off the railing with his shoulders. He had stashed his war bundle somewhere secret, somewhere safe. There was no point in advertising his intentions. They had underestimated him so far and that was just the way he liked it. He operated best like that. They expected the trickster and the fool, so he would play the fool. It was time for a little controlled folly.

They crossed the street, Coyote striding with purpose, Richard hurrying to keep up.

"Remember, Richard Green, through this door, no matter what it looks like, it is no longer your world. Do not speak unless spoken to. Do not eat or drink anything offered. Decline, but decline with grace."

Richard looked Coyote up and down.

"Right. Know my place. I've been told that all my life, and look where it's got me."

Nonetheless, Richard found himself polishing the toes of his shoes against the backs of his calves as Coyote rapped the huge brass lion's head knocker. A sonorous boom echoed on the other side of the door.

Coyote looked over at Richard, who screwed his eyes shut and shook his head, as if trying to dislodge a thought. It was the psychic wash of a concentrated number of gods. The proximity of so many deities was clouding Richard's mind. He hoped that what he had told Richard would help protect him, if he remembered it.

The door opened, and a man in a butler's uniform looked them up and down, his brief unctuous smile falling away into disdain.

"Good afternoon, sir. You have been expected."

Richard looked at Coyote. "Expected?"

"They're gods," Coyote reminded him gently.

THE BUTLER BECKONED them to enter. The door shut behind them with an ominous echo as they entered the lobby hall. It was all marble floor and pillars, with a wide stone staircase leading to the upper storeys.

Inside, Richard flinched under thin sharp migraine pains, as if a bird had sunk its talons into his mind. Then they faded. It felt as if honey or amber were slowly enveloping him. His thoughts slowed. They were there, but sluggish; anxiety and worry sluiced away. Like someone had wrapped his mind in a snug, warm duvet.

The butler indicated that they should follow him.

"They'll see you in the Supplicant's Room."

COYOTE STEPPED OVER the threshold, just as he would step into any trap: confident, without hesitation or trepidation, knowing it could not hold him. Once inside, he could feel the psychic trails of gods moving about within the building.

He didn't know why they did this: cut themselves off, close themselves in, and barricade themselves away. He preferred the open spaces, to be part of the world, not apart from it.

The butler showed them into a drawing room off the lobby. Shelves of leather-bound volumes lined the walls. A fire of blue and white flames crackled in the grate, flanked by large leather wingback chairs. There was a sheaf of the day's broadsheets on the table beside them. The slow, meticulous tock of a grandfather clock in the corner measured out the moments of silence, each second falling lightly like an autumn leaf, its almost imperceptible weight adding to the inexorable press of time that the gods had been exiled, slowly crushing them under its weight. It was an exquisite form of torture.

Across the room, Richard yawned. The heat from the fire was making him drowsy. It reminded Coyote of the sweat lodge. He recalled the giant he built it for, and smiled to himself.

As he walked to the middle of the room, he noticed someone already occupied it. A man sat in the armchair that had had its back to them when they entered. He wore a suit and a tie with a Celtic design, held with a Club pin. He looked middle-aged, his face lined and worn. Wan. He had a full head of white hair and a full beard and probably looked very good in a crown. Regal, even. Coyote decided the suit didn't do him any favours.

The man struggled to get up out of the chair. One too many brandies, perhaps.

"Bran," he said, extending a hand, "of the Celtic pantheon. Founder of the Club. It's a pleasure to have one of our Colonial cousins visit us, and a Raven Brother, too. A rare honour," he said, holding out his hand.

"Brother Raven," said Coyote with a nod of his head.

He shook Bran's hand. He felt it tremble in his grip. The god wasn't feeble; he had strength. So it wasn't fear that made it shake, it was something else. He looked Bran in the eyes, saw the golden swirls in the irises; roiling, shifting, like the surface of the sun. Coyote had seen that look before, that thousand year stare. Bran had recently taken Ambrosia, the so-called food of the gods. Opiate of the gods more like.

Bran, still clasping his hand, pulled him in and leant forward to whisper a confidence. "These days, as in yours, it's the east you have to watch out for. The Slavic pantheons are eager to expand. They're trying to muscle in on our territory." He released Coyote. "Barbaric deities. There used to be a sense of honour among pantheons. Not these days."

Bran dropped into the chair, gestured around the room. "I'm sorry about the hospitality, but I'm afraid you're not a member." He gestured towards Richard who was inspecting the bookshelves.

"And there is of course the matter of your bringing a mortal here. Hence the Supplicant's Room."

For a moment, Bran's eyes lost their focus, as if he could see something Coyote couldn't. That was Ambrosia for you. What puzzled Coyote was where they found it. By rights, the supply of Ambrosia should have dried up with their enforced exile. Nobody could believe that old guff Zeus spouted about it being delivered to him by doves everyday. Yeah right. Coyote sniffed. At least, it *smelt* like Ambrosia, but with an odd, sour tang. It was tainted, impure. It wasn't so much Ambrosia as an Ambrosiate, something akin to the food of the gods, but synthetic, processed. More like a fast food of the gods.

Since the Great Usurper had cast them down, some gods couldn't face the deep sense of loss. It was like losing a loved one. Losing a limb, an organ. A penis. They couldn't face the incarceration on this plane and sought to ameliorate their pain. Ambrosia could give them moments of their once precious godhead back. However, once the hit faded, they were still cast out, still trapped. So they took more. To Coyote that seemed more like a torture than relief. He wondered how he would feel if he knew his penis was lost to him forever. Not that it was, because he was Coyote. But if it was?

"So what brings you here, Trickster?" said Bran eventually.

"A member."

"One of ours?"

"No, mine."

"I'm afraid I don't understand."

"My younger brother was stolen from me."

Bran's face crumpled in confusion. "I'm afraid I still don't see—"

Coyote sighed. "I'm looking for my pecker. Todger. Wang. Willy. Cock. My phallus?"

"Ah."

Coyote rolled his eyes with exasperation and shrugged, palms out, Mea culpa. "I know. I was careless. Someone put one over on me. Kudos." He raised a finger. "But now I want it back. I followed a trail here, east to the Old World. I was told you might be of assistance. I was hoping that if anything was worth knowing, someone at the

Club would know it. Perhaps one of your members might have heard something. It can't have been easy, moving an object that powerful."

"Well, yes, rumours do spread around the members' lounge. To be honest it's often hard to know how much stock to put in them. Half of them are planted by members themselves for their own ends. You know what we're like. I can ask around. Discreetly, of course." Bran frowned. "There was... something. No. No, I can't remember. It's gone. Sorry." He shook his head. "Hmm? Oh, perhaps you might tell me something. There have been rumours abroad. Something about Kansas? I don't suppose you could enlighten us, at all? In your travels you must have heard things."

"Oh, that?" Coyote inspected a fingernail. "It was nothing. I heard it was a vendetta. Eros was killed. Aphrodite didn't take kindly to it. You know what we're like."

"Eros? Killed."

"That's what I heard."

"You mean murdered?"

"Yup."

"Who would murder a god?"

Coyote shook his head. "Deicide. I know." He leaned forward and looked into Bran's eyes, hunting the truth. "Who would do that? Murdering gods is a serious business."

"Aye," agreed Bran. "Has it come to this, that we turn on ourselves like trapped wolves, gnawing our own leg off in frustration to be free?" He gestured to the window. The original sash was still there, but there was an added frame of aluminium secondary glazing. A fly was buzzing, trapped between the panes. Bran watched it, mesmerised.

"Gods trapped on this plane, like flies between double-glazing and just as impotent for all their angry buzzing," he said. Bran braced his large hands on the arms of the chair, pressing into the leather as he pushed himself up. "Well, if that's all."

The interview was over.

Coyote stepped up and clasped Bran's hand again. He was disappointed. There was nothing to be gained here. Perhaps this was all the Club was; an Ambrosia den, a place where fallen gods could crawl into their broken dreams and relive the glories of their past.

Coyote had no regrets himself. He never looked back. Well, not often, and only then to make sure nothing was chasing him.

Bran offered an insipid smile. "I'm sorry I can't be of more help. If I hear of anything, I'll be sure to let you know. There can't be many gods who have want of a phallus. Unlike you, most still have hold of their own."

Ouch. He supposed he deserved that one.

Bran tugged on a bellpull by the fireplace.

"Someone will show you out."

They left Bran slumped in the chair, watching the fly in the double-glazing, buzzing angrily and butting the glass.

No, wait. Something Bran had said. Of course. It was so obvious when Coyote thought about it. Perhaps he should have been a detective after all. There *were* those who had lost their manhoods to misfortune and treachery. Maybe there *was* a pattern. Maybe *he* was just the latest victim on the list. He wished he had a corkboard and photos and coloured string. He began to tick them off on mental fingers. Uranus, Odin, Osiris, Mot, Mahadev, Attis, Kumarbi...

Oh, this was glorious. Once he'd questioned everyone, he was so going to summon them to a room like this, all the suspects, when he had some, and reveal who the pecker thief was. Now *that* was a plan.

As THEY STEPPED out into the lobby, Coyote heard the distant sound of laughter as a door opened above them somewhere. A party he hadn't been invited to. He hated that. Usually he'd just invite himself, but he could sense now wasn't the time.

The cold lobby filled with the warm smell of palm oil and myrrh. Well, that was unexpected. Maybe this hadn't been a complete waste of time after all.

He watched the bald, tanned man descend. He had a groomed black chin strip of a beard beneath his bottom lip. The mighty Osiris, Egyptian god of the Afterlife. What a judgemental prick.

Coyote smiled. "Fancy seeing you here."

"I'm a member."

Coyote's smile slipped into a smirk. "You can say that again."

Osiris's eyes darkened, and it wasn't just the kohl.

"And you're not, trickster, which rather begs the question, what *are* you doing here? You're a little off your reservation, aren't you?"

"Well, you know me. Led by my boner. Speaking of which, what about yours? How's it hanging? Oh, I forgot. As a god of fertility, having to wear a golden strap-on must really chafe. Wait, that's it, isn't it? After all that, this is just about plain old penis envy, isn't it? You know, I'm almost disappointed. You didn't think I'd figure it out did you? You stole my pecker to replace your own. Back of the net. QED. Well, I want it back. Where is it?"

Osiris glowered at him. "I have no idea what you're talking about."

Coyote stepped forward and grabbed Osiris's crotch. There was the hard arch of the pubic bone against the heel of his hand, but under his fingers, nothing. He held his hand there, a moment longer than he needed. Just because.

The Egyptian's face contorted with shock and rage. Osiris clenched his fists.

"How. Dare. You. Perhaps you forget what I am."

"Dickless?"

"God of the Underworld. King of the Living. Lord of Persons. God of the Staircase. Lord of Terror. Devourer of all Slaughtered Things."

Coyote raised his eyebrows and shook his head. Gods. Not content with being gods they had to give themselves all these honorifics. As if just *being* wasn't enough. Gods and their egos. "So you haven't got my pecker then?"

Osiris stepped forward and bellowed, spittle flying from his mouth. "No, I haven't got your bloody member! I wouldn't stick that rancid disease-ridden thing anywhere near my wife, Isis, after you've been using it to whore with nymphs!"

Coyote held up his hands and stepped back. "Whoa. Okay."

Osiris's eyes narrowed. "Choose your next words carefully, you totemic savage."

Coyote couldn't resist. He leant in, lowering his voice. "In that case, how *is* that gold strap-on working for you? Just asking. You know, for a friend."

"Get out!"

The front door flung itself open, slamming back on its hinges, the crash echoing about the lobby.

Richard tugged at the sleeve to Coyote's jacket. "Coyote, I think we should go."

"Listen to your pet, trickster."

With that, Coyote put his nose disdainfully in the air and strode towards the door.

"Come, Richard Green. We are done here."

Osiris watched him go before gesturing toward the door, slamming it shut behind them. He took the stairs two-by-two up to the landing where he stormed into a room.

"Are you sure we need him alive, Lugh?" he demanded.

The auburn haired god glanced up from his paper, regret in his eyes. "Yes. With the All Fathers having gone to ground, this is tricky enough as it is. So, for the moment, yes, we need him alive. Sorry."

Osiris dropped into a chair. "Do you think Coyote suspects?"

Lugh folded his paper and put it down. "No. The Roman didn't get a chance to tell them anything. He's just a fox nosing about in rubbish bins. He's an irritant, but ultimately unimportant. It's all in hand. Don't worry."

"Good, and are the Slavic mob happy?"

"Yes, we shipped them another batch yesterday. Thanks for that."

The Egyptian answered with a distracted grunt.

Despite Lugh's reassurances, he *was* worried.

CHAPTER NINE
Coyote Wings It

WHEN RICHARD CAME out of the Club, it felt as if he'd just stepped from stifling heat into a cool refreshing breeze. For a moment, the relief was palpable. Then he felt a wave of migraine-like nausea. He bent over and threw up in the gutter. A post-vomit sweat prickling his brow in the cool breeze, he wiped the back of his hand across his mouth.

People tutted as they passed by, making judgements, reinforcing prejudices, reaffirming their own petty little mortal perceptions of the world, the one out of which Shu had jolted him. He caught sight of himself in a shop window. Mind you, he wasn't surprised. He hadn't had a shower, a shave or a change of clothes since he left Las Vegas. How long ago was that? He didn't even know. Days? It felt like weeks. This was no way to live. He felt drained and lethargic.

All of a sudden, Coyote tensed. Richard felt his guts tighten. He looked back over his shoulder towards the Club.

Coyote yelled at Richard and bolted off down the street. Overcome with terror, adrenalin pumping, Richard took off after him, as if his life depended on it.

Quarter of a mile away, Richard caught up with Coyote, who was leaning against a railing, waiting for him.

"What... what was all that about?" panted Richard.

Coyote shrugged. "I needed to get you away from there."

Richard waited for an explanation, but there was none forthcoming. "Fine," he said, once he'd caught his breath.

Coyote inhaled deeply through his hawk-like nose. "Well I must say, that all went better than I expected."

Richard looked at him in disbelief. "You pissed people off. No, not people, gods."

Coyote shrugged. "It's what I do."

"In that case, I'm surprised we got out of there in one piece."

"Well technically, I didn't, but I'll let that pass."

Coyote glanced up and down the street then set off towards the nearest Tube station. "They're up to something, I can tell," he said as Richard hurried to keep up. "As sure as gods is gods, some of them are plotting something. Schemes within schemes. Premeditated plotters and schemers are gods."

Not him though. He was more of a pantser than a plotter.

He also knew trickery when he saw it and there was trickery here, though it was blunt and childish. No finesse. Someone wanted Bran out of the way and easy to control, so they doped him with Ambrosia, and a synthetic impure Ambrosia, at that. Where were they even getting that stuff?

And the way Bran talked about the castratos, did he even know Osiris was there? And as for the Egyptian, how did he know he'd been with nymphs in Vegas? He didn't like his disparaging remarks about his penis, either. He was a god. It was magic. He never got STDs. Where would the fun be in that?

There was definitely something going on. He would have to go back to find out what. It was very possibly a trap, but that thought just gave him a boner; well, it *should* have given him a boner and that was frustrating.

Impatient, Coyote strode ahead.

"Come on, Richard Green."

Richard caught up quickly. "Where are we going?"

"To see Weyland. We'll pick up my war bundle on the way."

Coyote put his hand in his back pocket and fished out the business card the Anglo-Saxon had given him. It wasn't just a rune embossed on the card. It was a set of psychic directions.

As they descended into the Tube station, Coyote took out his phone, his thumb fidgeting over the touch screen as he texted. Shu was going to have a hissy fit.

The thread is fraying. Send.

Reply: *THEN DON'T LET IT.*

Easy for him to say.

THE OLD LADY followed them at a distance, muttering to herself in a tongue not heard abroad in millennia. Cerridwen always found that this form made her invisible. She could be more commanding in her mother aspect and more alluring when a maiden, but being a crone was like the old days. Rather, people looked on indirectly, out of the corner of their eye. They didn't linger, as befits gazing on a goddess, although this unfortunately was indifference, not deference. Nevertheless, people parted for her, glancing away, crossing the street to avoid her. Let them think her mad. Mortals were such shallow beings. No wonder they were incapable of seeing the truth.

She followed the trickster and his man down into the underground.

If you wanted a job doing, do it yourself. Osiris and Lugh would tackle him head on. Morrigan would turn the whole of London against him. Besides, they needed him alive for the time being. All they had to do was guarantee his cooperation. The trickster, by his nature, thought only of himself and that was his blind spot. It left his mortal vulnerable. There was no need to tackle the trickster at all.

A young man on a mobile phone stumbled into her. He started to apologise, then his eyes met hers. His brow furrowed and he looked away in revulsion.

Big mistake. Especially today. She may want the trickster alive, but she had no such compunction about this mortal. She turned and watched his back with eyes the colour of raw egg yolk, and bared her two peg teeth. She brought her hand up, like an upturned claw, and squeezed the air.

The young man staggered into the side of the tunnel, to the inconvenience of others as they tried to pass. He slipped down the tiled wall, his skin becoming translucent, yellowed and mottled with liver spots, his bones becoming brittle, his hair thinning. His hip fractured as he hit the ground. His wrist snapped as he put his hand out to steady himself. Arteries furred as the youth drained from him and, one by one, his organs failed.

Cerridwen smiled, full lips framing white teeth, her face now plump and glowing. She lowered her clenched fist, having exchanged decrepitude for pulchritude. The voluptuous middle-aged businesswoman that she had become spared a single glance back as a crowd of curious commuters gathered round the fallen old man. Cerridwen flicked a stray lick of hair back behind her ear and stepped onto the escalators after her prey.

Two Tube changes later, Coyote and Richard stood in a dirt road riddled with potholes and oily puddles, looking at the run-down units under railway arches as a train rumbled by overhead. The rune on the business card in Coyote's hand glowed strongly now, like a red-hot iron. When Coyote had decided to look for Weyland, various portions of the runes began to glow, directing them, like a mystical satnav, glowing stronger the closer they got.

In front of them, faded, flaking white letters on peeling blue paint simply said 'Smiths'. There was a small door set into the semicircular frontage of the viaduct unit.

Richard jiggled the handle.

"It's locked. He's not here."

"Then we'll wait."

"What, for another one of your omens?"

The road was empty. Coyote had gone. Godammit.

Richard turned round, but before he could call out, the door opened. Coyote stepped out and beckoned him inside.

"Jeez, will you stop doing that?"

He followed Coyote into the workshop.

In the light from the doorway, Richard could make out chains hanging from rails above, and in the corner was a workbench and tools; metals shelves full of stacked boxed parts, and in the far corner a little plywood office by a pile of tyres. There were dark patches on the concrete floor, from decades of leaked sump oil. It smelt of rubber, oil and damp brick.

"So this is Weyland's forge?"

"One of them, I suspect."

Richard groped around by the door, found some light switches and flicked them down. *Chunk chunk chunk chunk.* Lights went on overhead, forcing the shadows into retreat, revealing the unsuspected treasure. The walls shone with burnished shields and armour, and swords of intricate craftsmanship. There were ornate silverwork boxes and caskets, and jewellery so exquisite that it took your breath away, and under several tarpaulins, large intricate devices at whose functions Richard could only guess.

There, by the back, old fashioned and out of place, was a forge, a trough of water, an anvil and, on the anvil, a hammer.

All of a sudden, Richard didn't care anymore. He was tired of all this. He was tired of not having a routine, not having a job, not having a purpose. He was tired of all this running. He wanted to sit and take stock. Since he met Coyote, his life had been trashed and he had been carried along on Coyote's boundless energy.

"We're being dragged from pillar to post in search of your dick, which you couldn't keep in your trousers, by all accounts. Count me out. I've had enough."

Coyote sat against the workbench, having stored his war bundle beneath it, arms folded, watching him.

"Really? Have you finished, Richard Green, because I have to go."

"So that's it, you're abandoning me now?"

"Sure, if that's what you want. You can go any time you like." Coyote swept a hand towards the exit. "There's the door."

"You're not going to try and trick me?"

"Frankly, I have no interest in that. It would be a poor challenge and no sport."

"Oh, thanks. I was good enough when I had money."

"Oh, if money's all you want, no problem. We can go to an ATM right now. But can you honestly go back to what you were, having seen what you've seen, knowing what you know? It's a choice. But is it the interesting one? Is it the warrior's choice?"

Richard's shoulder slumped. "I don't care. I don't care any more."

Coyote gestured around the lock-up. "I brought you here to this place because it is a place of power. This negativity you're feeling is not you. Your encounter with the gods of the Club has drained your personal power. Your awareness, your perception, wobbles like a loose tooth. I had to yell at you back there to give you enough power to move. Unless you learn how to accumulate it, to hunt power for yourself, you will die in this new world you find yourself in." He pushed himself off the workbench and wandered into the middle of the space. Arms out. He turned round. "This place is a beneficial power spot. Here, you can restore your balance, rearrange your feelings. Here, if you have the will, you can accumulate personal power. It's your decision. But right now I have to go."

Richard sighed heavily.

"God stuff, huh?"

"God stuff. You have not the power for another encounter yet. Besides someone has to be here should Weyland return."

Richard sank down on a pile of tyres. "Then go. I'll think about it."

Coyote paused in the doorway. "Very well. If you're not here when I come back, I shall not come looking for you. Make the right choice, Richard Green, for your sake."

Richard, too tired to argue, nodded and waved him away.

He watched as Coyote stepped out of the lock-up, his body framed in silhouette against the doorway for a moment. Then, suddenly, he was gone and the flapping of wings taking flight echoed round the lock-up.

FROM THE ENTRANCE to the side street, the businesswoman watched the Coyote-raven fly away. As she walked down the dirt track in her heels, dressed for the city, she was oddly out of place in a street of dismal shuttered shops and graffiti, as was the smile that played upon her lips.

THE MOMENT HE took to the air in raven form, Coyote gave little thought to Richard. He thought only of his younger brother. He flew over London, tracing threads on the Tapestry, threads that would lead him back to the Club.

Below, the human huddle raced around their great city like ants, but he paid them little heed, for today he was sure he would be reunited with his younger brother.

Seeing the Club below, Coyote-raven circled down, landed on the balustrade of the piano nobile, and hopped along, looking in each window until he found Osiris. The Egyptian was not alone. He was at a long table, talking with several others and laughing.

Coyote-raven was sure they were laughing about him, about how they had tricked him and fooled him. Well, Coyote-raven grew angry at that, but made sure not to lose his temper, not just yet. He had to find out where his younger brother was, and then he would show them. To that end, he hopped closer to the window until he could hear what was being said.

"The time for the ritual approaches," said Osiris, addressing the others.

"For which you and Cerridwen are key, Osiris," said Lugh. "For our part, I believe the preparations are almost complete. Gobannon?"

A large, dark haired man with a ruddy complexion answered from down the table. "The parts have arrived at the old dock as the Slavic pantheon promised and they are being assembled on site. The sacred vessel is being constructed under my command and on schedule. The armature is being assembled as we speak. When complete it will be a wondrous thing to behold. Cerridwen will be proud."

"You have done your job well, Gobannon," said the slim clean-shaven man sat next to him, wearing a black open-necked shirt and shoulder length hair, his eyes completely black. "I'm sure the bards will sing of it when this is done." He leant forward and spoke down the table to Lugh. "We have enough phials of ichor now for the ritual. The Farm doesn't suspect a thing."

Lugh nodded. "Your discretion and hunting skills are appreciated, Pwyll."

"And what of the other aspect?" asked a woman with startling emerald eyes and long flaming hair, the colour of villages put to the torch.

"Safe, Morrigan, safe," said Lugh, lifting something onto the table.

Coyote-raven blinked. There, in the middle of the table, bound and contained by a fiendish ornate casket with crystal panes in the sides, like a reliquary, was his pecker, limp and shrivelled.

Morrigan peered at the thing from the far end of the table and curled her lip in disgust.

"Are you sure this... *thing* is powerful enough. It looks like it wouldn't satisfy a shrew."

Lugh patted the reliquary. "Be assured, Morrigan, when the time comes, this thing will have power enough to help grant all our desires."

Morrigan sat back, staring at it warily, not entirely convinced. "Forgive my scepticism. I have been disappointed by male members before."

Osiris laughed. "Worry not, Morrigan. It is not pleasure we're concerned with here, but procreation. It will serve its purpose."

"And what of the trickster? Now the Roman has failed to bind him, is Coyote going to be a problem?" asked Gobannon.

Lugh turned to him. "As I told Osiris," he said, "it is all in hand. Leave Coyote to us."

CHAPTER TEN
Coyote Takes Flight

OUTSIDE, ON THE balustrade, Coyote-raven sighed. It grieved him to be so close, yet so far, from his penis. "What have they done to you? Do not worry, younger brother, you will soon be free."

After all, Coyote had stolen daylight, filched fire and ventured into the land of the dead. He would surely be able to rescue his younger brother.

He thought about smashing through the glass and stealing his pecker away there and then, but with so many gods around, and so many wards and sigils protecting the building, even he didn't think that was a wise move.

No, he needed a plan, a good one, and what a plan it would be once he thought of it. Perhaps he would fly down one of the chimneys into the kitchens. There, he would bake a bread that resembled the size and shape of his confined member. Once it had risen (heh) all he had to do was find out where they were keeping the reliquary, sneak in, open the casket, make the exchange, yadda, yadda, yadda. Couldn't fail.

As he fidgeted in thought, from above Coyote-raven heard a challenging call. Two ravens perched on the lip of the roof above, watching him with all the glee of bored mall cops who had found some amusement.

"Good day, brothers," he called.

They did not answer, but flew down in silence, and landed on the balustrade either side of him. They were bigger than he was, with sharper beaks and longer talons. Heavyweights.

He looked from one to the other.

"Did my raven brother Bran send you, has he become aware of the vipers within his lodge?" asked Coyote-raven.

One raven cocked his head with an insolent stare, but said nothing.

"Then perhaps are you Odin's. Huggins and Muggins, no?"

The other mocked him with a raucous caw of laugher.

"No," said Coyote-raven. "I can see by the vacant look in your eyes, that thought and memory would be too much to hope for."

One of the ravens, its beak wide, cawed in his face and flapped its wings in threat. Its breath was rank with foul meat, its muscles grown strong on the carrion of the battlefield. Its feathers were black with blood.

Coyote-raven sighed. Just his luck, battle ravens. His plan was going to have to be a little more complicated than he first thought. Still, two battle ravens shouldn't be a problem.

There was a thrashing of wings. Coyote-raven glanced up. Along the edge of the roof, eight—no, nine—*ten* ravens settled. Make that twelve.

Okay.

RICHARD ROOTED ROUND in the little office for a kettle. An old transistor radio he'd found played in the background. He'd discovered a packet of digestive biscuits and eaten half of them already. He was starving. As he moved about, waves of static swept over the music, but the songs grounded him, reminded him of his life, of when he had one. All he needed was money. Enough so he could build his life again. Buy a better house. Get a better job. Meet a better girl. Coyote could have done that for him, pulled a couple of grand out of a cash machine, bought him a winning lottery ticket, dropped him off somewhere and let him get on with his life.

But how could he, knowing what he knew now, that humans were just ants to be stepped on or played with or burnt with magnifying glasses? How could he go back to that? He wished he could.

"Hello?" A woman in a business suit peered round the lock-up door into the gloom. "Excuse me?"

Richard looked up. Great. He didn't need this.

"I'm sorry. We're shut," he called. Okay, it wasn't his business, he shouldn't have been there and, besides, it was shut. At least it had been until they arrived. He just wanted to deflect any attempt at conversation. He wasn't feeling very sociable right now.

"I just heard that you did MOTs, and I was wondering—"

She was old enough to be his mother, well, aunt, but nevertheless her full figure won a blush of appreciation from him.

Wary of her footing, she stepped inside, trying not to touch the door and soil her hands or suit. Her heels clacked on the concrete, her footsteps unsteady on the uneven floor.

Her ankle gave on the uneven ground. She staggered. Richard was there before she could fall and caught her elbow. The scent of vanilla filled his nostrils, dousing the acrid male aroma that filled the dank enclosed workshop. The perfume seemed oddly out of place. A young girl's scent, but it suited her.

"Are you all right, Missus—?" he asked.

"Cerridwen. Oh, I'm fine," she said, looking up into his face and smiling. "You, on the other hand—"

It was as if his brain was filling up with warm water. Richard didn't have time to panic. Like a deep scented bath, Richard soaked in the feeling. It was calming.

"The time is coming when we will put things to rights," she said. "We will rise once more and take our appointed places. Change is coming." She studied him, as if picking up micro tells he wasn't aware of giving out. Something sifted through his mind, turning it this way and that, like a mother inspecting a wayward child's face for dirt or injury. A half smile. "And I see *you've* already started. A pity, then, that you will never complete it."

"You're one of them aren't you? A god," he said in languid tones, fighting the comforting warmth that enveloped his mind, the warmth of a mother's love. He felt himself yielding to it, unconditionally.

"Very astute," she said sharply. She idly surveyed the workshop-come-forge. "Coyote isn't interested in you, you know. You're an idle curiosity at best. You're like a bauble to a cat. He could have set you up with money any time he wanted. But the trickster isn't like that. He can be cruel and deceitful."

He tried to escape the warm feeling, but he was like a child trying to escape its mother's grip. His mind struggled and squirmed, a little act of rebellion, but he couldn't work loose.

His face was puce with effort as he forced the words out. "Why don't you just leave us alone?"

An arched pencilled eyebrow. A flash of temper. The warm, cosseting feeling in his mind withdrew and he was lost somewhere alone, somewhere cold and dark and deep. He felt panic rise. He wanted to cry out for her, beg her for succour, and say he was sorry, but he bit down on his cheeks until he drew blood.

"For the most part we did, for millennia in fact, and we were content for the most part, but now we're trapped down here in the gutter with you, suffocating in the stench of decay and mortality. It's like living in a midden heap. But no more. We have had enough. The Great Usurper can keep us cowed no longer."

He looked at her. Somewhere he felt pity. They had lost everything, like him. Only they hadn't learnt the lesson. Perhaps that's what mortals had over gods. Humans could adapt. They could evolve. For all their vaunted power and immortality, could they do that? Even now, they still clung to their sense of divine entitlement. Were they just theological dinosaurs? Is that what this was all about, survival of the fitter? Maybe this Great Usurper was a Darwinist. Wouldn't that be a laugh?

"Come with me."

He felt a not too gentle tug at his mind and, unable to resist, followed her as she left.

*　　*　　*

FROM A WINDOW of the Club, Morrigan turned, alerted by her battle ravens' caws of alarm as they mobbed the intruder outside. She watched, fascinated, in expectation of blood. She was disappointed.

COYOTE-RAVEN BROKE FREE of the murderous mob and flew up across the rooftops, startling a flock of dull-witted pigeons into the air. The battle ravens raced after him in single-minded pursuit, tearing through the hapless birds as they flapped frantically.

Bloody-feathered pigeon corpses dropped out of the sky to the screams of pedestrians below.

The battle ravens pursued Coyote-raven so relentlessly, they reminded him of a rock he once knew. He shuddered at the thought and flew on.

The beat of their wings was like a martial drum, their harsh calls, bloodthirsty war cries urging each other on.

If he had his penis, this would have been so easy...

Coyote-raven swooped down through the buildings, along the street and over the traffic, the battle ravens on his tail, their strident battle caws cutting through the city's cacophony.

Coyote-raven flew lower, as low as he dared, over the top of cars and taxis to the sounds of blaring horns.

Scared by the sudden aerial activity, docile junk-food-grazing pigeons took to the air in a flurry of wings and coos of alarm, causing pedestrians to flinch, squeal and flail their arms, adding to the chaos.

A double-decker bus loomed. Coyote-raven caught sight of his reflection in the windscreen—and those of the battle ravens closing in behind him. He saw the bus driver throw up an arm as he flew over the cars at the bus, only to swoop under it at the last minute. Two battle ravens on his tail tried to follow, smashing into the engine grille and vanishing in puffs of black vapour that soon dissipated, mingling with the exhaust fumes.

Wheeling left, over the heads of screaming pedestrians who ducked, yelped and squealed, some taking swings with attaché cases, newspapers or umbrellas, Coyote-raven beat his wings, climbing up past the shiny glass walls of an office block. This close it was almost invisible, its mirrored surfaces reflecting the skyscape around it. He banked sharply round the corner, smirking to himself as he heard the deep reverberating *thung* of a bird strike on toughened glass. Another one down. He banked round the building, doubled back round the other side, put his beak down, and dived, picking up speed as he headed towards the fast approaching mouth of a corner Tube station.

Coyote-raven heard a caw as a battle raven, claws forward, slammed into him. Dazed, Coyote-raven lost control and fell from the air, a tumbling bundle of flailing wings and ruffled feathers. As he sought to come out of the spin, the pain hit. A sharp flash along his left side that melted into a sense of heat and burned as ichor oozed from the wound.

Now the others began to mob him as he fell, swooping in for opportune slashes and pecks.

Coyote-raven made for the opening of the Tube station, dispersing the gathering commuters, some of whom had taken out smartphones to film the unusual avian behaviour. Coyote-raven landed in an untidy ball by the ticket machines. He had no time to catch his breath before the mob of battle ravens descended. Commuters fled the station foyer in a panic. As the triumphant cawing of iridescent black battle ravens fell upon their victim, Coyote-raven cried with pain at each slice and rip. His caw lengthened and deepened into a howl as he transformed. The battle ravens' cries of triumph turned to ones of pain as the coyote, its fangs bared, shook his body, throwing them off. It snapped at the nearest raven, seized it by its wing and shook it violently until it dissolved into a greasy black vapour in his mouth. He pounced and seized another, clamping his teeth down hard on its body, feeling the bones crunch in his mouth before the red light in its eyes died like embers, and the body turned into a foul tasting mist.

By now, people were screaming at the wild dog in the Tube station as it charged the diminished flock of battle ravens.

They took to the air, over the heads of shocked onlookers, leaving the coyote bloodied and panting in the foyer.

Coyote howled in humiliation and the crowd of gathered

commuters yelled and parted as he loped out of the station, across the road and down an alley.

SOME OF THE shallower cuts were beginning to heal by the time Coyote walked upright and human into Weyland's lock-up under the arches. He was tired and sore, but this was a power spot and a good place to replenish his personal power.

"Richard Green!" he called out.

There was no answer. He couldn't say he was surprised. He wasn't even disappointed. Trust the human to make the boring choice. Well, the choice had been his. Coyote was Dickless again. The truth was he'd just wanted sympathetic noises while he licked his wounds, while he remade the story of his defeat into one of heroic triumph. However, for that transformation he needed an audience. Anyone would have done. It didn't have to be Richard Green.

There was a loud retort as several short high-pitched farts filled the silence.

"Oh, there you go," said Coyote. "Where were you when I was being chased down by battle ravens? You could have guffed them to death."

A single loud wet one followed.

"No, I wouldn't call you a James Bond gadget."

Still, now he could concentrate on getting his pecker back without the mortal whining all the time. And once he did, those raven mofos better watch out. Oh, yes. Wakdjunkaga had a long memory.

He took his deerskin wrapped war bundle from under the workbench where he'd stashed it, and laid it reverently on the top.

He rolled a shoulder and winced, kneading his neck muscles.

He was healing nicely but the humiliation of defeat still smarted and it would take longer to fade.

Something large shifted in the shadows. There was a glint of metal.

"Someone has been in my shop."

A figure stepped from the shadows, holding a gleaming sword. It looked odd in the hand of a jump-suited biker mechanic. Odd, but no less fearsome.

"Weyland," greeted Coyote, as he gingerly felt the left side of his ribcage. "Yes, sorry about that. You weren't here. We didn't think you'd mind."

"I didn't mean you, trickster."

"Oh, sorry." Coyote fanned a hand round his backside and pulled a face. "He does that sometimes."

Weyland stepped over to the bench and put the broadsword down next to the war bundle. "Where is Richard Green? My radio's been retuned, the digestives have all gone and someone's been at my teabags."

Coyote looked up at him. "It's not my fault. I wasn't here."

"And Richard isn't here now," said Weyland.

Coyote shrugged, as if that cleared it all up. "Well, there you go. I knew he'd run out on me. Still, it's one less thing to worry about."

Weyland sniffed the air. He wandered round the lockup, still sniffing. He turned back to Coyote with a frown.

"Personally? I'd say it was one *more* thing to worry about."

CHAPTER ELEVEN
Coyote loses his Dick

RICHARD WANTED TO please Cerridwen, as a child wants to please its mother. To be honest, after the last few weeks, it felt like blessed relief to give up all his worries. He wanted to bury himself in her bosom and be comforted, but he knew the cruel sting of her hand could be waiting. Nevertheless, his love for her was unconditional. He wanted the approval, not the rebuke, so he followed Cerridwen into the Club.

Although he would do anything for her, there was a small part of him, locked away in his head, banging behind plate glass. He could feel her hold on his mind exerting just enough pressure to let him know she was in there.

The front door opened of its own accord. He walked through, bracing himself for the psychic pressure wave of nearby gods. Coyote had helped alleviate that by giving him a push, jolting his awareness by lending him a small amount of power. What he felt on leaving before was psychic decompression. However, this time it didn't feel as overwhelming. No doubt, Cerridwen's constant hold on his mind acted as protection.

Richard followed her through the lobby and up the stone stairs to the landing, and along a wood panelled hall. There, double doors swung open silently at their approach. They passed through a large room full of leather armchairs and walnut tables. The members' lounge, the Inner Sanctum. There, sat in the chairs, reading or chatting in low voices as mortal servants moved quietly between them, were gods.

Their passage warranted barely a glance from the few members that were about as Cerridwen led them to another door.

Beyond was a drawing room.

Richard felt a churn of nausea as the door opened and the minds of the occupying deities turned their attention towards him.

"Bow before my Lord Lugh, the Shining One, a god of great skill and art," said Cerridwen sternly. Richard could not resist.

"So this is the trickster's stray?" said Lugh. He laughed as Richard bowed for his mother-mistress.

Richard felt like a child in the company of adults—insignificant, powerless, and uncomprehending. They seemed larger than their size, as if their physical bodies could barely contain them, and looking at them gave him a kind of vertigo. Despite that, he tried to speak. Richard's face screwed up with the effort of trying to move, a child wriggling and fidgeting against a mother's firm grip.

Lugh leaned forward, eyebrow arched, and glanced at Cerridwen.

"He resists you."

"The trickster has put a little of his power into him to protect him, though little good it has done him," said Cerridwen, her smile tempered by an occasional wince as she tried to retain her grip on his mind. "Instead it has just weakened the trickster further. Without his member, he is not complete. Without Richard here, he is weaker still. Coyote cannot hope to stop us now."

Lugh seemed less amused at this news.

"If this mortal possesses even a fraction of the trickster's power, I want him out of the way. Take him down to the catacombs."

"I—" began Richard as if trying to cough up something lodged in his throat.

"Stop it!" Cerridwen scolded, and he felt the removal of a mother's love, a slap of bone-numbing cold, like falling into dark, desolate water. The shock was profound. He would do anything to crawl into the warmth of her affection again. Anything, if only she would reach out to him.

"Wait," commanded Lugh. He sat forward. A look of amusement crossed his face. He nodded toward Richard and flicked a finger. "Let him speak his mind. *His* mind."

Cerridwen nodded her permission to him. "Answer."

"I... I thought Bran was the chair of this club," said Richard, his mind slipping Cerriwden's grip like a recalcitrant child.

Lugh shook his head. "Bran is weak. He did not see the glory of our proposal, so Ambrosia allows him to relive his own past glories. It seemed fitting."

Richard cleared his throat. He tried to produce saliva enough to speak.

He caught sight of the silver reliquary on the table; through its crystal windows, he saw the shrivelled red protuberance.

"That's—"

Lugh raised his eyebrows and nodded encouragement. "Yes?"

Fighting Cerridwen's increasing grip on his mind Richard managed to spit out the words. "Coyote's penis."

Lugh patted the casket.

"He's coming for it," Richard blurted before Cerridwen's mind clamped down on his once more.

Lugh tutted, shook his head, and gave Richard a look of deep disappointment, as if he were a wiry little terrier that had just fouled the carpet.

"Bored now." He dismissed Richard with a wave of his hand. "Take him to the catacombs."

As Cerridwen led Richard from the room, Lugh called after him.

"Cerridwen is right. He has no hope of success. Our plan will come to fruition. How can it not? Cerridwen inspired us. My art conceived it, Gobannon's skill realised it and Osiris will help implement it." He placed his hand on the reliquary and smiled broadly. "And with, or without, his consent, the trickster is about to become a father."

* * *

By the time Cerridwen led Richard down a set of small, cramped servant's stairs, she had changed again. He was not aware of it happening, but it happened nonetheless. It felt as if she had always been as she was now and he willingly transferred his devotion to her new form, as if there had never been any other.

She appeared now as a young black-haired girl, gamine in appearance, with blue eyes that made Richard's heart drum a tattoo, and a complexion that was all roses and cream. She was aware of it, too and the maiden played him without mercy, like a cat with a mouse: a coquettish look, a fleeting touch, the swing of her hips, and the rise and fall of her breasts under the simple shift she wore.

She tripped along lightly behind the floating greenish nimbus of light that went before them.

Below the Club, brickwork tunnels with barrel ceilings led to wine cellars and other storage rooms before giving way to deeper passages hewn from the bare bedrock, lit by misshapen skulls set into regular niches, each burning with a cold blue- green ethereal flame.

"The heads of slain Formorii," said Cerridwen, pirouetting lightly on her feet as she turned to explain, her hair floating out with her shift as she did so. "An ancient enemy. Makes the place feel like home."

"Uh huh," agreed Richard with all the sincerity of a love-lorn youth.

She tripped gaily on and Richard followed. They passed branching tunnels. From some came the sharp clangour of beaten metal, and the red glow cast on the walls warped the shadows of repetitively falling hammers.

"Gobannan's brethren of the Trí dé dána labour to finish their delicate task, so we may succeed in our goal," said Cerridwen, now as prim and proper as a school prefect, Estelle to his Pip.

From other passages, strange whispers issued, while others still reeked of unfamiliar sour musky odours.

Cerridwen stopped and threw out her arms. The passage was lined with barred cells cut into the rock. "This is where we keep the monsters and misbegots," she said, "and this is your stall."

She thrust him into an empty cell with a hand in the small of his back and the bars clanged shut behind him, setting off a cacophony of howls, bays, barks and growls as things paced and rattled their stall doors around him.

Richard, face against the bars, peered into the shadows. "What... what's down here?"

"Things that aren't gods," she said, "things we don't want wandering around free. Things you don't want to see. Things you wouldn't want to see." She paused, a mischievous smile playing across her petal soft lips. "Do you want to see?"

Richard shook his head in fear. "No." Then, despite his terror, desperate to impress her, he blurted out, "Yes!"

She swung a skull lantern towards a barred cell. The swinging light set the shadows dancing wildly.

Richard screamed.

The last thing he heard as she left was Cerridwen's scornful laughter. It tore him apart, as sure as any beast.

HE MIGHT HAVE been there minutes, or hours. Not days. No, not days, surely.

There were things down here, not just corporeal creatures, but creatures of ideas and concepts, on the edges of perception, that could not be bound by bars or chains. He'd noticed them before when Shu jolted his awareness and when he fell asleep in Nataero's car. The rough stone beneath his feet vibrated with a rumble that he hoped was the Underground deep below, but he knew wasn't.

Outside, in the passage, there was a flicker of light. He shuffled his way to the barred door, saw a floating light approach, and heard footsteps behind it.

"Hello?" Osiris stopped in front of his cell. "You. Shouldn't you have a crop and a flail and one of those long beards?"

"The Egyptians imagined me after their own image. The myths aren't the full story. They're spin. PR. Just as this isn't my true form. I'd show you, but I don't have the gift of transformation like Cerridwen. Be thankful for that."

"What do you want with me?"

Osiris smiled at the impudence. "You? Nothing. I came down here to feed Ammit."

"Ammit?"

With a wave of his hand, Osiris sent the glowing nimbus to a nearby cell. Behind the bars, there stood a creature that should not exist. Richard saw a large crocodilian snout, larger than it had any right to be, questing towards the god with a mucus-ridden snuffle. Behind it, acquisitive reptilian eyes watched the pair, while the clawed front paws of a lion pawed the ground of the passage within its reach. In the shadows, its rear legs were heavy and covered with thick hide, like a hippopotamus.

"The Eater of Souls," Osiris said by way of introduction. "Ammit sat with me in the Hall of Judgement, devouring those unworthy to join me in the afterlife. When the Great Usurper's winged abominations swept across our realms, she was lost in the fall.

"For years she had to fend for herself. They found her roaming the world, devouring souls indiscriminately. They brought her here for her own good, and for that of humanity. Until the Halls of Ma'at are open once again, Ammit is a danger."

Osiris reached into the pocket of his jacket, retrieved something small and tossed it towards the creature, like a doggy snack. The elongated jaws caught it and snapped shut on the feeble glowing gobbet. Ammit shuffled against the bars, hungry for more.

"The soul of a small time gangster and rapist," said Osiris. "It's the souls that concern me. The halls of Ma'at have been sealed and empty since the Exile and since then the Great Usurper has sought to gather all the souls to himself, for what purpose I cannot say, but in recent times souls have not been passing on. Good and bad, they have been backing up. Something has changed.

"And now there are pantheons that seek to trade in these surplus human souls, indiscriminately, the good and the bad, like a celestial commodity. There are others who buy them, flensing the souls, sifting and refining them to a concentrate, to make a form of synthetic Ambrosia. Others traffic it. It's impure. It's addictive. An opiate of the gods. It hurts me to see it. It's what they feed Bran to keep him quiescent.

"Lugh came to me with a proposition. Should I choose to aid them, and their plans succeed, then I shall once more be able to sit in judgement and all souls will come to me, as they should."

"And you're down here justifying yourself to me because...?"

"I don't have to justify myself. I am a god. You are a mortal."

Richard curled his lip. "Well, that's a parasitic relationship."

Osiris cocked his head. "I was going to say symbiotic."

"You prey on us."

"You pray on *us*."

"Without humans, what would you be?" said Richard.

"Without us, what would *you* be? Do you shape us, or do we shape you?" Osiris was amused by the question.

He turned and looked Richard straight in the eyes. He felt as if Osiris were examining him under a microscope, that nothing lay hidden to his gaze. "You have an interesting soul. It would be a shame if anything happened to it."

"Is that a threat?"

"I don't threaten. I judge. You are young enough that the balance has not yet tipped. Watch the weight of your heart, Richard Green." He began to walk away, retreating into the dark. He called back, "Make sure it does not grow too heavy for, if it does, I shall be waiting for you."

CHAPTER TWELVE
Coyote on the Warpath

COYOTE PACED ABOUT Weyland's lock-up. He scratched his head. "How is it that Richard is a worry now? He's gone. The choice was his."

"No, it wasn't," said Weyland. "He's been taken." He sniffed the air again. "You smell that?"

Coyote gave him a quizzical look and tilted his head back. His nostrils flared as he inhaled. There was a smell. He didn't know about mechanics or forges; he just assumed it was some kind of air freshener. After all, the place certainly needed it.

"Bergamot and vanilla," Weyland informed him. "Cerridwen's essences."

"And who's Cerridwen?" The name meant nothing to Coyote.

"Cerridwen, of the Celtic pantheon. She is a threefold goddess of rebirth and transformation and she is a member of the Club."

In other circumstances the thought of a threefold goddess—maiden, mother, crone—would have stirred Coyote's baser instincts, but today he wasn't interested, which was a first.

"They have my younger brother, penis," he said in a petulant tone. "They have him confined in a box and want to use him... force him to conceive something. Nataero mentioned a birthing." He pulled a face.

Weyland went pale and sat down heavily on the workbench, crushed by the pressure of a sudden guilt.

He hung his head, unable to look Coyote in the eye. "I am afraid this is all partly my fault."

"What?" That was the last thing Coyote expected.

Weyland sighed. "Cerridwen was the keeper of the Cauldron of Rebirth and Transformation, once used by Bran to resurrect slain warriors, until it was destroyed. A year ago, someone contacted me. A patron who wished to remain anonymous, wished to know if I could make an object to certain... specifications."

"Well, you're a forge god," said Coyote, unsure where this was going.

"They wanted a bespoke piece made. It was a component, a part of a larger design, although what that was, I had no idea. I was flattered that they asked me, for it took a great deal of craft to forge. It was a challenge. I rose to it; they accepted my workmanship and I thought nothing more of it.

"When we last met, at Hillstone Howe, I went in search of the blade that killed my kin. I visited fellow smiths, Lepsch of the Circassian pantheon, Brontes, Hasemeli of the Hittites, Ogun and Ilmasepp. Some told tales of similar commissions, each piece different. Each by and of itself was odd, but innocuous enough. Commissioned in secret by a third party, one of the Slavic gods, we never knew our true patron, or their purpose. For what did we care? We were pleased to show off our skills, to have them acknowledged. None of us knew then that the others had been commissioned. Pooling our knowledge now, it's clear that we were part of the secret reconstruction and recasting of Cerridwen's cauldron."

He lifted his eyes and looked at Coyote.

"That's what all this is about. The cauldron is a symbol of the womb, of female fertility, a vessel in which things can be born and reborn again. Your member is a potent male symbol. I believe now that they mean to bring the two together, powered by the ichor sacrifice of my kin, to give form to this... *birthing*."

"It's a primal act of creation." Coyote shook his head in wonder. "And that they dare all this in secrecy, without the knowledge of other pantheons, without the guidance of the All-Father creators, and with my penis! Unbelievable. Although they do have Osiris, who is a god of fertility, too. They said his part was crucial."

"Aye," said Weyland staring at the ground, as if he might scry the future there. "But to what end? Some elder entity with a prior claim to the universe, who might, reborn, overthrow the Great Usurper itself? Or perhaps some assassin god-killer, so they can eliminate their own competition? Who can say? The minds of gods are multifarious and perverse."

"Old Man Shu hinted at something that threatens to warp the Tapestry. I see it now. A pattern forming from the slaying of your kin, spreading out, warped by the reconstruction of this cauldron. Richard was a loose thread. If we hadn't have found him—" Coyote sagged with realisation. "Wait. If Richard didn't leave of his own free will, I'm still bound to him. There are still laws."

"I thought you didn't care for rules?"

"He caught me in a moment of weakness. There are some things that should not be broken. A personal oath is one, the connection between a man and his manhood is another."

"Richard might have to wait. We have to find out what they are doing first."

"Back at the Club, I overheard the one called Gobannon say something about an old dock?"

"I know it. There have been psychic ripples from there recently, but nothing I thought untoward. If their scheme is this far advanced, then the place will be guarded."

"Well, we do have one advantage," said Coyote, brightly. "Nataero told me they need me alive, at least until the ritual is complete, so that my younger brother would live, too. That was why they wanted me out of the way in the belly of a wyrm."

Weyland gave him a weak smile. "They underestimated you."

Coyote chuckled. "They always do."

He was silent for a moment, lost in thought, then Coyote's face split like a ripe fruit, revealing a pithy grin.

"I have a plan to get us in there, but first," he said, holding up a finger, "we need an elk."

SHORTLY AFTER SIX in the evening, a fleet of black cars left the Club. Behind their mirrored glass, no drivers sat, yet still they drove east, the direction of the rising sun, towards a new dawn.

At the same time, a flock of ravens assembled from the leaden clouds that hung over London. They swarmed round the Club and headed out over the cars, swirling and surging in synchronous flight, pouring eastwards like a living entity.

As the murderous murmuration continued down the Thames, the ravens at the Tower of London abandoned their posts to join their brethren.

Richard was sat in one of the cars with Cerridwen and Lugh. She was in her mother guise again. The scent of vanilla and bergamot that he'd recently found so enticing, he now found cloying in the close confines of the vehicle.

Cerridwen was preoccupied. She seemed nervous and her psychic grip on him had loosened slightly.

Lugh sat in the seat facing her; he leant forwards and took her hands in his. He spoke to her calmly and softly.

"The time approaches. Gobannon is there, overseeing the final preparations. Morrigan's battle ravens and Pwyll's hounds patrol the site. Decades of planning and here we are, on the brink of our achievement, one Bran said couldn't be done. You should be proud. You brought us to this and you shall take us further."

He lifted her hands to his lips and kissed them.

She gave him a distracted smile.

THE FLEET OF cars pulled into the yard outside the abandoned warehouse, bought and owned by a front company for the Club. Already, the ravens were flocking on the building's roof, their cawing filling the air. Gods and goddess deplaned from the cars as if they were celebrities arriving at some red carpet event. Mortal thralls of the gods, the servants and staff of the Club, provided another level of security.

Cerridwen got out of the car, Lugh escorting her, a hand on her back. The strain of responsibility showed on her face, all the years of searching for the scattered pieces of her cauldron, commissioning the missing pieces to remake the whole. Then there was the refining of the rituals so that it would bypass the need for the All Fathers, from whom all things came, then finding gods who were willing to die in order to fuel it, and last but not least a potent enough male member capable of fulfilling the role the cauldron and the ritual required of it. It was just unfortunate that the only viable organ belonged to a trickster, and there was just no way to deal with them. All this involved delicacy, secrecy, and a number of conspirators working quietly and covertly below the notice of the Farm's protectorate. But, here, now, at the end, it all came down to Cerridwen. She sighed and tugged absentmindedly on the psychic leash.

Richard followed behind, like a duckling blithely following its mother.

Osiris and Morrigan came after, the goddess of war's eyes ever alert; flashing up to where her battle ravens kept watch on the rooftops.

Pwyll's red-eyed hunting hounds gathered round their master as he stepped from his car. He grinned, rubbed heads, patted backs and greeted favourites, before ordering them off. The Lord of Otherworld had a role to play in the night's proceedings, too.

Kubera, the god-dwarf, followed him. A select number of gods and goddesses spilled out of other cars; all had contributed to the task at hand in one way or another, and had earned the right to be here.

From the boots of two cars, thralls carried two locked and chained trunks into the warehouse.

Last came Bran, stumbling, escorted by human thralls. He looked around, confused, fresh Ambrosiate flowing through his veins, his presence an act of sheer hubris on Lugh's part.

* * *

CERRIDWEN'S CAULDRON STOOD in the vast iron-pillared space of the warehouse, remade. Whole. She wandered over to it. Richard could not help but follow.

This was no ordinary cauldron, this was a ritual object of great significance. It stood six feet high, was six feet wide across its mouth and its entire surface was covered in intricate Celtic patterns and designs of great power.

Richard could feel her joy through the psychic link and could not help but share in it. He watched as she ran her fingers lightly over the metalwork, tracing the designs. It was hard to tell the difference between the original fragments and the new parts. The smiths had done their work well and Gobannon had excelled himself, forging the pieces together. You could barely see the joins, even on a psychic level.

Gobannan also circled the cauldron, but with less joy and more professionalism, checking his handiwork.

The gods' thralls had built a small platform to ensure that those who performed the ritual had access to the cauldron's lip. Several thralls were already stirring contents into the vessel's depths in preparation for the ritual ahead.

Others were lighting the fire beneath the cauldron, a sacred fire kindled from the bones of holy men and sacred oils gathered from a thousand religious sites around the world.

Two more servants placed the trunks on the platform and opened them, revealing phials of ichor and, Richard noted, the silver reliquary containing Coyote's penis.

COYOTE WAS DISAPPOINTED to find there were no elks in Britain.

He and Weyland stood in Richmond park, eyeing up the deer. It had been closed to the public for some hours, but Coyote was no respecter of social boundaries or commercial opening times.

"Wait for me here," he told Weyland.

His war bundle over his shoulder, he went to talk to a deer as it grazed. He sat down before her and the pair conversed. The deer, recognising her older brother, bowed her head to listen.

When Coyote had finished talking, the deer nodded her head solemnly.

Coyote thanked her profusely, apologised out of respect, then slit the deer's throat. Its body dropped to the ground and he cut into its abdomen.

He strode back to Weyland, a sack in his hands seeping blood from its contents.

Weyland opened his mouth to ask a question, but Coyote glowered angrily and shook his head, cutting off any discussion.

"Let's just do this," he said.

CHAPTER THIRTEEN
Coyote and His Bag of Tricks

BACK AT WEYLAND'S forge under the railway arches, Coyote took the deer's liver and fashioned a vulva for himself. Then he took the deer's kidneys and made a pair of breasts from them. Then, using old magic and medicine paint from his war bundle, he used them to change his sex.

When he'd done that, he dressed himself in a woman's business suit and then he was a she, transformed under Weyland's guidance into one of the very likenesses of Cerridwen herself. In this way, he convinced Weyland that he could get them near the warehouse without raising suspicion.

WEYLAND STARED AT the change. It was uncanny. It could *be* Cerridwen in her mother phase, if you squinted, and didn't look too carefully. He walked round the transformed Coyote, shaking his head in wonder.

"I don't know how you managed that, trickster, but that is one hell of a trick."

"I know, right?" said Coyote-Cerridwen, with a playful wink.

"While it may not fool gods up close, it will certainly fool their servants and thralls. That's the plan, anyway." He took one last look at himself in the dirty scratched mirror Weyland had provided, and wiped away a stray smear of lipstick from the corner of his mouth. "Right," he said. "Time to go."

Weyland was already arming himself with his hammer and chain.

"Oh, and one small favour?" said Coyote-Cerridwen. "You wouldn't carry my war bundle for the moment, would you? I daren't touch it in this form. It contains powerful and sacred magic and the only thing that can destroy its power is menstrual blood." He pulled a face. "Awkward."

Weyland raised his eyebrows. "You mean you can get pregnant in that form?"

"Oh yes," said Coyote-Cerridwen, brightly. "Several times."

THEY APPEARED NEAR the river warehouse. It wasn't hard to miss. The psychic emanations were intensifying as they watched. Whatever Cerridwen and her coven were planning, it was already under way.

They surveyed the long four-storey red brick building. One flock of battle ravens wheeled and swirled round the warehouse before landing on the roof, then another flock would rise and do the same, so there was a constant aerial agitation.

The hounds of Pwyll patrolled the ground around the building, their red eyes glowing in the twilight, and surrounding the building itself were human thralls.

Coyote's phone beeped. A text message.

It was Shu: *WHAT ARE YOU DOING? THE THREAD IS STILL FRAYING!*

Honestly, Shu wanted to do this now? He really didn't need the pressure. Did the old man know how hard it was to keep this form? And as for the feeling of liver between his legs, let's just say it reminded him of how much he missed his younger brother.

Coyote texted back: *Not now, I'm working!*

He pressed send.

Message failed.

Psychic interference. Oh well, Shu would have to wait.

He put the phone away in her jacket pocket.

"I know there's no point in asking you, of all people," said Weyland, keeping watch on the distant warehouse, "but what is the plan?"

Coyote-Cerridwen paused and thought for a moment, tapping a manicured finger on his lip. "I just figured I'd get my penis back before I become a sperm donor. That ought to stop them, don't you think?"

Weyland nodded in agreement. "I expect so, yes."

THEY SET OUT across the vacant concrete wasteland surrounding the warehouse. The hounds bounded towards them, barking.

If they smelt the deer's liver and kidneys, this was going to get messy. Weyland tensed, wrapping another set of chain links round his arm.

There was only one thing to do. Coyote-Cerridwen didn't like it, but needs must.

"Younger brother," he said, out of the corner of his mouth. "Younger brother anus, I know we've had our differences, but right now I need you to work with me on this. Okay?"

There was a shrill unlady-like trump from the skirt area.

"Bergamot and vanilla, you hear that, younger brother anus? Bergamot and vanilla. This is a chance to redeem yourself."

The trickster's anus expelled gas in quiet puffs, the sweet smelling fragrance that he recognised from Weyland's lock-up. Bergamot and vanilla. He began to walk with more confidence.

Younger brother anus kept it up. *Pfft. Pfft. Pffffft!*

The huge black hounds slowed to a lollop as they approached, sniffing the air, recognising the scent and whining. They walked round them, tongues lolling, before bounding off into the dark again.

Coyote-Cerridwen and Weyland breathed sighs of relief as they continued on to the building.

* * *

THERE WAS A wet plop as the deer liver fell out onto the ground.

Useless bloody deer. Next time he'd wait for elk offal. That lasted for months. You could have sex, get pregnant and give birth with that stuff.

Coyote and Weyland looked down at the bloody mess at the same time and exchanged glances.

"Run?" suggested Coyote.

THEIR SUDDEN MOVEMENT attracted the curiosity of several battle ravens. The air filled with caws as they swooped down. Distracted by the offal that had fallen from Coyote's disintegrating disguise, they set to squabbling over it and tearing great gobbets off it with their beaks.

Also drawn by the scent of offal, the hounds came running toward them. Coyote shed the rest of his disguise as they fled. It peeled away and turned to dust.

Weyland turned and swung his chain round his head, building its speed. The whirling links took out several diving battle ravens that disintegrated into black vapour under the impact.

"War bundle!" cried Coyote.

Weyland tossed him the deerskin package as the first of the dogs charged, fangs bared.

By now, the sky was alive and writhing with eruptions of agitated battle ravens.

They needed to get inside, quick.

Coyote glanced toward the building as he rooted in his war bundle. They needed to get through the line of thralls that was advancing toward them with menace.

"Remember! This was all *your* idea!" roared Weyland over his shoulder as the chain flailed through the air and several more ravens and a hound burst into sprays of black vapour at its bite.

"Shut up and make for the building," said Coyote taking out a flute.

Weyland didn't need telling twice. With a flick of his arm, he wrapped the slack of the chain about it and ran for the building.

Coyote played a melody that was old when even he first walked the Earth. While he played, it would paralyse the running power of the enemy.

Within the sound of it, the hounds cowered and whimpered, turning round in confusion, and the human thralls slowed to a drunken stagger. The battle ravens lost control of their flight, colliding with each other and tumbling from the sky, impacting on the side of the building and bursting into thick black balls of mist.

Weyland and Coyote flinched and ducked as the birds dropped, exploding like water bombs into mystic gas.

Coyote stopped playing. "The confusion will last a little longer, we might make the building," he told Weyland.

They dodged past the last few falling birds and whining hounds, and swerved round the bewildered and clumsy thralls.

They made it into the building, drawn by the sound of chanting and incantation.

Weyland abandoned his chain for stealth, pooling it quietly on the floor and taking his forge hammer from the tool loop at his thigh. They used the shadows and kept the iron pillars between them and the watching gods gathered round the large cauldron in the centre of the warehouse.

It was an impressive piece of workmanship, even to Weyland's eyes.

"They've really done it!" he whispered to Coyote. "I never thought it would be so beautiful."

"You said it had been destroyed before," said Coyote in an urgent whisper.

"What? Oh, yes. It was Bran's half brother, Evnissyen, who destroyed it."

"That's good to know," said Coyote "because it may come to that."

"There's a catch," said Weyland.

"I'm a trickster," said Coyote with a sigh, "there always is."

Weyland turned his gaze from the cauldron to Coyote. "It can only be destroyed from the inside."

"Ah," said Coyote. "That's quite a catch."

A soft blue-white celestial light began to issue from the interior of the cauldron, fluctuating, illuminating the warehouse and casting long shadows from the surrounding gods.

Despite their predicament, Coyote had to smile. Gods! Even after thirty years down here, give 'em a taste of the old mumbo jumbo and they loved to slip back into traditional costume.

Lugh stood on the raised platform, next to Cerridwen, who had her hands stretched out over the mouth of the cauldron, fingers splayed as she continued her unearthly chant. By her side, Osiris held the instruments of his office, looking every inch a hieroglyphic prig. The silver casket that contained Coyote's penis sat between them on a plinth. Among the others, he made out Morrigan, Gobannon, and the unmistakable dwarfish silhouette of Kubera.

"Why the dirty double crosser!" muttered Coyote.

He slipped along to another pillar and caught sight of Richard, looking up in adoration at Cerridwen.

"At least he's got an excuse for being a toady," he muttered.

RICHARD WATCHED THE gods, a smile on his face. He had tried struggling against Cerridwen's grip on his mind, but she had been too strong. She was his whole world and he did not want any other. His eyes fell on the silver casket. It reminded him that she wasn't his whole world, at all. That's just what she wanted him to think, but somewhere, there was Coyote. That red shrivelled thing through the glass in the casket was a part of him. He kept the tiny sliver of his mind she let him keep focused on the reliquary. As the ritual took up more of her concentration, her hold on his mind weakened. Little by little, he was able to flex a thought, without rebuke. He kept thinking, gently easing his own mind out of her grip, waiting for an opportunity to slip out of it entirely...

COYOTE SLID ALONG from one pillar to another, trying to get closer.

The intensity of incantations over the cauldron increased as Osiris joined in the recitation with Cerridwen. Lugh unstoppered the phials of ichor and poured them into the cauldron.

The blue-white light dimmed as the ichor was absorbed, and then flared again, brighter than before.

There, in its light, he noticed a recent acquaintance. Standing slightly apart from the others, tears running down his face from golden Ambrosia tinted eyes, was Bran, muttering to himself, his lips moving inaudibly.

"Raven brother," whispered Coyote.

Bran's lips stopped moving and he glanced toward Coyote out of the corner of his eye.

"Are you another wraith come to torture me?" Bran asked in a whisper.

Coyote slipped in behind him until the old god's shadow hid him from sight. "No, brother. I have come to stop this. This madness is warping the Tapestry."

"It will do more than that," said Bran, returning his gaze to the cauldron. "It will tear it asunder. And I will have to watch."

"Why? What are they trying to accomplish? What are they trying to conceive in that cauldron?"

"An idea. They're trying to conceive a concept that will grow into a reality."

Okay, too much Ambrosia talking. Perhaps a more direct approach?

"What do they need my penis for?"

Fresh hot tears welled from the old god's eyes and rolled down into his already sodden beard. "They are going to create a new heaven, a new Otherworld for themselves." His shoulders racked with silent grief-ridden sobs.

Coyote didn't know what he was expecting, but it wasn't that.

"But they *can't*," he said. "The Great Usurper sealed off all dimensions upon our exile and folded them into this one. It is constrained by the laws he set in place to contain us. There is no longer any place for a new heaven to grow. That was the whole point. All reality itself will crack and shatter under the strain!"

He remembered the fly Bran pointed out, buzzing in the double-glazing of the Supplicant's Room back at the Club. He imagined the panes of glass shattering.

This could not be allowed to happen.

He had to stop it.

Caught unawares by a wash of warmth and a sudden pulse of pleasure in his groin, Coyote froze.

He looked up in confusion.

Cerridwen had opened the casket and held his penis in her hands. As Osiris held out his crook and flail over the cauldron, and worked a counter chant, Cerridwen, with an exultant climax to her charm, cast Coyote's member into the cauldron.

And Coyote howled.

CHAPTER FOURTEEN
Coyote Erectus

THE LIGHT FROM the cauldron intensified until those on the platform were lost in its glare. Sound ceased, as if the noise had overloaded reality.

Coyote watched, unable to hear his own scream.

Within seconds, (was it seconds?) the light began to fade as it rushed back toward the cauldron mouth. Ethereal matter licked the air above the cauldron, as something inside sought to come into being. Tendrils of chaotic light reached out, twisting and dancing round each other in fractal sworls and loops, like some miniature celestial event.

The proto-heaven was beginning to gestate.

"You'll destroy everything!" Coyote cried.

There had been precious few times since the creation of the world that Coyote recalled the Earthmaker's purpose for him so clearly. Contrary to what many believed, he did have a purpose, when he cared to remember it: it was to protect this world for the People.

CERRIDWEN TURNED AT the shout, distracted by Coyote's interruption.

Richard felt her psychic grip slacken. He knew he might have only moments to act.

"It's too late, trickster, your penis has done its work. You're expendable now," crowed Lugh. He beckoned to Gobannon and Morrigan. "He's interfered enough. He's an uninvited guest and we don't want him along in our new Otherworld. Kill him."

Unsheathing their swords, they looked only too pleased to try as they advanced on Coyote.

Damn. Those tables turned quickly.

Gobannon charged toward Coyote, his face contorted with bloodlust as he swung his sword. Coyote braced himself for the inevitable impact when a roar of rage and a blur of orange swept in from the side, intercepting the Celt.

Weyland and Gobannon crashed together like bull elephants.

Outside of the melee, Coyote spotted Kubera, hedging his bets and doing a runner. Coyote smiled to himself. Let him run. Coyote never forgets.

He then turned his attention to the cauldron platform where Cerridwen and Osiris continued their incantation of making.

Before he could get there, Morrigan waylaid him. He reached swiftly into his war bundle, pulling out a weasel skin and tying it round his neck. In battle, it gave him the ability to evade trouble. Every swipe and thrust of Morrigan's blade he was able to weave and dodge, until she grew furious at his luck and impudence. Her strokes became wild and careless until he ducked a blow that bit deeply into an iron pillar. As Morrigan struggled to free her sword, Coyote slipped away toward the cauldron.

Cerridwen was continuing to chant in an almost trancelike state, but Osiris he might yet reason with. He grabbed him by the shoulder and turned him round.

"Coyote!" the Egyptian spat. "You're too late. We have defied the Great Usurper and our birthright is ours to claim once more. I shall sit in my Halls of Judgement, with Ammit at my side."

Okay, Coyote was going to have to try the unthinkable here. No tricks, no lies. Just the plain unvarnished truth. It felt a little odd. "Osiris, listen, if they succeed they will have their new heaven, yes, but at the expense of everything else. Do you see what that means? As it grows, it will devour reality around it. There will be no more mortals. There will be no souls to judge. There will be their heaven and you, sat in your empty Hall of Judgement alone. Forever. Is that what you want?"

Osiris' eyes flickered with doubt.

As CERRIDWEN CONTINUED to chant, her mind was totally focused and Richard was able to slip easily from her psychic grasp. He was free. Blinking, as if he had been doused in a bucket of ice-cold water, he took a moment to get his bearings. He saw the cauldron and Cerridwen, lost in her art. He saw Coyote remonstrating with Osiris.

And he saw Lugh.

Lugh seized his spear and, with a roar of rage, flung it across the warehouse at Coyote.

Richard had been here before on Hillstone Howe, knowing he was out of his depth and that in a battle between beings of myth, there was nothing he could do. But that was then, this was now. Now he could buy Coyote time.

He threw himself towards Coyote. Lugh's spear tore through Richard's abdomen and vitals, impaling him.

"Interesting choice," Richard thought as he glanced down at the shaft of spear projecting from his stomach, and at the blood fast spreading across his shirt.

Still, his luck hadn't changed one bit. Bloody Coyote.

He convulsed once and died, his body toppling through the yet insubstantial proto-heaven into the cauldron.

COYOTE TURNED AND saw Richard fall through the expanding nimbus of light. Soon it would be too large to be contained and too voracious to stop. Once the proto-heaven was birthed, nothing could stop its expansion, and this dimension would be destroyed, gods, monsters and men alike would perish.

Ah, crap. Shu owed him one.

Coyote leapt into the mouth of the cauldron.

LUGH ROARED TRIUMPHANTLY. The trickster was gone. There was nothing now that could stop the birth of their new heaven.

He turned and forced Bran to his knees. With the blade of his sword beneath his chin, he lifted the old man's head up to look at him.

"See, old man? You were wrong to oppose us. We have beaten the Great Usurper. We have our own Otherworld again, at last. Our own realm once more, where our laws will be sacrosanct."

"I know what you have done, and it is monstrous," said Bran, his voice shaking, but its tone of reproach unmistakable. "I have failed to protect this land as I once swore to do, so if you have won, then I am ready to die."

For a moment, there was a flash of steel in the old man's eyes.

Lugh sneered. He raised the sword, brought it down and cut off Bran's head. The god's body flopped lifeless to the floor and Lugh tossed the head aside.

COYOTE FOUND HIMSELF between worlds. All about him, in whatever direction he looked, he saw an almost featureless roiling soup of potential and possibility cooling, coalescing and expanding. It had been like this in the beginning times, before the worlds were formed, so the Earthmaker had said.

The temptation to fiddle was almost too much, but he resisted.

Somewhere in the celestial miasma, he heard a weak voice cry out, "Older brother, older brother!"

He moved towards the sound and looked round. There he saw his younger brother, penis, limp now and spent.

"I am here, younger brother. I have been looking for you," he said.

And he gathered him up and put his penis in a pouch around his neck.

He went a little further, but whether it was on two legs, four legs or wings he could not say. There, he came across Richard's lifeless body. He pulled the spear from it, cast the weapon aside, and stood astride the corpse.

Then Coyote closed his eyes, reached out his hands to either side, like wings, and focused his awareness. Here, now, he could perceive the limitless heaven coming into being around him. He shifted his perception repeatedly, up and down the thread until he found himself stood within the cauldron and his hands felt warm metal. He braced them against the sides and pushed.

In the warehouse, the birthing was almost complete. Rising above the neck of the cauldron, the slowly expanding heaven, patterns of fractal light roiling across its surface, was now all but free of its artificial womb.

Weyland recognised the sounds of stressed metal. He took hurried shelter behind an iron column as tortured shrieks and bangs rang out from the cauldron. His foot kicked something. It was Bran's decapitated head. It opened its eyes and blinked.

"It seems my work is not yet finished, then," said Bran. Weyland hastily gathered the head to him and bent over to protect it.

The light of the coming heaven began to flicker like a cheap light bulb until, without even a pop, it abruptly contracted as the cauldron warped and shattered in shards and twisted fragments.

A shockwave of psychic energy followed, blasting shards and cauldron fragments out in all directions.

Gods screamed as they were pierced and cut by the sacred shrapnel.

Amniotic potions, spilt from the shattered vessel, sluiced Richard's body and Coyote across the warehouse floor.

Coyote coughed, raised himself up on his arms and took in the scene of devastation. Flung across the far side by the psychic shockwave, Cerridwen lay slumped and broken against the wall. Nothing she wouldn't heal from eventually, but it would be painful.

Psychic wounds always were. Coyote was glad. Shards of cauldron had partially crucified Lugh against the opposite wall.

Of Osiris, there was no sign.

At the epicentre, amongst the doused ashes of the fire, Coyote spotted the remains of the potential heaven. Without the ritual or the power of the cauldron to sustain it, it had collapsed in on itself. All that remained was a small glowing sphere the size of a hen's egg, a sphere that dimmed slowly, turning black as the final spark of potential at its core winked out and it died, stillborn.

Watched by Bran's head, Weyland had salvaged the silver casket used to imprison Coyote's penis from the wreckage of the shattered platform, its wards and sigils still intact. Carefully, with all the delicacy of a smith used to handling hazardous items, Weyland lifted the stillborn heaven and placed it within the casket before closing it. He would take it to his forge and seal it properly. Although the proto-heaven seemed inert, there might be those who would seek to divine its mysteries. As far as he knew, as a magical artefact, this was unique and that alone made it worth possessing for some. It would be better hidden.

COYOTE GRINNED, EVEN though it hurt to grin. The world was still here. The thread was intact, the Tapestry in one piece. Chalk up another one for the Kai-man. Shu would be pleased, not that he would ever show it, or thank him for it, but hey, that's tricksters for you.

Coyote's grin evaporated when he turned and saw Richard's lifeless body.

Shit. Despite everything, this mortal had made the interesting choice and that choice defined him. He had to respect that.

Coyote wondered whether he should say a few words. Give a eulogy. It seemed fitting.

Richard coughed.

"You're alive!" said Weyland.

"Well *I* am, but he shouldn't be," said Coyote, getting to his feet.

Richard looked up. "What-what happened? How the hell am I

here? I was dead... wasn't I? I remember... dying."

"It was the cauldron," said Weyland. "Birth and rebirth. Bran used to immerse his best dead warriors in it and they would be restored to life."

Coyote clamped his hands on Richard's upper arms. "You, my friend, are what we call in the trade, one lucky sonofabitch."

Richard looked down at his stomach and scrambled to pull open his bloodstained shirt. There was no wound underneath. That shouldn't be possible, but this was a new world. A world not just of men, but of gods and monsters. The question was, which one was he now?

"There is one thing you should know, Richard Green," said Bran's head. "Though your life is now mythically imbued, those reborn in the cauldron return to this world without their soul. That is the price of being Twice-born."

Richard frowned. It was odd, losing something you never believed you had. He didn't know quite how to feel about that, or what the consequences were.

Coyote beamed and put an arm round Richard's shoulder. "Don't listen to him. You got lucky! For a brief moment, it was a time of creation. Different laws of physics. I did tell you, remember?" Coyote's smile vanished. "The shock of your death has permanently shifted your awareness. You now perceive the worlds of both gods and men. Which path you walk from here on is your choice—make it an interesting one."

Richard rubbed the back of his neck and tried to take it all in. He was sure shock would set in soon.

"On the plus side," continued Coyote, brightly. "I've recovered my penis *and* I've given your life back, as I promised. I'd say we were quits, wouldn't you?"

ABOUT THE AUTHORS

Chuck Wendig is the author of the published novels: *Blackbirds, Mockingbird, Under the Empyrean Sky, Blue Blazes, Double Dead, Bait Dog, Dinocalypse Now, Beyond Dinocalypse, Unclean Spirits, The Cormorant, Blightborn* (*Heartland* Book #2), *The Harvest* (*Heartland* Book #3, *Dinocalypse Forever, Frack You*, and *The Hellsblood Bride*, and a compilation book of writing advice from his blog, *The Kick-Ass Writer*.

He, along with writing partner Lance Weiler, is an alum of the Sundance Film Festival Screenwriter's Lab (2010). Their short film, *Pandemic*, showed at the Sundance Film Festival 2011, and their feature film *HiM* is in development with producers Ted Hope and Anne Carey. Together they co-wrote the digital transmedia drama Collapsus, which was nominated for an International Digital Emmy and a Games 4 Change award.

He currently lives in the forests of Pennsyltucky with wife, two dogs, and tiny human. He is likely drunk and untrustworthy.

www.terribleminds.com
@ChuckWendig

Pat Kelleher is a freelance writer. He has written for magazines, animation and radio. He served his time writing for a wide variety of TV licensed characters, translating them into audio books, novels and comics. Yes, he's written for that. And that. And even, you know, them. He has several non-fiction books to his credit and his educational strips and stories for the RSPB currently form the mainstays of their Youth publications. Somehow he has steadfastly managed to avoid all those careers and part-time jobs that look so good on a dust jacket.